The Best
AMERICAN
ESSAYS
2018

GUEST EDITORS OF
THE BEST AMERICAN ESSAYS

1986 ELIZABETH HARDWICK
1987 GAY TALESE
1988 ANNIE DILLARD
1989 GEOFFREY WOLFF
1990 JUSTIN KAPLAN
1991 JOYCE CAROL OATES
1992 SUSAN SONTAG
1993 JOSEPH EPSTEIN
1994 TRACY KIDDER
1995 JAMAICA KINCAID
1996 GEOFFREY C. WARD
1997 IAN FRAZIER
1998 CYNTHIA OZICK
1999 EDWARD HOAGLAND
2000 ALAN LIGHTMAN
2001 KATHLEEN NORRIS
2002 STEPHEN JAY GOULD
2003 ANNE FADIMAN
2004 LOUIS MENAND
2005 SUSAN ORLEAN
2006 LAUREN SLATER
2007 DAVID FOSTER WALLACE
2008 ADAM GOPNIK
2009 MARY OLIVER
2010 CHRISTOPHER HITCHENS
2011 EDWIDGE DANTICAT
2012 DAVID BROOKS
2013 CHERYL STRAYED
2014 JOHN JEREMIAH SULLIVAN
2015 ARIEL LEVY
2016 JONATHAN FRANZEN
2017 LESLIE JAMISON
2018 HILTON ALS

The Best AMERICAN ESSAYS® 2018

Edited and with an Introduction
by HILTON ALS

Robert Atwan, Series Editor

A Mariner Original

HOUGHTON MIFFLIN HARCOURT

BOSTON • NEW YORK   2018

hmhco.com

ISSN 0888-3742 (print)   ISSN 2573-3885 (e-book)
ISBN 978-0-544-81734-0 (print)   ISBN 978-0-544-81743-2 (e-book)

Printed in the United States of America
DOC 10 9 8 7 6 5 4 3 2 1

Contents

Foreword

THE ROOM HAD three views: "At one sweep," he wrote, "I command a view of my household . . . and see below me my garden, my farmland, my courtyard, and into most parts of my house."[1] The house, the Château de Montaigne, was built in the fourteenth century and purchased in 1477 by the essayist's great-grandfather, Ramon Eyquem, a prosperous fish and wine merchant who laid the foundations of the family fortune. About thirty miles east of Bordeaux, the château has gone through many renovations, but the famous tower remains intact, a monument to the great writer who once resided there and its fortifications a reminder of the violent religious conflicts he endured. The château is where Montaigne will be born in 1533, grow up with Latin as his native tongue, be paternally indulged and spared a country life's ordinary chores. And then in 1571 at the age of thirty-eight, shortly after his father's death and the inheritance of both the estate and a large fortune, the château is where he will retire from public life, construct a private library, and devote himself to study and leisurely reflection. The new lord of the manor will eventually abandon the family patronymic and assume the name of his beloved estate: Montaigne. Was ever a room, a study, a house, a piece of property, a person so closely attached to a literary genre?

Situated on the third floor of one of the château's stone towers, just above his bedroom, and two floors above his Catholic chapel, the library was his favorite place on earth. It had originally served as a wardrobe (*une grande garderobe*), which he considered the most useless room in the house and so converted it into a library when he established residence. A self-proclaimed klutz, inept at most practical endeavors, Montaigne surely had a talented carpenter construct the five semicircular shelves that housed his personal collection of some one thousand books. He also probably didn't paint the inscriptions from Greek and Latin authors on the room's ceiling beams, some of which can still be seen. But it's very likely he alone designed the interior space (including the ten-by-eight-foot adjoining study with a fireplace for colder days) of his personal "kingdom" where he would spend so much time alone with his precious books and fluid thoughts. I've never visited the tower, and perhaps someday will, but in all of my reading and research I've also never come across any information from anyone about the dimensions of this historic library, even though it has been a prominent tourist site for centuries. My only information comes from Montaigne, who writes that the diameter of his library was *seize pas* — sixteen paces.

"Paces" is perhaps the most accurate word, since Montaigne preferred to compose in motion ("My mind will not budge unless my legs move it"), pacing back and forth, often dictating to someone who sat, one imagines quietly and patiently, at a small writing table facing the bookshelves. And this is how the modern essay takes its shape. A solitary, restless individual, perhaps one experiencing what we might call a "midlife crisis," circling the floor of his library, now and then consulting one of his books, now and then peering out of one of his beloved windows to enjoy a momentary interruption of thought, and occasionally looking up at the ceiling for philosophical inspiration. And so, in a tentative fashion, he gradually figures out how to document his innermost thoughts and originate a suitable mode of vernacular expression. He had a later start than most. Although he had recently published a long translation of a theological work from Latin to please his father, he didn't consider himself a writer or a scholar: he had no craft, no subjects, skills, or style. If, like some literary geniuses, he did have a sense of destiny, he presumably thought that his destiny would be achieved only if he avoided a destination. He didn't retire with essays in mind. They slowly emerged out of the relentless reflective process, the endless pacing.

His was a mind filled with doubt. His genius evolved with his writing and it essentially consisted in making doubt a source of creativity, not an intellectual liability or a spiritual affliction. When he looked up at his ceiling beams he could absorb his favorite maxims from his cherished classic authors, and many of these came from one thinker cited frequently in the essays — the third-century physician and philosopher Sextus Empiricus. In his influential *Outlines of Pyrrhonism*, Sextus, not himself an original thinker, conveniently handed down the essentials of the ancient schools of skepticism, mainly those based on the philosophy of Pyrrho of Elis (c. 360–c. 270 BCE), whose brand of skepticism especially interested the early Montaigne. Put briefly, Pyrrho believed we could know nothing for certain and that every opinion could be countered by an equally convincing opposite opinion (for more on Pyrrho and Sextus I recommend the excellent entries easily found online in the *Stanford Encyclopedia of Philosophy*). Temperamentally opposed to dogmatism and having witnessed the ways dogmatism fueled the religious persecutions of his time, Montaigne clearly found a skeptical attitude to be both illuminating and salutary.

But the skeptical philosophy promoted by the ancients was not intended to be an epistemology, an investigation into the limits of human knowledge. It had a practical goal, one that may appear quite peculiar today. The skepticism practiced by Pyrrho was an introduction to a set of skills that enabled his followers to produce opinions that would effectively counter or refute other opinions. This systematic process, however, was not devised for the sake of testing public arguments to arrive at the truth (there was no truth or it was irrelevant) but rather to attain by a "suspension of judgment" what the skeptics termed *ataraxia*, a mental state of tranquility and imperturbability.

How a deliberate clash of conflicting opinions could result in tranquility is not especially clarified by Sextus; the process appears to take a Zen Buddhist form of sudden enlightenment or, as Sextus admits, tranquility follows the suspension of judgment somehow "by chance." Apparently, if we can convince ourselves that one opinion or one course of action is no better than another we needn't worry about selecting the correct one. As we come to understand the futility of possessing a dogmatic belief in any philosophical, scientific, or religious opinion we can reach *ataraxia*, which is perhaps best translated literally, though clumsily, as "troublelessness." This psychological goal was a large part of Montaigne's attraction to ancient skepticism. Uncertainty could be as therapeutic as essaying while pacing. And consequently the essays, as he began to shape them, embraced two large converging vectors — the dynamics of skepticism and the quest for happiness. "What do I know?" and "How should I live?"

Some readers may wonder why, given his adherence to skepticism, Montaigne took comfort in his title, his possessions, his estate, his routines, and his Catholicism. But this, too, is derived from Pyrrho via Sextus. Since no single way of life could be proven to be superior to another, no one government to another, then one may as well relax and accept the customs, laws, traditions, morals, and standards of life that one's community offers. This "traditionalist" approach based on the "suspension of judgment" would be abhorrent to many people today, even those who would not for a moment consider themselves dogmatic in their beliefs. But it was understandable to Ralph Waldo Emerson, whose well-known essay on Montaigne focused on skepticism. For Emerson, Montaigne represents the skeptical mind, and his essay largely contends with skepticism as a lived philosophy.

At one point, Emerson confronts the inherent conservatism that seems to be at the heart of the skeptical mind-set. "The superior mind" (i.e., the skeptic), he writes, "will find itself equally at odds with the evils of society, and with the projects that are offered to relieve them." He then goes on to say something that the ancient skeptics, with their acceptance of social conventions, would disagree with: "The wise skeptic is a bad citizen; no conservative; he sees the selfishness of property, and the drowsiness of institutions. But neither is he fit to work with any democratic party that ever was constituted; for parties wish everyone committed, and he penetrates the popular patriotism."

Montaigne provides a pretext for Emerson to test his own skepticism. It is not easy to see where Emerson stands, as he appears to advocate skepticism while at the same time disavowing it. No matter how necessary it may be for an open-minded individual to suspend judgment, skepticism will be swallowed up by life's larger forces. "Although knaves win in every political struggle, although society seems to be delivered over from the hands of one set of criminals into the hands of another set of criminals, as fast as the government is changed, and the march of civilization is a train of felonies, yet, general ends are somehow answered." Emerson's skepticism may be tough-minded and unsympathetic, but it is always optimistic.

The skeptic is always faced with an internal contradiction: to say that knowledge consists of knowing that nothing can be known for certain is to express a certainty. This puts it simply, yet the core inconsistency (which didn't perturb Sextus) caused Bertrand Russell and, before him, the essayist and founder of British Empiricism, Francis Bacon, to dismiss much of skeptical thought. But there is another problem with skepticism, especially with extreme forms: to follow a rigorous Pyrrhonic suspension of judgment would seem to make everyday life impossible. The Pyrrhonists, like Sextus, knew this and it's why they didn't feel they had to doubt certain beliefs, and thereby accepted the laws, customs, and moral codes of their community. But to read Sextus is to see that his radical system of skepticism is not without its internal contradictions. And there's also the dubious claim that the strength of any opinion can be nullified by an equally persuasive counteropinion.

One of life's troubles, of course, is in determining which opinions are open to the vigorous give-and-take of discussion and which are so settled that discussion becomes an unproductive waste of energy. And which are so taboo they cannot even be mentioned. These are not easy distinctions; what seems eminently debatable for one person is off-limits to another; what is obvious or self-evident to you is perhaps mysterious and complicated to me. Although Montaigne could enjoy being a contrarian, he is — as I read him — a reasonable skeptic who proceeded in discussion and debate with an open, receptive, and tolerant attitude ("No propositions astonish me, no belief offends me"). As he gained experience in essaying, his reliance on Sextus diminished and his love for Plutarch grew. Montaigne realized that one needed to be skeptical of skepticism; it could serve as a useful intellectual tool, especially if we grew overly confident of human reason, but skepticism, too, will often fall short of supplying us with the answers we need.

What to me is most important from a literary and philosophical point of view is the extent to which Montaigne created the essay as an exercise in self-scrutiny and free inquiry. As Emerson suggests, through Montaigne the essay became closely, and perhaps permanently, identified with a skeptical sensibility. The essays were forms of expression new to the world and for centuries they characterized what it is like to possess an open and inquiring mind. It remains to be seen whether the future will any longer respect or care for such a mind, with its amazing scope, tolerance for opposing opinions, and delight in trying out — not proselytizing — ideas.

Assuming it can continue to be the humanistic principle it once was, the old (now discredited?) ideal of free and open discussion begins in our dialogues with ourselves. If we don't continually test even our firmest beliefs and opinions they will calcify into unquestioned dogma. Montaigne knows this; and he knows that there will always be those who welcome such calcification of thought and opinion, who — either for moral, political, or professional reasons — would rather accept dogmatic positions than entertain the expression of opposing perspectives. In an increasingly polarized society, skeptical free inquiry can easily lead to slippery-slope conclusions: you contemplate opinion X or Y or Z, and the next thing you know you're a bigot, a communist, or a Nazi. For a moment you pace back and forth in your room essaying, and suddenly the reputed tolerant are no longer tolerating.

Stefan Zweig understood the powers of unchecked dogmatism. Escaping from a Nazi-dominated Austria, he accidentally rediscovered the *Essais* while exiled in Brazil. In his admirable book on Montaigne, written just months before he and his wife committed suicide together, Zweig finds distressing parallels between the essayist's time and his own troubled era. Although from the outside Montaigne "appeared to be a model citizen," he lived an exciting and authentic interior life energized by an unrestricted spirit of free inquiry. For Zweig, Montaigne's skepticism is what kept him free, and Montaigne's commitment to freedom is what readers should take to heart in troubled times.

"In such epochs where the highest values of life — our peace, our independence, our basic rights, all that makes our existence more pure, more beautiful, all that justifies it — are sacrificed to the demon inhabiting a dozen fanatics and ideologues, all the problems of the man who fears for his humanity come down to the same question: how to remain free?"

And Zweig concludes:

> It is to this question and this question alone that Montaigne dedicated his life and his strength . . . And this quest, which he undertakes to safeguard his soul, his liberty, at a moment of universal servility before ideologies and parties, makes him today a brother to us, more intimate

than any other artist. If we love and honour him today more than any other, it is because he devoted himself more than any other to the most sublime art of living: *rester soi-même.*[2]

"To remain oneself." That sounds perhaps too static a goal for a personality as mercurial as Montaigne's. Yet, he knew the self, *himself* at least, to be a shifting, protean phenomenon, and his own human mutability was exactly what he hoped to record in the essays, just as his near-contemporary and admirer William Shakespeare captured it for the stage. To remain oneself is to remain variable. Montaigne often felt divided over issues and decisions, seeing several sides or choices at once, or different sides or choices at different times, and he thought candor and honesty required that we admit our self-contradictions, conflicting views, and turnabouts instead of striving for what might well be an artificial consistency. This, of course, may be where literature separates itself from the world of law and politics, where "flip-flopping" or "walking back" is an unpardonable offense.

Zweig found Montaigne to be an intellectual hero primarily for his ability to maintain a free and inquiring mind in the midst of turmoil and oppression. His book was designed to promote Montaigne's relevance to a world heading precipitously toward another horrible war. But I'm not sure that Zweig's argument for Montaigne's relevance wouldn't seem romanticized by many readers today. Perhaps Sextus, Montaigne, Emerson, and Zweig would all be considered "bad citizens" now, with their emphasis on the solitary spirit of independent thought as opposed to the solidarity of collective action. Will Montaigne's essays remain relevant and vital? Will his formidable reputation endure? Will the essay as a mode of unconstrained expression survive? I'm growing skeptical, but I guess it all depends on how much future generations will prize free inquiry and open discussion.

The Best American Essays features a selection of the year's outstanding essays, essays of literary achievement that show an awareness of craft and forcefulness of thought. Hundreds of essays are gathered annually from a wide assortment of national and regional publications. These essays are then screened, and approximately one hundred are turned over to a distinguished guest editor, who may add a few personal discoveries and who makes the final selections. The list of notable essays appearing in the back of the book is drawn from a final comprehensive list that includes not only all of the essays submitted to the guest editor but also many that were not submitted.

To qualify for the volume, the essay must be a work of respectable literary quality, intended as a fully developed, independent essay (not an excerpt) on a subject of general interest (not specialized scholarship), originally written in English (or translated by the author) for publication in an American periodical during the calendar year. Note that abridgments and excerpts taken from longer works and published in magazines do not qualify for the series but if considered significant they will appear in the Notable list in the back of the volume. Today's essay is a highly flexible and shifting form, however, so these criteria are not carved in stone.

Magazine editors who want to be sure their contributors will be considered each year should submit issues or subscriptions to:

The Best American Essays
Houghton Mifflin Harcourt
125 High Street, 5th Floor
Boston, MA 02110

Writers and editors are welcome to submit published essays from any American periodical for consideration; unpublished work does not qualify for the series and cannot be reviewed or evaluated. Also ineligible are essays that have been published in book form — such as a contribution to a collection — but have never appeared in a periodical. All submissions from print magazines must be directly from the publication and not in manuscript or printout format. Editors of online magazines and literary bloggers should not assume that appropriate work will be seen; they are invited to submit clear printed copies of the essays to the address above. Please note: due to the increasing number of submissions from online sources, material that does not include a full citation (name of publication, date, author contact information, etc.) cannot be considered. If submitting multiple essays, please include a separate cover sheet with a full citation for each selection.

Writers should keep in mind that — like many literary awards — the essays are selected from a large pool of nominations. Unlike many literary awards, however, writers may nominate themselves. A considerable number of prominent literary journals regularly submit issues to the series, but though we continually reach out with invitations to submit and reminders of deadlines, not all periodicals respond or participate, so writers should be sure to check with their editors to see if they routinely submit to the series.

The deadline for all submissions is February 1 of the year following the year of publication: thus all submissions of essays published in 2018 must be received by February 1, 2019. There is no fixed reading period, but writers and editors are encouraged to submit appropriate candidates as they are published during the year and not wait until the final deadline.

With the passing of William H. Gass late last year, the essay lost one of its great modern practitioners and champions. In the first volume of *The Best American Essays*, Elizabeth Hardwick paid him tribute by featuring one of his remarkable essays and by relying in her introduction on his memorable distinction between essays and articles. His brilliant criticism of prose style and his insights into the aesthetics of the essay have had a lasting impact on this series.

It's a pleasure each year to thank Nicole Angeloro for her superb editorial talents and uncanny ability to keep everything on track given the tight schedule of an annual book. And for their expertise, a heartfelt thanks to other publishing people at Houghton Mifflin Harcourt, including Larry Cooper and Megan Wilson. I also want to thank my son, Gregory Atwan, for all of his generous help throughout the year. It was especially enjoyable to work on this thirty-third volume of *The Best American Essays* with one of my favorite essayists and critics, Hilton Als. He brought to this edition a sensibility keenly attuned to the varieties of literary and artistic performance. This volume of twenty-four essays expresses a multiplicity of passions and perspectives; it is both highly eclectic and — as readers will detect — subtly interlaced.

R.A.

Notes

1. *The Complete Essays of Montaigne*, translated by Donald M. Frame (Stanford, CA: Stanford University Press, 1976). I use this translation throughout.
2. Stefan Zweig, *Montaigne*, translated by Will Stone (London: Pushkin Press, 2015).

Introduction

SOME MONTHS AGO—actually it's over a year now—I moved from one part of Manhattan to another. The distance wasn't tremendous, less than a mile, but the psychological shift was sizable: I was vacating a kind of way station that passed as a home for a room of my own. Even though I'd lived in the apartment I was leaving for over twenty years, I'd shared it with a number of friends, some gone now, and too many ideas about what constituted generosity and receptivity: if you had a roof over your head, then it behooved you to share it with others, no matter the financial and spiritual cost. Giving might make someone else, anyone else, better.

That was my mother's ethos; she raised me and my five siblings in Brooklyn. My father did not live with us. He was more or less supported by his mother in her large house not too far way. He had a room in her house, at the very top of it, and it was sacrosanct: you didn't enter it uninvited. I never questioned my parents' arrangement; it was the way it was. But in the last years leading up to my leaving my first Manhattan apartment — which, by the way, I'd moved into the year my mother died, in 1989; I was born in 1960 — I'd felt crowded in it or, more accurately, crowded out of it.

Let me explain. Even though I ostensibly lived alone in that flat surrounded by piles — books, records, photographs, magazines — my body had been afflicted by emotional piles for a long time before I left all that junk behind. You see, everything I'd learned about hospitality from my mother — she who is every child's moral barometer, even if she's broken — had caved in on my soul. I could no longer sustain the platonic soup kitchen I'd been raised to stock, and preside over. I could no longer maintain my mother's lessons of the heart.

By the end of my stay in my first New York place, all those bodies, sometimes excellent and sometimes not, that had crossed my threshold had impressed themselves on me no matter how the relationship was defined. It didn't matter if the day-to-day friendship had dissolved, or the person had died, or what have you. Those former friends, bodies, were now a part of my body, and I could no longer bear their weight, or the weight of any of it. Then Love called, rather unexpectedly. Love didn't so much edge those bodies out as ask for a different place to house itself — a new home with less of everything that was not Love. No *Pilgrim's Progress* burdens, or treating time as though it was valuable to others but not to myself. Love taught me that my time was my own. Mine. To say "mine" was evil if you came from the Ma school of things; it was a way of killing off Ma and her brand of goodwill, a way of being like all those others who hurt Ma, and in hurting Ma, hurt me. Love pushed against that. And how "mine" was forbidden when I was growing up.

Our ma supported us in part with "help" from public assistance — welfare. Some images from those days: caseworkers going through her cabinets to make sure she didn't have a crust of bread or a man or anything that could contribute to her well-being, let alone that of her children. If anything was found, no more government "help." No more standing with my sister to get welfare food off a truck. No more social workers asking what your daily life is like, as a way of finding out what your mother is up to personally, or whether or not she was mothering you at all. Love pushed against all that, and wanted something else, including the right to ask the questions I never thought of for myself, given that "I" I had been trained by Ma's idea of love not to love. Another question Love asked: Why didn't Pa, during all those years of lying and not lying about his absence, give his family any nourishment, take his kids in before making at least one kid sick with tinned meat? Love pushed against all that, and this, too: the feeling that if I had my own place and a lock and key, I would be no better than Pa, wrapped up safe as can be and soft in his cocoon of a room, nursing on the overly sweet milk of self-protection, a mother's indulgence, constant self-regard. Love assured me that having a space to work, one that wasn't entirely at the mercy of other people I had known, which is to say Ma's legacy of giving unto death, didn't have to be a thing. In fact, it could be dismantled brick by brick, so that out of the prison of Ma's days I could be a free man taught to praise.

Love was the principal architect of my new place and the principal dissembler of the past. The primary feature of my new apartment is light. There are windows on either end of a floor-through in a part of town notable for its proximity to the Hudson River and its vestiges of bohemian New York: trees, a square, crooked old streets with Dutch or Flemish names. Few if any of us know the stories behind those names. History takes too much time. We are Manhattanites and preoccupied by our lives in Manhattan. Sometimes Love stays for the night, and other nights Love cooks meals, and in between these pleasures there's the fear of Love removing its presence. How will it go? Must it go? What is it doing now? What is it doing without me? Have I done enough for it to stay? Are you my mother? If you love me enough, will I be my father and lock the door, letting no one in? Love encourages me to get to the desk built in the room where I work, and even to shut the door from his Love in order to get whatever it is I need to get done, done. Love can't always stay. Love weighs on me, not in the same way those other bodies did in the days when I followed Ma's ethos to a T. Love is not here sometimes — is out working or making a meal or sitting in a room far off, on the other end of a joke. And yet there is Love's presence in a disfiguring world. And then there is your disfigured body—the one that is misshapen by words and events Love cannot follow you into and you do not want Love to follow you into, shaped, as it is, by the once-irrefutable loneliness I thought was the world.

The street leading to my house runs east to west, a trajectory that takes you from a once-bad neighborhood to a very nice one. (In any case, it's difficult to find a bad neighborhood in lower Manhattan now. Everything has been bought and made better here in the land of the plenty, the horn of the good.) I spend several mornings a week on the east side of my block, dealing with personal stuff, including learning how to physically and mentally defend myself against those who do not feel my "I" should exist at all. Sometimes this begins even before Love finds me for the day, or night. That ill wind follows me down my street the way thoughts followed Virginia Woolf down the road in her essay "Street Haunting," written in 1930:

> How beautiful a street is in winter! It is at once revealed and obscured. Here vaguely one can trace symmetrical straight avenues of doors and windows; here under the lamps are floating islands of pale light through which pass quickly bright men and women, who, for all their poverty and shabbiness, wear a certain look of unreality, an air of triumph, as if they had given life the slip, so that life, deceived of her prey, blunders on without them. But, after all, we are only gliding smoothly on their surface. The eye is not a miner, not a diver, not a seeker after buried treasure. It floats us smoothly down a stream; resting, pausing, the brain sleeps perhaps as it looks.

But I am not gliding down the surface of my thoughts as I make my way from the east side of my street down to the west, in part because I am not Virginia Woolf, which is to say, I do not go unobserved in the world of my street, thus making me free to observe in relative safety and peace. In the world of my street I'm observed for a variety of reasons, and this individual and collective surveillance shapes my thoughts and my writing in ways that I resent. Who wouldn't want to spend an evening walking in search of a pencil and coming back home without incident to think about it? The way I'm observed means my brain can't sleep as I look; that's a luxury I can't afford as I try to not kill the world that means to kill me. From the time I moved into my new home—the windows let in as much nature as is possible in Manhattan—but really several years before that, I felt something in Manhattan that even Love couldn't protect me from, and what shall I call it? The *May I see your ID* syndrome?

On my block there's a big store, part of a chain that sells electronic devices. I've been in the shop exactly three times—once to get a device fixed, once to buy a Christmas gift with my white German goddaughter, and once to replace a missing something to fix another device. Each time I've gone into the store, done my business, and am about to pay, I've been asked for my ID. I am not asleep to the fact that none of the other customers—usually affluent Europeans, yuppie mothers, and the like—are asked for anything but their credit cards once they belly up to the electronic bar to make a purchase. For those of us who are not them, the exchange of capital for goods becomes a kind of sickroom: *May I see your ID?* The sickroom glows with blood, the blood that floods your face your neck your back as you hand over your ID instead of—what? A fuck-you? And why not a fuck-you? Because the worker who asks you for your ID is black or Hispanic and male, too, and he needs to make a living, even if it's at someone's literal and figurative expense. He can't look at you. (A side note: this is always the point in the story when you become a third-person figure. Your body can't bear it and so becomes a different body, watching as things happen but trying not to feel, despite the rush of blood to the face the neck the back. In this situation and others like it, your "I" recedes, running further and further back into the hidden world housed in the body the world hates.) He looked at you before, smiling, as you decided to purchase the shit you needed, but all of that changes when he asks, *May I see your ID?* The tone was the same as it was when he was showing you the junk you needed, friendly like, but now there's a threat: If you don't have ID, who are you other than a thieving threat? There's a bright lift to his voice: *May I see your ID?* Surely someone trained him to say that, just as my mother and father, respectively, showed me how important it was to despise racism and its various inevitable humiliations, and to empathize with workers who were oppressed by a corporate system that puts their head in a yoke just so they know who's boss. Who is the slain, who is the victim? Speak! So wrote Sophocles in *Antigone,* and maybe that's the start of the essay in my head that I can't write because of the blood pounding in it as the young man swipes my card and swipes my reason several blocks away from my home, away from Love. The transaction closed, the thing I needed now bagged, weighs heavy in my hand like evil, like shame: Why couldn't I forgo my mother's ethos and "read" that young man to filth? Because by not looking at me—*May I have your ID?*—he was, perhaps, frightened to discover what he would find on the other end of his learned question/inquisition: at the beginning or end of his own street, rocky with the stones of compromise, smiling all the while, the better to survive.

The first time I experienced the *May I see your ID?* syndrome, outside of when I tried to enter Pa's room—*Whose child are you?*—I was fourteen or so and wearing white ballet slippers. I was a stu-

dent at the School for the Performing Arts, which was then on
West 46th Street. There, I majored in theater. To get to the school
from my home in Brooklyn, I took the IRT express—the 2 or 3
train—and got off at Times Square. I always wore ballet slippers
then, and, frequently, tights. Sometimes I carried a bag, a kind
of pouch my mother had made for me. A queer costume for her
queer child. One day, as I hurried through the filthy labyrinth that
was and is the IRT subway system at Times Square, a cop stopped
me. *Give me your ID.* I showed him my train pass. I didn't have
any other ID. The blood was pounding behind my eyes. Something—instinct—told me not to show my real face—the face of
my fear and hatred. I was no longer myself: I knew what it was like
to be almost annihilated or have some part of your natural trust
annihilated by men. Become "nothing" and maybe they won't kill
you. When I was a kid, my boy cousins used to try to suffocate me
with plastic bags. They wanted this faggot to die. Maybe that long-
ago cop wanted this faggot to die. With no provocation at all, he
walked me down some more filthy corridors and we ended up in
his headquarters, where I was booked as a truant. I said, once, that
I was not a truant, that I was on my way to school, but that wasn't
the story he wanted to hear or his buddies wanted to hear, and
something in me went silent. How could I contradict his idea of
my body? With what? My ballet slippers? My mind? My love of art
and theater and movie lovers in anguish? And let me just say that
what I felt then is not so very different from what I feel as I walk toward my new home where Love waits. I'm adrift in a stop-and-frisk
universe that has always been a stop-and-frisk universe. My silence
is a form of protection: Do I want them to cut my tongue out, too?
Or an equally effective private part of my anatomy? This feeling
goes back centuries, no doubt, and is in my DNA and has saved my
life in the past, all the way back to the ships and the lash. But it has
also stomped on my heart and given Love quite a job. Call it what
you will—white backlash, Obama-era payback, or whatever—but
I find our present condition difficult to write about. Part of what
drew me to the pieces collected here is how the writers managed
to discover, during a hard rain, times even of humor, and sometimes beauty, and a great heaping of pain and incomprehension
that they wanted to make sense of. These voices encourage me to
not *not* speak, despite history and most evidence to the contrary
saying otherwise.

*

Even before I moved out of my old apartment with all those bodies, one could feel the need for blood to be spilled in the streets,
an extension of all those shot bodies in North Carolina or mowed-
down bodies in Lexington, Kentucky, not to mention other parts
of the world, now and forever, somewhere, always. As I've said,
some folks call our present condition white backlash, but I call
this wave of violence the tedium of having to give a shit. All those
years in college reading *Beloved,* all those seminars on women's
bodies, including reproductive rights, and Dad down at the office having to deal with hearing about equal pay even if he never
forked it over. All those years of talk of immigrant care and elder
health care and social security this and fair that. Even entertainment wasn't safe. Tender movie and TV shit about lesbians and
gays and trans people, and will it never end? So says the guy sitting
in that classroom or in that movie theater, emboldened by the vile
slime that comes via the airwaves night after night, so says this guy
as he watches TV reflecting the rich and his constantly rightly exas-
perated-by-all-this-difference president. Lock those immigrants up,
says this guy following his commander in chief's example, sterilize
them, separate them from their children like in the slaves' days,
and let me get mine, my *stuff.*

Once, in my old neighborhood, a guy with a BMW was looking lov-
ingly at the stuff under the hood of his shiny car as his little son, a
toddler, walked out into the street and was minding his own unsu-
pervised baby business when the world stopped but reality didn't: as
the child toddled, a taxi suddenly rounded the corner near where
he was, and I screamed, the car stopped, and the man stopped
looking at his stuff for a moment to pick up his living stuff. Then,
holding his neglected child, this dad followed me home to make
sure that I wasn't going to report him to the police. I should have.
Ma's ethos interfered: Perhaps the man had "learned" something,
Ma said in my heart, while my body said, If I went to the police,
who would believe us? Would I be the dude who pushed his baby
into the road, while caring rich fathers looked on helplessly? Looking at his BMW stuff, that father—a version of my father?—was,
perhaps, tired of giving a shit even when it came to his own child
and its baby needs. Maybe he was tired of all those other baby
needs over the past eight years or so, when he had to deal with

imagining how someone else might feel. Maybe he was tired of living through some version of the civil rights era again, all those Obamas. It was exhausting to be made aware of the world's concerns, all the moral bullshit of the underprivileged and whatnot, including those guys in ballet slippers who scream when a child may be harmed, who the fuck wants to deal? Now it's my turn, the same guy may think, my time, mine, and what I want to ask is how long will it be before even the most enlightened person starts calling me a nigger? This guy may say: If all those niggers and cunts out there can't take what we've had to swallow all these years—all those years of trying to empathize with crap that has nothing to do with us at all, that has nothing to do with power—surely it's all those niggers' and cunts' time to deal with us guys who have had to listen to what they've had to say, all that whining, ignoring the fact that America was never theirs and always ours, ignoring the fact that America has always heard them first. And because these guys are American, they want me to hear them first.

Here's some stuff they've said that they are surprised you don't want to listen to as you listen because of Ma's ethos, the body that took it all because Ma considered it her job. At a memorial service where I eulogized a white woman I didn't like but her family asked me and what can you do?, one of the bereaved came up to me and said, I've been reading you for years, I didn't know you were black. And so big. Then, at a party, out of nowhere: I really like *Dear White People*—as if you're in the cast. At a business meeting with a potential producer: Don't you miss that comedy troupe that used to say, "I'm black and I suck dick"? At a small theater, a small black female performer in a solo work. The show is over, and when I retire to the men's room, a gentleman in the opposite stall: You were so great in the show. Then there is the usual, someone mistakes me for another writer of color, and when I say, No, I'm the other one, he looks at me cockeyed: Was I sure? Then there's the guy you go out on a date with before you find Love who tells you that his relatives owned a plantation in Haiti years ago and the people who worked it looked like you. Sometimes you try to convince others, these guys, that you are yourself—*Where's my I?*—especially, hideously, if they are your friends. Remember the moment when the dying woman you were trying to help said, You see that black guy crossing the street, my grandfather would have called him a mook. Remember the former friend who loved to tell the story of how, when her father thought someone was unattractive, he'd say, They're uglier than a bag of nigger rectums. Or the other, dying friend who said, while bending over to kiss her, Whoa, this is just like the Tennessee Williams story "Desire and the Black Masseur." This casual and not so casual hatred and aggression, even in presumed love, is as old as America, a country defined in part by people defining who they are least *not*. While America is happening to my mind and body, I try to make sense of it as I walk toward home and Love, but my mind can't make writing of it somehow, because how can you tell a story that all the metaphors in the world can't enhance or help make into art?

Love wants so many things, wants your story without metaphors if it comes to that. Love says, Tell it, baby, tell about that walk from east to west, marred and marked by others, that which makes for a different kind of reflection. Tell it, because Love is interested.

All a writer has is his epoch and how it shapes him. In her very interesting introduction to the first volume of *The Best American Essays* series, Elizabeth Hardwick wrote that the essay was a "slithery form, wearisomely vague and as chancy as a fish in the open hand." In short, the essay, like love, like life, is indefinable, but you know an essay when you see it, and you know a great one when you feel it, because it's concentrated life, whole and in bits. Indeed, the essays I'm attracted to—and I think the present volume shows that—have something unfinished about them, a circle that cannot be closed, filled with dread—even or especially when humorous—anxious that certain national politics, say, are generated by nothing more and nothing less than certain revenge fantasies vis-à-vis identity politics, say, all those bodies rising up out of the dust and grief of racism and sexism to say "I."

In "Why I Write," a 1976 talk about her early years as a writer, Joan Didion said that she borrowed the title of her essay from another—George Orwell's "Why I Write"—because, first off, she liked the sound of the words: *Why I Write*.

> There you have three short unambiguous words that share a sound, and the sound they share is this:
> *I*
> *I*
> *I*

In many ways writing is the act of saying *I*, of imposing oneself upon other people, of saying *listen to me, see it my way, change your mind.* It's an aggressive, even a hostile act. You can disguise its qualifiers and tentative subjunctives, with ellipses and evasions . . . but there's no getting around the fact that setting words on paper is the tactic of a secret bully, an invasion, an imposition of the writer's sensibility on the reader's most private space?

And in her *Best American* introduction, Hardwick said, "The aggressiveness of the essay is the assumption of the author to speak in one's own voice."

Rereading Didion and Hardwick, I wonder if, indirectly, these authors were telling us something about their experience as women, and that their description of aggression was the result of having been aggressed upon, told what to do, claimed, putting their "I" aside on more than one occasion to make a difficult situation work, to pacify a husband, to not be a target. Just as queer writers of yore, and writers of color who had to smile and twirl in between bitter descriptions about life in America in order to be read at all, often told the reader more about who they were in between the lines, saying "I," if you are a different person, can feel like a dangerous proposition, let alone reality: being a target hurts. And since writing is the author's deepest self, writing about one's "I," standing up for it, can feel like an aggressive act, I suppose, given how we targets are programmed not to. I wonder how many heteronormative men and some queer ones worry when asking for your ID, or saying, in so many words, stay out of my room, or worry about how aggressive their language is after they put a plastic bag over your head, trying to smother your faggot voice and concerns. How did we get here? That's the subject of many of the essays that we read and remember. How did we get here, and are we stuck here as men and women and Other?

Living as we do in a broken world, essays are bound to become more broken, fractured, as power becomes insistent on showing its power further by breaking more backs, jailing the innocent, cracking Love in the knees. The majority of us are not whole individuals, because there is no such thing as a whole society. Sometimes, on my walk home, in the short space between the rest of the world and my front door, I will have a moment to dream and reflect, and I speculate on what the essays to come will look like, read like.

Of course they'll be made up of many things, including questions and images and gestures, because we live in a world of too many things and half-understood selves. But the essays of the future will or should start with questions, generally political in nature, and if you don't think so, think again.

Here's one essay born out of these times: The comedian Richard Pryor asking once why targets on shooting and archery ranges were always black. Add to that the sound of the woman crying, "Why are they shooting?" as she filmed Antwon Rose being gunned down in East Pittsburgh. Another essay: Looking at Jean-Michel Basquiat's 1983 painting *Defacement* (*The Death of Michael Stewart*), which the artist produced after Michael Stewart, another graffiti artist, was beaten to death by policemen in the subway. I remember Michael Stewart, the guy my female friend went home with the night I told her we could not be lovers. We were in our early twenties, players in a club on lower Broadway, in Manhattan. After we parted for the night, my complicated companion wasted no time finding herself a guy, a thin man of color with dreads who seemed to be drowning in his overcoat. (Interestingly, she had been involved with Basquiat himself off and on for some time before and after he made that painting dedicated to her murdered friend.) Basquiat, on hearing of Stewart's death: That could have been me, that could have been me. I didn't have the presence of mind to say then: But it is.

Another essay: The music video "This Is America," starring the performer Donald Glover. Directed by Hiro Murai, who oversees many of the episodes of *Atlanta,* a history-making series about race, relationships, and place, also starring Glover. In "This Is America," Glover performs under the name Childish Gambino. The look of the clip is airy and claustrophobic. Folks record acts of violence on their cell phones. A KKK figure rides in on a horse. Glover plays both sides of the racial coin. As a "white" man he blows away a chorus of black singers in a church, impersonating Dylann Roof murdering nine black people in a church in South Carolina. As himself, Glover critiques how blackness can become a pose, commodified, and how that commodification repeats itself, for bigger and bigger bags of cash. At one point, he stands on a pile of cars, just as Michael Jackson did in his 1987 "Bad" video, and just like Beyoncé did in her 2016 "Formation" video. This is black anger as entertainment. Is Glover doing the same thing by putting out a video at all? At the end of the piece, Glover, black and naked with fear, is chased down a seemingly endless corridor by white people.

The terror in Glover's eyes and open mouth, gasping for breath, is familiar to me, and now to Love, as Love holds my body, not seeing it as the wrong one but as *the* one. And that's the thought and feeling that gets me down the stairs on most days when I leave my house to walk east to west. I have a little ritual when I close my apartment door and face my day, after checking to see if I have my ID, checking to see if I'm ready to make the journey once more. (Joan Didion: "Every day is all there is.") I look across the street at the colored lobby guy sitting at his station. He's an essay unto himself. Every day I go out and he's at work in his glassed-off world. We wave to one another, quietly happy and satisfied to find that we're still here, each in the other's world.

HILTON ALS

The Best
AMERICAN
ESSAYS
2018

MARILYN ABILDSKOV

The Trick: Notes Toward
a Theory of Plot

FROM *The Gettysburg Review*

THE HOSPITAL SAT high on a hill. The city smelled of coffee and salt. When I wrote my name, I thought, "There's a record now."

Beside my name, *friend*. Beside others' names, *mother, sister, wife, wife, wife.*

His hands were bare. The first time we'd met, both his hands were covered in rings. The rings repelled me. I was surprised to be so repelled. But here he was, alive and ringless, in a sweatshirt and khaki pants. He'd just finished dinner. His feet looked funny in beige socks and flip-flops.

I told him about a movie I'd just seen, set in Japan. There had been a lot of scenes involving feet. He said he would like to see it. He said, "This is the first time I laughed all day."

We talked in one of the anonymous waiting rooms where everything, the walls and chairs and atmosphere, was beige. He still had a half-eaten container of pudding nearby. "Do you want to finish that?" I asked. I thought if he still liked pudding, he'd be okay.

There were advantages. I came to understand that right away. I always knew where he was. I knew where he was yesterday, and where he would be tomorrow, and where he would be the day after that and the day after that. I did not worry about him meeting someone else.

A car, a subway, a taxi — it took these three forms of transportation to get to the hospital every week. I had a lot of time to think. And I remember the day after each visit as heightened, saturated, a day of attention and high alert. The color of the pumpkins growing in the neighbor's yard across the street, the taste of the apple pastry and dark coffee at Peet's, the feel of the paperbacks at Half Price Books — it was all ordinary, important, memorable.

At Le Bateau Ivre, on our first date, I told him all I remembered from junior high school French was *Je suis bibliothèque.*

He said he'd lived an eventful life. I said I'd lived an uneventful one and wanted to keep it that way.

I wanted to make sure I understood the timeline. So when, over lunch, he told me bits of his history — that he sold cheesecakes once, a long time ago; that he worked for a radio station after that; that when he lived in this neighborhood, he rode a purple bike; that he spent a year traveling in France — I reached for a napkin to write it down: "Cheesecake, radio, bicycle, France." I wanted to fix the details along a line of time. But he put his hand over mine. I closed my eyes so I didn't have to look at his rings. "No," he said. "These things have to happen organically."

After lunch at Le Bateau Ivre, we took a walk. Kissed on a street corner. Went to my apartment, where he said he needed to lie down. When he woke, we walked across the street for coffee. We sat on a bench. He said he needed me to drive him home. I'd never driven to the city. I was afraid of its steep hills. I was afraid of water. I was afraid of the bridge. I told him all this. But I said I'd try. "For you." Now that I'd told him my darkest fears, I insisted he tell me his. "I'll tell you later," he said. Then all at once, his face darkened as if thick black curtains dropped to cover the stage of an unsmiling mouth.

He could have just as easily disappeared. We'd only gone out once. We'd made plans to go out a second time, to hear jazz in the city on Friday night, something I thought sounded like what people who lived in the city would do on a Friday night. He called me on Thursday night to cancel, saying he was in Langley Porter, that he would be there for a few days, but I could call tomorrow night if I wanted. Afterward, I looked up Langley Porter online. I looked up 5150 online. I called him Friday night. I called him every night. I had just moved to town. Who else would I call?

When I asked him how he was doing, what he had done that day, what he had eaten for dinner, he answered simply: "Not well." "Watched TV." "Meatloaf and mashed potatoes." When I asked him what was going on in his head, he said, "Nothing." And I came to believe that happiness was an ability to elaborate, to chatter, to embroider, to cluck over how dry the meatloaf tasted.

I was forty-two years old. I'd lived alone for many years. I knew how to get by, how to go without.

And the situation was not without its comforts. There was comfort in calling, comfort in learning the names of his doctors (Dr. Lee, Dr. Nyeem, Dr. Housner), comfort in learning the names of the others on the fourth floor (Daniel, Chris, Isabel), comfort in writing down the names of the drugs he went on (Effexor, Lamictal, Ambien, Seroquel), comfort in learning what all the drugs were for (depression, moodiness, insomnia, anxiety attacks).

Did I have an agenda? Yes. Soon enough, I believed, he would be fine, and then, just imagine how grateful he would be, beholden really, to the woman who'd called every night, the one who'd waited so patiently, the person who'd seen him through his darkest hour.

We went from nothing to something, the plot of a story I knew. Stories, or fragments of stories, began to leak through.

The first time, he said, was with sleeping pills. He was thirty-three. His father had just died. He had been visiting his mother. He had wanted his mother to find him.

The second time, he was going to jump. I was sitting on the floor of my apartment for this. I had a little black couch, but the couch was uncomfortable, and I wanted to buy a new one, but I didn't dare because I didn't know yet if my job would work out. I wanted my next couch to be bold, not black but red. I had in mind that if I had a red couch, my love life would improve. He kept stopping to say, "Are you okay?" "Do you want to hear this?" And I kept saying yes, I was okay, yes, I wanted to hear. I was thinking about balconies, how high up his had been. I was thinking about flowers, if he'd had geraniums growing out there. I was thinking about rhythm, how after the first comes the second, and after the second? Three would be the charm. The third time would do the trick.

The trick is to find some reasonable plot. A thread, a through line, a timeline, a string. The trick is to move beyond the image, the fragment, the list. The trick is to find someone to hang it all on. To trade in the black couch for red, to have hope for the future, to learn how to shake things up, to stay out of the head.

"My childhood was consumed with my mother's passions," he said. "It was like a Greek tragedy."

I read online to learn how it might go: how he would get an IV

of Brevital; how, once unconscious, he would be given succinylcho-
line; how doctors would insert a rubber block in his mouth; how
the worry is that the brain will be deprived of oxygen. I wrote down
the steps: how doctors would rub jelly on his temples then connect
him to electrodes; how they would push a button; how there would
be a shock; how an electric current would run through his brain;
how a grand mal seizure could last twenty seconds; how thirty minutes later he would wake up with a headache.

After the first electroshock treatment, I asked him how he was,
and he said, "Great!" and I said, "Great!" But when I asked him
to elaborate, to tell me more, he said, "The thing is, with this
treatment, my memory's shot. Did you know I've been here two
months?" I asked him if he remembered why he went to the hospital, and he said, "The doctors told me that I wanted to kill myself."
I asked him what he thought of that, and he said, "I can't imagine
it. Why would anyone want to die?"

Later I asked him if he remembered me, and he said, "Yes,
of course, don't be ridiculous." Later I asked him where we had
lunch that one day, in the summertime, and he said, "Can you
give me a hint?" Later I asked him what he'd ordered for lunch at
the Drunken Boat, and he said he wasn't sure, then he turned it
around and asked what *did* he have? I didn't remember but said
chicken. "You had chicken. You said it was very good." And I tried
to sound definitive.

(I remember ordering crab cakes. I remember thinking they
were the worst crab cakes I'd ever had. I remember when I shared
my crab cakes with him, I wasn't sharing to be generous; I was sharing because I thought the crab cakes tasted like shit.)

I remember calling a friend and saying, "The thing is, the situation suits me. He can't remember the stupid things I said. He
can't remember that we never had sex. And this way, I don't have
to worry about him fucking around. It's like dating someone in
prison. I know right where he'll be. Plus, it makes me feel like I'm
doing something in the world."

Romance as charity. Romance as service project. Romance as
the plot that makes the world go round.

("Did you know," my friend Michael told me, "there was a plot-
line on *Sex and the City* just like this?")

Each time we talked, each time I visited, he asked me how I was.
I liked that. I'd been waiting for that. No one had asked me that in

a very long time. It was a very simple thing. I'm embarrassed now to say it meant everything.

Once, when I visited him, he asked me, "No, really, how are you?" and I said, "To be honest, I'm not so sure. This whole thing scares me." It took two hours to get to the hospital every week. Sometimes it seemed like a lot of work. And for what? But he said not to worry, that we were learning about each other, that this was a good thing, how much we were learning. "Don't forget that," he said.

So I began pushing him. "What do you know?" I asked on the next visit. "What can you say you know about me?" It seemed this whole thing had become too much about him. His face looked stricken, then worried, then blank. "I know you're a teacher," he said. There was a long pause. "Isn't that right?"

One night I didn't call. The next night he asked if something was wrong. I told him I was busy. He sighed and said, "It *was* Friday night. I'm sure you want to go out with your friends to have fun." But it wasn't that. I didn't have any friends yet. I wasn't interested in fun. Instead I had classes to teach, papers to grade, facts to face — I might be in love with someone who can't remember my name.

Sometimes I came home from work exhausted and fell into bed with Goldfish crackers and a bottle of wine, and on these nights, I'd think of Langley Porter with its locked windows and big-screen TV, its steady meals and someone calling every night — it didn't sound so bad to me.

In November someone new took center stage. The plot demanded it. What else was the spotlight — ever searching for drama, for action — to do? Isabel. He talked about Isabel all the time. The more than a dozen times Isabel had tried to kill herself; the hundreds of medications Isabel was on; the years of institutions where Isabel had lived and not even thirty yet; she wasn't even thirty years old. Impressive.

I imagined Isabel with long, dark, wild hair and a dancer's fragile build, her wrists covered in delicate markings.

One night when he talked about Isabel again and at great length, I got quiet, and he asked what was wrong, and I said, "I'm sorry, I just can't get into this." "Into what?" he asked. "Into feeling sorry for Isabel." He said she was sick, really sick. He said he was afraid she was really going to do it this time, succeed in killing herself if they let her out. "I hope she does," I said. "It must be terrible to be such a fuckup at being a fuckup all the time." He said, "You don't mean that." But I did. I was tired of hearing about Isabel all the time. I was tired of him worrying about poor Isabel. Why Isabel? Why not me? "Because you're okay," he said.

But I wasn't okay. I had a cold, a terrible cold. Nothing helped. Not NyQuil. Not tea. Not peeling and eating oranges religiously. I wrote on student papers: "It isn't clear if you're analyzing the cause or effect." I watched TV. I walked outside for fresh air. Near my apartment was a French boutique that sold handmade baby clothes in delicate shades of blue, yellow, and red. In the window, the tiny mannequins had no heads.

What causes two people to come together? What causes a man to write about himself online? Or a woman to answer? Or for someone to turn her head left before leaving a bar? What causes his eye to rest on a plain, unadorned face? What causes her to stop and talk at the bus stop? For two people to realize they are part of a new-old plot, glowing in a new-old kind of heat?

At Le Bateau Ivre, I'd asked him if he wanted to hear my theory of plot. It wasn't mine exactly. It belonged to a professor I loved and before him, thousands of others. But I wanted to say something that sounded smart. "There are two strands," I said. I cut my crab cake in half to make my point. "What happens and also what the person thinks about what happens. The more interesting part." He got quiet. When I asked him what he was thinking, he said he was just trying to take in the atmosphere, the Marilyn-ness of it. Then he wrapped his fingers around his water glass and said he was thinking about how he would think about this afternoon later on.

After my first visit to the hospital, I'd waited for a taxi, the fog so thick I couldn't see across the street. I'd started to cry, imagining that this was it, a kind of slide into gray oblivion. Part of me wanted to run back upstairs, to tell him something big, to talk about something other than a small film with feet. Part of me wanted desperately to be home, alone.

The plot was simple; the plot was old. Cities are filled with bridges and balconies and the smell of fresh bread. Cities like this one are filled with sad people who want to go home.

He was released from the hospital. Now there was no reason for me to call, no reason to visit. Now he could call me anytime. And sometimes he did, but not so often, not like before. He wasn't as devoted as I had been. He must not have had any agenda in mind. So part of me missed it, the old routine, the steadiness of it, the way I could control it, count on it, the way it all depended on dependable me.

When he called, ANONYMOUS came up on caller ID.

One night we went to the Elmwood. He ate popcorn. His hands were covered once again in rings. He'd had to quit smoking while in the hospital, but he'd started again. The holidays were approaching, and there were previews for a lot of sappy family dramas. Catherine Zeta-Jones came on the screen. He leaned over to me, said, "She does nothing for me. I'm like a baby now." Later he told me that the Anafranil had rendered him "chemically neutered," a dreaded side effect for many men, so much so that one guy he met at Langley Porter asked to have Viagra prescribed at the same time. "As for me," he said, "I couldn't care less. In fact, it's a relief. One less thing to worry about."

And in the end? What happened happened fast: a quick succession of arguments. He suggested a movie on Tuesday night. I arranged to take Tuesday night off work, then he told me Tuesday was no good, that he'd promised to go to Isabel's daughter's Christmas pageant. In an email, I wrote: "So Tuesday's off now? But I moved heaven and earth to make Tuesday work!" And he wrote back that everyone — except me — had given him wide latitude on his memory slips, and that if I got pissed off so easily, he would happily step aside. "This drama," he concluded, "is getting a bit much."

We never saw each other after that. We haven't talked. But when ANONYMOUS appears on caller ID, I think of him.

NOAM CHOMSKY

Prospects for Survival

FROM *The Massachusetts Review*

LIKE IT OR NOT, we happen to be living in the most extraordinary period of human history.

In recent years, humans have constructed two huge sledgehammers poised to destroy us, with others waiting in the wings. Along with these achievements, the dominant forces in global society have instituted policies that systematically erode the best line of defense against self-destruction. In brief, human intelligence has created a perfect storm. If it continues to rage, the human experiment is unlikely to survive very long.

It appears that we are dedicating ourselves to confirming a grim thesis formulated by one of the leading modern biologists, the late Ernst Mayr. He was considering the possibility of finding intelligent life elsewhere in the universe, and concluded that the prospects were dim. His reasons have considerable bearing on our current plight.

Mayr observes that we have one sample: Earth. There have been, he estimates, about fifty billion species on Earth, so we have fairly good evidence on biological success. The evidence, he argues, is quite clear. The most successful organisms are those that mutate quickly, like bacteria, or that have fixed niches to which they keep, whatever happens, like beetles. As we move up the scale of what we call intelligence, biological success declines. Large mammals never did very well. Humans are a statistical blip in the past few hundred years. The history of life on Earth, Mayr concludes, refutes the claim that "it is better to be smart than to be stupid." In other words, what we call intelligence may be a lethal mutation.

Mayr adds that the average life span for a species is about a hundred thousand years.

Modern humans emerged about two hundred thousand years ago. They now appear to be engaged in a dedicated effort to confirm Mayr's thesis — to show that we have perhaps outlived our allotted time on Earth. This enterprise has been under way particularly since the end of World War II, when two imminent threats to survival were constructed by human intelligence, and followed by systematic erosion of the means of defense.

The two awesome challenges to decent survival are, of course, nuclear weapons and environmental catastrophe. The best defense would be a functioning democracy in which informed and engaged citizens join together to develop means to overcome the threats — as can be done. However, policy making during the neoliberal years of the past generation has significantly enhanced the threats. For principled reasons, the policies enacted tend to exclude the general population from participation in policy formation, often even awareness. These policies have sharply concentrated wealth, and thereby political power, undermining institutions that might be responsive to the public will. They are well designed to diminish authentic democracy. Associated with the erosion of democracy is principled assault on an effective regulatory apparatus that might mitigate the threats. In the most powerful country in world history, the leader of the free world, we see all of this very dramatically right now.

But the roots run deep.

Let me try to bring together some strands of recent history that intertwine, I think, in order to show that a perfect storm is all too plausible.

The end of World War II was one of the most important moments in human history. It was a time of joy, and also of horror, with the dawn of the nuclear age, an age overshadowed by the dark realization that human intelligence had created the means for terminal destruction.

It was not understood at the time, but the end of World War II also signaled the beginning of another era that threatens organized human existence: the Anthropocene, a new geological epoch in which human activity is dramatically changing the environment. There have been debates about its inception. The World Geological Society has settled on 1950, partly because of radioactive elements dispersed across the planet by nuclear bomb tests, but also other consequences of human action, including a sharp increase in greenhouse emissions. So the nuclear age and the Anthropocene coincide.

One index of the severity and imminence of crisis is provided graphically by the famous Doomsday Clock of the *Bulletin of Atomic Scientists*. Scientists and political analysts meet regularly to evaluate the state of the world and to determine how close we are to terminal disaster, midnight on the clock. The clock was first set in 1947, with the minute hand at seven minutes to midnight. In 1953, after the USSR exploded an H-bomb, following a much larger H-bomb explosion by the United States, it was advanced to two minutes to midnight. It has oscillated since. In 2015–16 the hand was again moved forward, and set at three minutes to midnight — the closest we had been to terminal disaster since the early 1980s, when there was a major war scare. The reasons in 2015–16 were the mounting threat of nuclear war and the failure to deal with climate change, which had not been considered before. In the wording that accompanied the setting of the clock, "The probability of global catastrophe is very high, and the actions needed to reduce the risks of disaster must be taken very soon." That was 2016.

At the outset of the Trump term, the analysts reset the clock, moving the hand still closer to midnight. The reason, in their words, is that they found "the danger to be even greater, the need for action more urgent. It is two and a half minutes to midnight, the Clock is ticking, global danger looms" — the closest to terminal disaster since 1953, when the United States and the USSR tested H-bombs.

That earlier close brush with terminal disaster is worth attention. It tells us a good deal about policy making and world order.

The obvious question is: Was the crisis avoidable, and what efforts were made to avoid it? The answer is startling, and fraught with grim lessons for today.

At the end of World War II, the United States was remarkably secure. It controlled the entire hemisphere, both oceans, and the opposite sides of both oceans. It enjoyed overwhelming economic and military superiority. It largely controlled the major industrial states, which had been severely weakened or almost destroyed by the war, while the American economy boomed: industrial production almost quadrupled, and the basis was laid for rapid postwar expansion. The United States had long had by far the largest economy in the world, with unique advantages, but had not been a major player in world affairs, ceding that role to Britain and France. The war left the United States in a position of power with no historical precedent.

Though the United States was indeed remarkably secure, there was one potential threat: ICBMs with nuclear warheads. They did not yet exist, but surely would. There is a standard scholarly study of nuclear strategy by McGeorge Bundy, national security adviser in the Kennedy and Johnson administrations, who had extensive access to internal documents. Bundy's *Danger and Survival: Choices About the Bomb in the First Fifty Years* does touch briefly on the possibility of averting the one potential threat to US security. Briefly, because the possibility was apparently ignored. As he writes, "I am aware of no serious contemporary proposal, in or out of either government, that ballistic missiles should somehow be banned by agreement."

That comment deserves close attention. It may be one of the most remarkable and revealing statements in all of the relevant literature on this subject. In short, there was apparently no thought of trying to prevent the sole serious threat to the United States, the threat of utter destruction. Security for the citizenry is a marginal concern, even for its security from instant destruction. Rather, the institutional imperatives of state power prevailed. Furthermore, the potential victims, the population, were left completely in the dark — and still are. Though all of this is public, it is unknown.

Let's look further. Were there some possibilities for diplomatic initiatives to avert the threat of destruction? We cannot be sure, because apparent opportunities were ignored. One was in March 1952, right at the time of the events that moved the clock to two minutes to midnight. Stalin made a remarkable offer: he proposed unification of Germany, which would have largely ended the Cold War. A settlement might have led to elections, which the Communists were sure to lose. There was one crucial condition: that a reunified Germany not join NATO, a hostile military alliance — hardly an extreme demand in the light of recent history.

Stalin's offer was taken seriously by the eminent and respected

foreign policy analyst James Warburg, particularly in his important
1953 book *Germany: Key to Peace*. He was ignored. Later references
to the possibility were dismissed with ridicule, as I can recall even
from personal experience.

Since the Russian archives were opened, attitudes of scholarship
have changed. The bitterly anti-Communist Soviet scholar Adam
Ulam took the status of Stalin's proposal to be an "unresolved mystery." Washington "wasted little effort in flatly rejecting Moscow's
initiative," he writes, on grounds that "were embarrassingly uncon-
vincing," leaving open "the basic question": "Was Stalin genuinely
ready to sacrifice the newly created German Democratic Republic (GDR) on the altar of real democracy?," with consequences
for world peace and for American security that could have been
enormous? One of the most prominent Cold War scholars, Melvyn
Leffler, writes that scholars who have studied documents released
from Soviet archives were surprised to discover that "[Lavrenti]
Beria — the sinister, brutal head of the secret police — propos[ed]
that the Kremlin offer the West a deal on the unification and neu-
tralization of Germany," agreeing "to sacrifice the East German
communist regime to reduce East-West tensions" and improve internal political and economic conditions in Russia — opportunities that were squandered in favor of securing German participation in NATO.

Were these possibilities real? We cannot be sure, of course.
What does seem clear is that what mattered was global power, not
security for the irrelevant and uninformed population.

The episode illustrates one of the starkest and most consistent
lessons of policy formation. There is much talk of security, but it is
not about security of the population, which is at most a marginal
concern: rather, it is about security for systems of power, state and
private. The topic is much too large to review in detail, but let's
proceed for a few more years into the 1950s and '60s.

Not long after Stalin's death, Nikita Khrushchev took power.
Khrushchev was committed to economic development and understood very well that it would be severely hampered by an arms
race with the far richer United States (and with western Europe,
which alone more than matched the Russian economy). He therefore proposed sharp mutual reduction in offensive weaponry, and,
when he received no response, undertook it unilaterally.

What happened next is described by the late Kenneth Waltz,

one of the most respected international relations scholars. After considering Khrushchev's offer, he writes, the Kennedy administration "undertook the largest strategic and conventional peacetime military build-up the world has yet seen . . . even as Khrushchev was trying at once to carry through a major reduction in the conventional forces and to follow a strategy of minimum deterrence, and we did so even though the balance of strategic weapons greatly favored the United States."

There was a Russian response. Khrushchev sent missiles to Cuba in October 1962 to try to compensate slightly for the strategic imbalance that was greatly enhanced by Kennedy's huge military buildup. A second reason, it appears, was to defend Cuba against the murderous Kennedy terrorist campaign against Cuba, which was to culminate in a likely US invasion in October 1962. What followed did almost lead to terminal disaster.

Once again, the decisions made harmed national security severely while enhancing state power. What happened was concealed behind the enthusiastic rhetoric of the Camelot years. And largely remains so, serious scholarship apart.

The crucial conclusion is once again glaringly clear: security of the population is not a major concern of planners. The conclusion prevails right to the present moment. When investigating foreign affairs and government decisions, we routinely discover that peaceful options exist, but are dismissed, though they might well avert disaster. There is no time to review the record, but let's turn to today's headlines.

Today, we are instructed that the great challenge faced by the world is how to compel North Korea to freeze its nuclear and missile programs. Perhaps we should resort to more sanctions, cyberwar, intimidation, an antimissile system that China realistically regards as a serious threat, even perhaps direct attack.

Another possible option was ignored as the crisis developed, and has only belatedly and often misleadingly been mentioned: accept North Korea's offer to do exactly what we had been demanding. China and North Korea had proposed that North Korea freeze nuclear and missile programs. Their reasons are much like Khrushchev's. North Korean leaders are seeking economic development, and understand that they cannot make much progress while facing the overwhelming burden of military production.

The North Korean proposal was rejected at once by Washing-

ton, just as it had been two years earlier — and just as Khrushchev's
initiatives were rejected by the JFK administration, leading to the
closest brush with total disaster in human history.

The reason for the instant rejection is that the Chinese–North
Korean proposal has a quid pro quo: it calls on the United States
to halt its threatening military exercises on North Korea's borders,
including simulated nuclear-bombing attacks by B-52s, sent by
Trump in recent months.

The Chinese–North Korean demand is hardly unreasonable.
North Koreans, of course, remember that their country was literally flattened by US bombing, and some may well remember the
gleeful reports in American military journals about the bombing
of major dams when there were no other targets left, the rejoicing
about the exciting spectacle of a huge flood of water wiping out
the rice crops on which Asians depend for survival — very much
worth reading. A part of history that it would be useful to retrieve
from the memory hole and to ponder.

The Chinese–North Korean proposal could lay the basis for
more far-reaching negotiations to radically reduce the threats
and perhaps even bring the crisis to an end. Contrary to much
inflamed commentary, there are reasons to think that negotiations
might succeed, so the record reveals.

But the offers are rejected in the usual interests of securing
power interests.

Let's look further into how we are carrying forward our verifica-
tion of Mayr's thesis.

Last March, the *Bulletin of Atomic Scientists* published a remarkable report on the vast nuclear modernization program initiated
by President Obama and now being carried forward under Trump.
The report discusses how US nuclear force modernization is undermining the strategic stability on which survival suspends, by a
slender thread.

The current modernization programs include "revolutionary
new technologies that will vastly increase the targeting capability of the US ballistic missile arsenal. This increase in capability
is astonishing — boosting the overall killing power of existing US
ballistic missile forces by a factor of roughly three — and it creates
exactly what one would expect to see, if a nuclear-armed state were

planning to have the capacity to fight and win a nuclear war by disarming enemies with a surprise first strike."

All of this has "revolutionary impact on military capabilities and important implications for global security," the report continues. The implications are clear. Russian strategic analysts are of course aware that the US now has the capacity to wipe out their deterrent. The Russians do not have our sophisticated satellite-based advance warning systems, and would have little advance notice of a possible attack. With the deterrent at serious risk because of the nuclear modernization programs, at a moment of crisis — and there are all too many possibilities — Russian leaders may be tempted to undertake a preemptive strike just to assure survival, an act that would end organized human life on Earth.

Once again, is a diplomatic avenue possible? It surely seems so. Is it being pursued? If so, it's not detectable.

All relevant to Mayr's thesis.

Turning to the second existential threat, global warming, anyone with eyes open should be aware that the dangers are severe, and imminent. How are we reacting? Here's a recent report from the US business press (*Bloomberg*, March 2): "The boom looks like it's back. The number of oil and gas rigs drilling in the US has almost doubled . . . While two dozen nations are coordinating to cut oil production and rein in the global supply glut, US producers are moving in the opposite direction. Over the last four months, output increased by half a million barrels a day. If that rate of expansion continues, the shale boom will break new production records by summer. The US now produces nine million barrels a day."

The report, one of a flood, illustrates a remarkable fact of current history: while the world is taking halting steps toward facing the existential challenge to survival, the richest and most powerful state in world history, virtually alone, is racing toward destruction, with enthusiasm and dedication. That has been true since November 8, 2016, another date of great historical significance.

There were three significant events on that date, one important, one extremely important, one astonishing.

The important event was the US election, which virtually monopolized reporting for days.

The extremely important event, which received virtually no coverage, took place in Marrakesh, Morocco, where almost all nations of the world were meeting to try to put some teeth in the Paris agreements (COP 21, December 2015). A verifiable treaty could not be reached in Paris, as had been hoped, because the US Republican Congress would not accept it. On November 8, the World Meteorological Organization issued a review of the state of the climate. Along with other dire reports, the review confirmed "that 2016 was the warmest year on record: a remarkable 1.1 [degrees] C above the pre-industrial period," sharply above the previous record set in 2015, approaching the desired limit set in Paris. Deliberations effectively ended on November 8. The operative question became: Can we survive with the leader of the free world racing toward the precipice? The countries of the world turned to China as the hope for survival. China!

The astonishing event is the dog that didn't bark, the reaction to these amazing events: silence.

No less astonishing is that while the richest and most powerful country in history is leading the effort to intensify the likely disaster, efforts to avert catastrophe are being led, worldwide, by what we call "primitive societies": First Nations in Canada, tribal and aboriginal societies around the world. Ecuador, with its large indigenous population, sought aid from the rich European countries to allow it to keep some of its oil reserves underground, where they should be. The aid was refused. Ecuador revised its constitution in 2008 to include "rights of nature" as having "intrinsic worth." Bolivia, with an indigenous majority, passed the Law of Mother Earth, granting nature rights equal to humans. In general, indigenous populations are well in the lead in seeking to preserve the planet. The countries that have driven indigenous populations to extinction or extreme marginalization are racing toward destruction.

Perhaps something else we should think about.

There should be no need to sample the grim reports on threats to the environment that appear regularly in science journals, sometimes making it to major media. Meanwhile, the Republican wrecking ball is systematically dismantling the structures that offer hope for decent survival. The Environmental Protection Agency, established by Richard Nixon, is being virtually dismantled. More important still is the Department of Energy. Its Office of Science is scheduled to lose $900 million, nearly 20 percent of its budget. Even mention of climate change is coming under a ban, while regulations are being dismantled and every effort is being made to maximize the use of fossil fuels, including the most destructive, like coal.

It's not just Trump. In the Republican presidential primaries, every candidate either denied that what is happening is happening or — the moderates — said maybe it is, but we shouldn't do anything about it. There is virtual unanimity among party leaders. A remarkable spectacle, which passed with little notice.

The major media play along in other ways. A Fairness and Accuracy in Media (FAIR) study of interviews and press conferences with Trump since he took office on January 20, 2017, found that not a single question had been raised about climate change. Hardly surprising. After all, it's only the most significant policy position of the administration, enhancing a truly existential threat.

Even if sea level rise is more limited than what is anticipated, it will inundate coastal cities and coastal plains, as in Bangladesh, where tens of millions may be forced to flee in the fairly near future, many more later. Today's refugee issues will be a tea party in comparison. The chief environmental scientist in Bangladesh has said that "these migrants should have the right to move to the countries from which all these greenhouse gases are coming. Millions should be able to go to the United States." That certainly agrees with the current mood in the West — and not just the United States, which is extreme (or Britain). Those who think it is better on the Continent can turn to a recent poll showing that a majority of Europeans want a total ban on immigration from Muslim-majority countries.

In general, the idea is that first we destroy them and then we punish them for trying to escape from the ruins — calling it a "refugee crisis" while thousands drown in the Mediterranean fleeing from Africa, where Europe does have a certain history. In fact, the so-called refugee crisis is actually a serious moral-cultural crisis — in the West.

Let's return to the other sledgehammer, the nuclear threat. The major nuclear powers, the United States and Russia, are both expanding their arsenals, in quite dangerous ways. And flashpoints are becoming more serious, particularly on the Russian border. On the *Russian* border, not the Mexican border — a result of the ex-

pansion of NATO right after the collapse of the USSR, in violation
of verbal promises to Gorbachev that NATO would not expand
"one inch to the East." At the time, the immediate referent was
East Germany — if Gorbachev agreed to unification of Germany
within a hostile military alliance, a pretty remarkable concession
in the light of history. Gorbachev's vision of a European common
home, a security system from Brussels to Vladivostok with no military alliances, is a fading dream.

George Kennan and other senior statesmen had warned early
on that NATO expansion would prove to be a "tragic mistake, [a]
policy error of historic proportions." It is now leading to rising tensions along the traditional invasion route, through which Russia
was virtually destroyed twice during the past century by Germany
alone. To make matters worse, in 2008 NATO membership was offered to Ukraine, the Russian geostrategic heartland, efforts later
pursued by Obama and Hillary Clinton.

Let's return finally to the main line of defense: functioning democracy. We can begin with the leader of the free world, the model of
democracy for centuries.

In a democracy, the voice of the people is heard. Let's ask what
might happen in the United States if this principle were upheld.
One consequence would be that the most popular and respected
political figure in the country would have an influential role,
maybe even be president. That's Bernie Sanders, by a very large
margin.

The Sanders campaign was the most remarkable feature of the
2016 elections. It broke the prevailing pattern of over a century
of US political history. A substantial body of academic political science research establishes very convincingly that elections are pretty
much bought: campaign funding alone is a remarkably good pre-
dictor of electability, for Congress as well, and also for decisions of
elected officials. Research also shows that a considerable majority
of the electorate, those lower on the income scale, are effectively
disenfranchised, in that their representatives pay no attention to
their preferences. As wealth increases, political representation
does too, though only slightly — until you arrive at the very top, a
fraction of 1 percent, where our policies are pretty much set.

The Sanders campaign broke sharply from that well-established
model. Sanders was scarcely known. He had virtually no support

from the main funding sources, the corporate sector and private wealth, was derided by the media, and he even dared to use the scare word "socialist." Yet he probably would have won the Democratic nomination had it not been for shenanigans of the Obama-Clinton party managers.

Suppose he had won, or even that he had a major public platform today. We might then hear statements like this concerning labor rights: "I have no use for those — regardless of their political party — who hold some foolish dream of spinning the clock back to days when unorganized labor was a huddled, almost helpless mass . . . Only a handful of unreconstructed reactionaries harbor the ugly thought of breaking unions. Only a fool would try to deprive working men and women of the right to join the union of their choice."

That's not Sanders, however. The candidate who said that was Dwight Eisenhower, when he was running for president in 1952. Such was the voice of conservatism during the days of the great growth period of regulated state capitalism, often called the economic "golden age."

We've come a long way since then. Now we are on the verge of seeing the demise of even public unions, about the only sort that remains in the United States. Real democracy would be quite different, so public opinion studies show. Much the same holds for a host of other issues as both parties have shifted well to the right during the neoliberal period, with the Republicans now at a point where respected conservative political scientists describe them as a "radical insurgency" that has abandoned parliamentary politics.

One consequence is anger, frustration, and contempt for the formal institutions of democracy, reactions that often take ominous forms.

The basic fact is that a true majority of the population would never vote for the policies designed by elites. Some simple figures give a good indication why.

In 2007, before the crash, at the height of euphoria about the Great Moderation and the grand triumphs of neoliberalism and neoclassical economics, real wages of American workers were lower than they had been in 1979, when the neoliberal experiment was just taking off. One important reason was explained by Federal Reserve chair Alan Greenspan when he testified to Congress on the wondrous economy he was managing. He informed Congress that "greater worker insecurity" was keeping wages and inflation low. Workers are too intimidated to ask for decent wages, benefits, and working conditions, even in the late 1990s when unemployment was low — by neoliberal standards a sign of health of the economy.

Social justice measures also deteriorated through this period — the United States, in fact, ranks at the very bottom of the developed countries of the OECD in such measures, alongside of Greece, Mexico, and Turkey. But profits are booming, particularly in the largely predatory financial industry, which exploded during the neoliberal period, accounting for 40 percent of corporate profit right before the crash (for which they were, once again, largely responsible). One motive for the so-called reforms of neoliberalism was to reverse the falling rate of profit that was largely a consequence of popular activism and worker militancy in the 1960s. That was achieved, so in that sense the reforms were a success — for corporations, not for the population as a whole. Under such conditions, democracy can hardly be tolerated.

Much the same has been true in Europe under the lash of neoliberal austerity programs, which even IMF economists recognize to be unwarranted. But IMF bureaucrats listen to different voices — mostly those of the rich northern banks. Those are the voices that control the unelected troika that determines policy in Europe: the IMF, the European Central Bank, the European Commission.

In his important critical analysis of neoliberalism, *Failed*, economist Mark Weisbrot has carried out a careful and revealing investigation of the political agenda guiding the destructive economic policies. He studied the reports of the regular IMF consultations with member governments of the EU, and discovered "a remarkably consistent and disturbing pattern." The financial crisis was exploited as an opportunity to lock in the neoliberal reforms: spending cuts in the public sector rather than tax increases, reduced benefits and public services, cuts in health care, undermining of collective bargaining, and in general moves to create a society "with less bargaining power for labor and lower wages, more inequality and poverty, a smaller government and social safety nets, and measures that reduce growth and employment." "The IMF papers," Weisbrot concludes, "detail the agenda of Europe's decision-makers, and they have accomplished quite a bit of it over the past five years." An agenda that is quite familiar where the neoliberal assault has proceeded.

In Europe, too, populations would not vote for these measures, so democracy must be sacrificed on the altar of locking in neoliberal reforms. The device in Europe is straightforward: transfer decision making to unelected bodies: the troika. The public response in Europe resembles what has been happening in the United States. Centrist political institutions are discredited, public disillusionment, fear, and anger are running high, sometimes taking quite ominous forms. Those old enough to remember the 1930s, as I do, cannot fail to be alarmed at the rise of neofascist parties, even in Austria and Germany, of all places, and not only there. And bitter memories are not easy to suppress when a majority of Europeans call for banning all Muslims from Europe, and many want to reverse the real achievements of the European Union, such as free movement of populations and erosion of national borders — which would be quite consistent with strengthening of cultural diversity in liberal and humane societies.

We cannot attribute all of these developments across the West to the neoliberal assault, but it is a common and significant factor.

Neoliberal policies are specifically directed toward undermining the regulatory power of the government, hence undermining the capacity to avert the blows of the sledgehammers. But the effects are more far-reaching. In our state capitalist societies, the power of the government is the power of the population, to the extent that the society is democratic. Neoliberal programs, by their very nature, tend to concentrate wealth in few hands while the majority stagnates or declines. Functioning democracy erodes as the natural effect of the concentration of economic power, which translates at once to political power, by familiar means but also for deeper and principled reasons. The doctrinal pretense is that transfer of decision making from the public sector to the "market" contributes to individual freedom, but reality is quite different. The transfer is from public institutions in which people have some say (insofar as democracy is functioning) to private tyrannies in which the public has no say at all: the corporations that dominate the global economy.

The policies are dedicated to making sure that "society no longer exists." Such was Margaret Thatcher's famous description of the world she perceived, or, more precisely, hoped to create. With these words, Thatcher unwittingly paraphrased Marx's bitter condemnation of repression in France, which had left society as a "sack of potatoes," an amorphous mass that cannot function. In the contemporary case, the tyrant is no longer an autocratic ruler, in the West at least, but instead concentrations of private power and bureaucracies that are free from public control.

There is also no guarantee that functioning democracy, with an informed and engaged population, would lead to policies that address human needs and concerns, including the concern for survival. But that remains our only hope.

All of which brings us back to Ernst Mayr's question: Is it better to be smart than stupid? A question for you to ponder, and like it not, for you to answer.

Without too much of a delay.

From a talk delivered in Montevideo, Uruguay, on July 17, 2017

Bibliography

Bundy, McGeorge. *Danger and Survival: Choices About the Bomb in the First Fifty Years.* New York: Random House, 1988.

Gardiner, Harris. "Borrowed Time on Disappearing Land." *New York Times,* March 28, 2014.

Kristensen, Hans, Matthew McKinzie, and Theodore Postol. "How US Nuclear Force Modernization Is Undermining Strategic Stability." *Bulletin of Atomic Scientists,* March 1, 2017. http://thebulletin.org/how-us-nuclear-force-modernization-underminingstrategic-stability-burst-height-compensating-super10578.

Leffler, Melvyn P. "Inside Enemy Archives: The Cold War Reopened." *Foreign Affairs,* July/August 1996.

Mayr, Ernst. "Can SETI Succeed? Not Likely." *Bioastronomy News* 7, no. 3, 1995.

Osborne, Samuel. "Most Europeans Want Immigration Ban from Muslim-Majority Countries, Poll Reveals." *Independent,* February 7, 2017. http://www.independent.co.uk/news/world/europe/most-europeans-want-muslim-ban-immigration-control-middleeast-countries-syria-iran-iraq-poll-a7567301.html.

Ulam, Adam. "A Few Unresolved Mysteries About Stalin and the Cold War in Europe." *Journal of Cold War Studies* 1, no. 1, Winter 1999.

Waltz, Kenneth. "America as a Model for the World?: A Foreign Policy Perspective." *PS: Political Science & Politics,* December 1991.

Warburg, James P. *Germany: Key to Peace.* Cambridge, MA: Harvard University Press, 1953.

Weisbrot, Mark. *Failed: What the "Experts" Got Wrong About the Global Economy.* New York: Oxford University Press, 2015.

WMO Statement on the State of the Global Climate in 2016. https://public.wmo.int/en/resources/library/wmo-statement-state-of-global-climate-2016.

PAUL CRENSHAW

Cadence

FROM *Hotel Amerika*

EACH MORNING BEGAN with music, military speakers mounted
from flagpoles playing reveille, and from a deep sleep of dreams
not about this place, we heard the horns. Then came the quick
switch of lights, and fluorescents flickering overhead, accompanied by the crash of something thrown, a trash can or gas canister.
The voices of the drill sergeants rose out of the chaos, and we fell
out of bed to the floor and tried to sleep for another two seconds
under our bunks until the black boots came crushing down the
aisles and forced us to rise.

We ran to the latrine then, our new song the turn of taps and
rush of running water. The fluids and flatulations, the scrubbing of
teeth, the groans and grimaces as new aches arose on our beaten-
down bodies. This was Basic Training, and there were always new
injuries announcing themselves as we woke and prepared ourselves for the day, our bodies like tired old men, our pain another
part of the song we heard each morning, whines and cries joining
with the farts and shouts of "fuck" as we tried to rouse ourselves.

We dressed staring at the darkness out the windows, silent now
but for the rustle of clothing and our low curses about what was
to come. When we had finished dressing, our lockers slammed
closed together and our feet hammered the stairs in rhythm as
we rushed down to the drill pad. The air lay thick and heavy in
summer, Fort Sill, Oklahoma, 1990, just before the war began, but
we didn't know that then, only that a long day lay ahead of us and
here was only the beginning.

The streetlights were still on and the air smelled of bitterweed
and heat as we stretched on the concrete, calling cadence, our

voices echoing beneath the big building. Our drill sergeants' voices hung hoarse in the hot morning, and our own voices came harsh as hounds over the hill as we finished stretching and marched to the road for our morning run. All up and down the area other batteries were doing the same, and already the voices rose like a choir, calling cadence softly into the coming morning, the fading night.

> In the early morning rain,
> in the early morning rain.
> In the early morning ra-a-a-ain,
> in the early morning rain.

And so we sang, the sky lit up not with light but with litany, a thousand or ten thousand voices all calling cadence out of the darkness. Flashlights bobbed and weaved along the road outside the barracks buildings, vast edifices drawn into shape now by the yellow lights ringing them all around. The sun had not yet come up and the air still felt heavy and there was a pit of fear forming in our stomachs at what lay ahead, but for a time there was the song to focus on. While calling cadence we could forget about everything else: the future, friends and family, what forces were at work in the world.

We started slow, still marching, singing about the early morning rain, about going off to fight a war, a common old cadence, one we sang every morning in the darkness before dawn drew the world into familiar forms. As we marched, the dark shapes of other batteries moved past, men just awoken from sleep now singing of cold hills in foreign countries, the desolation and destruction of war, the loneliness and despair that can creep into a soldier far from home, and Fort Sill felt like a foreign country on those hot mornings, Perez and Talley and Alvarez and Buist marching beside me, each of us looking at the other with something like kinship, or at least the common bond men in uniform share, men who are forced to suffer through such conditions.

Already our T-shirts were soaked, sweat springing up on our shaved heads. Already the sides of the road were littered with men doing push-ups and sit-ups and jumping jacks, then sprinting to catch up with their platoons. Already the voices were deep-throated as despair, and were it not for the songs we sang we might have given in to despair.

Just past the next barracks the call came for double-time and

we took off, the cadence rising now, quicker, the flashlights passing like searchlights at sea. We did not know how far we would run
each morning, whether a mile or ten miles, only that we had to
keep up, to lock our bodies into the rhythm of the run, to focus
on the cadence to get us through. The first gray glow lit the far
horizon and a thousand voices raised themselves in song. Our feet
hammered the road, creating a rhythm of its own as the day began.

> C-130 rollin' down the strip
> Airborne ranger on a one-way trip.
> Stand up, hook up, shuffle to the door,
> Jump right out on the count of four.
> If my chute don't open wide,
> I got another one by my side.
> And if that chute don't open round
> I'll be the first one on the ground.

I forget now how far we ran on those first mornings, but by the
end of Basic Training, about the time the hammer came down
and Hussein invaded Kuwait and we were told we were going to
war — by then we were up to six miles every morning, ending out
of breath, our shaved heads steaming and slick with sweat, our
shirts soaked, all the song run out of us. We gathered once again
on the drill pad to stretch and steam and catch our breath, our
voices gone now. The sun had come up sometime while we ran
and gray light filtered over the drill pad, which was always a revelation because we had been running for what seemed forever and
thought the night might never end. It was easy in those days to
forget where you were and how long you had been there and what
you were doing. Easier to put the body on autopilot, to follow only,
to respond when called to. Easier to run into the morning singing.

I've learned since that someone knew that, perhaps Private Wil-
lie Duckworth, who created, on one long march through swamps
and rough terrain and night, the "Duckworth" chant, which raised
the spirits of other soldiers during World War II. Or maybe Baron
von Steuben when he brought close-order drill techniques to Revolutionary War soldiers as a way to perfect timing and to create a
greater sense of camaraderie. Or even further back, to Africa, and
slaves who brought call-and-response to cotton fields in order to
lighten the workload, to make the day pass quicker, to give hope
to those without any.

But we knew none of that then, only that here was a way to pass the interminable mornings, the long runs on a hot base. And some mornings the world began exploding as we ran, when artillery was fired in the far distance and the ground trembled beneath us and the coming light bent at the horizon when the bombs went off. And some mornings it seemed, as we sang about soldiers on a hill or a C-130 rolling down the strip or what to do in case we die in a combat zone (box us up and ship us home) that we were in a combat zone, which was, I suppose, the point.

> Mama, Mama can't you see,
> what the army's done for me?

After first light the song changed.

I should say now part of what I am calling cadence is only rhythm — our days were planned. Sectioned into smaller parts: run, chow, marching. First class, marching, chow. Marching, second class, marching, third class, marching, chow. More marching. More cadences called through the long white afternoons, and finally, as night came, another run, this one with the heat of the day still on us but the weight of the day gone. We had survived once again, and we ran with night falling, clapping our hands, happy with our place in the world, at least for this moment. After the run we would wash our clothing and write letters and hopefully receive them. We would lie on our bunks and feel the exhaustion of a day's work and still hear the songs thrumming through our heads about the soldier on the hill, about the early morning rain. About Mama, and what the army had done for us.

But we're not there yet. When first light fell and our run ended, we double-timed back to the barracks, still steaming, to wipe ourselves with towels — no time for a shower — and dress. After the run the aches and pains were gone but for a stitch in our sides that would fade on its own. The blood was pumping and adrenaline flowing and there was only this day to get through, only this day to worry about. Whatever cadence we had called was still in our heads — a C-130, an airborne ranger, an unnamed enemy — so that any worries seemed unimportant, any aches easily forgotten.

From the barracks we ran back to the drill pad, where we assembled, and then marched to chow. Our cadences here took on a different tone, one I've tried to figure out since the years I left the army and have watched the world explode in war, most of those ex-

plosions from bombs of our making, our missiles and men always
in the forefront, our technology always ready to shock and awe. If
our morning runs needed some motivation, our marches in the
daylight must have needed to teach some lesson. We knew we were
being broken down and then built back up in the army way, but
it only occurred to me years later that the songs might have had
something to do with that as well. That songs stick in the head and
filter down to the heart. That a rhythm moves on its own, and the
words can become lodged like a bullet in the brain.

We marched to chow calling cadence through the open corridors. In the mess hall even our eating took on a rhythm. We
shuffled down the line, speaking only to point out what food we
wanted, then ate in silence. We had four minutes to finish, and
then we were out again, marching toward our first class of the day,
where we would learn to treat sucking chest wounds or what to do
in case of a nuclear, biological, or chemical attack, and it seems
logical now that our cadences took on a different tone.

> Gonna kill some dirty commies,
> Turn around and burn their mommies,
> stab their babies in the back,
> put 'em on a roast and rack,
> place 'em in a barbecue,
> it makes them very soft to chew,
> pick 'em clean down to the bone,
> and back to the jungle I will roam.

We called this cadence on the way to the rifle range or the gre-
nade course or hand-to-hand training. To the bayonet course or
the pugil-stick ring. Anytime we held a weapon in our hands, anytime we were about to simulate killing.

We loved this cadence. Called by a drill sergeant named Kuykendall, whose big booming voice made us think he really wanted to
kill commies, that he missed roaming the jungle in search of them.
Drill Sergeant Adams carried seventy-five pounds of extra weight
in his rucksack when we went on long marches, because, he said,
if war ever came, he would not fall behind — he was conditioning
himself for battle. Drill Sergeant Camacho had arms the size of
missiles. Jackson was a Golden Gloves boxer. First Sergeant Pem-
berton's favorite phrase was "Fuck 'em and feed 'em fish heads,"
and we thought all the drill sergeants were only biding their time

until another war broke out and they could be released from garrison duty and go kill something.

This might be a good time to mention that when we fired our M-16s, the targets were painted to look like Soviet soldiers, complete with hammer and sickle, so that when we were firing or punching or throwing grenades we were imagining commies, and burning and eating their children. Kuykendall's "Commie" cadence must have been a holdover from Vietnam, because by my time in the military the Cold War had ended and the Berlin Wall had fallen, but we did not yet (soon, very soon, I promise) have another enemy to hate in the world, so we called this cadence, which, I must repeat, I loved. I say this first to hold to truthfulness, and second so that I will not be able to absolve or exonerate myself, to set myself apart from the other soldiers I served with or give myself special treatment. I loved it. We all did. We thought it funny. We sang louder when this one came — about killing commies, about stabbing mommies. Burning babies. Barbecuing them. We were only eighteen and had never heard of the My Lai massacre. Or the Siege of Stalingrad. We might have read *Slaughterhouse-Five* but didn't know about the firebombing of Dresden. Nor Nagasaki nor Hiroshima except in the distant way of history books. We hadn't seen that little girl running down the road with napalm on her skin. But this is what I want you to know, because this is important — we fucking loved it.

> Don't bludgeon a seal,
> just to make a meal,
> do it 'cause you want to hear
> that little fucker squeal,
> and stomp them in the head,
> until you get your kicks,
> then poke them in the eye with
> your eye-pokin' sticks.

We sang this one in the mornings as well. Before first light and after night fell were the times for emotional cadences, full of heartache and loneliness, that soldier on the hill again. But mornings were for killing. "We kill more before 9 a.m. than most people do all day," the drill sergeants said, and we sent up a cheer. Remember now we've only been here a few weeks. Our morale is still shaky. We still miss our mothers, our girlfriends. We cry at night and everyone else ignores it. For those in on the long haul, those who enlisted for six years, there's no going home, not for a long, long time, and the days seem longer.

So mornings are for killing cadences, dirty commies and baby seals and yellow birds on the windowsill. We loved this one even more than eating babies. Because although there's a rhyme, there's no reason. Or rather there is a reason — there's joy in killing. Delight in destruction, pleasure in causing pain. We don't kill for any honest reasons — not to feed or clothe ourselves, but to satisfy the craving for killing inside all of us.

So the song says. Do it 'cause you want to hear that little fucker squeal. And who can deny there is a fascination with death inside us, at seventeen or eighteen, carrying an M-16 on the way to the rifle range, artillery exploding in the distance, low rumbles like distant thunder, the earth shaking in response. We packed inside what were called cattle cars, all of us standing like cattle, and perhaps there were those among us who thought we might be headed for the slaughterhouse, but instead of thinking, we sang of baby seals, and stomping and bludgeoning and eye-poking them.

At the rifle range we fell out of the cattle cars and into formation, where we were told to keep our rifles pointed downrange and always on safety, but we were thinking of killing. We fell out of formation and lay prone on the shaking earth and zeroed our rifles in, some of us drawing baby seals and baby communists on our zero targets and trying to put their eyes out, some of us calling our M-16s "eye-poking sticks" because they seemed so. We sat in the ungodly heat and slipped cartridges into our clips, and after we had zeroed our weapons in, we went to the line and opened them up on rock-n-roll, another cadence here, this one of three-round bursts, of the bullhorned drill sergeant's voice asking if there is anyone downrange is there anyone downrange is there anyone downrange. The heat stabbed down like a sword and the distant targets shimmered and the rifle reports echoed to the far hills and back, and inside our heads was the song of it all, the cadence of these hot days.

> Ain't no need in calling home,
> Jody's on your telephone.
> Ain't no need in going home,
> Jody's got your girl and gone.

Jody is a recurring character in army cadences, a lazy shiftless bum, but one who has the power to attract females formerly attracted to us. Absence, it seems, does not make the heart grow fonder, at least according to our cadence calls, and Jody, in verse, took over everything we once had. While we were marching, and firing our weapons and tossing hand grenades in the direction of America's enemies, while we were learning to be soldiers, Jody was sleeping with our girlfriends. He was driving our cars, eating our food, using our telephone — all the things we didn't get to do. He lived a luxurious lifestyle, one we no longer had. He took over our houses for himself, threw our clothes out the window, and we believed this could happen because we had left our homes and had our clothes taken away and did not know when we would see our girlfriends.

Jody in cadence became an instrument, a tool to shape men into soldiers. He served to detach soldiers from home life, and all the things they could no longer have. He was a mark at which to aim aggression. When mail time rolled around every night, someone — Buist or Talley or Sykes — got a letter from home and learned his girlfriend had left him, his fiancée had called off the marriage, his wife had slept with another man.

"I'll kill that motherfucker," Sykes, who was from the South Side of Chicago, said, and sometimes on the rifle range you could see in a man's eyes the need to kill. The anger and aggression, the hurt that comes out as hate. Then the disconnect, for after a few days Sykes or Talley or Buist would say he didn't need that fucking bitch anyway, and we'd all agree he was better off without a woman who slept around on him, which was another thing the Jody cadences taught us, that women were never to be trusted, for they had no control over themselves and were often swept away by someone as sorry as Jody.

Jody then served also as a symbol of civilian life. The world will take your girlfriends, your wives, your house, your car, your respect. But here, in this man's army, none of those things will happen. The army is your wife, your lover. The army will feed and clothe you, will give you shelter. What else, the idea is, do you need?

My girl's a vegetable,
she's in the hospital.
And I would do anything,
to keep her alive.

She's got no arms or legs,
that's why I call her peg,
but I would do anything,
to keep her alive.
She's got a new TV,
it's called an EKG,
and I would do anything,
to keep her alive.
One night I played a joke,
pulled the plug and watched her choke,
but I would do anything,
to keep her alive.

There was another version of this cadence titled "My Girl's a Chorus Girl," a Chicago girl, and the unnamed narrator would buy
anything to keep her in style, the unspoken argument here that
the girl is a prostitute, but we liked the vegetable version best. Like
the clubbing of baby seals or eating of barbecued children, we
found it funny. I would say we didn't take it seriously, but there
must have been something in our dark hearts it spoke to, some
suggestion of the tragedy we might have been looking for.

Despite the narrator's repeated claim that he loves this girl, and
would do anything to keep her alive, he makes fun of her plight.
He calls her names. He makes fun of her life-support system (he
is, obviously, not her life-support system). He plays a joke by watching her die a little. As if she is an embarrassment, or a thing which
holds little value.

This one was only ever called by the male drill sergeants when
the female commander wasn't around. Which brings up several
questions about its intention, about women in the military and how
they are viewed, about how men are supposed to view them. As a
motivational tool, then, quadriplegic girlfriends rank evenly with
the burning of communist babies or bludgeoning baby seals — a
joke, a thing to lift morale.

The drill sergeants knew, of course, that every night letters
came in, Sykes's girlfriend leaving him, Billings's wife asking for a
divorce. After a long time as military trainers, the drill sergeants
knew how men serving longed for the women they had left behind,
so they attempted to deconstruct them into parts: a prostitute for
sale; a woman with no arms or legs and no hair, just patches of it
here and there.

See the soldier on the hill,
he is not afraid to kill.
See the soldier on the hi-i-i-ill,
in the early morning rain.
See the soldier in the sky,
he is not afraid to die.
See the soldier in the sky-y-y-y,
in the early morning rain.

In the evenings we came back to this one again. We sang it so often the refrain echoed in our heads at all times. It's a sad, slow song. We could hear the rain falling in the drill sergeant's trembling, hoarse voice. As if this had happened, was happening, would happen. As if there were always a soldier on a hill, and always would be.

We sang this one in the morning and the evening. At the beginning and end of day, as if all our days should end thinking of the soldier. Our days were long and hot and lonely, full of despair, but this soldier on the hill, the one who is not afraid to kill, the one who is not afraid to die, has sacrificed everything, and here we only have a few rough days to get through. That is the lesson of this song — when a man wearing the same uniform as you has given everything, you have no right to complain about a run, or a few push-ups. Or being tired. Or hungry. Or hot or wet or cold or tired or afraid.

We were often all these things. And marching back from the rifle range, sweat-soaked and streaked with dirt, burning in our boots, we sang of the soldier. After a sudden storm soaked us through and our clothes clung sodden to our wet cold skin, we thought of the soldier on the hill. Through long nights with fake artillery flashes going off overhead and real ones in the distance, we hummed to keep ourselves awake, and always our humming was of this make-believe soldier, this creation of cadence that rattled around in our heads at all times.

The soldier dies in the end, of course. This is what soldiers do. They die. While laying here to rest, he caught a bullet in the chest. But he wants his wife not to cry, in the early morning rain.

A yellow bird,
with a yellow bill,
was perched upon,
my windowsill.

I lured him in,
with crumbs of bread,
and then I smashed,
his little head.

Cadences fall into one of a few categories. The soldier on the hill in the early morning rain is meant to motivate, a romantic image of death in a foreign country. There is no defined enemy, only the image: the tireless soldier who has yet grown tired but still stands in the cold rain, who left his wife and left his child, who went off to fight a war, and there is in these words a sense of pride, of self-lessness, a sacrifice for some undefined greater good. He will be mourned but also idolized. He is a symbol of a soldier. Freedom, as we will learn, is never mentioned.

Another category is what I'll call madness. Jody sleeping with a soldier's wife or girlfriend instills anger. Clubbing baby seals or eating communist children incites aggression, a gleeful delight in killing, in reducing death down to a humorous cadence. A soldier who would barbecue babies is a soldier so caught up in the war he has become mad, but there's the lingering idea in the lyrics that war can become something he loves, the enemy a thing he hates so much the soldier loses all sense of rightfulness, but in doing his job of killing the enemy, whatever he chooses to do is rightful.

All cadences are designed to help morale. A soldier may laugh at Jody's antics but they also prepare him for what may one day happen. (Almost half of all military marriages end in less than ten years.) The girl lying in the hospital hooked to her new TV (it's called an EKG) reduces women to a burden a soldier must bear, and the idea in this one is that women are not worth the trouble they cause. Pulling the plug to watch her choke is an ominous foreshadowing of what a soldier might finally do to rid himself of whatever keeps him from serving the army. The "othering" of groups: women, communists, baby seals, draws men closer together. Us versus them. Good versus evil. You're either for us or against us, and if you aren't for us, you must be against us.

One word we never heard in any cadence or calls is freedom. We sang often of death and killing and communism, of the ideal soldier standing in the rain or jumping from a plane, but never freedom. Nor democracy, nor right nor righteousness. Not a force of good in the world. Not peacekeeping or peacekeepers or bring-

ing peace. Soldiers know what their job is, and it has nothing to
do with peace.

To soldiers, these are abstract concepts. Freedom is a weekend
pass. It's going home, getting out of the army for a few days or a
few weeks or forever. Freedom is sleeping past 4 a.m. It's seeing a
girlfriend, a mother, a father, a brother, a wife. Freedom has nothing to do with foreign countries. There is no freedom in war, just
more of the same thing the soldier experiences every day: long
hours of waiting, endless drills, bad food, boredom, preparation
for what may never occur but must be prepared for anyway, only
now the threat of death is thrown in as well. Bombs may fall from
the sky. Missiles streak in through the clouds. Land mines stepped
on, IEDs hit, snipers striking from the blue hills all around.

Freedom is a word politicians and civilians use, not soldiers.

> Here we go again,
> Same old shit again.
> Marching down the avenue,
> I don't know when we'll be through,
> But I'll be glad and so will you.

But we sang of death often, for death is a common recurrence in
cadences. I suppose now these cadences were in some ways medita-
tions upon death, a glorification of dying in war, a preparation for
it. Or, in some of the others, preparation to kill. To create unthink-
ing men, unafraid to stab babies in the back, put 'em on a roast
and rack. To see women as jokes, to pull a plug and watch them
choke. In war, every death means a kill, and by preparing for one,
we must have been preparing for the other.

We didn't know that then. On August 2nd we would return
from a morning run, singing of soldiers on the hill and C-130s
rolling down the strip, to learn that Saddam Hussein had invaded
Kuwait, and we stood in silence on the drill pad as our leaders
announced that it looked as if we were going to war. The United
Nations passed Resolution 660, condemning the invasion and demanding the immediate withdrawal of Iraqi troops. They did not
need to tell us what would happen if Iraq did not withdraw.

In the next few days the 101st and 82nd Airborne Divisions
were mobilized. The aircraft carriers *Eisenhower* and *Independence*
slipped through the Suez Canal. The first F-15s arrived from Langley, and each morning, before we ran singing of soldiers dying in

foreign countries, we came down to see the news from the Gulf written on a chalkboard, the mobilization of forces, the resolutions and sanctions passed by the UN.

Then we ran, farther and faster than we had before. I want to say our voices were louder. Many of us would go home after training and never see the Gulf, never stand on a hill or jump from the sky, but we went through our last days singing, adhering to the old rhythms, the old songs. We ran in the mornings and evenings. We marched to class with our young voices echoing off the walls of the barracks all around us. And when we returned to our temporary homes in the barracks late at night, we lay dreaming not of home but of war, what form our futures might follow.

Our last night in Basic Training our parents had flown in or driven through the night to see us. They were waiting on the drill pad as we came back from wherever we had been, and the drill sergeants marched us in place for what seemed forever, our voices louder and louder and louder, echoing off the buildings all around as bombs exploded in the far distance. The drill sergeants wanted our parents to see us and hear us, to feel our voices ringing out into the summer night, and caught up in the cadence, the sheer joy of singing, whether about dirty commies or women lying dead in hospital beds, whether about soldiers dying in the early morning rain or soldiers falling from the sky, we didn't know that we were only marching in place.

Which is to say we never knew where we were going, and would only realize later that we never went anywhere. We woke every morning to reveille and dressed with the dark outside the windows, then ran down to the drill pad and all over the base, past the old WWII cannons and the fighter jets, past the tanks and helicopters and bronze statues of men long dead, past the base commander's house, everything dark, lit only in pools of yellow light that threw our shadows out large beside us. We might have been circling forever, as if we had always been here and always would be. We might have been lost in the darkness. We might have been on any base, wearing any uniform in the world, blindly following the men chosen to lead us, who could have taken us anywhere.

EDWIDGE DANTICAT

All the Home You've Got

FROM *Freeman's*

Faith

MY UNCLE, THE Baptist minister, whom I lived with in Haiti from the time that I was four years old to the time I was twelve, often used the expression *enfants de la promesse*, children of promise, to refer to children like me. The phrase was not meant to refer to our overall potential, but to the fact that we were born to Christian parents. Being a child of promise, in my particular case, also had to do with being born as a result of many promises.

It took five years from the time my parents were married for them to have me. And between their wedding night and the day I was born, there were a lot of prayers and tears. My father once told me that he'd wondered whether he would have to wait to be a hundred years old to become a father, like Abraham. So there were many promises made before I showed up. My mother had promised that she would consecrate her firstborn to Christ, that she would make sure the child walked no other path, that her first daughter or son would be a servant of the Lord. And my father promised God that he would stop smoking, that he would never so much as look at any other woman but my mother. He promised that he would never leave his children if he could help it. But there were many things that were beyond his and my mother's control.

A few years after my birth, my parents left Haiti to seek a better home and future elsewhere, to escape a brutal dictatorship, to find work, to make money. And for all that to happen they had to leave me and my younger brother behind. So I was a child of promise, born out of pure faith, but a child, and later an adult, whose faith in any kind of home, would, just like my heart, completely break.

Witness

When I was ten years old, an older boy moved into my aunt and uncle's house and every night for a few weeks, he would walk into the room where I and several girls slept and he would slip his hands under our nightgowns and touch our private parts. Our bunk beds were lined up near the linen-filled armoire from which he needed to get a set of sheets at night, and before he'd pick up the sheets he would touch us. Sometimes it was one or two of us. Sometimes it was all four of us, all of us too terrified to discuss what was going on even among ourselves, all of us too afraid that he might kill us if we screamed or told anyone else.

In that moment I would pretend that my body was no longer my own and that I had merged with the bedsheet. During the day, I would find certain objects to keep me from thinking about the night: self-made amulets in the form of beautiful black and brown women on toothpaste boxes. I would cut out these faces and their gleaming white teeth and I would think how lucky these women were because, since they neither had homes nor beds, no one could touch them in terrible ways. These ungrounded women could also shield me, I thought, by drawing me into whatever imaginary world they lived in, where people laughed all the time and had no vulnerable flesh.

I was afraid to write openly about these nights while my parents were still alive. I was afraid that it might upset them. My parents had left Haiti in the middle of a thirty-year dictatorship during which most people were being terrorized. A woman or girl being raped, or even killed, was not all that unusual. A girl could be walking down the street, she could even be on her way to school alone, and if one of the dictatorship's henchmen decided he liked her, he could take her away. My aunt and uncle managed to protect me from the street threat. Yet they were not aware that the terror had walked inside their home.

As an adult at family gatherings, at mine or other people's homes, I would sit quietly and listen to story after story of female relatives who had been asked to go to private houses, prisons, police stations, wearing their prettiest dresses to "convince" the colonel, general, foot soldier, or militia man who'd arrested their father, brother, uncle, cousin, not to kill their men. Sometimes the price of a loved one's release was a young female relative's virginity. But no one spoke about any of this until our female heroines had died.

Many of the women in my family covered up being abused with piousness. They wore white clothes and wrapped their hair with white scarves. They wore no jewelry or makeup. They prayed a lot. They tried to make themselves as white as the snow we had not yet seen, as white as light itself. They tried to become invisible.

The less of you that was seen the better, my aunt Denise liked to say. But it was no guarantee of protection, even in the dark, even inside your own home.

"I can't always be where you are, but the more time you spend in church, the more eyes you have on you," my father would say when I joined him and my mother in New York at age twelve.

Having eyes on you made it harder for people to hurt you because there were not only human eyes on you. God and his angels were also watching over you.

Prayer

When I first wrote about this — as fiction — when I was twenty-three years old, this is some of what I wrote:

> When I was a little girl, I had a small notebook made of a few folded sheets, held together by bamboo syrup. There, I sketched a series of stick figures, which were so closely drawn that they almost bumped each other off the page. My effigies were of a child who woke up in tears every morning to find her panties gone. There were never any bubbles over her scalp. No expressions nor conversations. There was just a burning ache between her thighs and a head that bent down to look and then somehow was never raised again . . .
>
> I was forced to press my pillow farther against the wall when Aunt Denise's godson Joel moved in. He was a tall, thin fifteen-year-old who looked like a man on account of a shaggy beard. He had just come from the hills of Léogâne and his whole body smelled like the wet clay that was still clinging to the straps of his brown sandals.
>
> After he spent the first night in the far corner of the room, way over on the boys' side, I woke up and found my panties gone.

I couldn't string together the words to tell. ("Lost Shadows and Stick Figures," *The Caribbean Writer*, volume 6, 1992)

I asked that this be published as fiction, but I am not sure it was. I find it interesting that in my fictional version, I put him in the same room with me and the other girls, "way over on the boys' side." I also gave myself a notebook to write and draw images in. Reading this now, I wonder whether worse things happened to me than my protective childhood mind has allowed me to remember. But what I most want to hold on to now is the fact that words and images had become an alternate home, my safest place. My imagination had rescued me. My prayers had saved me too — I consider writing a kind of prayer — even though they had not been answered in the way I'd yearned for or expected.

A few years ago, I ran into Joel at my aunt and uncle's house in Haiti after my aunt had died. I stood away from him, and though I had both dreaded and rehearsed this encounter over and over in my mind for years, I did not publicly blurt out what he had done to me. I did not cry or run away either. I did not even cringe. I answered his hello and looked into his eyes, and though I saw no visible sign of remorse or soul-searching there, it was the first time in my life that I stopped praying for his death. He was now a shadow to me. I had escaped his grasp, and strangely enough, my imperfect faith in God, which had led me to supplement my prayers with my own protective visions of those bodiless women, had been a big part of my being able to stand in the same room as Joel and mourn the same loved one.

I am still waiting to experience both perfect forgiveness and perfect faith, though. I am not yet able to love my enemies the same way I love my friends. I am unable to pray for those who persecute me beyond praying for them to stop persecuting me. But I am still praying that this particular persecution will not follow me all the days of my life.

Grace

I have always had low religious self-esteem. Whenever I am in a church, be it my home church or a church I am visiting, there is always a moment when I expect someone to walk over and escort me out, saying, "This is not your place. You don't belong here. We are kicking you out."

The feeling that God let me down by allowing Joel to touch me sometimes makes my faith plummet in a way that is as clear to me as a special-effects meteorite in a movie. But it is much harder for me to express how my survival of this ordeal is what keeps making my faith rebound — not just my being alive, but being able to love my husband, and my two daughters, being able to write my stories, and also to contribute some things, both tangible and intangible, to the world we all live in.

Many of the people I grew up with, some of whom are now pastors and choir directors and other functionaries in different types of churches, are very happy to see me in church. But others, armed with public revelations that writers directly or indirectly make in their work, are hell-bent on seeing me draw a line in the sand and make a clear declaration of "pure and absolute faith," as one friend put it.

For a long time, a childhood friend would email me accounts of dreams that she'd had about me and my family. Her most consistent dream about me involved my having sold my soul to the devil, unwillingly, in my sleep. She could tell by the things I had been writing, she said, and by the fact that I refused to write Christian stories.

"You might have strayed too far from home," she once wrote me, "a little or a lot from the path your uncle and parents taught you. Jesus does not do in-between or lukewarm. You're either inside his kingdom or out in the cold."

I felt condemned by this person because she had very accurately described my often wavering faith, which could be lukewarm or sometimes cold. At times it was because of gatekeepers like her, whose level of certainty I could never match. But most of the time it was because my imagination would not allow me to constrain myself to one set of beliefs, one set of people, and one set of "certainties." As a writer, I told myself, I had to live in other spaces, in other bodies, in other homes, in other minds, in order to convincingly create my characters, which, if I am lucky, represent a whole range of beliefs, lifestyles, moralities, and hopes and dreams.

"This kind of thinking is a certain road to hell," another *enfant de la promesse,* who actually fulfilled her religious promise and was attending a theological seminary, told me.

None of this shocks or offends me; I grew up with a minister after all. Hell was not just other people, but even deviant thoughts, which is a minefield for fiction. I understand drawing lines and un-ambiguity. I understand not compromising. I understand you're either with us or against us. But that is just not me. Besides, I'm not always sure who "us" is. Is it the gatekeepers to our celestial home? Is it God? Might "us" not also be a group of wounded people whose faith often wavers but who are still seeking a home in God?

Whenever my faith wavers, I try to stick to the basics. I am not expecting any cookies for it, but I still believe in prayer and I still believe in God. I understand, as my minister uncle used to say, that the Bible has many contradictions. I am still struggling with the way these contradictions are often used by human beings to hurt, and even assault, others. Yet I want to respect other people's reli-gions. I want — need — to seek inspiration in the stories of strong people from a whole range of faiths and religious paths.

In the strict religious environment in which I grew up, that makes me a heretic, and a messy one at that. A heretic who refuses to wander off too far, to not believe at all, yet still continues to walk around with a messy and incomplete faith that sometimes feels like living in a half-finished house.

One thing trauma and the resulting restlessness keeps remind-ing me is that we are all born vulnerable. Unlike an actual house we are not made of wood, stone, concrete, mortar, or cement. We are easily broken, and we might end up spending the rest of our lives trying to find some way to fix that brokenness. One can still learn, though, from other wounded people — real or fictional — whose faith seems complete, "finished," people whose faith is — or feels — actually like home. One of those folks for me is the lay preacher Baby Suggs in Toni Morrison's novel *Beloved*.

I sometimes find myself prayerfully muttering a few lines from one of her outdoor sermons.

"Here," she said, "in this here place, we flesh; flesh that weeps, laughs; flesh that dances on bare feet in grass. Love it. Love it hard."

Reading this, I always imagine her meaning that sometimes our bodies are all the home we've got.

Then I whisper, *Amen, Sister, Amen.*

STEVEN HARVEY

The Other Steve Harvey

FROM *Michigan Quarterly Review*

IT DOES ONLY happen on the telephone.

A woman — it is always a woman — and I may be talking about insurance or a credit card or my medications, while I'm standing in the kitchen twirling the telephone cord and the subject of my name comes up. The voice at the other end of the line that had started off businesslike, polite, and unaccented, suddenly breaks into a nervous laugh, sheds its formality, and is full of attitude.

It turns black.

"Are you *really* Steve Harvey?"

It happens to those of us with the name of someone who is famous, in my case a black television star known for his charisma, chutzpah, and thick moustache. "I'm here with Steve Harvey," Ellen DeGeneres once joked, "and Steve Harvey's moustache." He is an entertainer who presents himself as saucy, sexy, and full of good cheer.

"I just *love* that man, hmm mm," the voice on the phone once added. "He's *some*thin'."

It is the voice of a black woman letting down her defenses. A woman among friends, and I hear in it an opening, a thinning of the distance between us, even, perhaps, a call to kinship from a confidante, and I usually try to join in with a self-deprecating joke. "No, he's the rich one," I say. Or I might be a little evasive. "Me, Steve Harvey? Only on the telephone." Usually I just tell them what they know already: "No, I'm the *other* Steve Harvey."

What I don't say is what I am thinking.

The Other Steve Harvey

I remind people that I had the name first. I was born in Dodge City, Kansas, seven years before the TV star, and my parents chose the name because they liked the sound of it. No one else before me in my family was named Steve as far as I know. My mother called me Stevie.

As for the name Harvey, my dad's father was a cattle rancher in Dodge City and the last name has a question mark beside it, since that side of the family, unlike my mother's side with a lineage that runs back to a witch in Salem, is not well known. There may be a reason for this blank spot in the record since my dad liked to joke that the Harveys were probably cattle rustlers and thieves.

Aside from the name, I have little in common with the comedian Steve Harvey. I was blond when I was young though I am bald now and most of what is left of my hair has turned gray. I live in the North Georgia mountains and for many years taught at Young Harris College, the only source of racial diversity at all in our area at the bottom tip of the Appalachian range, a part of the country long ago settled by Scotch-Irish immigrants after the removal of the Cherokees in the 1830s on the Trail of Tears. When I look at my hands while typing I see that — despite the faded freckles — they are a kind of wheatish white. Not fish-belly white as Mark Twain liked to say, but plenty white, and no one who sees me mistakes me for *the* Steve Harvey.

The Other Trayvon Martin

After George Zimmerman, a white neighborhood-watch volunteer in Sanford, Florida, shot and killed Trayvon Martin, a black high school student, President Barack Obama responded to a question about the shooting. "If I had a son," he said at a White House press conference, "he would look like Trayvon." After the acquittal of Zimmerman more than a year later, the president, in an attempt to put the events in context, reiterated the idea more forcibly. "Another way of saying that is Trayvon Martin could have been me thirty-five years ago," he explained, and at the phrase "thirty-five years ago" he shrugged slightly and a wistful smile briefly crossed his lips, the smile of recognition at a simple truth that had rocked him.

The president said that "there's a lot of pain around what happened here," speaking softly and deliberately though his voice came down hard on the word "pain." Holding it for an extra beat, the word sounded like two syllables, and he extended his cupped hands before him, palms upward, as if they held a great weight before letting them drop down to the lectern again.

"The African American community is looking at this issue through a set of experiences and a history that doesn't go away," he explained, pausing, bowing his head and closing his eyes briefly, and, as he gave his examples, I — the other Steve Harvey — began to register some simple truths myself, truths I have known intellectually all of my adult life but had somehow failed to take in as felt experience until I heard the president put them into words.

"There are very few African American men in this country who haven't had the experience of being followed when they were shopping in a department store," the president said, looking down at the audience. "That includes me," he added. "There are very few African American men who haven't had the experience of walking across the street and hearing the locks click on the doors of cars. That happens to me, at least before I was a senator." And as he gave this example he lifted his hand to make the clicking motion with his thumb, and I immediately registered that small gesture as a blow. Yes, I have seen that, I thought leaning in toward the computer screen mesmerized by the president's hands and words. I have *done* that. "There are very few African Americans," the president said finally, "who haven't had the experience of getting on an elevator" to find "a woman clutching her purse nervously and holding her breath until she had a chance to get off. That happens often." At the phrase "clutching her purse" the president pulled his hand close to his body reenacting the frightened woman's gesture, becoming her briefly as he remained by reason of his skin color the object of her fear.

That includes me.

That happens to me.

That happens often.

Yes it does, I admit resignedly, implicated in these scenarios. Steve Harvey and the other Steve Harvey face off across a passenger window, a moustache between them, and I click the lock.

"Where do we take this?" President Obama asked, opening both of his hands outward toward the future, toward all of us, toward me.

He suggested a reexamination of racial-profiling practices by police, a review of "stand your ground" laws, and the development of long-term projects to "bolster and reinforce" African American boys, but he also called for "some soul-searching."

He did not look directly into the camera at this moment — he was focused on the reporters sitting in front of him — but he was talking to me, the other Steve Harvey. He asked that Americans be "a little bit more honest" about race and that they at least ask themselves this question: "Am I wringing as much bias out of myself as I can?"

As he said those words he moved his hand three times in a semicircular motion as if twisting a washcloth.

The Other Barack Obama

The facts in the Trayvon Martin shooting are important and in dispute, but, for the purpose of wringing as much bias out of myself as I can, what other people do does not matter. I don't know why Zimmerman was suspicious of an African American teenager walking through his neighborhood wearing a hoodie. I don't know if the words from a dispatcher saying "We do not need you to do that" when he was following Martin in his car was a direct order to stand down. I don't know if Martin broke Zimmerman's nose though it seems pretty amazing to me that we cannot figure that one out. I don't know if racial slurs were exchanged that night.

Did Trayvon Martin say "You are going to die tonight" moments before the shooting as Zimmerman's father said? Or did Zimmerman say that? Like Martin's father I'm pretty suspicious of the detective's claim that Trayvon said "What's your problem, homie?" because they also claim he said "You got me!" when he was shot, which sounds like some terrible line from the script of *Gunsmoke*. Was Zimmerman on top of Martin during the scuffle as one witness claimed, pinning him down with his knees or was Martin on top grinding Zimmerman's face into the concrete as another witness said? Or did positions shift during the struggle? And those cries heard in the background of one of the 911 calls — is that Zimmerman screaming or Martin pleading for his life?

I don't know, and I suspect that we will never know for sure, important facts about what happened that evening, but for my purposes here they don't matter. I don't even care what Zimmerman saw when he pulled up in his car beside Trayvon Martin and looked at the young man's face.

What I do care about is what *I* see. What would catch *my* eye on a winter evening in Sanford, Florida, during rounds of my neighborhood watch when I pull up beside a lone figure and look at the face under a hoodie staring back at me through the passenger window?

And what matters most is what I see first.

The Other?

Even before I lift the hood up over my head, the hoodie feels cozy. When I zip it up, the soft lining wraps around me tighter than a sweater and the pockets go deep in front pulling my shoulders down. In order to drape the hood over me I bow my head a little, and the suggestion of fetal isolation is complete. The mother's other. The only other. The world goes away, and I am ready to wander its empty streets alone.

Well, sort of.

My wife bought the hoodie for me as a Christmas present when I retired from teaching, and my children urged me to wear it, going against type. I was always a sweater guy, my favorite an old blue cotton cardigan with knitted ribbing and tattered cuffs that hangs from a hook in my study. In fact, I knew it was time to retire when I noticed at faculty meetings that I was the only man in the room who wore a cardigan. I would *never* trade one in for a sweatshirt.

But the minute I wrapped myself up in the soft warmth of a hoodie I was a convert. "What was I thinking!" I announced when I lifted the hood over my head and dug my hands into the pockets. "I *love* this!"

Trayvon Martin loved his hoodie too. "It could be a hundred degrees outside and he always had his hoodie on," his aunt told

USA Today. The iconic — and controversial — photograph of him that appeared on newscasts and in newspaper reports shows Trayvon in his gray hoodie looking directly at us with soulful eyes and smooth and youthful skin. The photo is undated, leading some to believe that it misrepresents Trayvon as an innocent-looking boy, though his defense attorney claims it was taken within a year of the shooting.

Was Martin shot because he was a young black man in a hoodie? Many think so. One of the largest rallies after his death was the Million Hoodie March at Union Square in Manhattan to protest the racial profiling of nonwhite youth wearing hoodies. In a photo of the march a crowd gathered to hear Trayvon's father and mother speak, many of them expressing their solidarity with Trayvon as a victim of profiling by draping their hoodies over their heads.

George Zimmerman did not see a person but a hood when he decided to follow Martin in his car — that is the sentiment behind the protest. When he rolled down the window and spoke to Trayvon, he spoke to a dark and hooded face. And when he fired his pistol, he did not shoot Trayvon Martin, a high school student carrying a bag of Skittles. He shot a hoodie with blackness in it. He shot the other.

The hoodie invites otherness. The hood isolates. It hides the wearer from the world. Surely this is why young people wear them as expressions of adolescent rebellion. To be one among a million hoodies — well, more like several thousand — gathered in Union Square, is not to be lost in a crowd, but to be lost to the crowd. The isolation, not the community, gives the wearer a feeling of protection. You can't touch this, the hood says, but the protection is false. Just look at the bloodstains and the stippling of powder burns around the bullet holes in Trayvon's hoodie, entered in evidence at the trial.

But there is more to this story of otherness than the hood. Something deeper and intractable. I lift my hoodie from its hanger and put it on, draping the cloth over my head, and walk into the living room to stand before a full-length mirror. Shoving my fists into my pockets I peer into the glass, looking hard at that shaded, freckled face, wondering if I can see the other there.

I can't, of course, but it is not because it is my own face in the mirror.

It is because of what I don't see first. *The* Steve Harvey in my hoodie could be the other, but the other Steve Harvey that I am can't. Anyone who shot me would be aiming at me, not at my hood.

The Mother

Sybrina Fulton, the mother of Trayvon, met with *New York Times* journalist Charles Blow twice to talk about her son's death. In the first interview, conducted at a restaurant near her home five weeks after the shooting, she was accompanied by her mother. "She grows distant when she talks about her loss," Blow wrote, "occasionally, seemingly involuntarily wrapping her hands gently around her mother's arm and resting her head on her mother's shoulder like a young girl in need of comfort. The sorrow seems to come in waves." A year later, in their second interview, she is alone and stronger — her sorrow replaced with a "reservoir of resolve" — but her magical thinking reveals that she is still in mourning. Unable to go to Trayvon's grave, she had begun to collect the gifts given to her in Trayvon's room. "I miss him hugging me," she laments, yearning for no other than her son, and she is puzzled by his death. "I don't know if it's real or not."

The Other Mother

When a racist Valentine card fell out of the envelope of a letter that my mother wrote more than fifty years ago, I was surprised. These cards, popular in the 1950s, show black children with stereotypical bulging eyes and big, red lips, as well as a sexualization of body parts that is particularly offensive. I no longer have the postcard, but it looked like one I call up on my computer showing the caricatures of two black children with exaggerated features and coy expressions on their faces standing back-to-back and holding hands. In their free hands the boy clutches a heart and the girl a fan, and in the fingers of their clasped hands there is a note that says "All About Necking." They look to be about three years old.

My mother died when I was eleven, so I cannot ask her about the Valentine, but I was surprised when it tumbled into my lap because I don't remember overtly racist language or symbols from my childhood when she was alive. I never heard the N-word spoken in my house. My parents used the word "colored" instead, which was common in the 1950s, and did so out of politeness or as a refinement preferable to alternatives, I think, unaware that they were labeling another race in a way that could be offensive. My parents were moderate Republicans, the party of Lincoln, which was, at that time, associated with progressive views on race.

But I suspect, under the surface, an unconscious but pervasive racism was built into my youth, a suspicion that the Valentine card makes manifest. When my parents shopped for a house in the North Shore area near Chicago, they talked openly to each other about housing values and race. They chose Deerfield, which Harry and David Rosen called "the Little Rock of the North" in their book *But Not Next Door,* the town becoming notorious in 1959 when a developer attempted unsuccessfully to build integrated housing units there. In a letter my mother, aware of the controversy, was relieved that the residents of Deerfield blocked the project by voting "to build several park areas" in disputed neighborhoods of the town. "Deerfield is truly a town of nice, wholesome people," she wrote, the word "wholesome" covering over a host of unspoken sins.

I think if my mother were alive today and in an elevator when *the* Steve Harvey walked in she would clutch her purse nervously and hold her breath until she had a chance to get off.

The Other Father

In his speech, President Obama said that "things are getting better." "Each successive generation," he explained, chopping the air above the podium into segments with his hand, "seems to be making progress in changing attitudes when it comes to race." Gesturing toward the family residence in the East Wing, he mentioned his daughters as examples: "When I talk to Malia and Sasha, and I listen to their friends and I see them interact" — here the president paused, composing his thoughts — "they're better than we are — they're better than we were — on these issues." He admitted that America was not "postracial" and that racism had not been "eliminated," and that we needed to work on these challenges. He said that leaders needed to "encourage the better angels of our nature" rather than use episodes like the shooting of Trayvon Martin "to heighten divisions," and he paused after the word "divisions" for a full four seconds, looking off into the middle distance, before returning to the optimism his children represent to him. "But we should also have confidence that kids these days, I think, have more sense than we did back then, and certainly more than our parents did or our grandparents did; and that along this long, difficult journey, we're becoming a more perfect union — not a perfect union, but a more perfect union."

The Other

When I pull off at the Tenth Street exit in downtown Atlanta and a handful of black men rush at the car armed with Windex bottles and washcloths as a scam to get money, I click the lock on my door. When I drive through the inner city to visit my daughter, I click the lock on my door. When I walk into downtown neighborhoods, I move my wallet to my front pocket. When I go to a Braves' game at Turner Field, I walk behind my family to keep an eye on them. I don't say the N-word or tell racist jokes, and at a party when someone does, I don't laugh or acknowledge the ugly word, but I do remain silent.

And as I make these admissions to myself and vow after the president's speech to do better, I picture in my mind a hand turning slowly as if wringing a washcloth.

Then suddenly it stops.

Many years ago I was at the house of a friend in the mountains where I live, admiring a framed photograph he had taken of black children at a playground. The kids were scrambling to get into the shot, their faces alive with mischievous delight, especially one of the girls in a white dress who clearly had elbowed her way to get her big smile in front of the camera.

"Racism will be with us," my friend said, nodding toward the picture, "as long as the first thing you notice about these children is that they are black."

I turned and looked hard at the picture again. When I had

looked at it before I had registered delight, playfulness, mischie-vousness, and spunkiness, but the first thing I saw was that their faces were black.

I think my friend is right.

It is prejudice, this *first* thing I see, a judgment based on race before any other facts are known. President Obama asked us — asked *me* — to be a "bit more honest." Well, if I met Barack Obama on the street, a man I voted for twice to be president, I'm pretty sure the first thing I would in all honesty see is that he is black.

Another Trayvon

So what do I see when I look at the face of Trayvon Martin under his hoodie? In reverse order, I see the smoothness of his skin. I keep coming back to that. He really is just so damned young under that gray hoodie, a kid and nothing more.

And he really could be Barack Obama thirty-five years ago. I see that in the wounded innocence of his seventeen-year-old face, the hint of mischief in his smile, and a dreaminess about the eyes.

I could see menace here, too, a twisting of these features in an-ger that could be a threat, but in repose it is a face that a mother, a girlfriend, or a father would love.

I see his black hair forming a kind of crown around the face, framing it, containing it.

The pupils of his eyes, highlighted with flecks of light, are oth-erwise black and penetrating. They float dolefully from the upper eyelids in the eggshell white of his eyes. And the eyebrows rise up, almost elfin.

His nose has a small hump in the middle and a hint of a mous-tache appears above his upper lip.

His skin is buttery brown and there is something feminine about its smoothness, inviting the touch.

But the first thing I see when I look at the face of Trayvon Mar-tin as I imagine him bending down to speak to me through the window of my car on a cool winter night in Sanford, Florida, is not the buttery brown skin, the suggestion of a moustache, or the doleful eyes under the hoodie.

The first thing I see is that he is black.

And what I see first is what I think first.

The Other Steve Harvey

So I tell my Steve Harvey jokes. "He's the rich one," I say. Or "I had the name before he did." Or "only on the telephone." What I don't say is the first thing that comes to my mind when anyone asks me if I'm really Steve Harvey. "No, he's the black one." Under the hoodie of my silence, that thought floats into my mind first, revealing an unconscious bias I cannot wring out of myself. When I tell the jokes — being self-deprecatory, of course, to disarm the situation — I drive my prejudice down in me where it is not apparent but does not die.

"Where do we take this?" President Obama asked, opening both of his hands outward toward the future, toward all of us, toward me. If I am an employer, it takes me to a tendency to say no too quickly, and if a juror to say guilty too easily, and if a cop to shoot before a threat is real. When I judge the death of Trayvon Martin and other black men killed by authorities under mysterious circumstances, it takes me to a conclusion contrary to all I have been taught: that the burden of proof is on the killer. And it takes me to an ugly truth hidden in my own name. With each repetition of my joke, an offensive Valentine card tumbles from the fingertips of memory, and I'm secretly clicking the lock on my car door. I'm surreptitiously checking my wallet in the elevator. I'm following Steve Harvey through the aisles of a department store, watching his hands.

LESLIE JAMISON

The March on Everywhere

FROM *Harper's Magazine*

I WAS AT a Maryland travel plaza just off I-95 when I finally saw them, en masse and outfitted: the women. They were emerging from the fog like visions, their bodies spectral and streetlamp-lit, walking alone and with friends, with canes, with glowing ciga-rettes between their fingers; with boots over their jeans, with their daughters and mothers, with paper cups of coffee in their hands. They were headed into the rest stop, its vertical windows rising from the mist like church spires. They were holding doors for one another, asking, "Did I just cut you in line?" They were buying sodas and bananas. They were going to the bathroom. They were letting pregnant women go first. They were in utero, they were in wheelchairs, and they were all headed where I was headed: to the corner of Third Street and Independence Avenue.

When I arrived at that travel plaza — with my friends Rachel and Joe and their eleven-week-old baby, Luke — it felt like a mythi-cal village of Amazon women had been transplanted from the jun-gle to the harsh fluorescent lighting of a highway rest stop. That night on I-95, arms full of licorice and chips, we didn't yet know the statistics of our surge. There would be half a million people in Washington, three times the size of Donald Trump's inaugural crowd, and more than eight hundred demonstrations on seven continents, with an estimated 4.2 million people marching in this country alone: probably the largest protest in American history. But already, we were made of nerves and excitement. We were buzzed on coffee. We were breastfeeding babies. We were part of a creature with four million faces. We were a bunch of strang-

ers intoxicated by our shared purpose, which is to say: we were
a we.

The DC Metro was jam-packed at eight the next morning. People were practically embracing strangers to make room for other
strangers. Trump and Putin were French-kissing on five different
pins. One hat said MAKE RACISTS AFRAID AGAIN. One pair of
sneakers showed a uterus painted in pink glitter glue. The left
foot said PUSSY. The right foot said POWER. A voice over the loud-
speaker said: "Women's-rights fighters from all over the world, welcome to your Red Line!"

We marched past the Capitol — which I barely recognized at
first, because we were marching past the back — and then down to
Independence. We did not need directions. We just followed the
human stream. Our friend Erin, five months pregnant, put a sign
around her neck that said FEMINIST FUTURE, with an arrow pointing down at her belly. I saw a sign that said VIVA VULVA. I saw a
sign that said FIGHT LIKE A GIRL. I saw a sign that said I'M WITH
HER. It had arrows pointing everywhere.

A woman my age wore a sign that said FOURTH-GENERATION
FEMINIST. It made me wonder who counted, whether feminists
existed before the phrase itself was invented. My grandmother was
raised on a farm in rural Saskatchewan, bathing once a week in
kettle-heated water, and grew up to work in a university laboratory. She was one of the founding members of the Shattuck Neighborhood Action Coalition, in Oakland, California, a community
where she put down roots decades before it started to gentrify.
She led cleanup missions around Bushrod Park, collecting piles of
garbage for trucks to haul away, and had everyone over afterward
for soup and homemade bread. Until her diabetes made it impossible, she delivered voters-alliance newsletters to eighty homes
in her neighborhood. She wore bright flowing skirts and we took
walks together pretending to be aliens from the planet Algernon,
trying to figure out the purposes of all these mysterious objects:
garden hose, fire hydrant, wind chime. She believed in the latent
magic of the proximate, and in community as something actively
built, not passively inherited. She put her body and her time — her
self — into work she felt was important.

As for my own mom, I have always understood her commitment
to social justice in worshipful, often cinematic terms. She fell in

love with her first husband while they were protesting the Vietnam War in Portland, Oregon, at a liberal arts college where the students figured out ways to make their sex lives count toward the PE requirement. At one demonstration in San Francisco, where federal agents started photographing the crowd from nearby buildings, she and everyone held up their driver's licenses.

I grew up hearing stories about the season she spent picking crops in the South of France, with the woman I eventually realized had been her lover — which only made these tales more intoxicating, their days spent harvesting olives and Roma tomatoes, staying in a small cottage in the woods, getting paid in jugs of wine, stacking the fireplace with roots at night and watching their knotted, whirling patterns burn. My mom told me about a strike she had led among the olive pickers, who were forced to work long hours in the brutal cold wearing only cotton socks as gloves.

As I saw it, my mother had repeatedly shown up for something larger than her own life. She'd been desperate to join the Peace Corps. She worked as a precinct leader for the McGovern campaign, in 1972, while she was pregnant with my oldest brother. (She called him George while he was still in the womb.) She brought my brothers, just five and six years old, to rural Brazil when she was doing her doctoral research on infant malnutrition. She spent decades working on maternal-health research and advocacy in West Africa, and I carried in my mind's eye a vivid memory that wasn't mine: the night in Togo when she accompanied a woman in obstructed labor to the hospital in Sokodé, driving along muddy, rutted roads while the rain pelted down.

It wasn't just the things she had done that I admired but the spirit in which I imagined her doing them: selflessly, putting her own comfort aside, choosing the path of most resistance. Her life in social justice was always intertwined with her life as a primary parent. She was committed to her children — and to children who *weren't* her children.

In her early seventies now, she is still at it. As a deacon in the Episcopal Church, she recently protested unjust immigration policies by giving Communion through the mesh of the border fence in Tijuana. She was also arrested with unionized hotel workers in downtown Los Angeles, wearing her clerical collar as she was handcuffed. As I construct the story of her life, it shimmers with valor, with purity of motivation, and with endless, altruistic work.

*

I have always found a kind of mission statement in the story of her very first protest, a march around Portland's Pioneer Courthouse Square against the House Un-American Activities Committee. My mom was handing out flyers, and one woman handed hers back, looked my mom straight in the eye, and said, "I hope your children grow up to hate you." It was a female curse, a way of saying: I hope the gods of motherhood punish you. But ever since my mother told me that story, I have believed that loving her as much as I do is a political act.

I have also seen myself as a disappointing inheritor of her legacy. My own commitment to social action — while durable — has felt more like a series of do-gooder missteps and awkward incursions into activism: mixing concrete (badly) in a small Costa Rican village to build a footpath to the local church, as a naively well-intentioned fifteen-year-old whose parents could afford to fund her exercises in conscience; or tutoring mothers in a minimum-security prison to help them pass their GED exams, feeling so shy — so convinced I was doing a terrible job — that my stomach knotted up with anxiety.

My attempts at direct political action have been shot through with apathy and bumbling. When I canvass, there is the perpetual nervousness before each buzzer-ring, and an ongoing record of startling ineloquence. ("I'm not voting." "But you should!") My days organizing with my graduate-student union always felt grudging and full of discomfort: town hall meetings I didn't want to attend, follow-up emails I didn't want to type.

Whenever I compared my history of social engagement with my mother's, it felt meager and disheveled. I was a lurker, always ducking around the edges of the crowd, hovering near the snack table, drinking too much coffee. I was both too insecure and too egotistical to fully join group efforts, convinced I had better ways to spend my time than being one body among many. I was too obsessed with singular expression, with my own voice, to lend myself to the humbler chorus of collective action. This was the ego investment — the stubborn sense of my own identity — that kept me from being useful, from being subsumed into the whole.

When we got close to Independence and Third Street, and found no stage in sight, we wondered: Are we in the right place? We were definitely *some*place, with more people than I'd ever seen in my life. Every time we looked down a street, we saw endless bodies. We were looking for the core of it: the epicenter of the gathering, the departure point. Eventually we realized we were marching toward the wrong side of the stage, along with probably twenty thousand other people. I hadn't imagined the rally like this, with this abiding uncertainty about where the thing itself *was*.

We inched up C Street to see if we could hit Independence further back. We walked over hay and flattened horseshit, perhaps left over from the inaugural parade, though we weren't directly on its route. We passed circular black tanks labeled HORSE CONTROL. A woman stood in the back of a pickup truck hawking GET YOUR HANDS OFF MY VAJAYJAY pins at the top of her lungs. A few blocks away, bras dangled from the trees. A woman dressed in bright orange was looking for a group of other women dressed in bright orange.

The buildings of our government felt vast and indifferent on either side of us, made of cold pale marble. We flooded their inhuman scale with our human bodies. The crowd often stopped in its tracks, because there were so many of us and because so many of us were taking selfies. This did not seem like vanity so much as a useful motivating impulse, the desire to say: I was part of this. We all wanted our presence documented. If activism had to be entirely selfless — no affective payoff, no emotional or digital souvenirs — it would never happen at all.

For the first few hours, I couldn't hear or see the rally. Gloria Steinem was speaking somewhere, but at a certain point I couldn't have even told you which direction the stage was in. I tried to check on my phone, but I wasn't getting reception. No one was. There were too many of us. Our technology was blocked by the more ancient technology of so many bodies gathering together.

We weren't on the official route of anything. We weren't even sure where we were going. But this didn't mean we weren't at the march. We *were* the march — in our mistakes and our rerouting, in our circling back, trying again, taking the long way around. We were already part of what we had been searching for.

When Alice Walker arrived home from the March on Washington in 1963 after taking a night bus back to Boston, her relatives were sure they'd seen her on TV. They insisted they had spotted her "among those milling about just to the left of Martin Luther King Jr." But they had seen what they wanted to see. She wasn't anywhere near him. "The crowds would not allow it," she wrote later. "I was, instead, perched on the limb of a tree far from the Lincoln Memorial."

I liked this lineage, this tradition of the partial and obstructed view: the marginal experience as authentic experience. It was permissive. You felt what you felt. You saw what you saw. You took what you could get. The only thing you could say for sure was that you had shown up.

At the Women's March, I saw people perched in the trees all around me, straining to hear. I thought of their aching legs and wondered how long they would last up there. I wondered if they had remembered to bring snacks.

Activism isn't an oil painting. It's real life: a box of tampons, a forgotten cell-phone charger, a late-night car ride. It's many hours standing on concrete. It's not just the glorious surge, or the giddy feeling in your stomach when you're on the move, tucked into the thick of the crowd, voice hoarse from shouting. It's also everything it takes to get there. It's dealing with the low-tire-pressure indicator light, flat on your stomach in a Bed-Stuy parking lot, losing the little metal cap somewhere on the oil-pocked asphalt. It's getting stuck in bumper-to-bumper on the Verrazano, with barges chugging through the gloom below. It's a post-quesadilla stomachache in Jersey. It's changing the baby in the backseat because the changing table in the restaurant bathroom is covered in mouse shit.

There is no activism that isn't full of logistics and resentments and boring details. Commitment to anything larger than your own life often looks mythic in retrospect. But on the ground, it's all in-box pileup and childcare guilt; it's a lot of wondering if you're having the right feelings or the wrong ones, or confusion about which is which. It's messy and chaotic and imperfect — which isn't the flaw of it but the glory of it. It trades the perfect for the necessary, for the something, for the beginning and the spark.

My mother may have led olive pickers on a strike in France, or been cursed out by an angry housewife in Pioneer Square, but her life isn't myth. It's a life. Over the years, I've learned the counterhistory of whatever glorious legend I wrote for her — not its cancellation, but its supplement: the fuller version. Her life in activism was fraught with apathy, despair, an urgent sense of inadequacy.

In other words, it was full of humanity. There were other truths, other parts of the story. She couldn't fulfill her Peace Corps assignment because her marriage fell apart and she wasn't allowed to report to Botswana without her husband. After the first flush of her antiwar activism, she fell away from the movement and into depression. She was working as a telephone operator in Oakland, trying to connect calls across the Pacific, hearing wives and mothers crying as they failed to reach soldiers they hadn't heard from in months.

The whole arc of her story was punctuated by moments of doubt and disillusionment. When McGovern was crushed in a landslide, losing every state but Massachusetts, she felt as though she had been personally rejected by her country. Her career in public health didn't grow seamlessly or instantaneously from her days of early motherhood; it took her years to figure out that she didn't want to spend two decades at home caring for her children. She almost dropped out of grad school on her first day because she was afraid it would take her too fully away from her sons. In retrospect, she felt guilty about bringing them to Brazil, especially my middle brother, who didn't like his preschool and had trouble learning the language.

Not long ago, she met a Vietnam vet who had also become an Episcopal deacon, and she told him about heckling a train of returning soldiers, how much she'd always regretted doing it. She told him that she was sorry. He said she was the first person who had ever apologized to him for doing that.

My mother recently confessed to me that she had never liked canvassing. This was years after I'd written an internal script that imagined her knocking on doors with full-throated eloquence and confidence, the way I never could. She didn't knock on doors because she enjoyed it, she told me, or even because she felt she was good at it. She did it because it was the work that needed to be done.

The point of participating in large-scale collective action isn't glory. It's something close to the opposite: being a body among bodies. It's about submerging yourself, becoming part of something too large to see the edges of. Over chiles rellenos in South Jersey, at a strip-mall Mexican restaurant on our drive down, Rachel told me: "My goal is just to be a body in Washington."

We were bodies among bodies. We were with an old man with a silver beard and a green vest and a sign around his neck that said THIS IS WHAT A FEMINIST LOOKS LIKE. Feminists looked like many things. A woman in a coat covered with tissue-paper flowers had a sign that said FRIDA CHOOSE. Another woman was dressed up like a giant vagina, with plumes of purple and beige felt. We had our tampons and our cigarettes and our breast pumps. We were ready to rewrite Mailer's *Armies of the Night*. We wore American flags as miniskirts, as bandannas, as hijabs. The transparent backpacks mandated by the organizers showed Luna bars and sunflower seeds: the comet trails of preparation behind everybody's presence. You saw the internal organs of cell phones and city maps, little confessions strapped to everyone's backs. A first-time protester told me she brought homemade cookies, but noticed that the veterans brought throat lozenges.

I felt awkward chanting — I often do — but chanted anyway. If everyone felt too self-conscious to chant, then we would make no noise at all. I wanted to reframe my own awkwardness as part of the process going right, or getting started, rather than a sign that it had always been going wrong. I wanted to believe that submission to awkwardness is one of the ways you can show up for a cause. Awkwardness can be part of authentic presence, the same way doubt is part of faith. One guy's sign said I HATE CROWDS, BUT I HATE TRUMP MORE. Another said SO BAD EVEN INTROVERTS ARE OUT.

We passed a cluster of pro-life women standing on a traffic island. One held up a rosary and a poster of a dead baby. The baby in the photograph — the idea of the dead baby, the visual rhetoric of shame-mongering — was less real to me than the baby my friend was pushing in his stroller: the child of a pro-choice mother, surrounded by the children of pro-choice mothers. The women on the island held posters that said WOMEN DO REGRET ABORTIONS.

Did we? Speaking for myself, I knew I was grateful that I'd been able to make a choice, that I hadn't had to drive thirty-six hours across state lines or feel a wire inside my body. I couldn't speak for the thousands of women around me who had also gotten abortions. Perhaps some regretted them. They still had the right to get them. I could see one poster showing a crude clothes hanger drawn next to the scrawled words NEVER AGAIN.

*

I saw more uteruses that Saturday than I had ever seen before, more than I'll ever see again. I saw them painted on cardboard and scribbled on paper. I saw them in handcuffs. I saw them made of snakes. I realized I had never known whether the plural of "uterus" was "uteruses" or "uteri" — and the question had never felt more urgent. One sign said THERE'S AN ELEPHANT IN THE WOMB and featured a little GOP mascot lurking at the top of a fallopian tube. *Our* mascots were the ovaries, the Statue of Liberty, and the pussy cat.

I'd always thought signs were for external eyes: for the media, or for the president I imagined peering down at us from the Truman Balcony. During the march, I realized that the posters were also for us, a way to keep from getting bored. When you're standing on concrete with no cell reception and thousands of bodies packed all around you, and the crowd hasn't moved for hours and you're not sure if it's ever going to move again, the signs are a saving grace: a live-action Twitter feed with its own endless taxonomy.

There were the anatomy signs, internal organs made external and external organs on parade. PUSSY GRABS BACK was its own genre, its own little zoo: vagina dentata, fluffy kitten, big cat baring its teeth. There were the grandma signs, like NINETY, NASTY, AND NOT GIVING UP. Or the elderly Japanese woman with a sign sticking up from the back of her wheelchair: LOCKED UP BY US PREZ 1942–1946 NEVER AGAIN. One woman's cross-stitch read I'M SO ANGRY I STITCHED THIS JUST SO I COULD STAB SOMETHING 3,000 TIMES. The Trump signs were endless. One showed the president grabbing the Statue of Liberty between her legs, creasing the folds of her robe. Another told the straight truth: YOU RUINED HOME ALONE 2. I thought of the public service performed by that sign, how many people it must have made smile over the course of an hour, a morning, a day.

Our signs were joyous. We were united. We were glorious. We were uteri. We were a crowd-sourced poem! A scrolling song!

A group of men standing outside the National Museum of African American History and Culture held up a sign that asked WHO ELSE WILL YOU MARCH FOR?

At the Women's March, our "we" was not uncomplicated. I never wanted to pretend it was. "Community must not mean a shedding of our differences," said the writer and activist Audre Lorde in 1984, "nor the pathetic pretense that these differences do not exist." Her belief in difference as a creative force felt like the right kind of optimism for this moment, full of faith that did not depend on naïveté.

Feminism, after all, had evolved by way of self-critique. There were the first-wave suffragists, who abandoned the prospect of cross-racial solidarity when it threatened their campaign, followed by the second-wave feminists of the 1960s and 1970s, who fought internalized patriarchy in consciousness-raising groups and crusaded for reproductive rights and economic equality. They were followed in turn by the third wave, who criticized the second as myopically attuned to the struggles of privileged white women. From its inception, the Women's March offered itself as a vexed and imperfect manifestation of the third wave — not its resolution or consummation, but a continuation of its necessary reckonings.

By now its creation myth has become familiar: two women posting on Facebook just after Trump's election. In New York City, Bob Bland proposed a Million Pussy March. In Hawaii, Teresa Shook put out a call to organize a women's march just after the inauguration. She went to bed with forty replies, and woke up to ten thousand.

By the end of that week, Bland had responded to the criticism leveled at the prospect of a women's march led by two white women. She invited three women of color to take the helm, all prominent organizers: Tamika Mallory, a civil-rights gun-violence activist; Carmen Perez, a prison-reform advocate focused on incarcerated youth; and Linda Sarsour, a Palestinian American racial-justice advocate and mother of three, who had successfully campaigned for New York City's public schools to designate two of Islam's holy days as holidays. In their official platform, released a week before the march, these organizers purposefully highlighted certain issues — racial injustice, mass incarceration, police accountability, the persecution of undocumented migrants — that moved pointedly beyond the standard second-wave fare of reproductive rights and equal pay.

Nearly two weeks before the march, the *New York Times* ran a front-page story quoting a white woman from South Carolina who had decided to cancel her trip to DC because she had been offended by a Facebook post from a black volunteer advising "white allies" to listen more and talk less. She said it made her feel unwelcome. "This is a women's march," she said. "We're supposed to be allies in equal pay, marriage, adoption. Why is it now about, 'White women don't understand black women'?"

Feminism has always been about white women not understanding black women. But at its best, it has also been about women recognizing the shifting contours of their own ignorance, and trying to listen harder. That awareness of limited knowledge and past mistakes can be a source of strength, rather than the movement's shameful underbelly.

Decades ago, Audre Lorde told white feminists who were offended by her outrage: "I cannot hide my anger to spare you guilt, nor hurt feelings." She wanted shared oppression to enable vision rather than obstruct it. She wanted women to recognize what wasn't shared, to fight the perils of conflation, to acknowledge their own complicity. "What woman here is so enamored of her own oppression," she wondered, "that she cannot see her heel print upon another woman's face?" This felt just as relevant three decades later. The trick was seeing the patriarchal footprints everywhere, even under our own feet. Intersectional feminism wasn't just an abstraction, and it wasn't about getting paralyzed by the shame of privilege. It was about owning it. When my mom led the olive pickers on strike, she was aware that she could afford to lose her job more easily than most of them, that she could afford the risk.

I wanted to send every white woman offended by the Women's March a copy of *Sister Outsider,* with a bookmark tucked into Lorde's observations about the role of guilt in the feminist community. "All too often, guilt is just another name for impotence, for defensiveness," she wrote. But this guilt, if it led to change, could become useful as the "beginning of knowledge."

At the Women's March, a black woman carried a sign that said WHITE WOMEN VOTED FOR TRUMP. A white woman carried a sign that said WHITE WOMEN VOTED FOR TRUMP. When Jasiri X, a rapper I'd never heard of, came onstage, he said, "My mother raised me all by herself . . . As a man, I can never understand how she felt." He said: "Fuck white supremacy, white privilege, and white wealth." I could not see the woman in the pussy hat beside him, translating his message into sign language, but I could hear his words through the speakers. I felt implicated. I *was* implicated. My discomfort was the point: my discomfort and everyone's. There was something useful in gathering to feel powerfully uncomfortable together, rather than simply celebrating our numbers. Humility was as important as solidarity. Jasiri X admitted that too: "I can never understand how she felt."

When I attended my first Black Lives Matter march, in Portland, I felt uncomfortable. Was I wanted? Was I intruding? I stayed quiet and followed in the footsteps of others. But I'm glad I was there. My discomfort wasn't particularly profound. It was just a small down payment against the kind of collectivity I believed in — a collectivity in which we weren't cloistered by the silos of our backgrounds, but still didn't assume that solidarity would be easy, that its declaration would mean it had been fully realized.

At the Women's March, the leadership was largely women of color, but the attendance wasn't diverse. I could see this for myself, and during the weeks that followed, other women testified to it as well. "Simply put," a woman named Brittany Martinez told me, "the march was very white."* Brittany explicitly identifies herself as a queer feminist of color, to distinguish herself from the "pervasive and popular brand of default white feminism." At the Women's March, certain celebratory totems — like the vaginas everywhere — made her uneasy. "First," she told me, "all the 'pussies' were pink, which doesn't reflect what many vaginas look like for women of color." Because "women of color are hypersexualized by popular culture in ways that white women are not," she found that "putting so much emphasis on 'pussies' felt uncomfortable." Her observations made me aware of my own blind spots, which felt less like an argument against the possibility of solidarity and more like another argument for trying to understand how much I didn't understand.

When we chanted "Black Lives Matter!" on Constitution Avenue, I could feel our whiteness so acutely, the pale average of our collected bodies. I thought of the Suffrage Parade of 1913, our inspiring but deeply tainted lineage: a march led by a white woman on a white horse, with columns of black women in the back. WHITE SILENCE IS VIOLENCE, said one sign, twenty signs, a thousand signs. But a thousand white people holding signs saying WHITE SILENCE IS VIOLENCE didn't mean the violence was over.

*

*Brittany Martinez's name has been changed, as have the names of two other interview subjects, Vaeme Tambour and Andrea Chen.

We hit the central vein, the jugular of the rally, at Seventh Street. Catching sight of a Jumbotron felt like arrival. The National Mall was a sea of bodies with the Smithsonian Castle rising behind them, all red brick and turrets, iconic and occupied. Our crowd was articulated by dabs of pink, not homogeneous but shaded into hues — rose, salmon, watermelon, lemonade, bubblegum, fuchsia — and broken by rainbows and parkas.

We found a spot where we could see the screen but couldn't hear anything. Then we found a spot where we could hear the speeches but couldn't see anything. It felt so right to have the event blocked by the other bodies watching the event: they *were* the event. Somewhere out there, on a stage I'd never see, Gloria Steinem uttered the words I would read online the next day: "I wish you could see yourselves. It's like an ocean."

From the middle of the ocean, we couldn't see the ocean. But we could see one another's faces, squinting and hungry. My friend Heather had written to me beforehand, "I'll be somewhere in that sea of women, looking for a bathroom." I thought of her frequently, and it became a kind of mantra: Heather was out there somewhere, looking for a bathroom. It was a reminder that our collectivity was powerfully visceral: we were bodies that needed to eat and pee.

A union leader stood in front of our endless columns and addressed Trump directly. "I don't know what kind of president you'll be," he said, "but you're a hell of an organizer."

As I looked over that sea of bodies, I kept feeling the urge to specify them. I wanted them not in their plenitude but in their particularity, their fine-grained humanity. So I spent the weeks following the march talking to other women who had been there. Almost every woman described the sheer mass of the crowds as the defining part of her experience. Monica Melton found herself moved by the blunt force of accumulated body heat. "In the thickest part of the crowd," she said, "it was literally hot."

Anika Rahman, who had fled the Bangladeshi War of Independence and was marching with Amani, her thirteen-year-old daughter, realized at a certain point that there was "no correct route." Which meant that every route was the correct route. She told me she was marching to resist an administration that threatened every part of her identity, every part of her life's work: "I'm brown, I'm an immigrant, I'm a woman, I'm a Muslim." After coming to the

United States at the age of eighteen, she obtained a law degree, devoted herself to fighting for human rights and social justice, and watched the rising tide of anti-Islamic sentiment in her adopted country. She also raised Amani, who wanted to be president and was carrying a banner that said RISE AGAINST THE PREDATOR IN CHIEF, her arms aching from its weight.

Nadia Hussain was also deeply moved by all those bodies in the streets. She was brought to tears when Michael Moore called on the crowds to fill the George Washington Bridge if that was what it took to stop the deportations. Nadia had grown up the daughter of Bangladeshi immigrants, spending much of her childhood in public housing, one of the only kids of color in her high school. She married a Salvadoran man whose mother had brought him across the border at the age of five; he became a US Marine, and they were raising a twenty-two-month-old Muslim Latino son. Nadia knew it was important not just to show up for the march but also for the work that would need to be done every day after it. She wanted to keep putting her body on the line. "That's why we remember the civil rights movement," she told me. "They put their bodies on the line."

Amy Lewis, a mother of two and therapist from Pittsburgh, wanted to put her body on the line as well. "I wanted to break through the paralysis of racial shame I've grown up with," she told me, which came from "the privilege of our white skin." She still remembers the thrill of her first protest, taking the bus with her mother to a feminist rally in downtown Pittsburgh. "I was small and exhilarated," she recalled, "looking up past the faces of the adults surrounding me, to the tops of the office buildings I thought of as skyscrapers, and beyond to the night sky, feeling strangely safe in the loud crowd."

When Amy brought her own twelve-year-old daughter to DC, she felt protective. The most extreme bodily sensations she remembered were sensations of vigilance: "The strain of constantly watching for exit points, assessing the danger when we were on a bridge or in a contained space, amplified enormously by my concern for my kid." She described her initial response to the sheer volume of the crowd as one of panic: thoughts sluggish, limbs heavy, words slow and disorganized. She was supposed to meet her mother but started to panic when she realized that it might not be possible. Cell phones weren't working. The route on the map was jammed with thousands of strangers. When Amy finally made her way to their meeting point, via side streets and force of will, and found her mother waiting there, she felt "strong" and "complete." She said, "The sludge in my veins turned liquid, I felt cheerful, and we looked around with excitement and wonder as we walked into the thick of the crowd."

The physical act of marching wasn't simple. The plain truth was this: the Mall was packed all the way back to the Washington Monument. The march couldn't happen because the route was already occupied by half a million bodies. "When the word moved through the crowd that we had filled the entire route, we roared," Amy told me. "The irony of such numbers equaling physical paralysis struck us. We were many, we were powerful, we were unable to move." At one point, a rumor spread that the march was being canceled, a victim of its own success, but Tamika Mallory came over the speakers to assure us that it wasn't so. We were going to take Constitution Avenue all the way to the Ellipse.

Of course I didn't end up on the correct route. As Anika pointed out, there was no correct route. I ended up somewhere else — on Independence, I think, up to Fourteenth Street, then left on Constitution up to Seventeenth. The truth is, I can only tell you where I marched because I looked it up afterward. While I was marching, it was more like a dream, with no street signs or Google Maps. I was just following the flow of bodies. I was noticing how little trash there was on the streets, and how much glitter. I was listening to an old black man shout, "Mike Pence has *got* to go!" as he sold photographs of the Obama family to weeping white people.

Each time the march was stopped, which was often, I imagined the traffic had gotten clogged because of courteous marchers ceding the intersection to one another, manners manifest as gridlock: "You first!" "No, you!"

In the shadow of the Washington Monument, my friend Joe said that for the first time since the election, he was excited to read the news. We were helping to write the story we wanted to live. But we would need to read about it afterward, to understand what we had been part of.

Leaving the march, we passed hundreds of signs piled against a fence on Pennsylvania Avenue. They didn't look discarded. They looked defiant. Joe and Rachel changed Luke's diaper on a cold marble bench at the Ellipse Visitor Pavilion. We passed weary protesters resting on the bleachers that had been empty for Trump's inauguration parade. It felt good to think of them serving this purpose. We needed to rest, because we weren't done. It wasn't just Washington, and it wasn't over. It was everywhere. It was ongoing. It was people singing with candles in the Budapest night, spilling through the streets of Atlanta, Oakland, Jackson, and Macau. It was people in Calcutta wearing sandals in the sunlight and holding a banner that said RESISTANCE IS FERTILE. It was people in Fairbanks marching in full winter parkas under tree branches covered in snow, with the temperature nearly twenty degrees below zero, a girl in red ski pants, maybe eleven or twelve, holding up her own sign: I SURVIVED CANCER. TRUMP MADE ME UNINSURABLE.

My husband spent two and a half years fighting insurance companies while his first wife battled a complicated form of leukemia — the disease she died of. When she was diagnosed, their baby was six months old. Eight years later, that baby held a LOVE TRUMPS HATE sign on a cold afternoon in Prospect Park. Which is all to say that this election is personal for everyone. Day One of the new administration was personal for everyone. Also true: It's been personal for years. It's been personal for centuries.

A woman named Aditi Khorana later told me about crying jags after the election, feeling her lifelong sense of marginalization — as a woman of color, as the daughter of Indian immigrants — sharpening into almost unbearable acuity. Why did this country hate her so much?

Aditi loved watching the march flood her city: the Los Angeles subways were packed instead of empty, Pershing Square turned into an ocean. She lives just a few blocks from the knitting shop where the pussy hat was first conceived. When the conductor announced that they were rerouting her train that morning, because everyone on it was headed to the same place downtown, all the passengers started cheering. "It felt like a tiny victory," Aditi said. "Like you've got to accommodate the will of the masses."

She had begun her adult life in the aftermath of George W. Bush's election, and under the shadow of his wars. She protested the invasion of Iraq as often as she could, with "this sense that the world we were inheriting was being created by old, rich, white men for themselves and their kids." After Obama was elected, she felt safer, which enabled her to turn inward, toward her own life and career.

Trump's election brought Aditi back to the streets. She felt proud to share the Women's March with her parents, who had told her stories about living under Indira Gandhi's autocratic regime, and had committed their lives to fighting for the oppressed: her mother as a sociologist, her father at UNICEF. Trump's victory hit them "on all levels," she said — as immigrants, people of color, parents who had raised two daughters.

She was struck by the kindness people showed them that day: giving up subway seats, catching her mother's arm when the train lurched. Her mother said the march felt like a collective exhalation. Sikhs passed out bowls of *chana* and reminded Aditi of her grandmother, a Sikh, who had passed away years before. Afterward, she and her parents went to one of their favorite spots in the city — a hole-in-the-wall run by a Mexican couple — and had Cokes and ceviche. It felt good to support an immigrant business, Aditi said, and it felt good to see her elderly parents "light up with excitement as they spoke about the resistance."

What does feminist inheritance mean? For Amy, it meant going to a Chicago Seven protest in utero, and then finding her mother, decades later, amid thousands-strong throngs of women in DC. For Vaeme Tambour, a former Hillary campaign staffer, it meant going to the march with the women in her family — ages sixteen to ninety-three — and walking in a tight circle around her great aunt, who marched with a walker, to protect her. For Laurie Logan, a family physician and lesbian mother from La Crosse, Wisconsin, it meant marching on Washington with her teenage daughter, Annie — full of maternal guilt because she hadn't brought enough water or snacks — as the continuation of a lineage that began when she was young. She'd grown up with little sense of separation between politics and the rhythms of daily life. "I have clear memories of conversations about political issues being mixed with ordinary life," she told me, "my mother ironing and talking about the Prague Spring and our right to free speech and a free press, drying dishes while talking about the importance of legal abortion." Laurie learned her first chant at the age of four: *Humphrey, Humphrey, he's our man! Nixon belongs in the garbage can!* As for Annie, she had grown up looking at pictures of her mother marching at rallies — and in DC, she finally got to march beside her.

But feminist lineage isn't always a simple inheritance. Brittany, who marched in New York, told me that the second time she ever protested — at a demonstration supporting HIV education, when she was in high school — she was arrested in front of the White House for civil disobedience. Her father, who had been the president of his local NAACP youth chapter and a 1960s civil rights activist, was proud. He said activism ran in her blood. But her mother was furious.

Andrea Chen, a second-generation Chinese American raised in Queens, told me her mother disapproved when she found out she was marching. Andrea grew up in a "noisy, mercurial, dramatic matriarchy" of a family, with a single mom who worked full-time while raising her kids. She feels strongly that her liberal arts education — an education her mother and female relatives never got to have — was both their gift to her and a force that threatened to distance her from them. The women in her family didn't grow up thinking about identity politics, eventually preferring to define themselves as "taxpayers and as people who made it." Many of them voted for Trump, and see Andrea as "this somewhat radical naive bleeding heart." But as Andrea told me, "Everything I am has been a straight line from these women."

Andrea loves the urgency of marches, their powerful alchemy of compassion and righteous anger. But she found the Women's March more mixed, clearly full of first-time marchers — many nervous, hesitant to chant anything besides the most familiar anthems — and driven by diffuse objectives. It also felt disorganized. "I don't think you necessarily felt the history of the moment," she said, "while standing there silently in ten-minute stretches, waiting for the march to move along." But she also felt the joy of spending the night before Inauguration Day with friends, "making posters and thinking of slogans while eating takeout and watching *Star Wars*." At the march, she felt she was witnessing the "birth of something massive and collective that didn't quite know how to articulate itself yet."

"We know that we gather this afternoon on indigenous land," Angela Davis told us as we stood in the shadow of the Smithsonian. "This is a country anchored in slavery and colonialism."

A middle-aged black woman standing beside me said, "Yes, yes, yes!" She said, "*This is awesome.* I haven't seen this lady since 1986."

Angela Davis said, "The next one thousand four hundred and

fifty-nine days of the Trump administration will be one thousand four hundred and fifty-nine days of resistance."

The seven days that followed the march were a nightmare of presidential orders. Trump reinstated the oil pipeline that would run near sacred Sioux land in North Dakota. He mandated a gag on federal funding to global health providers that offered abortion counseling, and issued orders to start building a wall along the Mexican border. He announced his plans to publish a weekly list of crimes committed by undocumented migrants. On January 27, just a week after the march, he issued a ban on refugees coming into the country, and on all citizens of seven predominantly Muslim nations, which meant that passengers in the air when he signed the order were detained in airports upon arrival. These executive orders are offensive to reproduce in summary. Every part of me fights the possibility of their normalcy, fights the neutral tone of reportorial prose, fears what will happen between the writing of these words and their publication.

The morning after the Muslim ban (a term the president and his advisers have vehemently resisted), protesters started gathering at JFK's Terminal 4, where two Iraqi men were being detained. One had worked as a translator for the US Army for more than a decade. Word went out over social media, and hundreds, then thousands, of people began flooding JFK and other airports throughout the country: LAX, Dulles, Houston, Sea-Tac.

My husband and I took the A train to JFK from Manhattan after we bought posters and markers from a downtown drugstore and scribbled phrases from Emma Lazarus's Statue of Liberty poem: GIVE ME YOUR TIRED, YOUR POOR.

The protest began before we got to the protest, at the Howard Beach AirTrain station. As we were waiting to buy our tickets, we saw a line of cops forming on the other side of the turnstiles. "Only ticketed air travelers and airport employees allowed to board!" they said. There were so many of them, so quickly.

My husband asked one of them, "Is there a regulation allowing you to do this?"

He asked my husband, "Are you a ticketed traveler?"

"I don't know," my husband said. "Am I?"

I could feel the molecules of the room vibrating and rearranging. The cops were multiplying. The protesters — mostly strangers, all of them intent on boarding the same train — were gathering into a sudden, spontaneous collective.

"What you are doing is wrong!" a woman said. And then the chants began: "If we don't get it? Shut it down!" I'd been in this station countless times — running late for a flight, checking email on my phone — and it was strange to see it as the site of such fervent desire, such heated conflict. The turnstiles were the obstacles keeping us from the protest, which meant they had become the protest.

I wish I could say I stormed the barricades, or cajoled the conscience of a Metro Transit Authority employee. The truth is, I just started thinking of another way to get to Terminal 4. We ended up catching an unmarked cab from a pizza place across the street, sharing a ride with an immigration lawyer who was trying to link up with a group of immigration lawyers already there. "They say they're in the diner," she said. "Where's the diner?" We saw more cops approaching the AirTrain station, putting on their NYPD vests, heading upstairs to the showdown at the turnstiles. Were we making our way to the protest, or were we fleeing it? How could we tell?

When we finally got to Terminal 4, the crowds went all the way back to the parking lots. It was cold. Someone had projected the word RESIST on the concrete wall of the parking structure, and then the words LET THEM IN. People had filled the structure, were standing at the edges — in rows, dangling their banners — looking out.

This was protest. Not just the perilous electricity of the AirTrain station, bodies blocking other bodies by force, voices crying out in response; and not just the stark beauty of those luminous words across concrete; but also the tedium of an hourlong subway ride, the uncertainty of what to do or where to go when the protest did not go as planned. It was the immigration lawyer wondering, "Where's the diner?"

"Mic check!" someone called, and then proceeded to warn anyone undocumented that they should leave, in brief parcels of language that turned into communal chants: "The police may be coming! If you think you are in danger! Protect yourself!" Then another call-and-response began, its force only deepened by its familiarity. "Show me what democracy looks like!" And the response: "This is what democracy looks like!"

That answer gave me chills, in total earnest, every time.

*

Like my mother, the old mythic marches weren't myth; they were life. They were full of flawed people and bored bodies. But it matters that they happened. What would our collective story look like if they hadn't? What would our collective story look like if it didn't include a massive gathering after Trump's inauguration, if it held instead a vacancy — thousands of people in despairing, isolated, private disbelief? What if the ban on refugees came down and no one marched at all?

A few days after the election, Greenpeace hijacked a construction crane near the White House and hung a rainbow banner that said RESIST. The banner thrilled me, but I also knew that thrilling work wasn't the only kind that mattered. When Alice Walker said that the "real revolution is always concerned with the least glamorous stuff," she wasn't talking about flying giant flags from giant cranes. She wasn't even talking about the logistics of five hundred thousand people marching, bringing enough trail mix and backup onesies. She was talking about ongoingness: showing up past the first flush of indignation and sticking with it. She was talking about the daily tedium of tutoring, voter registration, helping people fill out food stamp applications. She said that one of the great achievements of her life was taking a bag of oranges to Langston Hughes when he had the flu.

"Militancy no longer means guns at high noon, if it ever did," Audre Lorde wrote in the 1980s. "It means doing the unromantic and tedious work." This will never be the stuff of cinematic grandeur. It's never satisfying, in part because it's not enough. It should never feel like enough. But invoking insufficiency as an alibi is just as dangerous as self-righteous satisfaction or comfortable despair — the very things Lorde warned us against.

A week after that chilly day in DC, I sat with my friends Greg and Ginger in their Bed-Stuy kitchen, along with their daughters — Sara, twelve, and Fita, nine, who had marched with them — and their pet rabbit, Oliver, who had not. Ginger had never marched before. When I asked her about her activist history, her first instinct was to say she had none. Zero. But then she started recalling things that might have counted as activism all along: tutoring students in her class who were falling behind, back when she was a student herself, or working with kids in her local community gar-

den. Ginger called this "lowercase-*a* activism." Alice Walker would
have called it revolutionary work.

Ginger said that for her, the march itself hadn't been about
sacrifice or service, it had been about sustenance. "It's going to be
a long four years," she said. Her family was from El Salvador, and
she felt the potential breakdown of civil liberties as a real peril.

As for Greg, his earliest memories of collective action involved
marching on the picket lines outside Newark International Airport
when his dad was part of an air-traffic-controller strike. Greg was
twelve. He and his father marched along the highway, and Greg remembered the chants, the union-hall meetings, the thrill of fighting Ronald Reagan as their personal enemy. Years later, he went
to the Million Man March with his father and grandfather, and
it made him feel connected to the black community in a more
tangible way than he ever had before. This was part of what communal action could do: it could introduce you to collective identity in a way that didn't feel forced or conceptual, that felt bodily,
emotional, palpable.

Greg described a moment during the Women's March when he
started chanting because he heard Sara chanting beside him. This
captured something true about chanting, and about inheritance:
Both work like contagion. Both work in multiple directions. You
never knew who might start chanting simply because your voice
gives them prompt or permission. Ginger wasn't a chanter — she
was firm on that point — but she described one part of the Wom-
en's March when she found herself chanting. It had been outside
the Trump Hotel, the historic post office that Trump had converted and bragged about — ceaselessly, it seemed, in lieu of policy
arguments — during the presidential debates.

As they marched past the hotel, Ginger told me, police cars
drove through the crowds with their sirens blaring. "If they wanted
to make us disperse," she said, "they had just the opposite effect."
The sirens got her riled up, made her want to resist, to keep moving, to raise her voice. This was activism as generative friction, activism as diversion from plan, off-roading away from script: a protest at the turnstiles, AirTrain as flash point, sirens as tuning fork.
This was guilt — or awkwardness, or showing up for uncertainty —
as the beginning of knowledge.

My mom texted me photos from her march at LAX while I

texted her photos from my march at JFK. She shared the news of her resistance, as she had always shared the news of her resistance, which wasn't the ticker tape of myth but the stumbling notation of the actual. She recounted the pain of McGovern's loss, the weeping voices on the other end of telephone calls, the protests she felt proud of, and the one she apologized for — decades later — to a veteran who hadn't been there. She told me about the olive pickers, their hands covered in socks, and how good it had felt to stand with them by a blazing fire, when they got inside, after they finally said: Enough.

That Saturday, before the march-too-crowded-to-become-a-march became a march, when the multitudes were already tired of standing — hungry, shoulder to shoulder, antsy — the singer Janelle Monáe took the stage. She said her mother had been a janitor, her grandmother a sharecropper. "We birthed this nation," she said. "It was a woman gave you Martin Luther King. It was a woman gave you Malcolm X."

She introduced five mothers who had lost their sons to police violence. Each woman said the name of her son, and we called back, "Say his name."

We heard "Jordan Davis," and we said, "Say his name."
We heard "Eric Garner," and we said, "Say his name."
We heard "Trayvon Martin," and we said, "Say his name."
We heard "Mohamed Bah," and we said, "Say his name."
We heard "Dontre Hamilton," and we said, "Say his name."

When you are talking about half a million people, saying something is more like a roar. You feel it in your body, in your bones. It vibrates the air. This wasn't intersectionality as the heading on a college syllabus, it was the sound of primal, indisputable truth.

Each time Monáe passed the microphone to one of these mothers, she said: "This isn't about me." We heard the name of Sandra Bland. We heard the names of Mya Hall and Deonna Mason, two trans women of color killed by the police. Many of the mothers' voices cracked as they said the names of their sons. To hear and feel the crowd around me saying "Say his name" and to feel my own voice as one small fraction of that crowd: it filled my whole body. It made me feel large and small at once.

This was one of the most important things a crowd of half a million people could do: stand in the capital of our country and listen to these mothers say the names of their sons. It wasn't about me. I mattered only insofar as the *we* would be impossible without five hundred thousand individual voices. The we: pink-hatted and extending beyond our range of vision. Our mouths were parched and our voices hoarse. We were fidgeting. We were loud.

What mattered? The surge and force of us: half a million strong, nameless, calling for their names.

BETH UZNIS JOHNSON

Your Friend/My Friend, Ted

FROM *Southwest Review*

DO YOU REMEMBER Ted from elementary school? Of course you do — I saw a picture of the two of you on Facebook eating at a restaurant. I don't know whether it was lunch or dinner, or whether the restaurant was in Illinois where you lived as kids, or Michigan where you live now. No matter the location or time of day, you have drinks in front of you: tall, red drinks over ice.

Knowing you, I suspect the drinks are something like strawberry iced tea. Not because you like fruit-infused nonalcoholic beverages, but I'd be shocked if it were a froufrou cocktail. If you and Ted were going to have a drink, it would probably be a beer. I say this knowing you drink beer or something stronger like Jack and Coke. The idea of you sipping a fruity cocktail makes me laugh, though I'm sure you've had one in the past. At least one time, somewhere with someone who probably remembers it, especially now.

I didn't know Ted before, but he and I are Facebook friends now. He travels all over the world; I have no idea how or why. It looks adventurous and fun, and he often has a beer in hand. That makes me pretty sure the meal in the photo is lunch and the drinks are strawberry iced teas. There's a basket of pita on the table, too, so it's Middle Eastern. Michigan has kick-ass Middle Eastern. You're probably waiting for the hummus.

Ted must have asked the waitress to take the photo. In the twenty-five years I've known you, I can't remember your ever taking a picture or asking someone to take a picture of you. Ted, though, has lots of photos on his Facebook wall. He's probably used to asking waitresses to take them because of all his travels. You're sitting opposite in a booth, wearing shorts and a checked shirt, with that relaxed look one feels with a childhood friend who's known you from the time your mom dressed you in a red turtleneck and plaid pants. There's a bond you feel with kids from elementary school, maybe because you share some of your earliest memories, like for example, if your third-grade teacher came back from the bathroom with her panty hose tucked into her skirt. You both remember the embarrassment hanging over the classroom and how relieved everyone was when the smart girl — the one who was a violin prodigy — whispered the truth into the teacher's ear.

Maybe you and Ted both remember it and laugh over your strawberry lemonades until your ribs hurt and you can't breathe. Maybe you both realize you learned a valuable lesson that day: that it's always kind to tell someone when their butt is showing so they can fix the problem. Who knows — maybe you both spent the rest of childhood worrying your moms might come out of the bathroom in the same predicament. Can you imagine?

Since the photo in the restaurant is just you and Ted, I imagine your wife stayed home with the boys while you spent time with your elementary school friend. The reason I know you aren't visiting Ted is that, after he and I became Facebook friends, I saw other photos from the weekend.

You probably experience that familiar guilt or sense of failure while you eat lunch. Despite having a great time with Ted and feeling like a kid again, you know your wife hates what you do and how you do it. If you don't bring the boys to lunch, she'll say you are an uninvolved dad. If you bring the boys, she'll be angry you let them eat too much bread and permitted them Cokes and dessert. Since she'll be unhappy when you get home, you tell yourself you'll make up for it by playing with the boys later. You and Ted can set up a game of backyard ball like when you were kids.

In the backyard photo, the boys wear only bathing suits so it must be summer. An inflatable children's pool sits within the frame of the shot. The boys have a white plastic ball and a yellow plastic bat. You stand close to the batter, supervising. Your hands are on your hips and, though it's a long-distance shot, it seems like you're smiling. I spot your little dog Scout nearby, which really hurts now. If there was one thing in your note you made clear, you did not want Scout living with HER. I imagine you probably thought she'd kick Scout or mistreat her. After all that's happened, I worry you're right. It's good Scout is with your parents.

Ted stands deep on the lawn to get the backyard shot. From all his travel photos, he seems to be single with no kids. I imagine he's thinking how lucky you are to be married to a tall, pretty redhead. You live in a nice house in the suburbs with your three redheaded boys and Scout. You have a wood deck and an inflatable swimming pool for the kids. I don't see any drinks or beers on the patio table, but there is a pile of towels. The hanging pot of begonias is a flash of bright pink in full bloom. Your wife keeps a nice house and waters the flower baskets like the other neighbors.

I don't really know Ted aside from his travel photos, but his interest in capturing the backyard scene is obvious. Even if he's out there just to man the outfield, he took the time to get a picture so he'd remember the day. I'll bet he's glad he did. Like the photo in the restaurant, the photo in the yard holds a quality of authenticity. No one is posing or posturing to look good or prove he's a certain kind of successful husband and father. The kids are fully immersed in the game. I imagine Ted is watching through the lens, comparing his life to yours. Not better or worse, only different.

Maybe you and Ted played baseball in elementary school. The game in your yard might feel like reliving the past, something neither one of you ever expected to do. How strange to stand there and see your friend in the outfield; only he's not a kid anymore — he's a grown man with features you couldn't have predicted when you were young. Now you get to see him all grown up. What a treat. And even though you don't play baseball with the boys all that often (your wife is usually in charge), the photo is a permanent reminder you *were* that kind of dad.

The backyard photo reminds me you're a big guy, well over six feet tall. Even though you're not an affectionate person, you look like a teddy bear. You're handsome. The hair near your temples has turned gray. You're wearing a white T-shirt and khaki shorts. Scout is by your side. The boys are playing baseball, happy. Though the grass is long, I see your Birkenstocks. I know they're the same ones. You're the kind of guy who wears his Birkenstocks until the soles are worn out. It takes a long time, especially in Michigan where you can only wear them half the year. Maybe they're even the same Birkenstocks from college, where we met.

It was fall when you jumped, the end of September. Such an unusually warm season for Michigan. The only reason you wore the Birkenstocks that day was that it still felt like summer. It was like eighty degrees. The clothes you wore the last time anyone saw you were just like the clothes you're wearing in the photos with Ted. Including the Birkenstocks. They found one on the bridge, near the car. I think a lot about the other one, where it went. Did they find it? Did you wear one shoe when you did it? Such a stupid detail, there's no way I can ask.

You probably weren't thinking about Ted when you jumped. So much has gone wrong with your wife. You're distraught she wants to keep you from your kids. She's gone crazy about it, even had you arrested for assaulting her. I know you didn't do it and not just because your note says so. She had her sister take a video. It takes four minutes before you finally swat the camera phone from her sister's hand. You never even raise your voice as your wife badgers you about drinking.

Scout is in the video, too. She likes to lie on the back of the couch while you sit in the basement watching TV. It's cozy down there, which is good since you've been banished. It happened over time as your wife grew more and more disappointed in her husband, and you grew more and more unwilling to argue. No, it wasn't the best move. I know you regretted it; you confided in my husband that you wanted to be a family again. He suggested you write your wife a letter, which you did. You stopped drinking. You spent more time with the boys. But your wife was done, which was okay until she tried to get full custody and the house, and wanted enough child support to keep a part-time work schedule.

Scout is your dog, everyone knows. I'm sure Ted noticed when he was there. She looks so cute, in the video, on the back of the couch. She can tell there's a situation, so she stays flat on her belly and watches. Your wife says the boys came down to play with you earlier. Lucky, their last time. Not so lucky because your wife thinks the play was too wild and that you've been drinking. Thus the video. Thus the demand for a breath test, the four minutes of "*no*'s" from you, Scout on the back of the couch, your wife's growing intensity and frustration, your swatting away of the phone. I actually laugh when you mutter "psycho" as she narrates how she's being pushed around. It is not a funny video.

Your lawyer warned you about this. He said some women become so unhinged during divorce proceedings they literally throw themselves down the stairs and blame the estranged husband for injuries. It's a tactic, a ploy, to get a judge's sympathy. You know this as you are handcuffed in front of the neighbors and hauled away to jail. You spend three days there because you don't bother to call your lawyer.

What happened to you in there?

She will not rest, you say. She will not rest until you cannot see your boys at all. You write this down after the police escort you to your house to pack up some belongings. They say you can't go back home. You're not allowed to see your boys unless you go to Detroit. Even then, it will be supervised. I can see how, after jail and police escorts and more filed motions, it seemed she would not rest. Obviously you believed it or you wouldn't have jumped.

Where is the other Birkenstock? My god, did it hurt when you landed? Wasn't it freezing there, up north on the Mackinac Bridge, compared to the lower part of the state? Weren't you cold? Did you think about Ted and the day you played baseball in the yard with your boys, and Scout, and the white ball and yellow bat? Maybe the memory passed through your mind, a comfort to have seen the adult face of a childhood friend, your boys immersed in the game, your dog Scout by your side on a summer's day.

My husband called me on a Tuesday to say the police found your car on the bridge. Your note was inside. The lone Birkenstock was nearby. You must have jumped; they think you are dead. We debate it for a few minutes; I mean, you weren't the suicidal type, maybe you parked on the bridge and walked off.

Or not.

My husband remembers Ted a few hours later. He says Ted was your childhood friend and he's sure no one's told him. Ted was important to you. He needs to know what happened. I check your Facebook wall to figure out Ted's last name. I send him a message to please call my husband and his phone number. Ted calls within the hour. I feel terrible we have to share such news. You probably never pictured any of us having to do that.

I send Ted a message later telling him how sorry I am. I ask if I can send him a friend request on Facebook. A friend of yours, after all, should be a friend of mine. When he accepts, I find the photos of the restaurant and the backyard, and I stare at them, trying to figure something — anything — out. I can tell Ted mourns you by the things he posts. He informs your school friends because, of course, they would want to know. It's been years, but they all feel terrible. You were always a nice guy, a good friend. I imagine that Ted, like me, thinks about you all the time. He revisits the photos at the restaurant and in the yard. Maybe, like me, he pokes around my Facebook photos looking for you.

When I post on your wall about Michigan State's victory over Michigan, Ted comments, too. We wonder if you had something to do with the botched snap that led to our final touchdown to win the game. The Ohio State game, too. It's been a hell of a season. Maybe you saw to it so your boys would feel closer to you. They're big Spartan fans.

Did you ever think Ted and I would remember you every time we watch a Spartan game? That Ted would reach out to your elementary school friends? That Ted and I would become Facebook friends? That I'd study the pictures of the two of you hoping to gain something back that was lost?

And this is just me and Ted. We're on the periphery. If you knew I'd take the time to write all this down, would you have considered not jumping? Would it have jolted you to the realization Jerry Garcia wasn't kidding when he sang about a ripple in still water. Me and Ted, we're on the outer rim of the ripple. If it's this bad for me and Ted, just imagine how bad it feels to those close to the center of the circle.

Your boys are with your wife. Your parents took Scout like you wanted. The weather turned cold. Christmas passed. Your body has still not been recovered. I wonder if the boys know you jumped? If you can see me writing this now? If knowing all this makes you wish you hadn't jumped? Could I have stopped you?

I imagine what would have happened had you not jumped. I picture you and Ted on a trip somewhere in the world having a beer, talking about playing backyard baseball with the boys and when you can do it again. Ted might tell you he never would have guessed things would go so wrong with your pretty, redheaded wife. You say it's for the best. Everyone is much happier now. You're so glad all that is over. Ted is glad, too.

I wouldn't know Ted if it had gone this way. That would be better. I'm positive Ted thinks so, too.

HEIDI JULAVITS

The Art at the End of the World

FROM *The New York Times Magazine*

WE WERE TAKING an airplane, I told our children, to see what I dramatically billed as "the end of the world."

"Can't we go to a beach?" they asked. It was February. They were sick of the cold.

I promised them sand and plenty of water, but unless things went terribly wrong, we would probably not be swimming in it.

"Where are we going?" they asked.

We were flying 2,000 miles to see more than 6,000 tons of black basalt rocks extending 1,500 feet into the Great Salt Lake in the shape of a counterclockwise vortex, designed by the most famous practitioner of '70s land art, Robert Smithson.

"It's called the 'Spiral Jetty,'" I told them.

I showed them pictures. I admitted that maybe "the end of the world" wasn't the best way to advertise what I hoped we would experience, even though previous visitors had described the landscape as hauntingly spare, as resembling how our planet might appear following a nuclear holocaust. Smithson's gallerist, Virginia Dwan, said the jetty "was something otherworldly, but I hesitate to say hell, because I don't mean everybody being tortured and so forth, but the feeling of aloneness, and of it being in a place that was unsafe, and something devilish, something devilish there."

Adding to the excitement I presumed we now shared: The road conditions near the jetty were highly variable, which was to say not always roads. The lake's water levels, too, needed to be below 4,195 feet for us to see it, and those levels were partly dependent on snowfall (this winter there was lots) and how much of that snow, by the time we arrived, had melted and sluiced down the mountains — water that also, en route to the lake, could turn the sixteen miles of unpaved roads into impassable mush.

Where we were headed, in other words, we might not be able to reach. And even if we were, what we traveled so far to see might not be visible.

"Will there be internet?" they asked.

I appealed, finally, to their desire to see me happy, a strategy that, thus far in our lives, had failed 100 percent of the time. I told them that, for more than a decade, I'd wanted to visit "Spiral Jetty," as though these years of compressed desire had become a diamond that I could flash in their faces, my little crows.

This ploy worked as well as it ever had. They grudgingly accepted their fate. I accepted mine. You cannot sell others on a pilgrimage. You cannot drum desire out of nothing. Unlike me, the crows had not once held a piece of the jetty in their hands. It was 2004. I was in Los Angeles. My friend, Christopher James, an artist and Smithson admirer, had been tracking the water levels around the jetty for years. Because, for almost three decades — roughly since the death of its creator, at age thirty-five, in a plane crash — the jetty, except for a few brief reappearances, was submerged. Around 1999, the lake's water started to recede (because of drought) so that by 2002 the jetty could, again, be seen; people, again, could walk it. People like James could get in their trucks and drive thousands of highway miles and then through the cow fields and out to the Great Salt Lake, where the coastline "reverberated out to the horizons," according to Smithson, "only to suggest an immobile cyclone while flickering light made the entire landscape appear to quake."

James arrived to find that the jetty's black rocks, following their lengthy submersion, had become coated in pinkish-white salt formations like barnacles affixed to the hull of a sunken ship. He took one of the salt formations — cracked free from the rock to which it had been affixed — home as a souvenir. This was how I came to hold not a piece of the jetty, exactly, so much as a commemoration — the material accrual — of its disappearance. "Time turns metaphors into things," Smithson wrote. The salt formation was the size of my fist and weighty, warm and damp. "It's half the size that it used to be," I remember James saying. Exposed to the air, and possibly to the dryness of California, he guessed, the salt formation was evaporating. Within a few months, the time in my hand would finish changing states, conclude its vanishing act and disappear.

We landed in Salt Lake City. We rented a four-wheel-drive vehicle because my husband, calling ahead to a ranger at the Golden Spike National Historic Site, where the asphalt ends and the dirt begins, had been warned that the road to the jetty was "pretty bad." We received a similarly grim prognosis from the rental agent, who, on learning our destination, asked us whether we had checked the water levels. "I don't think you'll be able to see it," he said.

We did not panic. Instead we rejoiced. The natural obstacles on and around which the jetty was built, along with Smithson's prolific writings, suggest he designed the jetty to be both difficult to reach and difficult to see. He constructed it during a drought in 1970; he knew the water would someday rise. While in Rome, in 1961, surrounded by art tourists, he wrote in a letter to Nancy Holt (who would later become his wife): "People want to stare with aggressive eagerness or they feel they must stare in order to grant approval. There is something indecent about such staring."

An underwater artwork is the perfect remedy for indecency.

On the highway, mountains surrounded us. The crows had never witnessed a landscape like this; save once when tiny, they had never been west of the East. I urged them to look out the car windows rather than at their phones, and confirm that they were totally undone by the awesomeness. I demanded their indecent staring. But the crows are predominantly city creatures. Nature didn't interest them as much as civilization and its inhabitants did. We passed an abandoned amusement park, the roller coaster coiling like a train track yanked skyward by a tornado. We passed defunct factories that, with their silos and peaks, resembled the Mormon churches we could see in the distance, isolated and chalk-white against the brown mountainsides in which they were embedded. The billboards advertised Bibles and services you could pay for to deal with local plagues (FIRE WATER MOLD STORM). At regular intervals we drove beneath a digital sign that read ZERO HIGHWAY FATALITIES. The smaller print told a slightly less cheerful story: 26 OUT OF 47 DAYS. The landscape thrummed with vastness; other than the highway's thin river of commerce, the world outside our car was unmarked and uncontained (and un-time-stamped) by buildings and sidewalks and people.

I could tell: the bigness of Utah was freaking out the crows. They didn't know what to make of such an uninhabited expanse. "I'm interested," Smithson once said, "in that area of terror between man and land."

Smithson did not begin his career as an earth artist; nor, given his intellectually garrulous persona, would he probably wish to be called one. Born in Passaic, New Jersey, in 1938, Smithson became keenly cognizant of how the local postindustrial landscape — what he described as "ruins in reverse" — shaped his sensibilities, as did natural features like quarries, which he said were "embedded in my psyche."

Contrary to popular belief, or maybe just contrary to my assumption, Smithson didn't extend beyond his New York City studio to work in the outdoors because he desired more space. "I don't think you're freer artistically in the desert than you are inside a room," he said. In his 1968 essay "A Sedimentation of the Mind: Earth Projects," Smithson noted the importance, to his thinking, of the nighttime drive by fellow New Jersey artist Tony Smith on an unfinished stretch of the Jersey Turnpike, in the dark, with students from Cooper Union. "[Smith] is talking about a sensation," Smithson wrote. "[He] is describing the state of his mind in the 'primary process' of making contact with matter." In the same essay, he noted that Freud referred to this commingling experience as "oceanic." When Smithson first started working outdoors, he made boxes and containers to hold, for example, slate from a Pennsylvania quarry, which he then displayed in a gallery. Still, the tension between freedom and restriction remained an exhilarating struggle.

"If art is art, it must have limits," Smithson wrote. "How can one contain this 'oceanic' site?"

Clearly the crows, while lacking Smithson's theoretical framework, were asking themselves the same question. One crow remarked fearfully, "Everything is dead here."

The littler crow stared out the window and sang a soothing song to itself, the lyrics of which consisted of one repeated sentence:

No people.
No people.
No people.
No people.

*

Before visiting the jetty, I was thinking a lot about interior landscapes, those uninhabited places inside of us that cannot be contained (or explained) by any map. Interior landscapes are shaped
by all kinds of forces: geographic or familial or cultural or genetic.
When I was the age of the crows, for example, I lived in Maine. It
was cold and dark the majority of the time. We were surrounded by
ocean that produced food and bracing relief from the annual week
of heat but was otherwise a gray, impetuous slab. People with some
frequency were snatched off rocks by waves and drowned. Also, it
being the '70s and '80s, we could not escape stories of nuclear annihilation, which was a perennial story line for television series and
books, many of them aimed at young-adult audiences. Like a great
number of my contemporaries, I became hooked on the narrative
of nuclear annihilation, and via that obsession I started to plan.
Because my home life was stable, I had the luxury of dreaming up
very bad situations and strategizing how to survive them. It was as
if my entire upbringing had bred in me a delight in destruction's
aftermath, as well as in destruction's problem-solving thrills.

Interior landscapes interest me because I am not only a parent
but also a college professor. I regularly encounter young adults
from similarly comfortable backgrounds who seem mentally undone by the often mild daily challenges they encounter (mild
compared to a nuclear apocalypse, at any rate). I do not want to
make uninformed guesses about why this is the case; I simply want
to state that it is the case. Stress, anxiety, unhappiness, they thrive
in these young adults. Which has, in turn, made me wonder about
the crows. How prepared will they be to handle daily challenges,
both banal and catastrophic? How might I help them cultivate
their interior landscapes so as to improve their chances of survival — even happiness? I am admittedly limited by nostalgia for
my own upbringing, which I like to think has served me decently.
Perhaps for no better reason, I've wondered: Are they enough
into their future annihilation? Should they be, as a means to gain
present-day control over the frightening and the uncertain, *more*
into it?

Basically, I wanted the crows to be more regularly scared.

But the crows (and their contemporaries), perhaps because of
the future catastrophes they face — those of the global-warming
variety, which are not "maybes" but "definitelies" — seem less receptive to destruction narratives that might shape their interior

landscapes. Nuclear war was avoidable (or so I optimistically chose to believe), but what they will encounter as adults is not. Their interior landscapes, thus, are the only landscapes that may not end in ruin. Those are the only landscapes over which they may have any control.

On the east-west road — the one that cut through Corinne, the last chance for gas — the even emptier terrain became entrancingly beautiful. The waterlogged fields suggested that a tsunami had recently receded, leaving the earth striated by long glassy puddles that acted as mirrors between the planting rows. What beat past our windows at 80 mph was land-sky-land-sky, and soon we didn't know down from up.

The crows remarked, with slightly more enthusiasm, "It looks like Minecraft out here."

The disorientation caused by so much natural beauty clearly explained the abundance of DROWSY DRIVERS NEXT EXIT signs we saw back on the highway. Or maybe Drowsy Drivers was a roadside service the state of Utah provided, a type of GPS device you strapped into your backseat so it could babble map coordinates to you from the dream world. Technically, we were driving over a former ocean floor, or at least this is what we were told at a hot springs by a man with a DREAD GOD tattoo on his arm. This, he said, accounted for the water's high mineral content. The land around us was still saturated by the residue of that vanished ocean and the life it once contained.

Smithson grew interested in salt lakes, in part, because the water was filled with salt-loving bacteria that turned the surface pink and sometimes "the color of tomato soup." He started to explore the Great Salt Lake, looking for a place to make an artwork, and eventually settled on Rozel Point, location of a defunct oil jetty and a handful of derelict structures, what he described as "manmade systems mired in abandoned hopes."

He chose the location first, without knowing what he would put there.

At the Golden Spike National Historic Site, a ranger gave us a copy of an internet map. He circled the places on the jetty road that he'd heard were flooded, though "flooded" proved a relative distinction. The road, even in its driest iteration, was the consistency of wet cement; it strongly sucked at our tires when it wasn't threatening to slide us into the adjacent pastures. Then we encountered the water, lots of it, opaque and brown and quick, traversing the road. It was basically a river made of thick, muscular currents. This water was not legible to me. It wasn't Maine water. Fail to read Maine water correctly, and you could return after circumnavigating an island on foot to find yourself boatless. Fail to read Maine water, and you could swim into a current that — had you observed the lobster pots creating deep Vs of tiny rapids to either side — would require you to fight with all your strength to prevent being swept out to sea.

Fail to read this water, and who knows? My husband and I eyeballed the flood. It didn't look impassable; it wasn't terribly wide. I gunned our vehicle; more accurately, I bulleted it. What I didn't anticipate was the depth of the water, which of course, I should have. The breach was obviously because of the lowness of this land relative to the land around it. Our trajectory was sharp. We crashed nose first into the brown. The crows screamed as we surged down and through and up again, back to the semisecurity of soggy landfall.

The crows also really loved the cows. Cows stood on either side of us, and then, as we approached the shore, the cows were replaced by cow-looking rocks, sturdy black lumps that grazed on the hillside like the previous cows' petrified ancestors. There was otherwise not a lot of life, unless dead rabbits count. In the road were a decent number of flat, dead rabbits, which somewhat boggled the mind, given how few cars travel this road. We saw no birds. Bugs did die against the windshield (we thought they were sticky rain); otherwise it was just a pastel-scape of pinky-white grasses and stiff, bleached bushes blown into wild, death-throe shapes, the frosted purple of the salt and sand flats, and far in the distance — more than a mile from shore, that's how receded the water was — the light pink surface of the Great Salt Lake.

Finally we saw what we'd come all this way to see. Not only was the jetty above water; it looked like a glyph marooned in a desert. It was smaller than I expected it to be. Also wilier. The jetty changed shape and seemed to actively grow or shrink as we drove parallel to it, forcing us to constantly recalibrate our perception of it.

In short: we were not in hell. This was no inferno. The sky was low and soft and gray-mauve or dark mauve, as were the isolated triangular crags of mountains in the distance. "From that gyrating space emerged the possibility of the 'Spiral Jetty,'" Smithson wrote. "My dialectics of site and nonsite whirled into an indeterminate state, where solid and liquid lost themselves in each other." The lake, with its pinkish cast, was difficult to differentiate from the sky, creating the illusion that there was no horizon line. It kind of did feel like the end of the world, though not in the way I originally meant it. The world hadn't been destroyed; it simply dissolved into a combination water-gas-solid substance that surrounded us. Salt lakes, I later learned, are also known as "terminal lakes" or "endorheic basins." "Endo" (from the Ancient Greek) means "within" and "rheic" "to flow." They are self-contained bodies that do not empty into any ocean. They are the self-contained end to an infinite means.

One of Smithson's favorite words was "dialectic," meaning he desired that things exist in productive tension with other things, thereby producing a "dialectical situation." Our situation, vis-à-vis the jetty, clearly qualified as a dialectical one. But what was the "site" here, and what was the "nonsite"? I'd been reading oodles of Smithson and still felt confused by these two words that crucially underwrote all of Smithson's earth art.

"What you are really confronted with in a nonsite is the absence of the site," he said in a 1969 interview. "In a sense the nonsite is the center of the system, and the site itself is the fringe or the edge," he said in a 1970 discussion with the earth artists Michael Heizer and Dennis Oppenheim. (If I occasionally tired of Smithson's gnomic tendencies, I was not alone. Oppenheim, in the same 1970 discussion, grouched: "Why do you bother with nonsite at all? Why don't you just designate a site?") But the most compelling definition, to me, is Smithson's claim that the nonsite is "based on my experience of the site." The nonsite is a drawing or a sculpture or a box containing slate from a quarry. It is the collaborative transmission, or so I like to think, that results when a geographical landscape moves through or commingles with a figurative, human one.

Sites and nonsites, in other words, involve the equal interplay of consciousness and matter. Which again made me think about the crows and what had thus far shaped their interior landscapes, the ones that might come to play (or interplay) on this trip, as well as on the vaster metaphorical trip that eventually their lives would comprise. How might they contain their interior landscape — their evolving selves, basically — and how will they productively, without becoming overwhelmed (or without imposing preconceptions that close down possibilities), deal with the deluge of feeling and information that exists both within a person and without?

Generally speaking, the crows did not consume traditional narratives. Reading did not interest them. Instead of stories, for example, the crows consume patterns of existence. They watched unpackaging videos on YouTube. They watched other people play video games. They had not been inculcated with a sense of duty to experience "the end"; ends, for them, don't exist or aren't significantly different from the middle.

(I'm not saying narrative is the superior thought container. In fact, my memory was misled by the ruling paradigm — the one on which I was raised — in the beginning of this essay. The souvenir salt formation James took from the jetty? It didn't disappear. That was just me, or rather my training, imposing an ending.)

Also, the crows played Minecraft, which is perhaps the closest analog to the apocalypse narratives of my youth. Minecraft is less a story with arcs and ends than it is an experience consisting of pattern and repetition. It requires planning and involves randomness. In Survival Mode, you wake up. You work to ensure you have shelter and resources. The sun sets. You lock yourself in your house before dark to escape zombies and other monsters that spawn in the night. You sleep. You wake up. You work. The sun sets. You barricade yourself in your house. You sleep. You wake up. You repeat. Time is not so much a story line with a beginning, middle, and end as it is a sequence of actions and events that, shape-wise at least, resemble distinct circles that stack one atop the other.

In his essay "The Spiral Jetty," Smithson included a list of materials a person encountered as she walked from the center of the jetty. He demarcated twenty directional points (North, North by East, etc.). The materials view from each point was the same:

> Mud, salt crystals, rock, water.
> Mud, salt crystals, rock, water.

The same materials, listed twenty times, the stack of repeated words gesturing toward sedimentary time layers while also, in replicating the many hash marks on a compass, implying the unseen presence of a circle.

Smithson completed "Spiral Jetty" in 1970. He died in Texas in 1973, while aerially surveying the artificial lake area where he hoped to build his "Amarillo Ramp." He hired a plane, a pilot, and a photographer. The plane crashed. All three were killed. The artificial lake is dry now. The ramp, completed after his death by his wife and friends, is eroding. The crash site — or maybe it is a nonsite — is a few hundred yards away.

We parked in the dirt lot. We scrambled down the rocky bank onto the flats. The push-pull of negative/positive space made the jetty seem even more kinetically alive and like the storm its shape resembled, one that messed with the intuitive logic of water behavior. The land we'd driven over was filling up with water, while the lake appeared to be emptying of it.

We walked the spiral many times; we developed individual jetty styles and jetty rules. The crows cut across the puddled sand between the concentric rings, but I did not, I never did that, I would never do that. I walked the line, or rather, the curve. Later we flung off onto the flats. My husband made mini-jetties with black rocks he found in the sand. The jetty, he said, was spawning.

We returned to the jetty and walked it again. Was it an ancient ruin? Was it the beginning of a new civilization? Was it an example of, as Rainer Maria Rilke wrote, "the revision of categories, where something past comes again, as though out of the future"? In always being both, it encouraged temporal slippage. We were not looking at the past or the future; we were in the middle of time. We were at the point of dislocation around which salt crystals spiraled upward like a staircase as they grew. The crows wrote their names on the sand, and because there was no rising tide — no ocean's clock — their names would possibly never be erased.

Smithson, in his 1966 essay "Entropy and the New Monuments," mentions a recent electrical blackout in the Northeast. "Far from creating a mood of dread," he wrote, "the power failure created a mood of euphoria. An almost cosmic joy swept over the darkened cities." (When Smithson wrote this, a far more economically destitute New York had yet to experience the subsequent 1977 blackout, the violent and anarchic results of which would probably not be qualified as expressions of "cosmic joy.") When we are in

Maine, we often lose our power, and yes, the promise of darkness inspires glee. I gleefully fill the tub with water and the lamps with oil and make sleeping situations nearer to the woodstove. I create in our domestic interior a much more active and dynamic conversation with the exterior, that thing we are so often unaffected by, or simply trying, with our house, to keep out. And while this skill set has mostly been of use in places where the power lines are aboveground, sagging, even in good weather, from tilted pole to tilted pole, the underground electricals of New York are now equally menaced by rising (and descending, into the works) water. My gleeful preparations are increasingly applicable to many more situations, and by that possibility I feel energized. Not because I crave drama or instability, but because I am rendered, in a kind of trippy and exhilarating way, both indispensable and irrelevant.

At the jetty I became entirely irrelevant, and the result was even more exhilarating. Smithson, when searching for a framework with which to explore both limits and limitlessness, found useful the concept of entropy, i.e., the second law of thermodynamics. Entropy proved intriguing to him because, as he understood it, energy was "more easily lost than obtained" and thus, "in the ultimate future the whole universe will burn out and be transformed into an all-encompassing sameness." I experienced that ultimate future. I experienced what the planet would be like when we were, every one of us, gone. I had, before our visit, worried not only about my crows but also about the loneliness of a planet that might someday have no one to see it, walk through it, feel intense things because of it. That is what made my brain and my heart fold in on themselves. Cities, yes, gone; ice caps, gone; but the beauty of the planet routed through a human consciousness, that's what I couldn't comprehend vanishing. This was what, more than my own particular death, I'd despaired at. But on the jetty, I understood what Smithson intuited so long ago in Rome: beauty did not need us.

"You don't have to have existence to exist," Smithson said.

If there were a sun, it would have been setting. As the sky grew subtly pinker and purpler, other cars appeared: two families, a lone woman and a couple. Some walked the jetty, but others struck out directly for the invisible horizon and soon became tiny black marks floating in the middle of the same-color distance. The young couple stood on the flats and hugged and kissed. The lone woman neatened the jetty; she found errant rocks and threw them back within the boundaries, redarkening its outline.

Back in the parking lot, as the rain finally started (it had been threatening), we talked to some of these people. All of them were longtime residents in the area. The jetty-neatener said: "I've never been here before. Today just felt like the day."

A man told us that in the summer the lake looked like the Arctic, because the sun hardened the salt flats into a pink "ice" crust. Another man told us about the speed races over the salt flats, the time records that had recently been broken because, as already established, time worked differently out here; objects could exist in relation to time differently.

The rain grew heavier. Everyone wished everyone else luck getting home. "Last week there was snow on all these peaks," one man said, gesturing to the many mountains in the near and far distance. His implication: that snow was water now, and it was heading our way.

At dusk the cows were frisky. By the time we reached the river, its flow had more than doubled in width and intensity. Should we get stuck, no one would have been able to exit the car. A person would have been swept away. In Maine I'd learned to wait: wait until the wind dies or the tide recedes. Hang out until the situation improves. But I had no idea if this situation would improve. Maybe this, right now, was the best the situation would ever be. We took our chances. We entered the water and sank above the bottom of the doors. The current rocked the car. We pushed steadily through the churn and up the eroding bank on the other side.

We quite easily survived.

It got envelopingly dark. We passed the shuttered Golden Spike National Historic Site. In Corinne, we were stopped at a railroad crossing by a train that moved at a constant, slow speed, as if unmanned and responding to dumb instinct. We all felt dozy yet alert and so pricklingly full of well-being. One crow, back at the jetty, had said, very happily and with evident pride, that they had finally, of this formerly scary place, established a point of common connection, "This is just like Maine." And the jetty was like Maine, minus the tides. Also unlike the flats in Maine, the land revealed by the receding water did not stink primordially, even though there were dead things in it. A bird, for example. It was preserved —

brined — and had been artfully abstracted into pieces, all of which were level with the ground that contained them, like fossils in the making. We had traveled all this way to see something we'd never seen, and what we found was what we always saw.

Or maybe the site's forsakenness had softened. The rocks of the jetty were scattering into the lake; like the dead bird, it was nearly level with its surroundings. Now that the jetty was visible (and was designated, just after we visited, as an "official state work of art" by Utah), more people would travel to see it and walk on it and erode it further. Already a fuss had erupted about what Smithson would have wanted to happen to the jetty: Would he want it restored? Would his championing of entropic thinking deem the opposite? Like the Bible, his writings aid the interpretive bias of the person reading them. I personally feel this quote contains all that need be said on the matter: "The world is slowly destroying itself," Smithson said. "The catastrophe comes suddenly, but slowly."

Back on the highway, we listened to radio news, and the world in general seemed to be in a state much like the jetty road, pretty bad. And yet the collective familial state of equilibrium — our state of "all-encompassing uniform sameness" — endured. We passed a DROWSY DRIVERS NEXT EXIT sign, and as if on cue, one crow fell asleep. The other, littler crow stared out the window, and this time, in a much more chipper tone, and as if he were voicing a pleasant dream experienced by the sleeping crow, sang his same song to the darkness:

No people.
No people.
No people.
No people.

JENNIFER KABAT

Rain Like Cotton

FROM *BOMB Magazine*

Part I: Sand

> Architecture, fashion — yes, even the weather — are in the inte-
> rior of the collective . . . They stand in the cycle of the eternally
> selfsame, until the collective seizes upon them in politics and his-
> tory emerges.
>
> — Walter Benjamin, *The Arcades Project*

PICTURE AN AREA the size of Manhattan covered in sand. It
rises and falls and disappears.

It begins twenty thousand years ago in an age beyond imagination. To talk of it is to speak in approximations. Ice two miles
thick licks down in lobes across New York State. "Lick" is too gentle
a verb for its progress. The earth's mantle bows and breaks under the burden. Lakebeds are carved; layers of rock sheered off,
ground down into sand and debris. Then a few thousand years
of warming. The debris, boulders, and gravel held by the ice are
picked up and moved hundreds of miles. The ice leaves a chain
of frozen lakes — glacial lakes Iroquois, Vermont, and Albany —
their names a bit of hubris, as if to help us picture these places.
The largest, Lake Iroquois, melts; its far end rebounds as the ice
lifts and tilts the lake east. Near present-day Rome, New York, one
hundred miles from the Canadian border, an ice dam contains
the water. Two hundred seventy miles south, glacial debris forms
another dam at the base of what will one day be Staten Island. The
weight of water is overbearing, and it rushes out at twenty-four million gallons a second, almost forty times the pressure of Niagara's

greatest falls. Fresh water spills into the ocean. Desalinization. The currents shut down; the Gulf Stream stops circulating; another ice age begins. Lake Iroquois becomes Lake Ontario; Lake Vermont disappears into Lake Champlain, and Lake Albany drains entirely, leaving sand where its shores had been.

It blows from west to east and settles in dunes. They stabilize, held in place by pitch pine and scrub oak. Animals move in. Blueberries grow. It is 8,000 years ago, 6,000, then the centuries we call the Common Era, but people don't live in this inland sand sea. They venture in and out, crisscrossing on footpaths. The trees burn periodically. Species that depend on fire live here. The pines will only release their seeds with heat. The Lenni-Lenape and Iroquois now cross these sandy planes and do the burning. The blueberries need the clearings. Hunting here is easy.

It will come to be called a "barren," a pine barren, the barrenness itself of this place leading it to be called in geographic descriptions a "waste" and "wasteland," because nothing seems to grow here, nothing of value, no crops. This is why it will become a dump, a trailer park, sold off in schemes and scams. People who are overlooked, or want to be, settle here. The Shakers in 1776; Loyalists to the crown hide in the dunes during the Revolutionary War. Thieves take cover in the woods, and, later, African Americans arrive running from slavery, then hanging trees and Jim Crow laws. The Shakers first live crowded in a single log cabin. They are led by a woman whose followers believe she is the second coming of Christ, and they hope no one will bother them as they straighten the streams and haul in arable soil to build a new society where men and women are equal. The footpaths become roads. Stagecoaches charge five cents per mile and armed guards accompany travelers.

By 1830 there is a railroad, and not even 150 years later: two interstates, a landfill, six-lane roads called "extensions," slip roads, on-ramps, and off-ramps. Cars blow by and the steady roar of tandem trailers passes in waves. Now it's one of the rarest landscapes in the United States, and it's just on the outskirts of Albany.

Part II: Roads

I also arrive by car, lost, to go to the mall. Next time: it's driving to the Albany airport off the poetically named "Northway," as

I-87 stretches to Canada. I turn onto a six-lane road of intermit-
tent stoplights, strip malls, and gas stations. It's the nowhere of
anywhere, no different than the six-lane roads where I grew up
outside Washington, DC: the Tile Shop, nail salon, gas stations,
Trader Joe's, and Whole Foods. They will eventually become my
Tile Shop, nail salon, Trader Joe's, and Whole Foods. The first
time I visit, neither exist here yet, and now when I'm there I think
about what soon won't exist — the small extinctions of Sears and
Regal Cinemas. I pull out from the Colonie Center Whole Foods
with an expensive bottle of probiotics, and across the street is
an empty beige building. A shadow of its past adorns the front:
Barnes & Noble.

This land of strip malls and sand is technically in Colonie, New
York, which itself didn't always exist, at least not in name. The
town was first called Niskayuna — "vast corn fields" in a bastardiza-
tion of the Mohawk word. ("Mohawk" itself is Europeanized and
bastardized and not how the Iroquois named themselves. That was
Kanienkehaka, meaning the "people of the Flint Place.") Niskayuna
disappeared to become the town of Watervliet (water-flood) in the
early nineteenth century, and now it's Colonie with that strange
-ie ending and an etymology stretching back to a Dutch patroon,
the land here belonging originally to the Van Rensselaer family. I
say "originally," but you should know that means "originally" for
European colonists.

Small splintered scraps are all that is left of the sand. They're
"relics" or a "relict," and I love the word if not the fragmentation it describes. It means an ecosystem that has been confined,
constricted, and cut off, or, where geomorphology is concerned,
a place formed by forces no longer active. The sands hint, too,
at an earlier era in the word's broader definition: some lost sur-
vivor. Or, there's its anachronistic meaning: a widow. Separated
by death. Meanwhile "relict" first arose in the Scottish Acts
of Parliament in the 1580s, where it meant land left by water's
retreat.

Water retreats, husbands die, land is isolated and confined,
floods and glaciers disappear. No doubt as James VI ruled Scot-
land in the late sixteenth century, no one considered glacial retreat, or the idea of what might lie across the seas in a place yet to
be called Albany.

In 1895 Colonie superseded the place that had been called

water-flood, and Watervliet decided to form a new town. Surveyors collected all the vacant strips of land they could find — less than three acres in total. The town would use them to collect debts. The state supreme court said no; ghosts can't file cases. Relicts have no protection under the law.

The first time I go to the airport, a decade ago, I know nothing of sand. I see no extinctions, no relicts or fragments. A sign with a silhouette of a plane points left, so does another that says SHAKER SITE. I follow the Shakers and the plane. I turn onto Albany Shaker Road. This is before liquids are banned, and people in bold Yves Klein–blue uniforms inspect bags, passports, shoes, and belts. I drop my husband at departures and decide to find the Shakers, thrilled that the celibate socialists could be nearby.

    After the airport the Shaker signs disappear. I keep going. I get disoriented. Time and space spread out. Marsh grasses wave at an angry sky hazed with heat. A sign says I am driving to Schenectady. A blue sign implores drivers looking for OLD ALBANY SHAKER ROAD BUSINESSES to turn right. I turn right. Trash billows on the verge. On all these roads, trash billows.

    There are no Shakers here, no history, no sites, nothing picturesque, just Hertz, the Comfort Inn, and rusting chain-link fences. The road dead-ends at the county jail, another fence, and the runway. I have no idea this is all the Shaker site. It will take me years to discover that.

In 1959 Nabokov says of the sand: "People go there on Sundays to picnic, shedding papers and beer cans." In a letter he writes, "Nothing else of popular or scientific interest is to be found in that neighborhood." Except butterflies. That's why he comes. He discovers a species here and returns to see it each June. The butterfly lives a few days and dies. His novel *Pnin* describes how they rose from "a damp patch of sand" and, "revealing the celestial hue of their upper surface, they fluttered around like blue snowflakes before settling again."

    The butterfly depends on one specific flower that depends on the sand and fire to survive. The butterfly is the Karner blue; Karner is a place that no longer exists, created by a man, Theodore Karner, who ran a land scheme in the nineteenth century.

The village he designed and its train station are gone. All that is left is a road named for him: New Karner Road. The butterflies *fluttered around like blue snowflakes.* Karner was first called Center. The Center is gone. Karner is gone, the butterfly nearly extinct. It is on the endangered species list.

A few years after Nabokov's visits, Governor Nelson Rockefeller stands in the sand breaking ground for a state university campus. It is 1962. He heaves a shovel over his shoulder. He dreams of universal education. It will level inequalities and create a meritocracy; all we need is access for all. Nabokov writes *Pnin* in the late 1950s. Like Nabokov, Pnin fled first the Communists, then the Nazis, to land in America. Despite World War II and the rise of totalitarianism, it's an era that believes the world is improving, that we control the land, that our possibilities are endless. A cloud of sand rises like smoke as Rockefeller grimaces, and I know this is the sand of history and hope.

I return to the sand, though, for a ghost: a woman whose bones were broken, born on leap year's day. She was the illiterate daughter of a blacksmith. She called herself "Ann the word"; others called her "mother" though all her children died. She is Ann Lee, founder of the Shakers, Christ incarnate as a woman. By now, like Nabokov, I have come countless times to this place. It is a rainy day in January. The weather is wrong, too warm, everything sodden and heavy — puddles, tarmac, and sky. One of the last three surviving Shakers has just died in Maine, and I have finally found the Shaker site. I walk into the Meeting House through one of three doors. Originally, this one was for the ministry; another was for women, and the third for men, but none for me. No outsiders could enter.

Inside, the floor gleams and ladder-back chairs line the walls. The mystic monk Thomas Merton wrote before he died, "The peculiar grace of a Shaker chair is due to the fact that it was made by someone capable of believing that an angel might come and sit on it." If you were a true believer, you could see the spirit world clear as day. This is what the Shakers called the "gift," and even Shaker scholars have talked of experiencing it. I want the spirits to talk to me; I study the room and its chairs, and I don't see angels.

Instead I find a single car parked by a pond that bears Ann Lee's name. Rain careens off the gray ice. Overhead, jets take off.

Signs warn of Lyme disease. I turn back. I don't have a gift. I'm cold and wet and worried about what that lone car is doing on an isolated road in the rain.

Here, the Shakers believed they would build the world anew, heaven on Earth. All would be equal, men and women, black and white. They were collective and utopian; their communities were the most successful experiment in socialism, outlasting that of the Soviets. In trying to find these spirits, I've combed documents and diaries, even urban planning schemes. One hand-drawn Shaker map includes a note by the cemetery: "Mother Ann Lee was buried but the land did not belong to the believers & she was removed to land belonging to the society in the spring of 1835. C." She was buried and reburied. Now all that survives her are four torn scraps of fabric.

According to the map, the county jail where I pull up next to a chain-link fence was *PASTURE*. The airport: *FIELD*. The letters for each of these places, for *FIELD* and *PASTURE*, are elegant capitals with scrolled lines snaking up them. *SWAMP* swerves across the page in a sidelong *S*. The map says *FIELD* was "originally a low muddy swamp, but is now (as Mother Ann prophesied it would be) a light, dry soil." These notes are included in an Environmental Impact Statement (EIS) Albany County commissioned in 1999 when it wanted to widen the road.

My gift, I realize, is in the roads. This is where I find my spirits: Albany Shaker Road, Watervliet Shaker Road. South Family Drive is all that remains of the Shaker "family" that took in new converts, "family" in quotes because the sect didn't believe in the nuclear family, only a spiritual one. They banned marriage and raised children communally.

A shiver passes over me as I arrive from the west. I cross Sand Creek Road, but there's no sand, no creek, not anymore. Subdivisions have been built on High Dune Drive and Pitch Pine Road, as if this endangered area will be preserved in name alone, as if after thousands of years these are the relicts.

To reach them, I drive by squat office buildings and Lasting Memories Taxidermy. The EIS reports on "inconsequential" sites. "Stained soil where a post for a hut wall once stood . . . a cluster of fire-reddened rock which was once a fireplace or less than a thumbnail-sized chert flake." These prehistoric details are so "inconsequential," they're hidden in parentheses. Meanwhile, the county needs wider roads.

On that January day too warm for winter, instead of Ann Lee I find two cop cars and three men outside a crumbling building, the Ann Lee Nursing Home. There's no one left to nurse here. It closed nine years ago.

The Shakers sold off their land to the county in the 1920s for a TB sanatorium, the airport, and a "preventorium" for children at risk of tuberculosis. A handful of Shaker sisters remained. Relicts? Widows? In 1929 Sister Lucy Bowers writes in her diary of the airport:

> *Jan. 27: Wonderful day, cloudless and still. The fliers are often in the sky . . .*
>
> *March 20: Truckloads of furniture get taken away. Feb 8, Feb 13, April 13: boys from the Pre come for candy. March 14 Lady comes in a car . . . More furniture gets shipped off . . . Two sisters go to the airport; 10 busloads of children come to see the airplanes . . . June 22: Rest a while and go over to the airport. Pay $10 of my own money to go up in the airship . . . July 4: Go to airport to see the highest flier come down — 19,900 feet high. Aug. 29: Two men come to talk about buying 200 acres for a golf course . . . Thanksgiving: A fine chicken dinner. Eldress Anna, Caroline, Ella and myself go to see The Golddiggers at the Madison Theater in Albany.*

Utopian dreams, socialist values, sand. The stock market crashes. The kids from the Pre collect pennies. *Gold Diggers*. The celibate sisters see a movie about sex.

The film is a play within a play where showgirls search for men and money, neither of which tally with Shaker values. There's drinking and dancing on tables. Girls sleep with married men. The story hinges on one dancer's failure to say: "I am the spirit of the ages and the progress of civilization."

Sister Lucy's diary ends on Thanksgiving. She never says if she likes the movie. Its hit song is "Painting the Clouds with Sunshine." In it the singer promises to chase away sadness and depression, to keep emotional clouds at bay with a forced gaiety. The Shakers and their socialist dreams are nearly extinct, and all that remains of the movie are the last twenty minutes. The rest has disappeared.

Part III. Clouds

I stand in the shadow of a mountain. It's early autumn; asters and goldenrod bob their heads. The mountain is fenced in, and the top is flat. On it a tanker spews water. The truck is so high and distant it looks like a toy. The mountain, though, is not a mountain; it is the Albany landfill, nearly two hundred acres of trash, 360,000 tons deposited a year. I'm here with a biologist. He first came twenty years ago to volunteer on the controlled fires set each summer that preserve the sand and butterflies, scrub oak and pines.

We cross a sandy track so fine and golden we could be at the beach. A few feet away, the ground turns gray. A tire tread is hardened into it. The biologist tells me it's clay like glaciers deposit today. They melt, leaving areas that pond and pool where the clay filters out. Same here, he says, just millennia ago. He's showing me a glacier in this shadow of the dump, a shadow of trash filled with what we've discarded. The dump is a shadow, too, or will be soon. It will close in 2020 to be returned to sand and scrub and Nabokov's butterflies, those blue clouds of snow.

The biologist waves across this meadow. Five years ago, he says, there were streets, sidewalks, and septic systems here. The stream, the pond, and nodding flowers are all new. Even the sand has been brought in. In the background, the incessant beeping of reversing trucks blends with waves of cars on the interstate.

At home, I zoom in on this spot with Google Earth. Shadowy lines appear onscreen over the sand and scrub. These shadows were roads. Hovering over them with a mouse, their names appear: Fox Run Lane, Brier Fox Boulevard, Tally Ho Drive, Fox Hound Avenue, Hunters Glen Avenue . . . They conjure British landed gentry, the sort who'd wear red tailcoats and jodhpurs, and ride to hounds, as if that could ever exist behind the landfill. What did were a hundred trailer homes. Google Street View shows images of them from 2007: a paneled home with an SUV outside, next door a sedan, and yellow siding on the house. Some lots just appear as grass and foundation. The street is already crumbling into tarmac. The county bought it up to transform it back into pine sands, which will burn regularly.

*

I do find a ghost at the Shaker site: Rebecca Cox Jackson. She dreamt of clouds and the atmosphere. She was African American, became celibate, left her husband, and traveled the East Coast preaching a vision of salvation before joining the Shakers. She'd been illiterate but discovered she could read. It was a blessing. It was God. She picked up a Bible and the words were alive. "Eldress," she became a leader, and in 1843, just after her first visit to Watervliet, she dreamed of rain and flowers.

> *Sunday, 12th of March, after midnight, I laid down, fell asleep and . . . looked up into the air, saw wonderful strange colored clouds coming from the east . . . It began to rain, as if it were cotton, until the earth was covered . . . All the house, trees, and everything else disappeared. And then the rain changed from cotton to sweet-smelling flowers . . . I stepped to the door, picked some up, tasted them. Their taste was sweet just like the smell. I then put some in my bosom, but I am not able to tell what they smelt like. The whole air was perfumed with their odor, yea, with their heavenly smell . . . In that storm came streams of light. And they came in the form of hoops, white as snow, bright as silver, passing through the shower of flowers. They went like the lightning.*

At the end of her vision she began ministering to people. "I comforted them with the words that was given to me for them. They were all colored people, and they heard me gladly . . . I, Rebecca Jackson, was two-score and eight years and twenty-six days old, when in 1843, I dreamed about my people . . ."

In her dreams there are strange clouds and cotton rain. "Sparks of light shower down like silver." She also writes about how the Shakers are too self-absorbed in their isolation. "How will the world be saved if the Shakers are the only people of God on earth, and they seemed so busy in their own concerns?"

I think of her in the shadow of the dump. How do we stop being so busy in our own concerns?

She cries. She loves a woman, Rebecca Perot. Together they join the community at Watervliet. "The two Rebeccas," the Shakers call them. Their relationship is hard to understand from our distance of 175 years. The Rebeccas don't fit into our time, maybe not even into theirs. Were they mother and surrogate daughter? Friends? Lovers? Companions? The two Rebeccas: inseparable, inscrutable.

*

I don't find either of their graves. The other Rebecca, Rebecca Perot, took Jackson's name when she died in 1871. She became the second Eldress Rebecca Cox Jackson. Together they established an urban ministry, mostly for women, mostly African American women. Most of them worked as domestic help in Philadelphia.

I find a single drawing of Eldress Rebecca Jackson online. Her head juts out, as if she's trying to fix on something in the distance. She wears a white Shaker cap and shawl, and holds a pen in one hand. Her two fingers are raised like Christ giving a benediction in some ancient icon. Two books are by her side, but I can read nothing into her. I see no rain, no hoops white as snow. I want to see her and the other Rebecca. I walk across the Shaker site past the two cop cars. The three men watch me warily. Or I am wary. I feel their watching. I try not to drift into their gaze. I try to look as if I know where I am going.

The picture turns out not to be Jackson at all but another woman, as if any black woman in modest garb might be her.

Jackson wakes up on January 14, 1848, dreaming that she was in Philadelphia in bed with the other Rebecca. "I thought someone might come in while we slept. And I said, 'Rebecca, go and get three forks, and fasten the doors.' . . . Rebecca rose immediately, and as she put the fork over the latch, a man rushed against the door . . ."

Soon a Shaker brethren appeared outside, so did a well and a tub, and intimations of violence. He threw watermelons. The earth shook. She "saw a river of ice . . . and three ice rocks in it, and three men upon the rocks . . . The shaking of the earth caused the river, the rocks and the men to move up and down, and the men moved their hands like a person shooting." They transformed into "one transparent brightness — white as snow and bright as silver . . . rays of light . . . a brilliant circle. And in my heart the sight was magnificent."

In my heart the site was magnificent. But I stand in the rain, sodden.

That afternoon in the shadow of the mountain when the goldenrod bloomed and nodded, I ask the biologist why the tanker is spraying water.

"Water?" he says puzzled.

"Up there," I point, "for the grasses, right?" I assume native grasses have been planted on the dump's plateau.

He laughs. "It's not water. It's air freshener . . . Febreze." Indeed, the smell wafts over us. It has a green chemical scent like drier sheets. He and I stand on these spectral streets, the air filled with clouds of water, of rain — and of chemicals sprayed to mask the smell of trash. Jackson's flowers fell in bunches after the rain. *I put some in my bosom, but I am not able to tell what they smelt like. The whole air was perfumed with their odor, yea, with their heavenly smell . . .*

I've come to the dump to find the future and the past. Both haunt me in this place once named for a dream of England that must have seemed distant living here in a doublewide, near roads that memorialize a disappearing wilderness.

The biologist tells me Nabokov's endangered butterflies probably won't survive. They can't even fly across a four-lane road let alone a highway, and the issue, he explains, isn't protecting one species but all species and their habitat. It is not one thing but all things. They're interdependent. *How will the world be saved?* Jackson wrote.

The butterflies rise like snowflakes. Rockefeller throws sand. It lifts like a cloud. Rain falls like cotton. Hoops white as snow, bright as silver, pass like lightning. I'm painting the clouds just like the song.

Online, looking at the landfill and lost streets and lanes, I think about relicts and widows, Eldress Rebecca Jackson and Rebecca Perot. I think too about the internet and our lives. Google's data centers use nearly three hundred million watts of energy a year. The internet consumes around 5 percent of all energy usage. Stream music, TV, movies, shop online, subscribe online, pay bills online — or read this essay online. All of this life — our lives — happens online — in clouds, in the cloud, the cloud that is run by farms, server farms. All of this needs energy. The quaintly named cloud, which can seem as ethereal as the air and the sky, uses thirty billion watts of energy worldwide. A third of this is eaten up by data centers in the United States — and that statistic is out of date, that was in 2012. One data center takes more power than most towns in the US, and our energy usage has only increased despite attempts to stave off global warming. By 2020 the number of connected devices drawing on data and energy will more than triple, and by 2030, information technologies in the internet of things could account for as much as 20 percent of total energy use.

This is what haunts me. The Gulf Stream is weakening; the climate will warm or cool precipitously, maybe even both in turn. The catastrophic changes that brought the sand to Albany happened in a timescale inscrutable to us, taking place over millennia instead of decades. In a human timeframe the dump will close. It will be planted with prairie grasses. Every year is the warmest on record, and glaciers melt. The Karner blue lives less than a week.

The butterfly depends on fire and smoke to survive. The Shakers got their start here in smoke and clouds. It was the Dark Day. At noon in mid-May 1780 the depth of night spread from Maine to New Jersey. The Revolutionary War languished. Many saw it as the end times. The Shakers decided it was time to proselytize. The darkness wasn't God, though, or the end — just a forest fire. The smoke had drifted east. As the ranks of Shakers grew, they cleared the land. An airport followed. They lent their tools to build it and the sisters fed the workers. Then a golf course, a dump, a university, the interstate, and climate change. That's the prophecy I find.

Lucy Bowers dies in 1935. The last three Shaker sisters leave Albany in 1938. In a newspaper interview, they say what they miss most are the airport's planes and floodlights.

When I'm blue, the song goes, all I have to do is paint the clouds . . . Shopping, self-creation, reinvention, reincarnation, faith . . . Longing has shaped this landscape. Or maybe this place has shaped them. They've all taken root here in the sand — airport, strip mall, suburbs. I find them in the wake of our dreams of progress. Throw something out and start over. Trash, sand, and highways, flight, clouds, silver orbs, and socialism's most successful experiment.

In a letter as Marx was dying, Friedrich Engels wrote, "Remember the Shakers!" He wanted to remind Marx that it had taken the Shakers years to build their community. This was the last thing Engels said to him, Remember . . .

Ann Lee died on September 8, 1784. She was forty-eight. During her life, she was forced to strip to prove she was a woman, dragged behind a horse, imprisoned for treason because as a pacifist she couldn't support a war. She didn't believe in the legitimacy of the state or even Christmas. She was exhumed in 1835, and it was clear her skull had been fractured before she died. I find her grave. The stone is new and white like bone. The day feels like spring. It is February. At the edge of the cemetery, a tree hides broken markers. So many shattered graves, the violence is inescapable.

Christ's second coming, she preached that celibacy would create equality and the community of believers destroyed the traditional family structure. One hundred years after her death, Engels wrote in *The Origin of the Family, Private Property and the State* that the family was a tool of capitalism and women's oppression. Rebecca Jackson saw herself as a second Ann Lee. Illiterate, they both left their husbands for faith and wanted to rebuild society.

By the time you read this, an ice shelf the size of Delaware will have broken off from Antarctica. As glaciers melt, fresh water is released into the oceans, slowing currents. The flood thirteen thousand years ago looks like prologue or prophecy. Touch the sand, drive the roads, go to the mall. Cotton rain falls in the shadow of the dump.

SUKI KIM

Land of Darkness

FROM *Lapham's Quarterly*

I AM THE only writer ever, as far as we know, to have lived undercover in North Korea, immersed within the system to investigate
the place. In 2011 I took my fifth trip into Pyongyang, where, under the guise of being a missionary and an ESL teacher, I lived for
six months with 270 North Korean males in a military compound.
For this act, I am often described as "fearless." People call me
brave. But even if it sounds illogical, I consider myself to be a very
fearful person. Even more, I believe my fearfulness is the only way
I can begin to explain my time undercover in the gulag nation.

North Korea is perhaps the darkest place in the world. The
country lacks electricity; everything is gray and monotone, and
the only meaning is given to the Great Leader, an authoritarian,
godlike persona now worn for the third generation by thirty-three-
year-old Kim Jong Un, who is considered the sun, though that sun
exudes no warmth for its people. No other contemporary country
is so entirely devoid of light.

I have always been afraid of the dark. I rarely dream, and I
used to sleepwalk as a child to escape the pitch-blackness of being asleep. Even now, I cannot turn the light off at night. This is a
dreary habit since artificial light is so disruptive that I almost never
sleep well. But my fear of the dark is overpowering; I would rather
forsake good sleep if it means keeping the darkness at bay.

Morning brings no relief. I often wake with a sinking feeling,
then spend many early hours staring at unopened emails with
dread, ill at ease with facing a shared territory of interaction. I
have even been avoiding emails about this essay, which I've been

afraid to start for weeks. I disabled the calendar app on my phone so that I would not be reminded of the approaching deadline. I recently had to fly from New York to Seoul, and the reasons for that trip became secondary to the flight itself, which suggested to me a fourteen-hour-long refuge when no one would be able to reach me or expect me to reciprocate.

I experience the world, that is, as a map of fears to navigate, its coordinates all shattering bits coming at uneven speeds. This feeling has dogged me for as long as I can remember, and the map operates as a knot growing more tangled within me each day. Parts of it — the toughest paths to fathom — have been there for as long as I can recall. One of these paths leads back to North Korea, which often seems to me the dark night from which I have run all my life.

My family was separated by the Korean War, and I was born and raised in South Korea. When I was twelve, my father, who had been a millionaire, suddenly went bankrupt. In the middle of night, I was awakened and shoved into a car and driven off to a city far away, to a relative's house, where I waited for my parents to join me. Because bankruptcy is punishable there by jail, my parents had gone into hiding. I was a child and didn't understand, so I waited, every day expecting their return. But I didn't see them again until a year later, at John F. Kennedy Airport, in New York, after our family had fled Korea.

Predictably, I don't remember much of that year of waiting; that time remains in my mind as a hollow darkness from which the only sensation I recall is that of a thirst, the huge, bottomless kind that cannot be quenched. The darkness did not lift even when I immigrated to America and became reunited with my parents, now penniless. I did not speak a word of English. Everything I knew simply vanished in one instant, and I got stuck, I think, in the shadowy nook where I hid as a girl, aged twelve.

Perhaps because of all this, I am good at waiting. I can wait for days and years, through rain and storm — even through darkness — and hardly ever ask questions. Somewhere deep in my mind, I must imagine that if I am quiet and good, my parents will come back. I could have made, I suppose, a very good wife to a very conservative man. But instead I became a writer in the English language despite, or maybe because of, the fact that English, which I adopted as a teen, was another road on my map of fear.

As I write this, I'm reminded of a well near my childhood home. It was a deep, old-fashioned, cylindrical well made of stone, and the neighborhood kids played around it, throwing things and shouting into its vault to hear the echo. I was always terrified of it and never went near. Later in life I became briefly fixated with the work of Haruki Murakami because he kept using wells as symbols in his novels. But eventually I got bored of reading him; I realized that it wasn't Murakami's writing that haunted me but the well from my childhood. My passion for his work was just the flip side of a stronger fear.

How all this relates to North Korea might seem, I realize, abstract. I can't say it provides direct explanation. Perhaps I traveled to the darkest place on earth because I empathized with its citizens, who are stuck in that darkness and cannot get out. Perhaps their voicelessness became mine because it reminded me of my own powerlessness. Or it's possible that North Korea, in some ethereal way, became a kind of darkest night, the longest wait, the well from my childhood.

I pursued coverage of the country for a decade, every step of the way nearly paralyzed with fear. I was not one of those intrepid foreign correspondents who jump into war zones, nor did I have a team of editors, fixers, and photographers working alongside to help figure out the logistics and arrange the precautionary backups. Although I signed a book contract long before 2011 — when I finally dove into Pyongyang for those six months — my meager contract was just a piece of paper with a vague deadline, never a support network I could rely on for protection. In Pyongyang I was watched around the clock by the minders who lived directly below me in a dormitory under complete surveillance. My classes were recorded and reported on, and I had to get permission for every lesson from the North Korean staff. I saved my notes on USB sticks, which I kept on my body at all times. I made sure to delete my traces from my laptop every time I signed off. I saved a backup copy on an SD card, which I hid in different spots in the room, always with the light off. I created a document within a document, burying the notes in the middle of what looked like class lesson material. I was utterly on my own and knew no one who could come to my rescue if I were caught with the four hundred pages of notes I had taken in secret. The most likely scenario was that I would vanish in that bleak, dark unknown.

*

North Korea is the most inaccessible country in the world, and
its regime has committed human rights abuses at a scale, according to the United Nations, "without parallel in the contemporary
world." It is a society built entirely on fears. Its dictators have ma-
nipulated and exploited human frailties to incorporate them into
its system of control and abuse. Its citizens cannot leave the country, and their movement within it is restricted. Information is cen-
sored, and every interaction is surveilled. Education is only about
the cult of the Great Leader, as is the media, and the citizens are
treated as slaves and soldiers to uphold the myth. Those who enter
its borders without permission or who commit acts that are forbidden by the regime — even something as seemingly innocuous
as ripping a poster of their Great Leader — can face sentences of
more than a decade of hard labor. Public execution is sanctioned
by the regime, which is also known for kidnapping foreigners. No
one with any sense of self-preservation would sneak into North
Korea to write a book.

This leads people back home in the United States, or in South
Korea or Europe, where I've traveled in recent years to give talks —
the same people who like to call me fearless and brave — to ask the
inevitable questions: Wasn't I scared? And why did I go?

These questions always give me pause. Perhaps it is a natural human instinct to look for a neat, rational motive for any story that
seems incredible. Readers often want to identify with their narrator and the reasons for her action, or perhaps they just want to be
assured that the author of a story is not out of her mind. Some
years ago, when I published my first novel, there were readers who
seemed to take personal offense at the story being open-ended. A
few even told me I should write a sequel to redo the ending with
a proper conclusion.

Yet such an instinct is self-defeating; no true story worth anyone's
time operates according to a predictable pattern. Accepted plots
are almost always contrived. It is entirely possible to be scared and
not scared at the same time, though this idea is rarely allowed. Such
a blurred line reminds us how limited our agency is to control our
circumstances; this mathematics of fear leaves no such gray area.
In our attempt to be satisfied with a story's arc, we like to contain
ourselves to a one-dimensional narrative of a hero fighting evil,
although we know that life is almost always somewhere in between.

One of the questions I am most frequently asked about North
Korea is whether the people there are "brainwashed under their
Great Leader." The question strikes me as deeply patronizing; citizens there are not simplistic robots. They may believe and not
believe all at once. My North Korean students would, in unison,
swear against the imperialist America and its puppet South Korea
as their chief enemies and say that if a war broke out, they would
kill their enemies without hesitation. But when I asked them,
"What about me? I'm both South Korean and American," they
looked embarrassed and laughed shyly, mumbling, "But you are
our teacher. You are different."

Isn't this the kind of paradox by which the human mind works?
There is a place in our being that allows for simultaneous belief in
something while knowing it not to be true — or for calmly speaking with students in a classroom while experiencing absolute terror about the consequences of being found out by authorities. I
think of it as a kind of blind spot.

Despite the differences in circumstances in America, we have
seen plenty of examples of the blind spot operating through the
recent election cycle. It appears that an overwhelming sector
of the population became convinced that a real estate guy who
played a boss firing people for eleven years on a popular reality
TV show was uniquely qualified to lead the nation. Even in this
country, where celebrity prestige seems to dictate the public conscience, it cannot be that people would confuse playing the boss
on television with having anything to do with being the actual boss
of a nation — but perhaps such was the comfort of indoctrinated
habit. It's of a piece with an American psychology that has allowed
joking about the Great Leader to be our cultural norm. Movies
like the animated *Team America: World Police* and the comedy *The
Interview* are among the most popular reference points for North
Korea; a country where twenty-five million people are currently being trapped and tortured has largely been figured into American
mainstream culture as the butt of jokes.

Every time someone in an audience asks me how and whether
all North Koreans are brainwashed, I am struck by how unintel-
ligible such a question is, and how much it assumes a fundamen-
tal difference between the operations of their own minds and the
minds of North Koreans. I often feel I am watching an object of
fear grow to dominate the audience member's brain and arrest

their understanding. Perhaps there is a comfort in denying North Koreans their humanity, distancing their experiences as unreal. To do so allows us to have no obligation and responsibility to them, and it frees us from the vague sense of our complicity. They cannot touch us. The blind spot allows a person in such a situation to feign an act of agency that masks a deeper lack of agency; it is at once willful ignorance and knee-jerk self-protection.

Each time someone calls me fearless, I think of this blind spot, as I believe it helps explain my time in North Korea. I do not mean to suggest that I was naive to its dangers, but that each time I thought about being caught, I blocked the matching pangs of fear that came, attempted to usher them away from the front of my consciousness as well as I could.

In Pyongyang I was allowed to leave the campus only in a group with minders for a few hours on weekends, and my days were meticulously mapped out, so the only break I got was to jog in a circle around the tiny campus. I wore the mini USB sticks containing the notes for my book on a necklace as pendants, and I always feared that the strand might loosen and slip off me while I was not paying attention. In those passing moments, when the possibility of being discovered struck me as an impending, inevitable doom, my breath would catch, and as a kind of survival mechanism, I would shut my eyes and push away the thought.

It often seems to me that the desire to comprehend fear strikes at a mystery at the center of life. We breathe toward death; each moment alive is a clock tick toward not living any longer. There is no happy ending, and to help all this make sense to us, we repeat histories, fight needless wars, recite prayers, and fall in love, often more than once, with people who will break our hearts. Life is born from those blind spots, with each mishap, every accident.

Because I identify with fear, I turned out to be, as much as one can be, well suited to pursue North Korea and to bear each frightening day there as if I were a researcher at a laboratory working on a case. I did not count on caring so much for my students, but I did, and that consequence was afforded to me by my own blind spot. Each interaction surprised me, shocked me from unknowing to knowing, gave me names and faces toward a deeper understanding of the North Korean horror. The dark stopped being dark for one illuminating second at a time, and even if night returned each time to blacken the sky completely, the darkness that followed was never quite the same.

There is no full circle, tidy conclusion, or simple solution to any of this. I am still scared of North Korea. My inbox is full of unread emails. Mornings are hard, and I try to avoid reading breaking news from above the thirty-eighth parallel, which is inevitably negative; two Americans from the school where I was undercover are being held hostage by the regime. When I finally do glance at the news, I don't look at photos because I am afraid that I might see the faces of my students, which would make me tumble and lose my precarious balance.

Sometimes I still fear that it will all come to haunt me one day, that someone sent by the Great Leader will find me while I am traveling somewhere far away from home, and that I will either be taken back to Pyongyang or be punished for writing about what they did not want revealed. But each time my mind goes there, I stop myself, and though it is not clear where my thoughts retract to, there is often a lull; for a brief moment I am numb, and fear cannot get to me.

DAVID WONG LOUIE

Eat, Memory

THE LAST TIME I ate real food, actually chewed and swallowed, was six years ago. During those final meals, I ordered a pastrami sandwich, a pork-belly bun, and vegetable soup. The sandwich needed more fat, the bun more seasoning, and the soup I barely touched, because by that point it had become too painful to swallow. More memorable than my soup was the lamb burger served to my wife. It was a thick, luscious disk of meat; she cut it in half to show me the perfect pinkness inside. I made a mental note that I wanted one of those, once I was cured.

With the tip of a spoon I fished a cannellini — my favorite among the beans — out of the tomato broth, chewed until a fine paste was achieved, then swallowed, chasing the bolus like aspirin, with water and a jerk of the head. Everything in the bowl tasted like a blurry version of its vegetal self. A bite of carrot caught in my throat. I reached up reflexively and there it was, cancer at my fingertips, a hard bulge like an Adam's apple, just left of the original.

The neck is crowded real estate, dense with activity and structures; more systems of the body converge, commingle, here than anywhere else. It is the site of biological and social essentials such as breathing, speaking, and swallowing. The nurses had warned me that radiation to the throat area is the most painful of cancer therapies. It damages soft tissue, causing ulcers to erupt in the mouth. Food tastes strange. Appetite leaves you. Eating becomes hell. Previous patients, the nurses said, had quit treatment midway and taken their cancers home. My symptoms kicked in around the third week. Sores flourished. I lost weight. My throat swelled — evidence, I hoped, that the mass was in its death throes.

A month earlier, my wife and I had been at dim sum with friends when my ENT, Dr. H, phoned with the pathology report. My wife took the call outside, turning her back to the restaurant as if to shield me from the inevitable. I could see her tilt her head into the phone and roll her shoulders inward, shrinking from the news. When my wife returned to the table she stared at the dishes: *shu-mai, har gow,* rice-noodle rolls, taro-root cake, *jook* with pork, and thousand-year-old egg, all getting cold or congealing. I pointed at her plate, urging her to eat the lotus-wrapped sticky rice, our favorite. She shook her head, too upset for food. Then she arched her eyebrows and said, "You eat it." Which, being a pig, I did.

Eating had been my one enduring talent. More gourmand than gourmet, I loved to chew and swallow. My desire for food had the urgency of lust; I was constantly horny. Breakfast. A second breakfast forty-five minutes later. Lunch. Snacks all afternoon: last night's meat, cold cuts, a hard-boiled egg. Happy hour with my wife: drinks, chips, cheese, and salami; if she wasn't home, just drinks and chips. Then dinner, with wine, until it hurt.

When Dr. H discussed my tumor with another oncologist, I overheard him comparing its size to a plum. My first thought: What kind of plum? Italian, Santa Rosa, Greengage? But I didn't need comparisons to stone fruit to know that cancer was flourishing. Every raspy breath, every hoarse word uttered, told me that it was in there. I was sent to Dr. L, a radiation oncologist who had a reputation for taking on the worst cases, for pushing the limits of what a body could tolerate. At the end of the appointment, Dr. L seemed gleeful; he was "very excited" about my tumor. My disease and I had stumbled beyond Stage 4. We had entered the realm of sport, had become a challenge like Everest.

Three weeks after the vegetable soup, when even scrambled eggs were too much to bear, I told my wife that I was through with eating. She looked at me as if the cancer had spread to my brain. I clarified: I would go on a liquid diet. A friend had given me a smoothie recipe that her mother had sworn by (until breast cancer killed her): yogurt, milk, protein powder, banana, peanut butter, chocolate sauce, flaxseed oil, honey. At first, the intense sweetness and big flavors astonished me. My taste buds were zapped; I had become unused to recognizing what I tasted. But the moment the cool liquid hit my tongue, there was a burst of intelligibility.

For the next two months I drank the same smoothie four times a day. Each feeding was a marathon. The lump in my throat — formerly the mass, now irradiated tissue — made swallowing a struggle. Treatments had ended weeks earlier, but the expected improvement in my physical condition never came. I felt as wretched as during the radiation's worst days. The swelling was pressed up against my larynx, crimping the airway and paralyzing the vocal cords. I lost the ability to inflate my words to their proper dimensions. My breaths were no longer automatic, they were always on my mind.

I was sent for a barium swallow, an X-ray of the pharynx and esophagus. A nurse served me a thick, chalky suspension of barium, a heavy metal that absorbs X-rays, making visible the passageways through which it travels. After swallowing the barium, I would graduate through a *mise en place* of green water, applesauce, and cookies, set up on a tray nearby. I shook my head. My wife, standing next to me, knew exactly what I meant: I didn't stand a chance against those Lorna Doones.

I never even got to the water. The test was called off when the barium, a thin black line on the monitor, veered off course toward my windpipe. My doctor had seen enough — food or drink inhaled into the lungs puts one in danger of myriad complications, including pneumonia. He said, unequivocally, "You're getting a G-tube."

I balked. A G-tube was a sick man's game. Sick like late-stage Parkinson's. Advanced dementia. Comas.

My doctor explained that the tube would be inserted through my abdomen, to deliver nutrition directly into my stomach. He said, reassuringly, that the tube would be manufactured from state-of-the-art silicone, installed by a state-of-the-art surgeon, at a state-of-the-art facility. But it was still a tube embedded in my gut. What's more base than sustenance delivered directly to the stomach, like gavage to geese? I babbled to my wife about bodily integrity, how mine was, after these many years, unmarred, unpierced, un-broken-boned. Never mind the human condition. You are a body, first and last.

In reality, though, I was relieved. My weight was down to 112 pounds, and I was sick of smoothies.

Dr. H assured me that the G-tube was temporary, a few months, tops. Once the inflammation in my throat subsided and I passed a

barium swallow, he would simply pull it out, no OR required; if I
wanted, I could do it myself. What about the gaping hole that the
disconnected tube would leave behind — the contents of my stomach leaking into my body cavity, septic shock? The doctor strapped
on his profession's *You silly patients* look, then informed me: "Holes
close, that's what our bodies do."

Putting a G-tube in, he said, was as easy as taking one out. The
first attempt failed. After sedation, prep, and anesthesia, the surgeon called off the procedure. He had seen my large intestine
eclipsing my stomach, preventing a direct strike. He decided to
wait for the bowel segment to retreat, and in the interim fitted me
with a nasogastric (NG) tube, which was threaded up nostril, down
throat, into stomach. I left the hospital with the tube bent into a
U and taped to my face. It wasn't until I sat down to feed the tube
that I discovered it measured a mere six inches nostril to valve; in
order to feed it I had to hold my hands high and off to the side, as
if I were playing a flute. The tube wasn't designed with self-feeding
in mind, which made sense, given its target clientele: comatose
patients, patients on ventilators, patients with broken faces, premature babies.

Ultimately my wife had to feed me. For hours each day she
painstakingly pushed enteral formula, called Jevity (as in "longevity"), through the tube as thin as uncooked spaghetti. The Jevity
had the viscosity of heavy cream, further slowing the process. Each
feeding lasted an episode and a half of *Downton Abbey*. I emailed
my son a photo of my wife and me, my way of letting him know
of my new acquisition. We're smiling, a knit cap low on my brow,
the NG tube curved across my cheek, the residual formula inside
bright as neon, the purple valve taped exactly where an earring
would dangle. The subject line: "Post-feeding bliss."

On the second try, the G-tube was properly installed. I fed it every
four hours, a total of four times a day, with formula — think baby
formula — and an equal volume of water. After trial and error with
brands and caloric distributions, I settled on Fibersource HN, 300
calories and 13.5 grams of protein, a product of Nestlé, the same
company that gives the world Gerber baby food, Häagen-Dazs, Kit
Kat bars, and Purina Dog Chow. On the package, offset within an
attention-grabbing oval graphic, was the word "unflavored," which

made me wonder: Are there *flavored* enteral feeding formulas? Other than on our tongues, we have taste receptors in the palate, larynx, and upper esophagus — but in our stomachs?

G-tube meals meant no muss, no fuss. No food prep. No risk of aspirating or choking. No smoothie stare-downs. No marital discord over what or how much was consumed. One feeding to the next, it was the same comforting routine: fill beaker with water; spread towel on lap; crush pills, add water, stir; shake and unseal two containers of Fibersource; pour formula into a second, empty beaker; clamp G-tube to prevent stomach contents from escaping when opening valve; open valve; unwrap fresh syringe, dip nozzle in formula, withdraw sixty centiliters; insert nozzle securely into valve; gently push plunger. The syringe empties slowly, and the formula gently pools in your stomach. If you "plunge" harder, the formula surges, the jet pelts your pink insides, and you feel the stomach lining flinch. That's all the sensation there is. Pleasure, satisfaction, beauty never crossed my mind.

I devoted myself to the G-tube. Feedings were inviolable. The dietician prescribed eight eight-ounce containers daily. Eight is an auspicious number in Chinese culture.

After ten weeks of daily infusions at 2,400 calories and 108 grams of protein, I cracked 120 pounds. At the rate of two pounds per week I could hit my target, 150, in four and a half months.

From my journal, March 29, 2012: "Woke, fed tube, went to acupuncture, came home, fed tube, napped, fed tube, emailed, fed tube." In the locution of the cancer ward: Your only job is to get better.

I am astonished, now, at how many of my first memories of places are related to food: goose in Hong Kong, *lardo* in Florence, cherrystones in Boston, pizza in New York. And milestones, too: my fortieth at ABC Seafood, my son's graduation at Lupa, my mother-in-law's seventieth at Providence, my daughter's haircut party at Hop Li. I fondly remember the ham-and-Swiss sandwich at Bay Cities, the crispy-skin cubes of pork belly at Empress Pavilion, the roast-duck noodles at Big Wing Wong, the grilled prime rib at Campanile, those perfect bites of charred, almond-and-olive-wood smoky, tapenade-smeared meat dabbed in flageolet beans and braised bitter greens.

With the G-tube, I did not eat — I fed the tube. My mind did not equate the formula with food, as other patients do — how could I confuse the two? Goose in Hong Kong is a meal, not a feeding; the table is laid with utensils, not a syringe; one dines, not feeds.

I'd been feeding the tube for three months when a PET scan showed, in the words of Dr. L, "hypermetabolic activity that is asymmetric." That meant trouble. A PET scan measures bodily functions, such as glucose metabolism, using a radioactive tracer; cancer cells, which require lots of sugar, light up the scan. That night, feeding the tube seemed futile. Why bother if all that five hundred containers of formula yielded was more disease?

I was referred to another ENT, who strode into the examination room and, without introduction, threaded a light and camera up one nostril and down my throat. On the color monitor my throat showed up gray instead of carnation pink.

In the world of abnormal healing, he said, my case was abnormal. He doubted my ability to heal.

I can't say if he was seated or standing, I just remember him towering over me, and me wondering why he wouldn't stop talking.

The day would come, he went on, when I would have to choose between speaking and swallowing. He didn't elaborate and I didn't ask. I just wanted to leave before he said any more.

Later, I turned to my wife for answers. Since when were talking and swallowing optional? And how did one go about choosing? A pros-and-cons list?

In the end, a surgeon made the choice for me. Radiation and chemo had failed me, the cancer was back, and the only option left was a total laryngectomy, in which the entire larynx is removed and the airway is separated from the mouth, nose, and esophagus. In the operating room, the surgeon reattached mouth to esophagus rather than mouth to trachea and reconstructed the upper esophagus as a funnel of flesh with skin from my thigh.

If it had been up to me, I would have chosen the same. Swallowing, every time. I imagined the first thing I would eat — hot ramen noodles searing my throat on their way down.

From an early age I had learned the price of things, a consequence of growing up in an immigrant household. "How mucha cent?" was one of my mother's signature English phrases. She wanted to know the cost of things to take your measure: Had you been duped? How big a fool were you? Her brain worked like *The Price Is Right,* all goods were pegged to a number, and if your purchase went over, she would click her tongue; if it was under, she would say, "Waaaa!" and you would feel golden. Of the oncological deal she would have said, "Waaaa!" Anything in exchange for the rest of your life is a good value.

You take that deal every time.

The cost has been steep, though. I breathe through a hole in my neck; my nose and mouth serve no respiratory function; I can't talk; I can't whistle, moan, sigh; I can't scream (once, while cooking for my wife and daughter, I cut myself badly and jumped away from the cutting board shaking my hand, silently spraying blood); I can't smell anything, not bacon, not diesel fumes, nothing; mine is a vestigial nose, on my face solely for looks. And I can't eat, either.

Now that I'm at some remove from the surgery, I wouldn't mind being replumbed, having my windpipe hooked up to my mouth. At least then I could sing again, blow out candles, laugh at my daughter's jokes. This eating thing has been a bust. I'm a hundred percent Fibersource via the G-tube. When someone texts me a photo of their lunch, if I happen to be feeding the tube and feeling bitter, I text back a photo of a beaker of ecru formula with the empty container posed close by: "Here's mine."

"Do you miss it?" my wife asked me recently. She meant eating at restaurants, dinner parties with friends. She had just polished off takeout sushi from a new restaurant that we would have already visited, back in my eater days. Her postmeal rundown was enthusiastic at first — the rice was the perfect temperature, as if the chef had factored in the time it took her to transport the food home. But then she seemed to lose heart and the review sputtered, her voice taking on an apologetic tone.

Four years ago, after living crisis to crisis for so long after the surgery, it finally seemed safe to exhale and dig out of the chaos. It was time to reclaim a measure of normalcy. I was going to surprise my wife with a dinner out with our daughter. We were celebrating our wedding anniversary, after letting the past few slip by virtually without notice. I made a reservation at Connie and Ted's, a New England seafood shack in West Hollywood. The menu was right up my culinary alley — raw bar, steamers, chowder — but I would go as a bystander.

It hadn't occurred to me that people would stare until I walked into the restaurant. I hadn't been out in public except for doctor's appointments and walks in the neighborhood. While I was getting dressed, my wife had asked if I planned to wear a scarf to hide the tracheostomy tube that poked from my throat. As we were seated, I wondered if she had asked for my comfort or hers.

At the table, though, we were back to the old normal, studying the menu in forensic detail. "They have Fanny Bays," my wife said, reading off the oyster list. "And Malpeques. Or is it Malaspinas that you like?" Our dinner out came crashing down around me. What did it matter which bivalve I preferred? I was here only to window-shop.

My wife was undeterred. She ordered enough food for three adult eaters. Nothing says festive like a crowded table, and she was determined that I not withdraw to the fringes of the party. She would eat the oysters, and I would sip the liquor from the shells. For my entrée she ordered Rhode Island clam chowder. It was undeniably briny and clammy, easily the most delicious thing I'd tasted since I stopped eating. But I didn't take a second spoonful. We were out in public now. I couldn't take in liquid without dribbling on my shirt. I wouldn't embarrass us here.

My wife couldn't maintain her good cheer. By the time the entrées arrived, she was overwhelmed by the accumulation of food — lobster roll for her, squid for the kid — joining the *We're still working* dishes that remained on the table.

In the photos of that night my daughter looks wretched. She was nine, and had entered the stage in which smiles for the camera are self-conscious, betraying little of what is going on inside. Even with a just-delivered plate of fried clams and french fries in front of her, her eyes mirrored how the rest of the table felt: We wished we were far away.

We faked it, played at dining out. We pretended that cancer was behind us, throwing a scarf over it. Whenever we remember that dinner, my wife says, "Never again," and I flash the thumbs-up: *I'll drink to that.*

*

People dine. We eat consciously, looking, tasting, smelling, gauging texture and temperature. We share. We talk. My wife and I seemed to talk differently when there was food between us. We loved restaurants, loved to go out and indulge in the rituals of a shared meal: settling in at our table, scanning the room, dissecting the menu, faking our knowledge of wine. After our orders arrived, we dug in, tasted each other's dishes, critiqued the kitchen's hits and misses. For hours we sipped and chewed.

Do I miss it?

I can tell you that eating nice food and drinking good wine with my wife was the best thing ever. In my memories of dinner together we are enveloped in gilded light that seems to emanate from the table's 720 square inches and the plates of food and glasses of red wine between us. "Communion," "spiritual," "intimacy," come to mind as words to describe these moments.

I can also tell you that chewing was glorious. Swallowing was king. I can remember specific dishes and name the ingredients, but I can no longer tell you what it felt like with a platter of Dungeness crab on the table, what the sight of the orange carapace, the aroma of garlic, ginger, scallion, aroused in me. I can't relate to the old, eater version of me. I don't remember how it feels to be in the presence of food and crave it, want to own it, or how it feels to know its pleasure and anticipate having that pleasure again. I can't relate to that kind of beauty anymore.

I am told that cancer has not changed the essential me. "You're still David," my wife says, tactfully omitting the rest of the sentence: *despite physical damage and eroded quality of life.* As much as I love her for saying that she sees me past the wreckage, I think she's lying, at least a little, because from in here things have changed. Five years without a morsel of food passing between my lips has made me a stranger. Seeing food now doesn't make me hungry; neither does reading about it or thinking about it. Drop a steak in front of me and what am I going to do? Will my mouth water or my blood pressure rise, my pleasure centers spark in my brain? None of this happens, because it can't. A plate of rib eye might as well be behind the glass of a Hall of Mammals diorama.

At home, in my kitchen, I watch the dog eat. She puts her head down and doesn't come up for air until she's emptied the bowl. All day she wants food, and as soon as food arrives, it's gone. She has all that mouth, all those teeth, all that jaw, and she doesn't chew, just mindlessly inhales the premium kibble. It's textbook carnivore behavior, I know, brutal at its core, tear and swallow, take in the largest hunks that won't choke you. All the dog does is ingest a substance for the sole purpose of loading up the gastrointestinal tract: the same joyless thing that I do. Breathe, I would tell her, if I could. Sniff. Relish the chicken-and-liver recipe. Chew.

AMIT MAJMUDAR

Five Famous Asian War Photographs

FROM *Chicago Quarterly Review*

That Nameless Afghan Girl on the Cover of National Geographic

HER EYES ARE green because they had to be green for the photograph to mean anything to us.

Her eyes' intensity, and their hunted look, depend on their greenness (and, admittedly, a slightly disproportionate size relative to the rest of her face). Recessive eye colors are associated by people of European origin with people of European origin, and hence with a fully developed personality. Her face loses the one-sidedness so often read into the Asian both by SEAL teams and college admissions committees: the default Asian, depending again on the eyes, "looks like" either a religious fanatic or an uncreative overachiever. But not an Asian with green eyes; such an Asian is set apart. Green eyes add mystery and a sense of recognition simultaneously. Green eyes, in the setting of this otherwise standard refugee-face, create instant empathy, forcing us to imagine, in this most unexpected place, Someone Like You or Me.

Of course, her green eyes are themselves a recessive trait. They penetrated that far east of Europe, or south of Russia, in the forced injections of genetic material brought about by the British Army's invasion in the 1800s or the Red Army's in the 1900s. Or the Macedonian Army's in the 300s BC, or the United States Army's a couple of millennia later. The girl is nameless; she does not exist, she *represents*. So there is a possibility our empathy for the Afghan female in wartime is being aroused, when we look at this photograph, by the genetic trace of the ancient rape of an Afghan female in wartime.

That Guy in Saigon Who Is About to Get His Brains Blown Out

This is a photograph that has a clear precedent in painting: Goya's *The Third of May 1808,* in which a row of Napoleonic soldiers have lined up firing-squad-style in front of a group of Spanish resisters. The center of the group is that unforgettable man in the white shirt with his arms up. The left sleeve (the right is obstructed by the head of a fellow Spaniard) is the second brightest spot in the painting, slightly brighter than its own light source, the small box that the soldiers have set down to illuminate their targets. The brightest white in the painting belongs to the tiny sliver of the white in his eyes. His eyes are open, and his head is tilted, as if he were pleading, or about to plead. This is a man who might be shot in the next instant — but then again, he might simply be arrested.

The guy in Saigon who is about to have his brains blown out has no arms at all; the twisted front of his shirt would suggest they are bound behind him, but in the photograph, his shoulders taper abruptly into nothingness. He cannot throw his arms up in surrender, and he cannot throw his arms across his face in futile defense against the blast. He is, *literally,* an unarmed man getting shot.

This is only one way in which the photograph improves on Goya. The second aspect is the intimacy. Firing squads *had* to be five to eight strong: military men knew that a few of the soldiers always shot wide on purpose, and that the close-quarters executions were psychologically sustainable only if the soldiers could offload the guilt onto their neighbors in the squad: *his* bullet made the actual kill, not *mine.* Even this pseudo-anonymity takes a toll on soldiers; hard as it may be to believe, the nervous breakdowns of SS men in Polish forests prompted Himmler's shift from conventional, bullet-based massacres to the gas chambers. The Saigon picture is much more intimate, with two men foregrounded.

Goya does not show us the executioners' faces; the Saigon photograph shows us the shooter in profile, and his chin is unexpectedly weak. His weak chin has a clear relationship to the smallness of his pistol. The guy about to get shot is unarmed, but the guy shooting him is unmanned. These details articulate visually a very basic, widely held truth about a soldier who kills a civilian: it is an act of weakness; it marks an inadequate man, who did not deserve to be granted the strength and dominance of the soldier. His weapon has shrunk in his hand, just as he is about to shoot. He is, in a sense, impotent.

The photograph also benefits from the surreal fast-forward effect of the civilian's face. Parts of his face are a few seconds in advance of the rest of the photograph. There seems to be blood about his mouth, and his right eye, closest to the pistol, has already shut.

Douglas MacArthur Wades Ashore in the Philippines

Several photographs were taken of this apparently staged procession from various angles, showing various water levels along the pants and boots, which must have been terribly soggy afterwards. The one that is most widely circulated, however, shows the general and several cronies from the right, facing away from the camera. They are still close enough to the boats for the boats to be seen in the background, and the water is roughly knee level. Most importantly, however, the shore is not included in the frame. MacArthur is *actually wading the Pacific itself,* with the mighty tread of an aroused giant. He is walking from left to right, which on a map would be from east to west — from the Philippines, toward Japan.

The brim of his hat parallels the upward angle of the prow immediately behind him. He is at once the white American avenger and the flagship of the Pacific fleet, the instrument of American vengeance. (The atomic bomb, that supreme *Vergeltungswaffen,* hasn't been built yet.)

To these Americans, treading the ocean floor, the Japanese home islands will be less than sandbars. In the photograph, MacArthur's pants seem dark to the hips, but later photographs of him on the sand prove that he was never more than knee-deep. He was set down very close to this quiet Leyte beach, on an island secured much earlier — by Marines who waded through water at navel level or higher, their rifles over their heads, taking fire.

That Buddhist Monk Who Has Set Himself on Fire

Thich Quang Duc in the fire, like MacArthur in the water, is another photograph that records an act of self-dramatization. The
monk is one shade closer to death than the Saigon civilian with
the gun at his head. He has crossed even farther, but every viewer
"knows" the photographed monk is still alive in the fire; a photograph of a burning corpse would fail to have this effect. It would
become a grotesque or obscene photograph: imagine the Saigon
civilian being photographed *after* his head was blown off. The
photograph would become something unfit for widespread replication. The moment *before* death is dramatic, and the closer the
image can get us to its threshold, the better: too far, and the image
instantly hemorrhages all its drama. This is why none of the truly
famous photographs of war, Asian or otherwise, are photographs
of corpses. Corpses leave us cold.

So the monk freshly burning commands our gaze, while no
photographs of the charred, humanish mound are available. Nor
are there any easily procured photographs of the people sweeping
up the monk's remains. Did locals pour buckets of water over the
blotch? Did they scrub at it? Assuming they didn't get it completely
clean, who pedaled the first bicycle over the black stain?

The Detainee at Abu Ghraib Hooded and Draped in Black

Of the roughly 2,742 photographs that emerged from Abu
Ghraib, 689 involved pornography or simulated sex acts, 540 were
of corpses, 37 involved dogs, and 20 involved a swastika between
the eyes of an American soldier. So a considerably smaller number of images were actually fit for potential widespread replication
in the media. If we subtract images of detainees either naked or
near-naked (although admittedly, the Pyramid of Naked Arabs did
gain some dissemination), it stands to reason that the cover of the
Economist, and countless other websites, should have replicated the
image of the prisoner standing on the crate in the black hood and
black poncho-like drape, with what appear to be wires leading to
his fingers.

Paradoxically, an excessively covered-up figure became emblematic of a torture facility that, in a clear majority of cases, stripped people naked. The arms are held out, which falls just short of the ninety-degree angle required for a parallel with the Crucifixion. The hint is unmistakably there, however. Notice that the image that provokes sympathy for The Muslim dovetails with the central image of Christianity.

Notice also that the face, and indeed the entire head, is *covered* — instead of hinting at Someone Like You or Me by the device of the green eyes, the photograph creates a black box (or bag) inside which we can imagine Someone Like You or Me. Even the smallest visual hint of sweaty black hair or overlong beard or large nose would estrange the viewer instantly; the image's power resides in its multivalence.

The torture scandal, represented most frequently by this photograph, managed to remain a self-examination regarding the *methods,* not the enterprise. Our pity for the enemy could rise to the surface without diminishing our sense of the cause's righteousness. The detainee's black hood and loose-fitted black drape resemble the veil and robe worn by women under the rule of orthodox Muslim males; the black hood, with its cone shape, resembles the white hood worn by members of the Ku Klux Klan. These are the cues that reinforce the detainee's guilt, subconsciously reminding the Western viewer of Arab Muslim misogyny and intolerance.

This photograph and the one of the nameless Afghan girl succeed on the same principle. To move us to empathy, one had to be photographed as a female child with green eyes. The other had to be photographed without a face at all.

RICK MOODY

Notes on Lazarus

FROM *Conjunctions*

WHAT DO WE know about Lazarus of Bethany? He lived thirty years after his resurrection, according to the Eastern Orthodox Church, and in these later years, he was said never to have smiled — for having seen the underworld.

"Jesus wept," it is well known, is the shortest verse in the Bible (John 11:35). This sentence describes Jesus's confrontation with the facts of the death of Lazarus of Bethany. There is reasonable consistency, among the many English translations, on this passage, although I have also found the much inferior "Jesus cried."[1] The strength of the passage is in its brevity. The brevity suggests, embodies, *incarnates* the feeling.

There are thirty-two modern cases (that is, cases here in the twenty-first century) of people whose hearts spontaneously restarted after they had been pronounced dead. A significant number of these deaths are owing to drug overdose. The technical name for a heart restarting without assistance is "auto-resuscitation." It's also called: Lazarus syndrome.

Why is it that Jesus feels such waves of grief at Lazarus's death, when he knows already that resurrecting Lazarus is possible? Is it simply because he feels the loss that the sisters of Lazarus, Mary and Martha of Bethany, also feel? Is the sibling relationship such as to suggest the pain of grief as no other does?

Maybe Jesus weeps so over Lazarus's tomb because he knows what is commenced as a result. According to John 12, the Jews of Jerusalem plotted to kill Lazarus a *second time* immediately after his resurrection (in various later versions of the story I have seen this same intent attributed to the Romans) — because they knew what the miracle would occasion in and around the ministry of Jesus.

The "grave clothes" of Lazarus are the bandages covering both face and body, at the time he climbs up and out of the tomb. He is, more or less, mummified. Covering the face as the body is buried removes what's most human about it; it's a recognition of the absence of self. The body of Lazarus will be evacuated of its spirit while decaying in the tomb. And thus: when Jesus wants to reveal what is human about the resurrected Lazarus, he first has to have the grave clothes removed, meaning uncovering the face.

Why Lazarus? Why Lazarus more so than any other deceased candidate who might have been proposed among those in the Jewish community? Lazarus is selected for his excellent abilities to serve in a heroic narrative capacity. Jesus must have felt as much. Lazarus was the Rosa Parks of the New Testament, in the right place at the right time. We might say that Lazarus had an honest face. Perfect for unveiling.

In John 12, Jesus goes back to Bethany later, to check up on Lazarus, after the miracle, and they have a meal together. Oh to have been a bystander! Did Jesus ask him about the four days in the underworld? Weather? Politics? That year's agricultural yield? "But Lazarus was one of them that sat at the table with him,"[2] according to John. Jesus knows, feels, comprehends what Lazarus saw! And yet the scene goes on to discuss the issue of poverty: "For the poor always ye have with you."[3] Lazarus is scarcely mentioned again at the table and yet always present (apparently without a smile).

Lazarus is not resurrected for all eternity, as Jesus promises the believers after Judgment Day. Lazarus gets his human death sentence commuted only temporarily. His is the kind of miracle that we all long for and are suspicious of, whether religious or irreligious. Lazarus is a revival-tent miracle. (After my sister's death, I remember any number of movies featuring dead characters returning, some of them profound, some of them imbecilic. I watched these films with envy.) I recently heard a sermon about Lazarus that spoke to this point: *Unfortunately I must disappoint those of you who, because of this story, are hoping for the resurrection of your own relatives.*

And what did Lazarus *feel?* The eternal repose, the sense of traveling down and into oblivion, must be reassuring in a way. I think of oblivion as potentially satisfying, lavender-hued. Imagine Lazarus of Bethany living at the edge of the Roman Empire, good friends with some itinerant Jew, some wandering mendicant, whom everyone wanted to put to death. An undeniable rabble-rouser, afoul of the authorities. Dying, for Lazarus, may have been a relief from constant political adversity and physical threats of the Romans, with their superior weaponry and numbers. And then having to be raised up from that repose, to face, again, contemporary political horror?

Or: maybe Lazarus suffered from the considerably rare Cotard's syndrome, in which he believed he was dead already. One can imagine, in the premodern era, when sanitation and medicine were not what they are now, when death was the kingdom at hand, that one could easily come to believe that one already suffered with the condition. And maybe Jesus of Nazareth did what he did (as when Jesus cast out the demons, in Matthew 8:28, by transferring them into a herd of swine) simply to commute psychic suffering. Maybe Jesus abbreviates Lazarus's preoccupation with death. Feels it and commutes it.

Maybe Lazarus was a member of one of those ancient mystery cults, one of those Greco-Roman schools of the forbidden and secret, as with the Dionysian cult, in which *chthonic rites* were prized. In this version of the story, Lazarus perhaps courted the underworld, according to the rigors of the cult, but was somehow lost in the process, and, at the urging of Martha and Mary, Jesus came to call him forth from the religion of error and schism, trying to bring him back to the true path. The weeping would have been, therefore, about the pointlessness of Lazarus's initial sacrifice.

This cultic narrative of Lazarus would nicely anticipate his value to Vodoun spirituality, where Lazarus is subsumed into the wild and anarchic presence known as Papa Legba. Or what about the feast day of San Lázaro in the Afro-Cuban tradition, which conflates the Lazarus of the Gospel of Matthew (a beggar) and the Lazarus of the Gospel of John (the resurrected guy). According to this tradition, San Lázaro was scourged on the flesh before being beheaded in AD 72. This San Lázaro allowed himself to be licked by dogs, too, after being scourged, and is therefore the patron saint of dogs. In Cuba, there is a pilgrimage to Rincón in honor of San Lázaro, to the former leprosarium there. Now they just treat skin diseases in Rincón. There is an insufficiency of lepers.

The insistence in the biblical account on Lazarus reeking upon emerging from the tomb is narratively admirable. In literature descriptions of scent make a passage more indelible. There should be more biblical smells. A friend of mine who was present on the set of Scorsese's film *The Last Temptation of Christ* tells the story of Scorsese attempting to re-create the horrible smell of Lazarus in a filmic way, instructing all the extras and the cast members to recoil visibly when Lazarus came forth, but, according to this same friend, this bit was mostly cut from the finished project. It just didn't look right.

Zeffirelli's *Jesus of Nazareth* (1977) has a nice Lazarus sequence. The white-guy-with-blue-eyes incarnation of Jesus (as played by Robert Powell) feels a bit dated, and there are all those British accents to lend *dramatic seriousness* to the undertaking, but despite the epic qualities of the project, Jesus manages to convey the immensity of his life and sacrifice. In fact, the raising of Lazarus, a miracle heavily outfitted with a retinue of observers, is the depiction wherein I best understand the sequential importance of Lazarus to the unfolding of the ministry of Jesus. This raising of the dead puts in motion Christ's own execution. What's at stake is this: if Jesus can resurrect the enemies of the state, the powerless, the Jews, the slaves, the indigent, then he has to be neutralized. And therefore when Martha and Mary stop Jesus on a footpath among cypresses to tell him of Lazarus's death, you can see a real dread cross the face of Jesus. He knows.

There's a moment of total black screen in the Zeffirelli miniseries, before Lazarus comes forth from his tomb in the hillside. The camera closes in on the blackness inside the tomb entrance, and then goes completely black to the edge of the screen. It's lovely and complete as a suggestion of the nothingness of the underworld. If I could put black screen in this essay I would. Right here.

More resurrections? There's "Po' Lazarus," the work song recorded by Alan Lomax, and made popular after the rerelease of some of the Lomax archive in the '90s, and again in the soundtrack to *O Brother, Where Art Thou?* by Joel and Ethan Coen. In the original (as opposed to the filmic recording), the words to "Po' Lazarus" are improvised by one James Carter with some other inmates who were chopping wood in 1959 at a certain penitentiary in Mississippi. James Carter, who therefore "wrote" the song, when presented with a royalty check after the release of the Coen brothers film (and at a point in his life during which he was working as a shipping clerk), could not remember having sung the song for the original Lomax recording. Couldn't recall it. He had to be convinced. He did attend the Grammy Awards, however, when the soundtrack to the Coen brothers film won album of the year. He died a couple of years later, in a state of redemption.

So adaptable is the Lazarus narrative to poetry and song of African Americans, so easily does it graft onto a civil rights dramatic arc, that it is possible to think of Lazarus as though he must have been black himself; thus, perhaps, an Ethiopian Jew, which would give the whole story an arresting subplot. Because if Lazarus were black, then so were Martha and Mary, his sisters, and there's a much more resonant intersectionality about the raising from the dead. It was to make central to Jesus's ministry the exiled community of *Beta Israel,* those who fled oppression, those who lived further out in the waste. This Lazarus, the black Lazarus, recurs again and again, and his struggle with prejudice and contempt in the Jerusalem of Jesus's ministry makes his narrative that much more lasting. Jesus, after the raising from the dead, goes to have dinner with the Beta Israel, with the Africans.

Terry Callier's powerful and moving song "Lazarus Man" finds Lazarus with a fever to narrate his journey ("Since he bid me to rise / I ain't been to sleep!").[4] Callier, an African American folk singer from Chicago who made a number of recordings in the '70s, completely dropped out of the music business, only to be rediscovered by British deejays (and Beth Orton) in the '90s, and he makes of Lazarus an allegory for renewal, both in the fact of his singing about Lazarus and in the words of his composition.

Callier's Lazarus, by inference, is African or African American, too, and it's interesting to think of the Lazarus narrative repurposed to describe the struggles of the disenfranchised (as the Jews themselves were in the Holy Land of Lazarus's own time). Callier's two chords, here, are modal like Miles Davis and John Coltrane ("Lazarus Man" feels closely related to Coltrane's "India"), so the song also situates Lazarus in the heroic liberation of jazz, the kind of music they play at New Orleans funerals: elegiac, tragicomic, mnemonic, celebratory, deep.

Terry Callier's Lazarus, moreover, seems to have something in common with the outlandish Provençal tradition in which Lazarus (and his sisters Mary and Martha) are put out to sea by hostile Jews, to drift all the way to Provence, where Lazarus becomes bishop of Marseille, after which he is put to death (he always dies eventually) during the persecutions associated with the reign of Domitian. In this French tall-tale, his head was preserved.

The Marseille narrative, which gets taken up and embellished by French believers of the medieval period, is Gnostic in the way it ties up loose ends (the Mary in the French Lazarus story is Mary Magdalene, even though there's no evidence for this; and Lazarus is a thief, like Barabbas, who was crucified next to Jesus of Nazareth). The Marseille narrative indicates that Lazarus is one of those pieces of the New Testament that is so powerful that people want to claim it, to manipulate its particulars, to bind up its disparate material. They want to make the story so plastic that it might, somehow, continue to grow, right before our eyes.

In the Eastern Orthodox tradition, Lazarus became a bishop in Cyprus. He may or may not have been appointed to the post by the Virgin Mary herself.

Henri Cole's poem "Hens" deals with a Lazarus, a pullet called Lazarus.[5] Cole's singular gift is for a richness of metaphor in which human struggle and human longing constantly appear recast into things observed in nature, and accordingly in the protagonist hen we feel both Lazarus's raising anew, in tragicomic form, a figure of sport, an entrée, or a layer of eggs. As in Cole's work elsewhere, the metaphorical layering is so dense that Lazarus's incarnations shimmer multiply before us at first. And some of these layers are very funny.

At least until Cole's Petrarchan turn in the sixth line of this pellucid sonnet-like form, when again Lazarus, the chicken, bereft of smile, comes face to face with the particulars of suffering and nonbeing: "Last spring an intruder murdered her sisters and left her / garroted in the coop."[6] The dread never far off, a muscular, exceedingly sober gaze at the facts of the world, where, as Cole puts it, anguish is inevitable and universal. Maybe, in this incarnation of Lazarus, his story tells a precisely human truth: that in the cycle of death and resurrection there is *eternal recurrence* of suffering.

Schubert never finished his oratorio about Lazarus.

Did you know that the site of Lazarus's tomb is contested? Like many places in and around the Holy City, it has been contested for thousands of years. There is a tomb, now underneath a mosque, the al-Uzair, which the Muslims sealed off. It was sealed off, that is, until the Franciscans cut a different entrance into the tomb. None can say for certain if it's the *actual* tomb of Lazarus or not, of course, but there have been churches in the area since the fourth century. It is more exactly an exemplary tomb from the days of the early church, a site plausible, and — because plausible — spooky. It is more exemplary than actual. The tomb, originally, was connected to Lazarus's house, or so it is said. He was buried right next to his house.

In "Dig, Lazarus, Dig!!!,"[7] Nick Cave (and his Bad Seeds) reduce Lazarus (nicknamed Larry in the verses) to a rock-and-roll drug adept, a hallucinating addict, a sort of fin de siècle decadent trying to achieve satori (I'm using the Beat terminology) through deformation of the senses, and this, in the chorus — "Dig yourself, Lazarus, dig yourself back in that hole" — indicates the coming-awake of Lazarus, in which Lazarus, realizing the enormity of his resurrection, the fearsome responsibility of it, tries to return to the underworld. It's more comfortable down there.

I sort of dislike this song. It's as if Nick Cave is the Susan Sontag of contemporary music: a popularizer of avant-gardes more trenchant elsewhere. The secret weapon of the Bad Seeds, once upon a time, was Blixa Bargeld, a founding member of the Bad Seeds (and lead guitarist at one point), and former member of Einstürzende Neubaten, whose inability was his mastery, and who gave the Bad Seeds a genuinely unpredictable element. The removal of Bargeld (and Mick Harvey) made the band sort of a pop band, the way I see it, and Cave tried to resist this transition into more palatable and socially acceptable material by making the *Grinderman* album (a garage-rock side project), after which came *Dig, Lazarus, Dig!!!,* somewhat in imitation of the *Grinderman* sound. It's a simulated punk rock album, therefore, and the song "Dig, Lazarus, Dig!!!" is obviously influenced by New York punk. When Cave, on "Lazarus," doesn't sound like Mark E. Smith of the Fall, he sounds a bit like Richard Hell (of the Voidoids), and the lyrics allude to New York (and San Francisco), and you know he means the drugs and chaos, the energy, the *Todestrieb* of punk.

It would all seem like self-mythologizing and lyrical excess of the kind that makes for great performance, but does not withstand close lyrical scrutiny. And yet notwithstanding this simulation of urgency Cave has made plangent and memorable remarks about the Lazarus of Bethany: "Ever since I can remember hearing the Lazarus story, when I was a kid, you know, back in church, I was disturbed and worried by it. Traumatized, actually. We are all, of course, in awe of the greatest of Christ's miracles — raising a man from the dead — but I couldn't help but wonder how Lazarus *felt* about it. As a child it gave me the creeps, to be honest."[8] "Traumatizing" is a perfect word for the Lazarus story, and the "actually" that comes after it here gives that beleaguered adverb, "actually," a force that it doesn't ordinarily have.

And so it becomes clear why there are three exclamation points in the title of Nick Cave's Lazarus song, when one would clearly do the job reliably: they are Trinitarian.

The other way that Cave gives us access to the Lazarus story is through Cave's son, Arthur. His son, as is well known now, fell to his death in Brighton, England, in 2015, and on *Skeleton Tree*, his recent album of compositions mostly written before Arthur's passing, but recorded after, you can feel the haunting of Arthur everywhere. (The jacket of *Skeleton Tree* is the same color as Zeffirelli's black screen.) "Jesus Alone," the first track on *Skeleton Key*, is where you feel acutely the Jesus of Nazareth who weeps over Lazarus's grave.[9] Jesus wept. Jesus wept. Jesus began to cry. Jesus started crying. Jesus wept. And Jesus wept. Jesus cried. Jesus wept. And at this Jesus wept. Jesus burst into tears. Jesus wept. Jesus wept. Jesus wept.

"With my voice I am calling you"[10] is the refrain of "Jesus Alone," and it's both Cave trying to call to Arthur across the trauma of loss, and it's Jesus alone, without the comfort of the divine, in dread of the human part of his mission, aggrieved by the loss of Lazarus, in the grief of a loss of a beloved friend, in the dread of knowing the numinous, in the knowledge of what comes next, his own sacrifice, when, after the dinner with the resurrected Lazarus of Bethany, he must enter the city of Jerusalem and proceed, well, to Golgotha.

"Evidently, this was needed,"[11] Franz Wright says of Lazarus, in a sort of a free translation of a poem by Rilke, "The Raising of Lazarus," perhaps a rehabilitation of a fragment of Rilke, a fragment that could not be completed to anyone's satisfaction, because looking accurately upon Lazarus is to be "traumatized," as Cave says, into fragmentation and silence, into failure. To know what Lazarus knew is to be *traumatized*. The antecedent of "this" in Wright's "Evidently, this was needed" is purposefully vague. The passivity of the sentence is exactly the kind of German abstraction that one

associates with Rilke, and the use of "evidently" is funny and sly, because in Wright's bloodcurdling rendering of Rilke's Lazarus, it's
all about *proof*, all evidentiary. As in the next line: "Because people
need / to be screamed at with proof."

Wright's account of the story is long on the horrors of the
scene, garish physical details, and all from the vantage point of the
Nazarene. Mary is a prostitute (evidently Wright is from Provence,
where all the Marys and all the Lazaruses are one), and all who
gather for the miracle are "Breughelian grotesques." It's an "on-
tological horrorshow," and we feel acutely Jesus preparing for his
doom (and glory), as he raises Lazarus, and removes the burial
garb. But what we don't get is much of Lazarus himself. He's "the
one young man"[12] who stoops at the entrance of the grave, coming
forth. The fact of the poem, its reiteration of Rilke, its apparent
long journey to completion, the sense of teetering on composi-
tional unworthiness, is an indication that it's Lazarus we're dealing
with. Lazarus is about the *telling* of Lazarus, where the dread and
completion shimmer just out of reach.

Or, *evidently*, what is needed is a transit across a dialectical pairing, a Hegelian opposition, life and death, a way to render the
longing of the one for the other, and: I wrote these lines after
spending time by the deathbed of a loved one, an ebbing out of
life, and what I found in the five days before and the two days
after that shimmering just out of reach, that marriage of particle
and wave, was not a dialectical pairing, a Hegelian opposition,
but rather an incremental development, in which self is pitted,
mottled, interstitial, but breath continues, and then, after breath,
a hovering of presence in the absence, as if the other who was no
longer was there again, and as I write these lines I can feel her
with me, inscribed in my inscriptions. I write these lines for her.
A death and not-death in language, a dissemination of fragments,
a broadcasting of residuary self, a hovering into this draft. There
are some ten minutes after medical death when the brain is still
responsive to stimuli, in a lavender-hued journey back and forth
across the entranceway to the next place of the black screen.

Caravaggio's *Raising of Lazarus*, which is in Sicily, where it was
painted by Caravaggio after fleeing Malta because of *legal problems*, has stories orbiting around it nearly as fanciful as those orbiting around Lazarus himself: for example, that he had a body
exhumed in order to paint Lazarus himself, and that there was a

prior version of the painting, which Caravaggio himself destroyed owing to criticism that he did not like. He got an enormous commission for the painting, but some of it may have been finished by assistants nonetheless, and it wants for the intense drama of other paintings by the master of high contrast. The arrangement of characters is powerful, though, with the women gathered around Lazarus's head. Almost exactly like a deposition. Christ looks extremely commanding, not the doubter that he would perhaps have been about the miracle of Lazarus. And though he *looks* commanding, Christ as depicted is just a backward version of a drawing Caravaggio previously used in *The Calling of St. Matthew.* As if one of the aspects of the story of Lazarus is that it features, among its reiterations, auto-plagiarism.

Rembrandt's *Raising of Lazarus,* from just fifteen or twenty years after Caravaggio's, is quite a bit more unsettling. I can't tell if it's because I have already gazed at length on Rembrandt's *Anatomy Lesson of Dr. Nicolaes Tulp* (1632), which has a cadaver in it, and which has so much intensity. (They only permitted one dissection a year in Amsterdam, and it was always a criminal, in this case it was Aris Kindt, a thief who had been executed the day before, a Barabbas character, if you like, and this you would know if you were to read *The Rings of Saturn* by Sebald, which discusses with great urgency this anatomy painting.) The arms seem to be on backward on the cadaver's body, and there's a shadow over the cadaver's face, which is the shadow of death, I believe, and there's something very claustrophobic about the whole. The mystery of death, the moment in which the soul flickers out of the body, is on display here.

Should it be impossible or unlikely that Rembrandt's *Anatomy Lesson of Dr. Nicolaes Tulp* could somehow have influenced his *Raising of Lazarus,* which was painted *before* the image of Tulp? In the uncanny event horizon of Lazarus, apparently it's not impossible at all, because failure, plagiary, repetition compulsion, and nonlinear time could all easily be coincident with a raising from the dead. Rembrandt's *Lazarus* trembles with unearthly lantern light from the left-hand margin, which shrouds Martha's face, and Lazarus, truly ghostly in white and gray, is given the vast majority of the pictorial space to be climbing up and out of the tomb, like an emissary from the underworld. It's as if the lessons of death, the way death is both absent and present, and most present when most absent, are catalyzed here for Rembrandt, and he keeps going back to them with the later anatomy lessons, such that his interpretation of Lazarus is affected by his later collision with Aris Kindt.

Both Giotto and Duccio painted Lazarus in their pre-perspectival, medieval way. (The bleached, nearly cubist backdrop of Duccio suggests the landscape of Zeffirelli's *Jesus of Nazareth.*)

I am so pained by "Lady Lazarus," by Plath, that I don't really know how to include it here, while giving over to it the confessional intensity that it has, the legacy of it, the importance of it to poetry by women and men. There are things about this poem that I find impossible to describe now, even as I admire it, and that is because everything about "Lady Lazarus" hurts so lastingly that it is hard to reread. It's a raw, lacerating disquiet that hovers about the poem. It is nearly vengeful, or perhaps "nearly" is unwarranted here. The threats of self-slaughter in its initial lines were ultimately successful, we all know, and that makes it seem less boastful and more the occasion for woe, and sympathy, and dread. Which is how we know that its allegorical appropriation of Lazarus is just. I dread turning the recto and arriving at this poem. And yet Plath, the suicide, the one-woman mystery cult of self-sacrifice, is raised again in the popularity of *Ariel.* In the literary sense, she is raised again, ever victorious in the matter of eternal repose.

Perfectly articulated, with respect to Lazarus, are these lines from Evie Shockley's poem about Barack Obama's (first) inauguration:

> ask lazarus about miracles:
> the hard part comes afterwards.

Ben Okri's memorable, singular, highly original novel *The Famished Road* is narrated by a character named Azaro — or at least that is the name he goes by, though his parents originally named him Lazarus. Azaro is an *abiku,* a spirit child, and the long, wonderful opening of *The Famished Road* concerns the many times the spirit world refuses to allow Azaro to be completely born. Thereafter, in the years of his childhood, he continually fends off spirit manifestations around the compound where he lives, and especially in the bar of his neighbor Madame Koto.

Okri's novel is often compared to Latin American magical realism, but in no way does this work feel reducible to this well-traveled subgeneric distinction. On the contrary, *The Famished Road* teems with its African spirits, even as, as Ben Okri has noted, it has some Western forbears as well. Azaro himself has Lazarus hovering albatross-like over his head, Lazarus's time in the underworld, and when Azaro goes *walking*, impulsively, in the Nigerian bush, as he does to his parents' chagrin, unfailingly mixing it up with the menace of the spirit realm, we can feel the incarnation of Lazarus in him, the Pan-African Lazarus.

Of course, there are many other improvisations upon the story and person of Lazarus. I haven't mentioned Van Gogh, or Chagall, or the episode of *Dr. Who* that alludes to Lazarus, or some software program named after him, or the prog-rock anthem by Porcupine Tree. I haven't mentioned Aleksandar Hemon's *Lazarus Project*, a novel that means to treat of a Jewish immigrant (Lazarus Averbuch) killed in Chicago in 1908, but which then goes further back to speak of the Lazarus of Bethany we are discussing here. I haven't mentioned a really astonishing sculpture of him by Sir Jacob Epstein, at New College, Oxford. There are more profane examples of our inability to stop talking about him. This is not an exhaustive list.

Yet I cannot stop adding to the list about Lazarus, which I have been keeping for over a year now, as though the intention to write about Lazarus is an analogy of his rebirth, and whenever I say I'm not going to write about a certain author or artist or filmmaker who has alluded to Lazarus I find myself going back and doing exactly that, and somehow adding this previously suppressed citation to the list. Lazarus calls to me and I answer his call.

And, so: David Bowie's "Lazarus," from *Blackstar,* his last album, combines different strata of meaning about Lazarus, and fuses them together. The song "Lazarus" is stately and slow-moving, it is the development of change, with fragments of melody on sax and guitar emerging out of a dirge of bass and drums. The first verse is narrated by a Lazarus-like figure from heaven and indicates some of the contradictions of a heavenly repose ("Look up here, I'm in heaven / I've got scars that can't be seen").[13] But the second verse seems to frame "up here" more as a place of isolation, perhaps the address of fame, and of danger ("I'm so high it makes my brain whirl"), which, in the significantly heartrending video for the song, is the space of the clinic, the space of illness, the place of physical destitution, like Lazarus's grave.

Then the song flowers into some sort of chorus/bridge, which

only occurs once (for such a rhythmically straightforward song it
is structurally rather odd and fragmentary), of the kind, in the
Bowie catalog, that invites biographical speculation. It's never
clear whether this song is *actually* autobiographical, or just has the
veneer thereof. What does "Then I used up all my money / I was
looking for your ass"[14] mean? The easiest interpretation of Bowie's
"Lazarus" would be that it articulates Bowie's feelings after his onstage heart attack of 2004. He did brush up against mortality then.
But the video for "Lazarus," with its hospital imagery, seems more
to describe the mortality of Bowie's later battle with cancer. It
transcends illness by celebrating illness, by speaking openly from
within the clinic.[15]

You could also argue that the song has a much deeper purpose.
You could argue that its purpose is simply to describe in modern
parlance Lazarus, the guy who died and who was raised from the
dead, in all his complexity, in his death and nondeath, with all the
mixed emotions, the awe and confusion and dread and trauma,
that attend upon the Lazarus story. The "Lazarus" video is rich
with irony, and the "I'll be free" out-chorus of the song seems especially ironic, and meant to convey just the opposite sentiment.
Freedom and nonbeing drawing near to one another.

In Bowie's portrayal of Lazarus, he's the character who occasions irony, as if irony is a thing that is best understood by those
who have experienced death, as if irony is the inevitable style of
those who have been to the other side, those who have come back
to tell of it, like Virgil and Dante. (I'm betting Tiresias understood
irony, having been both woman and man.)

David Constantine's remarkable poetical sequence "Lazarus to
Christ, Christ to Lazarus" goes to similar lengths in seeing into
Lazarus's complex impressions of his heroic journey. I admit that
I also really love the voice of Christ here, but I also feel I *know* that
Christly dramatic reconstruction — full of anxiety about his own
resurrection, given to complaint about being abandoned by the
apostles. I can get to that impersonation of Jesus, but Lazarus's
voice is more complex, because more surprising:

> What I mutter in nightmare
> I believe you lie awake to overhear.

This beautiful perception gets us much closer to the fearsome
mystery of Lazarus and nonbeing. Why is it that we need a re-

deemer, you ask? What is it about this trudge through the abattoir of the contemporary, with its stringy fibers of gristle dangling everywhere, that so leads the human heart to need a redeemer? It's what Lazarus said, it's what he mutters in nightmare, it's the black screen from the Zeffirelli, it's nonbeing.

Jesus of Nazareth is supposed to have descended into Hell, or to have *harrowed* Hell, during the period between the Crucifixion and the Resurrection, weeks after Lazarus was raised, but there's almost no scriptural support for the trip. There are sermons about it from the second century, and there are epistles that mention it or allude to it, during the period of the early church, but there is no real scriptural support. Why did he have to do it? Because all *humans* have to do it, experience death and the afterlife and irony and trauma, death and not-death, the black screen. Jesus of Nazareth was, lest we forget, one of us, and so he experienced what we experience.

Did Jesus know what Lazarus knew? Did Lazarus tell him about it at their dinner? And what does Lazarus tell us about death, *in the end?* If he could talk to us now, in our tongue, what would he say? That death is not the end, that life is not the end, that life is in the oneiric realm, full of deaths and endings that are commuted into beginnings, and beginnings that become endings, and that the feelings one has about all of this are of loss, and trauma, and regret, and humility? About what Lazarus knew, one can only weep.

Or: Lazarus didn't smile, and got decapitated for this and for other crimes, scourged, for the traces of his story, for the retelling of his story, for the implications of his story, for being a bystander to Christ's ministry. And in his bearing witness, again and again he is reborn for us to retell.

Notes

1. Here's a good list of translations of John 11:35: https://www.bible gateway.com/verse/en/John%2011:35. The International Standard Version gives "Jesus burst into tears."
2. Ibid., KJ, John 12:2.
3. Ibid., John 12:8.
4. Terry Callier, *TimePeace* (1998, Talkin' Loud Classics).
5. http://www.theatlantic.com/magazine/archive/2009/10/hens/ 307670/.
6. Ibid.
7. Mute Records, 2008.

8. https://en.wikipedia.org/wiki/Dig,_Lazarus,_Dig!!! (italics mine).

9. And maybe there is a mystery cult aspect to Arthur's death, as well, as it is said in the press that he may have taken LSD before his fall. "Jesus Alone," therefore, really conjures this reading of Jesus, bereft and uncomprehending, at the advent of Lazarus's death.

10. Nick Cave and the Bad Seeds, *Skeleton Key* (Mute Records, 2016).

11. https://www.poetryfoundation.org/poetrymagazine/poems/detail/ 58345.

12. The word choice here is powerful, because "young man" (*neaniskos*, in Greek) is used in the Gospel of Mark, and, elsewhere, in the forged or Gnostic *Secret Gospel of Mark* to indicate a character, not named Lazarus, raised from the dead by Jesus, and with whom Jesus may be in love. They even, it seems, spend a night together. "Jesus wept," in this case, would have much deeper implications. This thoroughly Gnostic Lazarus might be even more revolutionary than the canonical one.

13. *Blackstar* (ISO Records, 2016).

14. Ibid.

15. And this corresponds with the most recent timeline of *Blackstar*, namely, that Bowie didn't know that his cancer was untreatable until after the album was recorded. In fact, apparently Bowie didn't even know his cancer was terminal until he began filming the video for "Lazarus."

TIMOTHY O'KEEFE

You Are the Phenomenology

FROM *The Massachusetts Review*

IMAGINE THAT YOU'RE an insatiable reader — poetry, fiction, philosophy, plays, history, noir, CNF, DIY, cookbooks, travelogues, comic books, blogs, clickbait scrolling ad infinitum. Reading for you is no mere habit and, on some level, not even a proper activity, but a kind of experiential osmosis that positions language as primary and generative in the world to which it refers. You've always been struck by the elegance of that paradox, its call for exploration. One by-product of reading this way is that you've acquired a prodigious vocabulary. That's natural enough (and can't be helped), but another consequence that appeared somewhere in the osmotic flux is your desire to focus and channel it all toward some aesthetic end. Therein lies the first gauntlet.

Beyond that, it gets worse. Over the many years of your less abstracted moods, you've become aware of the alchemical effect that language can have on otherwise normal social situations. And this makes you think back on the times you've laughed too loudly, flirted too earnestly, or consigned yourself to brazen silences, the family all around and shooting looks over the holiday roast as you stare into your little well of gravy. However, after a stint of writing and reflection, you do find that you'd like to share your outlook with a friend, someone who's both similar and dissimilar to you, and this makes sense, feels right, since you've always envisioned the whole literary enterprise to be, at bottom, a collaborative enterprise, one that fosters a palpable boon in our understanding of what it means to be human. This, but also a vast, interpretive mire with countless systems of semantic ambiguity whose very purpose seems to be, at times, the enforcement of some totalizing

Ambiguity that brooks no definitive claims, no true resting places. So — this, in light of that — there you are, now, ready to listen and be listened to. It's an afternoon in mid-October. Brisk with a bit of tooth. You entered the café through a side door and quickly surveyed the room. You found your way to the back, made your salutations, shed your coat, and settled into the corner booth. Your interlocutor begins.

She is a classically trained singer and she speaks with a singer's reserve, one that knows and fears the strain of full-throatedness. She wears a green scarf patterned with gilt parrots. It is easy and safe to look at, but you can't just stare at her collarbone and expect to set a tone of candor and sensitivity. You must look up, at her. You must make eye contact — essential and intricate, concrete and wildly suggestive, the most exacting of all listening skills. Furthermore, your eye contact must be deployed in discrete intervals, and these intervals need to be tailored to your specific interlocutor, the gravity of the subjects under discussion, the nature of your relationship with said interlocutor, the circumstances of the meeting, the time of day, the temperature, the barometric pressure, the kind of week she seems to be having, the kind of week you seem to be having, and please be apprised that all of these variables are chain-linked and coordinated, which means none of them can be calculated before the conversation takes the shape of its unique moment, which means you're going to have to be optically nimble and vigilant and precise if you want what you've always thought of as your *listening practice* to shine through in a way that makes your interlocutor feel completely at ease and unsuspecting of the terrible demands that listening places on you and, frankly, anyone who's mindful of it. So, try to act natural. Sit straight but don't be stiff. Nod your head but not continuously — you're not a guidance counselor. Don't cross your arms against your chest — that expresses doubt, mistrust — and don't rest your folded hands against your belly — that's smug and creepy and paternal. Best to keep your hands on the table. Palms down, of course. If you've got grit under your fingernails, make soft fists. If not, you can let your fingers stretch out a bit, but loosely and with a curve at the knuckle. Keep them still but not statuesque, and don't fuss with the sugar packets.

Now your interlocutor has finished talking. Her face is slightly flushed, her eyes bluer than before, and her elbows are on the table with one hand supporting her chin. You have been good, you can see it for yourself — she turns to you in a pose of quiet relief and gives a half smile. Her green scarf nearly glows. It is your turn to speak. Imagine, now, that your interlocutor is an exquisite listener, the one from whom you absorbed, without even trying (at least at first), all the best attributes of your listening practice, and the one from whom, you must admit, you still have much to learn. The silent ball is in her court, and so you must begin. Of course you can't just say any rote thing that comes to mind in order to observe her listening prowess and further hone your own practice. You have to reciprocate, you want to reciprocate, and in order to do that, you have to give yourself fully to the speaking act, the one that will convince your interlocutor of the comfort and vulnerability that she has engendered in you, the one that will engender in her those intangible listening responses that you have yet to learn. But, again, make it natural or else it won't work. Not only will it (the conversation) not work, but its breakdown will introduce a rupture in the otherwise seamless, symbiotic rapport that you've both enjoyed, on and off, for years. Now, in the intervening moments that feel impossibly dilated, you find that you don't have an appropriate response to or segue from your interlocutor's speech act, which was compelling and honest and emotionally rich — so much so that it now seems to retreat into its own hermetic bastion, a kind of set piece that wants nothing more than to be acknowledged from a respectful distance. And this is no surprise — after all, your interlocutor is also a superlative orator, one who can modulate between public and private discourses and, more importantly, one who understands that in order to do the work of good listening, one must have something of significant scope and clarity to latch onto, that one simply cannot exercise the entire complex of gestures, looks, and body language on the topic of celebrity divorces or unseasonable weather. So you begin. It's a tentative maundering at first, but your interlocutor is patient. She is aware of her own towering presence and the difficulty of each sea-level beginning. Slowly the scale is laid, the blueprint is drawn, and your words start to amass and careen and conjoin within their centrifugal focus. You are watching her watch you. She blinks almost when you blink. She chuckles spontaneously. You both nod for a refill of coffee, and in this, even your silences agree. The sentences come easily now, fluidly, and you start to experience a kind of insular hearing whereby your words pass through a filter that is so deft and responsive that it doesn't feel like a filter at all. It feels like some ideal replica of you, thinking and talking outside of itself but also from deeply within. You can hear what you say before you say it. You can hear your own voice translating itself into itself. It is going well, isn't it. Yes, it is, she says in a look that holds you for an extra second, not quite erotic though it's hard to imagine a half measure, and that's what makes it perfect. Yes, it is going well.

But now, just when you've settled into the warmth of her reception, you begin to hear a glitch in the dark machinery of your own speech, and this glitch appears in its outermost mechanism — the fact that you yourself are also an external listener of the things you say. What you've been saying amounts to a diatribe against familial duty, which, once you've heard its outward form, you realize is just a conceptually souped-up lament against your older brother for snapping on you last July and later refusing to apologize. Granted, the causal chain leading up to that event is rife with subtext and interpretive blind spots that are themselves delicate and involuted, but let's face it: it's all tediously familiar to pretty much anyone who has active sibling relationships into adulthood. Somewhere along the way, your post-filter-not-yet-external voice has shifted gears or direction or you're not sure what, but it's no longer refining and pacing your own speech act; no, it now seems to imbue the words with a mild sneer, an ironic twang, barely noticeable at first, but you can feel it accelerating and you start to panic at the thought that your internal filter, which just a minute ago seemed a humble and apt servant, has somehow remapped its own circuitry and now threatens to undermine not just your interlocutor's nascent belief that *things are indeed going very well* (as her right hand tucked a lock of hair behind her ear and she dragged her fingertips lightly along her neck, so lightly that you could feel your pinkie ghosting its response along the lip of the creamer), but also your own long-standing conviction that language is the great arbiter of the world, and by harnessing it, we can perform our histories, actuate our futures, and finally concede that so much of the rest is not ours to navigate. Language as the one and the many, the first and the last, the very presence we live through — here but also distantly, like the mirage of water on a summer highway. Is its vanishing the same for everyone, you've often wondered, or is each person subject to a singular distance? No doubt you've met many people and some of them also work their language like a chisel struck by the mallet of their will, but you also get the feeling that some people (maybe even a lot of people) use their presence to assert not just the unimpeachable sharpness of their chisel's edge, but the apparent rectitude of their character for having merely uttered the words. This is to say: a lot of people stake their language to a site of moral power and then coyly invite you to stop by and make yourself at home as if their insignia weren't emblazoned on every wall and threshold.

You know you've met these people, and you know others have met them too. Maybe with even greater aversion. (Over the years, you've come to believe that education is, in its broadest sense, the granting of permission to speak your will and to offer presence, without the fear of being rendered invisible. Not a corpus of knowledge, not a skill set, and certainly not a license to grandstand or pontificate, but a steady belief in the legitimacy of one's identity. You've come to realize that this is *your* site of power — the one you've coveted and valorized, the one whose precincts have, in return, sheltered and galvanized you, and even now, as the internal voice transmutes into an externalizing self, you can feel another stake thrust into the ground, no matter if the ground now feels as though it's turning to sand. This is the sinking feeling you feel — the awareness that some presences may inevitably negate others, that negation is surely the worst aggression one can inflict on another, that every chisel defaces before it creates. Nonetheless, you can't deny that you are proud of your pedigreed education, not for the velvet on your doctoral robes or the perks of your alumni credit card, but because it took quite a bit of rerouting and recalibration for any of that to appear among your possible horizons, and the fact that you accomplished this first, formative task says more about you than any transcript ever will. This is a thought you like to think, and in a few cavalier moments, you've actually spoken it aloud. You're not proud of those moments, though you can't say you wholly regret them either.) You can now feel your face taking color, you feel the opposite of invisible, and so you pause, catch the server's attention, and order an iced tea. Moments later, it arrives having already sweated through the glass.

And so, no, not *maybe* — the more you think about it — but *probably:* those who wield language from a site of moral power are very probably met by others with greater aversion than you yourself have shown. Or, now, as you think harder and closer and come to the real crux of things, you-can-absolutely-bet-your-ass-on-it with much greater aversion. And so the likelihood that you are less repulsed by these people than others are — does this make you one of them, regardless of the site to which you pledge your allegiance? No, you think, that's a bit presumptuous, self-flagellating, there are some logical steps missing there, etc., but might it not mean that you are inclined toward using language in this way, as a kind of lexical producer? Or is this unpleasant solidarity yet more evidence for your savvy as a lexical consumer — that your empathy is capacious enough to include those whom you consider dangerous and manipulative bloviators of public opinion? Maybe. But, then again, to even begin to think *your empathy is capacious enough* — doesn't that smack of a narcissistic posturing that would preclude any sincere attempt to absorb the world from someone else's less grandiloquent station? Perhaps the obvious conclusion is to cut out the prolix bullshit and just talk about stuff in a way that (A) others can readily apprehend and (B) doesn't make you sound like the aloof, self-satisfied intellectual that you are dead-set against. To state the big questions in simplest terms — isn't that the goal? And yet, a deep-seated part of you — the same part that urged you toward a liberal arts education and an ecumenical worldview and a masochistic work ethic and the embrace of all things strange and mundane — this part senses that many issues have no denominator that is truly common to all parties involved. This part of you knows that the aforementioned Ambiguity of words and the structures they create is often irreducible, and while we may agree that this is axiomatic, the way of the world, not much doing there, etc., we still have the Herculean task of reconciling the innumerable lenses through which people perceive the world around them and inject their presence within it. And so, after much attentive listening, if your interlocutor now says that a rectangle defines some situation that you've always considered octagonal (so to speak), what's the use of debating how it fits into the larger, mosaic whole? Can we even assume that such a whole exists when the foundation often appears not just in rubble, but in multiform rubble? If the whole is merely the sum of contiguous experience, if each of us is confined to some half-swept corner of isolated consciousness — *where the dogs go on with their doggy life,* where the chance that any two thought-vectors meet head-on is roughly equivalent to the odds that two randomly chosen cars will arrive at the same remote crossroads at exactly the same day and hour and instance of their lifetime trajectories — then what was the point of all that unquenchable reading?

You've now spoken at length, and it is very hard to map an emotional hierarchy in the things you've said, never mind trace the desultory path between those things. And yet you can't shake the feeling that your internal filter has done right, that this is how things *are*, that your inability to encapsulate even the minor trials of everyday life says something crucial about the experience of language and what it really means to be present with others. Not to mention what it says about your so-called site of power. Your server brings the bill on a metal dish. He has drawn a smiley face at the bottom and discreetly covered the total with two peppermints. You now feel clear and cleared, and you begin to wonder if there is such a thing as transparency that is pure enough to render one invisible and hypervisible at the same time, a polestar that offers opposite roads out of the wilderness — both begin on mossy escarpments that descend into forest, both wend through shade flowers and waving boughs, both are mottled in the light and dark patches they've passed through when they open, at last, as all things must open, on the same native valley. You look up, as if through trees, and find that your interlocutor is staring right at you, unblinking. You have never seen her in this face. It is taut at the edges, tinged with gray, and there's a vague contortion to it, not discernible in any one feature but there all the same — a synthetic quality that soaks through her expression as if she were wearing a mask, or as if she were a palimpsest, or as if she had lived and died long ago and been undertaken and very carefully arranged. The mark of your valley is wiped clean off the map. Here, your hands regain their clamminess. Your undershirt sticks to your back. Some realities never leave the body. They are distorted, subsumed, and they are yours alone. How to speak to them, as they are. How to bridge them, when they themselves are the bridging. She does not say, and you cannot think how she would. The parrots on her scarf have alighted and will not turn away.

Your interlocutor stands up and excuses herself to the restroom, palms pressing the sides of her skirt. You watch her weave through the tightly arranged tables, and for the first time, you notice that the café is loud and bustling and indifferent. She knocks on the restroom door, disappears inside, and you are now alone in a throng of silverware and water glasses. You wonder why it is so, why it must be so. Then you wonder why the thought had never occurred, until now, that although you have seen wild animals along the highway, in a drought summer, making their cautious approach, bemused at the streaks of fatal cars that race toward latter distances, distance being itself the promise of more — perhaps you were wrong when you thought they had come to cross over. Perhaps this is the mirage they had sought. You can see them there in great masses, crowding the hot asphalt, predator and prey alike, stoic and noble. And perhaps, as if cued by some invisible conductor, something miraculous will happen: the animals will bow their heads together, and they will drink.

In Search of Fear

FROM *Lapham's Quarterly*

A VOID LIKE that is terrifying. Prisoner of a morsel of space, you will struggle desperately against occult elements: the absence of matter, the smell of balance, vertigo from all sides, and the dark desire to return to the ground, even to fall. This dizziness is the drama of high-wire walking, but that is not what I am afraid of.

After long hours of training for a walk, a moment comes when there are no more difficulties. It is at this moment that many have perished. But in this moment I am also not afraid.

If an exercise resists me during rehearsal, and if it continues to do so a little more each day, to the point of becoming untenable, I prepare a substitute exercise — in case panic grabs me during a performance. I approach it slyly, surreptitiously. But I always want to persist, to feel the pride of conquering it. In spite of that, I sometimes give up the struggle. But I do so without any fear. I am never afraid on the wire. I am too busy.

But you are afraid of something. I can hear it in your voice. What is it?

Sometimes the sky grows dark around the wire, the wind rises, the cable gets cold, the audience becomes worried. At those moments I hear fear screaming at me.

To imagine that one evening I will have to give up the wire, that I will have to say, "I was afraid, I met Holy Fear, it invaded me and sucked my blood" — I, the fragile walker of wires, the tiniest of men, will turn away to hide my tears — and yes, how afraid I am.

On the ground I profess to know no fear, but I lie. I will confess, with self-mockery, to arachnophobia and cynophobia. Because I see fear as an absence of knowledge, it would be simple for me to conquer such silly terrors. "I am too busy these days," I'll say, "but when I decide it's time to get rid of my aversion to animals with too many legs (or not enough legs — snakes are not my friends, either), I know exactly how to proceed." I will read science reports, watch documentaries, visit the zoo. I will interview spider-wranglers (is there such a profession?) to discover how these creatures evolved, how they hunt, mate, sleep, and, most importantly, what frightens the hairy, scary beast. Then, like James Bond, I won't have any problem having a tarantula dance a tarantella on my forearm.

The Body Language of Fear

The inner motion of fear is a thick book of old tricks that brims with almost invisible, almost silent improvisations — that's why it cannot be anticipated. Those who let themselves be brushed by that trailing shadow see their linear path transformed into a vertical whirlpool that carries them, in slow motion, into an abyss of angst.

The body language of fear is contagious. The body language of fear is devious. Before you feel it, strings are tied to your limbs. You are a puppet being made to dance. All spins and whirls, you never actually see the body of fear, only its shadow. The shadow of a doubt. It may glide behind you like a stealth hovercraft, tiptoe like a fox, or slither like a coral snake. If it runs out of deceptive moves, it will invent one on the spot.

Atychiphobia, the fear of failure, often focuses on the physical. That type of fear will do anything to block your path. It is responsible for the hesitation that delays some free-soloing rock climbers hundreds of feet above the ground from grabbing a tiny handhold during a crux move; it is determined to prevent them from continuing their ascent.

The Taste of Fear

Yom asal, yom basal. The Arabic proverb is true to life: "One day honey, one day onion." Honey is sweet and good, onion pungent and bitter. We taste both at once when our lips glue to the cup of fear.

There are signs. The good, the sweet, is what happens when a thought makes us salivate in joyous anticipation. The bitterness could be the acid taste blending with adrenaline on our palate just before we throw up in panic. Combined, the two opposite elements form a displeasing mixture that is hard to identify because nothing tastes quite like it.

The Music of Fear

It is a mistake to expect the music of fear to be like the soundtrack of a bad horror movie, door creaking, bat wings flapping, and the backward whispers of ancient Greek. At times the song of fear resembles rattling laughter. At times fear speaks in a devious tongue that transmutes your entire being from ears to toes into a frozen sentence from an unknown dialect that no one understands.

The music of fear is a deceptive blend. It may overlap a nice melody with a tune of an opposite style, an ice melody, like a radio stuck between two different channels. (For example, take a throbbing composition from Stephen Kent, the non-aboriginal master of the didgeridoo. Mix it with a musical opposite, say, Klaus Nomi performing his "The Cold Song.") The irritating potpourri you hear is akin to the music of fear. The more you listen to it, the more it dulls your senses — think of the Pied Piper, think of the mermaids serenading Ulysses — it lures you to surrender your sanity. At that point, fear is often so close, it sings while leaning against you. Then it starts to walk away. And you, already deaf, follow its song. You follow its meandering path to your doom.

The music of fear acts like the flute of a snake charmer I remember from Jamaa el-Fnaa square. From the first moment of fright when the lid of the wicker basket is removed and the cobra emerges, Marrakesh tourists are led to believe the snake's undulations are produced by the melody. In fact, having been hit on the head by the flute so many times, the cobra follows the subtle movements of the musical wooden stick, not its notes. The snake is not dancing for you, but avoiding corporal punishment out of fear.

How to resist being hypnotized by the central element in a portrait of fear; or for that matter, being swallowed by a larger-than-life moment of dread? Assemble weapons to destroy fear. Start by reacting to fright not by burying your head in the sand but by burying your mind in knowledge; then follow with specifics.

How to Disrupt the Body Language of Fear

Before my high-wire walk across the Seine to the second story of the Eiffel Tower, the seven-hundred-yard-long inclined cable looked so steep, the shadow of fear so real, I worried. Had there been an error in rigging calculations? No. I had just forgotten how high were my expectations, how mad I was to have conceived such a project. On the spot I vanquished my anxiety by imagining the best outcome: my victorious last step above a cheering crowd of 250,000.

If imagination does not work, turn to the physical side of things. Give yourself a time-limit ultimatum: start counting! Yes, choose a number — not too high — and when you hear footsteps on your porch at 3 a.m., unfreeze your trepidation by whispering to yourself, "At ten, I open the door! One, two, three, four . . ."

A clever tool in the arsenal to destroy fear: if a nightmare taps you on the shoulder, do not turn around immediately expecting to be scared. Pause and expect more, exaggerate. Be ready to be *very* afraid, to scream in terror. The more delirious your expectation, the safer you will be when you see that reality is much less horrifying than what you had envisioned. *Now* turn around. See? It was not *that* bad — and you're already smiling.

How to Eliminate the Taste of Fear

Use your intuition as well as your tongue to test the air. Since the taste of fear is hard to recognize, as soon as you taste something odd, unknown, strange, spit it out without a single thought and step on it with the sole of your shoe and grind it into the ground — like people do with a cigarette. That will short-circuit the chemical process. Do not look at what you've done; just move on.

Sometimes, to confuse us, fear transforms taste into odor. A smell by association can usher in anxiety and lead to phobia. Some people react drastically to the smell of fire; they think total destruction has already started. My brother dreaded the smell of garbage. He associated it with the kind of decomposition that invites final decay and death. He saw nonexistent rats gather, he heard them plot an invading plague, he smelled the annihilation of humanity. I pulled him into the nearest vegetable garden and served him a premeditated show-and-tell on a different kind of garbage, compost. I convinced him of the benefits of such a mixture and made its odor positive. I forced his mind to run off with a different association: the smell of rebirth, of growth, of the Garden of Eden. He is now cured.

How to Silence the Music of Fear

Never cover your ears. On the contrary, face the music and explore its layered construction. Sometimes you will recognize more than two musical pieces overlapping. No matter, note after note, extract the silences that fell inside the staves. Once the silences are caught, walk away with them swiftly and peacefully. You've just rendered fear speechless by altering its voice. You're done. You're safe.

One more weapon. When an inner howl assails me, the wild longing to flee an alarming situation, I counter the chorus of fear by amplifying it to the extreme. Distorted, it then exudes a single voice. The voice of courage, which I let scream at me because it makes me stronger.

Lastly, the Ultimate Weapon of Fear Destruction, Valid for All of the Above

When you're about to shrink with fear, instead do what the peacocks (and many mammals) do: frighten fear by enlarging your silhouette. Blow yourself up — mentally — feel unbreakable, wear self-confidence like a rhinoceros its carapace, appear immortal. Deadly fear will immediately run away, its scythe between its legs.

To fear in life is human. And difficult to avoid. And a rude awakening each time. If it seizes you, be proud of your fifteen minutes of fear. Like when you were about to jump from that ten-meter-tall high-diving platform and, well . . . had second thoughts. You forced yourself to go anyway — and it felt like suicide. You had the choice: disgrace or suicide. And, bravo, you chose suicide — your victory.

To live in fear of what's about to happen is for many people today — owing to our current political situation — a reality.

But *to live in fear*, period, is a horror, a torture. You have forgotten fear was the culprit, and you have been obliterated, replaced by a shameful black hole, which breathes — or not — in your stead.

This evening — outside, a murder of crows darkens the air with its flying formation, announcing the storm of the century, the end of the world — this evening, *to live in fear* will be my definition of death.

THOMAS POWERS

The Big Thing on His Mind

FROM *The New York Review of Books*

IT WOULD BE a grave mistake for anyone trying to understand race in American history to overlook the novels of William Faulkner. Beneath their literary complexity can be found the clearest statement by anyone of the core abuse that has driven black/white conflict since slavery times, but first you have to pass a test. Faulkner's French biographer, André Bleikasten, who devoted his life to understanding Faulkner, obviously passed the test himself, but it cannot have been easy for him. Bleikasten presents his readers with many examples of the test, but the one that seemed bluntest to me, impossible to mistake or ignore, emerges from an evening at Princeton in 1958 when Faulkner met J. Robert Oppenheimer. Both men were celebrated, Oppenheimer for building the first atomic bomb and Faulkner for writing the novels that won the Nobel Prize for literature in 1949.

Oppenheimer, when in the mood, could talk to just about anybody about anything, but Faulkner found conversation difficult with strangers; a bare *yes* or *no* was often all he could manage. Oppenheimer said he had recently seen a television play based on a Faulkner story and asked what Faulkner thought of television as a medium for the artist.

"Television is for niggers," said Faulkner.

This is the test: Are you prepared to believe that the Faulkner who said that might also have something important to say about black/white conflict in American history? The test was probably easier for Bleikasten because he was French, because he studied the books before he studied the man, because he was interested in literature, not history or sociology, and because at the beginning of his life Bleikasten did not yet understand that for many white southerners nothing changed with the end of slavery except slavery.

Bleikasten's long devotion to Faulkner began with a happy accident. In July 1962 he was nearing thirty and needed a safely dead writer of important novels in English for his doctoral thesis. He was close to committing himself to D. H. Lawrence when Faulkner died after falling from a hard-to-control horse in Virginia. Bleikasten devoted most of the next forty-five years to Faulkner, beginning with the novels, which he treated exhaustively in a book called *The Ink of Melancholy*, first published in 1990 and now reissued. Friends asked, why not follow the novels with a biography? Bleikasten resisted. "There are five already," he thought. "Why a sixth?" But then an editor at a small French publishing house "harried me gently for months until finally I gave in."

Bleikasten's book on the novels took decades, the life about three years. It was published in France in 2007 and won three big prizes. By that time he was already mortally ill with cancer, and he died in 2009 before talk of an English translation had gone anywhere. His wife Aimee took on the task, which was completed by Miriam Watchorn with the help of Roger Little. The result in English is heavy in the hand but the book marches with narrative vigor, the result principally of Bleikasten's clarity of thought. His points are never softened or simplified. Photographs capture Faulkner's wary reticence, and Bleikasten gets the rest. In 1949, Faulkner told the critic Malcolm Cowley that he thought a bare-bones epitaph would be enough: "He made the books and he died." Bleikasten puts the books first, too, but he sees things in them that the life helps make visible.

The big facts of Faulkner's life were place and time; he was born in Mississippi in 1897, when the eleven states of the old Confederacy were enacting anti-black Jim Crow laws to exclude African Americans from public life. The intent of the laws was reinforced by white mobs that brutally lynched blacks for real and imaginary crimes. They weren't just hanged but were often tortured as well.

Bleikasten notes that during one five-year period of Faulkner's childhood, 1903–8, more than eighty African Americans were lynched in Mississippi, including one in Faulkner's hometown of Oxford. The victim was Nelse Patton, charged with murdering a white woman with a straight razor. A mob broke into the Oxford jail with the help of local boys, including Faulkner's friend John Cullen, who were boosted through a window so they could unlock the door from inside. Patton was shot dead, castrated, attached to a car that dragged him through the streets of Oxford, and finally burned. Faulkner, who was eleven at the time and lived barely a hundred yards from the jail, wrote about the Patton lynching in two of his books, *Light in August* and *Intruder in the Dust.*

The world of Faulkner's childhood was obsessed with race. Faulkner was born lucky, since he was white, but his family held no great place in Oxford. A feckless farmer in Faulkner's short story "Two Soldiers" is described as always behind; "He can't get no further behind," a son remarks. Faulkner's father was like that. He failed in business repeatedly and was fired from his last job as comptroller at the University of Mississippi when he refused to contribute to local politicos. Faulkner's grandfather had been a bigger man locally but was disgraced at the end of his life after he ran off with some Oxford town funds and "a beautiful octoroon." The pride of the family was Faulkner's great-grandfather, who had fought in the Civil War, built a railroad, and was shot dead in the streets of Oxford by a former partner. Just as remarkable was the great-grandfather's huge popular success with a Civil War novel called *The White Rose of Memphis,* which prompted Faulkner at nine to say, "I want to be a writer like my great-grand-daddy."

The young Faulkner was a compulsive reader in childhood and did well in school but drifted out of college before getting a degree or knowing how to take the next step. He was short — five feet four by Bleikasten's account — and awkward with girls. His two early loves, Estelle Oldham in Oxford and Helen Baird in New Orleans, both abandoned him for men who were better bets. But Estelle's first marriage foundered, and she married Faulkner when he asked again. Faulkner told a friend, "They don't think we're gonna stick, but it is gonna stick." Why he wanted to marry her is a mystery. Both were alcoholics and had nothing else in common. When a daughter was born in 1933 (after the death in infancy of a premature baby girl named Alabama), they quit having sex and tormented each other for the next thirty years.

Bleikasten stresses the fact that Faulkner was a storyteller in both senses of the term. He loved writing complex stories of "the

human heart in conflict with itself" (a phrase he used in his Nobel
Prize acceptance speech in Stockholm in 1950), and he compul-
sively embroidered the bare facts of his own prosaic life. Writing
later about the months he lived in New Orleans in 1925, Faulkner
claimed that he supported himself by

> working for a bootlegger. He had a launch that I would take down
> [Lake] Ponchartrain into the Gulf to an island where the rum, the
> green rum, would be brought up from Cuba and buried, and we would
> dig it up and bring it back to New Orleans . . . And I would get a hun-
> dred dollars a trip for that.

Nothing about this story was true, but just as remarkable is where
he told it — in an American lit class at West Point in April 1962,
about two months before he died.

Yet bigger lies were told about his eventless months with the
Royal Canadian Air Force; after the war he limped from imaginary
machine-gun wounds suffered, he claimed, in aerial duels over the
fields of France. Faulkner was still in flight school when the war
ended, was never sent to France, was never wounded in combat as
he claimed, and never even took up a plane alone until years later.
Whether he lied to woo girls, or because he was desperate for distinction, or for the simple fun of it is hard to say. But Bleikasten is
blunt about Faulkner's fabrications and writes that "he lied to his
parents, his brothers, his friends, and later his son-in-law, his mis-
tresses, his editors, his colleagues in Hollywood, and his doctors."

In time Faulkner told fewer tall tales and had the deeper pleasure of constructing elaborate fictions in prose. He seems to have
been following the example of his friend Sherwood Anderson
in New Orleans, whose mornings-only writing schedule in 1925
appealed to Faulkner. "You've got too much talent," Anderson
warned him. "You can do it too easy, in too many different ways. If
you're not careful, you'll never write anything."

Faulkner set to work but was slow to find his subject. Two novels — *Soldiers' Pay* (1926) and *Mosquitoes* (1927) — came and went.
With his third he followed Anderson's advice to stick to "that little
patch up there in Mississippi where you started from." Faulkner
loved the sprawling complex novel that followed, but one publisher after another rejected the book, *Flags in the Dust,* until it was
radically cut and retitled *Sartoris* (1929). But that novel, loosely
centered on Faulkner's own struggle to fit into civilian life after

the war, showed him the way. "Beginning with *Sartoris* I discovered that my own little postage stamp of soil was worth writing about . . . so I created a cosmos of my own."

Faulkner's cosmos was Yoknapatawpha County in northern Mississippi, with a courthouse and the town of Jefferson at its center, a thinly fictionalized version of Oxford, Mississippi, where he had spent the largest part of his childhood, knew everybody, and heard many of the stories that emerged in somewhat altered but generally transparent form in fifteen of his twenty novels. Many of the characters in the books come from the same half-dozen families, both white and black, spanning a century beginning in the 1830s, when the first cotton farms were established on land ceded by the Chickasaw nation of Native Americans.

Few of the books sold well, especially in the beginning. Faulkner got by in the early years with frequent stints writing for the movies in Hollywood, where he met the great love of his life, in Bleikasten's view, Meta Carpenter, a script girl working for Howard Hawks, director of *The Big Sleep* on which Faulkner worked. Faulkner had other girlfriends as well, developed a reputation as a man hard to interview, answered contumaciously when pestered about politics, spent too much money renovating a house in Oxford, was churlish at the outset about accepting the Nobel Prize in person ("Everybody from the Swedish ambassador to my damn nigger houseboy has been telling me to do right!"), and stubbornly refused to admit that some horses were too much for him.

Bleikasten scants none of the life but is interested above all in the books. One or two might be called entertainments, using the term in Graham Greene's sense. Many can be as hard to read as the begats in the Bible or Heidegger on history. They are awash in detail, knotted, inexact, disturbing, and obscure in their fierce pursuit of elusive insights. It is hard to be sure what Faulkner is trying to understand, and hard to decide if he has understood it. Few Americans ever tackle Faulkner. Those forced to read him in high school or college remember little, perhaps Benjy looking at Caddy's drawers in *The Sound and the Fury* or Temple Drake's rape with a corncob in *Sanctuary*.

But there is a logic to Faulkner's dependence on difficulty. It serves two purposes. In some of the novels, and especially in *Absalom, Absalom!*, the difficulty ensured that Faulkner's neighbors would not know what he was talking about lest they burn his barn, if not worse. The second purpose was to force readers to struggle to get the story straight. A poem or a short story in Faulkner's view was too small, too soon over, to encompass the big thing on his mind — the great submerged obsessive guilty burden of slave times, when all whites knew but few said that slaves were not only unpaid laborers but unpaid sexual servants.

To say it flat out, as that does, is a way to get past the fact in a hurry. Faulkner was not in a hurry. The narrator of his story "Uncle Willy" notes that "Papa told me once that someone said if you know it you can say it." Faulkner knew it and somehow won permission — drinking may have helped here — to say it, "all of hit," as Mollie Beauchamp stresses at the end of *Go Down, Moses*. She is speaking of the life and death of her black grandson and also of the century of slavery and its aftermath that determined his fate. "Is you gonter put hit in de paper? I wants hit all in de paper. All of hit."

Five books address and wrestle with Faulkner's central obsession, which in one mood he called "the past" and in another "the South." These novels embody the second thing Faulkner learned from writing *Sartoris* — "that not only each book had to have a design but the whole output or sum of an artist's work had to have a design." About the past he famously wrote in a late novel, "The past is never dead. It's not even past." He meant that the meaning and the burden of the past are inextricably laced within the present. "There is no such thing as *was* — only *is*," he told his last girlfriend, Jean Stein, when she interviewed him for *The Paris Review*. About the South Faulkner was ambivalent, especially with strangers. "Well, I love it and hate it," he told reporters in Japan in 1955. "Some of the things there I don't like at all, but I was born there, and that's my home, and I will still defend it even if I hate it."

Faulkner's love and his hate are knotted together most tightly in the five novels that are primarily about race, but it would be perverse to describe them as a defense of the South. Indictment is more like it. As the books appeared, Bleikasten writes, southerners, generally, starting in Faulkner's hometown of Oxford, detested them all after a page or two. A partial exception was eventually made for the last of the five, *Intruder in the Dust* (1948), which they forgave and indulged when it was made into a popular film.

The other four are *Sanctuary* (1931), *Light in August* (1932), *Absalom, Absalom!* (1936), and *Go Down, Moses* (1942).

To understand how these books fit into Faulkner's grand design on the subject of the South, it helps to examine the chosen word in the South for the woman Faulkner's grandfather ran off with in 1887, ten years before Faulkner was born. The word is "octoroon." It means a person who is one-eighth African American, or in polite usage in the nineteenth century, one-eighth Negro. A quadroon would have one Negro grandparent, and a mulatto would have one Negro parent. The three terms were coined in slave times and refer only to African Americans; a person with one Chinese or one Pacific Islander or one Inuit great-grandparent would not be an octoroon.

The final point to understand is that "octoroon" neither says nor implies anything much about actual genetic makeup. The African American great-grandparent is any person who was identified, accepted, and treated at the time as an African American, whatever their actual genetic mix. Nothing about the physical appearance of an octoroon says "octoroon." In the South of Faulkner's childhood, somebody had to tell you who was or wasn't an octoroon. To find out you were one changed everything.

This point is crucial to *Absalom, Absalom!*, which some critics think Faulkner's greatest novel. The central character is Thomas Sutpen, owner of a huge plantation called "Sutpen's Hundred," who had once been married in the West Indies to a planter's daughter, with whom he had a son. He abandoned both when he learned that his wife was not "Spanish," as her father claimed, but part African American. Mixed race is a factor in all of Faulkner's core novels. Joe Christmas in *Light in August* agonizes over his "black blood." "Is it certain, proved, that he has negro blood?" a character asks. Faulkner never says, but Christmas is tortured equally by the taint and its uncertainty. He murders a white lover, is hunted down, castrated, and killed by townspeople infuriated by his refusal to act "like either a nigger or a white man . . . That was what made the folks so mad . . . It was like he never even knew he was a murderer, let alone a nigger too."

Sexual connection between master and slave is a principal driver of Faulkner's core novels, but it is never simple, never clearly told, and never without tragic consequence. In *Go Down, Moses,* the planter Lucius Quintus Carothers McCaslin has a daughter named Tomasina with Eunice, one of his slaves, who later walks into a creek and drowns herself on Christmas Day, 1832. The daughter is called Tomey and is of course McCaslin's slave as well; she dies giving birth to McCaslin's son, whose given name is Terrell but is called Turl and known by all as Tomey's Turl. He in turn fathers a son with Tennie Beauchamp named Lucas, who is the main character in *Intruder in the Dust,* threatened with lynching for a murder he did not commit. He refuses to defend himself, claiming "I belongs to the old lot. I'm a McCaslin," connected through his father (Turl) and his grandmother (Tomey) to L.Q.C. McCaslin. Popeye and Goodwin in *Sanctuary* are never clearly identified by race but are frequently described as dark or black, and suffer what might be called black fates — Goodwin lynched and burned, Popeye convicted and executed, both for murders they did not commit.

I have barely touched here on the driving force of gradations of race in Faulkner's work, where it is "black blood" that determines fate. Each horror is the consequence, often long delayed, of real crimes in the past that generate fatal confusions, push characters to madness and suicide, and fix everyone, permanently and without appeal, on one side or the other of the great social divide marked by the word "nigger." On one side of the color line in Faulkner's world people can call others "nigger" with impunity; on the other they must submit to it in silence.

What Faulkner contributes to this knotted history is the understanding that slavery's grip on white masters was sexual, and that the coping mechanism of the white South was denial. One of the few southerners to name the problem frankly was Mary Chesnut, daughter of one large slave owner and wife of another, who recorded the great fact in her diary before the Civil War:

> I wonder if it be a sin to think slavery a curse to any land. Sumner said not one word of this hated institution which is not true. . . . Like the patriarchs of old our men live all in one house with their wives and their concubines, and the mulattoes one sees in every family exactly resemble the white children — and every lady tells you who is the father of all the mulatto children in everybody's household, but those in her own she seems to think drop from the clouds.

The Sumner she credits with speaking the truth was Senator Charles Sumner of Massachusetts, who said as plainly as he dared that it was the lure of sexual license that explained the furious defense of slavery by slave owners. Everybody understood what Sumner meant when he attacked Senator Andrew Butler of South Carolina by name in 1856, saying, "Of course he has chosen a mistress to whom he has made his vows, and who, though ugly to others, is always lovely to him; though polluted in the sight of the world, is chaste in his sight — I mean the harlot, Slavery." Butler's kinsman, Congressman Preston Brooks of South Carolina — some say he was a nephew, some say a cousin — avenged the insult by beating Sumner nearly to death on the floor of the Senate with a gutta-percha cane, an act of violence that helped bring on the war that followed.

"As soon as the abolitionist Yankee North started to contest slavery," Bleikasten notes, "its justification drove all political discourse." He stops there, but we might go further and date the birth of the "solid South" to the 1845 split of the Baptist Church into a Southern and a Northern Convention, resulting from disputes over the issue of slavery. The solid South has never cracked but has continued to speak with a single dominant voice, justifying slavery before the Civil War and defending Jim Crow laws and lynching in the following century. During that century the solid South controlled the US Senate on the issues that mattered to it most, and it is no less solid in speaking with a single political voice now following its takeover of the Republican Party.

Faulkner learned about the history of race in the South from living there, not from books. His use of the word "nigger," of which Bleikasten offers a full spectrum of examples, along with much else, identifies him as indelibly white in the southern manner of the times. The day is probably coming when younger readers, bumping into "the N-word" repeatedly, can no longer pass the test I earlier mentioned. But the word was an ineradicable part of Faulkner's world. A walk through the streets of Oxford in his youth revealed the South's great either/or — black or white, one or the other, no exceptions. What Faulkner saw, and found a way to say that could not be silenced, was the fact of two centuries of sexual exchange, in which African Americans were compelled to endure exploitation that whites minimized, rationalized, and violently denied.

Faulkner did not ultimately disguise what he thought about the great fact. The thing he refused to admit to the Japanese reporters in 1955 was something he had already said plainly in the final words of *Absalom, Absalom!* when Quentin Compson is flatly asked, "Why do you hate the South?"

The question comes at night in Quentin's room at Harvard College from his friend Shreve, a Canadian. Quentin has been telling Shreve the story of Thomas Sutpen, his two sons, and the fate of his house at Sutpen's Hundred. Quentin had been present when Clytie, Sutpen's daughter by a slave, burned the house to the ground, killing both herself and her white brother, Henry, who had shot to death their half-black brother thirty years earlier.

Then Shreve's question and Quentin's answer:

"*I dont hate it* he thought, panting in the cold air, the iron New England dark; *I dont. I dont! I dont hate it! I dont hate it!*"

DAVID SALLE

Clothes That Don't Need You

FROM *The New York Review of Books*

THE FIRST TIME I visited Japan I fell hard for the highly abstract, ritualized form of musical drama called Noh. My Japanese
friends found this a little puzzling, since I couldn't understand
the dialogue, and there was no simultaneous translation such as
one finds at the opera. Even they didn't understand the arcane
Japanese dialect from hundreds of years earlier. There were syn-
opses of the plays, of course — usually just a few lines in a mimeographed program. My traveling companion and I were often the
only Westerners at these performances, which were held in the
late afternoon, adding to the oddness of the experience. The atmosphere was very different from the more popular Kabuki. No
beer. No cheering, no talking in the house at all. Pretty soon, as
the intricate rhythms and the rising and falling pitch of the atonal
chanting start to work on your brain, you begin to get a feeling for
the dramatic arcs.

Memory plays. Ghost stories.

Noh is the carrying forward of misfortune, of a stain of disgrace
that won't go away; fate unwinds in front of you. Most of the action
takes place before the play begins. Characters speak from beyond
the grave, recounting memories of betrayal, luckless love, suicide
by drowning. (George Saunders's *Lincoln in the Bardo* is American Noh.) The clacking together of two wooden blocks signals a
change of scene and releases a heavy sense of malaise into the
present. Visitations from the underworld are routine. The weeping cherry tree on a bare stage turns out to be the tears shed by an
abandoned lover waiting to tell her story.

What elevates these narratives of woe is the solemnity of their

staging, which contributes to a feeling that the boundaries between past and present, human and spirit, have loosened or dissolved altogether. The slowed-down movement across an empty
stage, the actors' white masks, the plaintive chanting and its shattering rhythmic accompaniment, the even, undramatic lighting —
the theatrical illusion is hard to account for, but after two or three
hours' immersion in the Noh world, I would begin to feel myself
overtaken by an immeasurable sadness, with tears spilling down
my face. Such exquisite perfection in the telling, so much suffering in the tale.

Walking mesmerized through the Rei Kawakubo retrospective at
the Metropolitan Museum was the closest I've come since to the
feeling of Noh theater. Without always understanding what I was
looking at, I was gripped by the kind of melancholy that seems to
accompany the toughest, most searching and demanding levels of
beauty.

The exhibition design, a collaboration between Kawakubo and
the Met curators, follows no perceptible chronology. Enclosures
of various shapes — inverted cones, flattened spheres and semi-
circles, keyholes, ovals, triangles — contain the clothes, which are
grouped by collection or theme. These frames are rendered in
white plasterboard and lit from above by dense rows of fluorescent
tubes, making a shadowless space, objective in tone. They are like
viewing platforms, some of which function as small proscenium
stages, while others are more like theater in the round. Still others
are like caves whose restrictive openings give only a partial view of
the clothes within. There is no attempt to make the clothes themselves look inhabited. Dresses and other garments are displayed
on mannequin forms supported by thin metal rods, like sculpture.
They are what Giacometti's figures would be wearing had they
taken the time to get dressed.

White muslin, bias-sutured Hans Bellmer dolls with steel wool
hair, their bulbous silhouettes like Jean Arp cutouts.

Call it an alphabet/poncho. A dress that, seen from the front,
is a near-perfect circle formed by a ten-inch-wide band of black
velvet, the top of which thickens to form a cowl-neck that hides
the wearer's chin. The interior of the circle is a complex pattern of
vertically striated pale beige lace, which is bisected in two places by

horizontal tiers of contrasting ruffles. The arms do not protrude, but stay inside the circle, and the head is draped with black lace, mantilla style, so that the wearer appears as a walking "O" with a soft, furry center.

Black, aggressively ruched satin bomber jackets over wavy black panel skirts. One sleeve of the jacket has an extra-long extension that hangs down below the skirt, as if for an elephant's trunk.

An antebellum-style dress with full and puckered cap sleeves, a low, scooped, and ruffled neck, and a skirt made of rows and tiers of short ruffles, all in a salmon-pink floral fabric, with brown and pale blue flowers. Sewn to its front and made out of the same fabric as the dress is a large stuffed bear, such as a child might carry, but with extra-long arms and an oversized snout, or maybe even a trunk, a bear becoming Babar; from another angle, the whole thing becomes a pink ruffled kangaroo.

Dome-shaped forms made out of gray-blue chenille, like an accumulation of upholstered headrests, gathered about the upper torso, shoulders, and neck; the meeting points of the heavily textured fabric recall the creased skin of a pachyderm. On top of this vertical Frank-Gehry-of-cloth is a "skirt" of shaggy black fake fur, which gives the whole composition ballast. Even though the dress falls to midcalf, to wear it without the articulated black froufrou would be like walking out of the house fully dressed but without pants.

Fruity shapes and silhouettes are everywhere. An apple perches on top of a pear; a kumquat floats above a doughnut peach; there are pumpkins, eggplants, and pomegranates, gourd shapes both rotund and hollowed out. Kawakubo is an Arcimboldo of cloth.

Some ensembles are reminiscent of the ecclesiastical raiments that you see in the store windows near the Pantheon in Rome. Loose-draped, knee-length robes in dark red floral brocade, the neck opening either a gathered cowl or a padded scoop, long loose sleeves that cover the hands. Now, using butch wax, pull the hair straight up and twist it into a point, so that it resembles a candle flame. Clothes made by a sorceress, for other sorceresses.

Who makes clothes like this? No one so flamboyant: the daughter of a university administrator, Kawakubo was born in Tokyo in 1942, studied the history of aesthetics at Keio University, did stints

in advertising and as a freelance stylist before founding her own
label, Comme des Garçons, in 1969, which has since grown into
a large and profitable business. Its name — "Like the Boys" — was
meant to signify the collaborative nature of the enterprise, and was
fun to say. Her early clothes were monochrome — dark gray, white,
and black — and drew on folkloric motifs.

In a lengthy interview with the Met curator Andrew Bolton that
opens the catalog, Kawakubo, speaking through a translator, is
adroit at not letting herself be drawn into generalities and disin-
clined to call herself an artist. "I make clothes," she says simply.
"I make objects for the body." Whatever name she gives to her
work, her clothes have the surprise, the emotional range, the formal imagination, and the gravitas — the authority — of art. To my
mind, Kawakubo, supported by her creative team, has been working, for decades, at a level that most artists can only fantasize about.

What kind of artist is she? Let's call her a combinatory formalist.
She is unusually adept at combining the many disparate influences
that course through her designs into unlikely, arresting, contra-
puntal compositions. She is first of all a creator of images — of pictures liberated from their original settings, and in this she belongs
with the Pictures Generation, that group of mediacentric artists
who were among her first devotees.

Fashion is the place where the associative, imagistic mind can
run riot with impunity; it's a postmodernist playground. Part of it
is practical: the need to come up with three or four or more collections a year, year after year, disempowers any will toward consistency. What makes a designer hold our attention over the long
term is the contour and shape of her choices, and their integra-
tion into a larger philosophy of beauty.

A designer traffics in associations, and even the obvious ones
in Kawakubo's evolution are like a long, multicultural roller
coaster ride through the history of style. They include, among
others, Elizabethan court dress, the France of Versailles as well as
the Belle Epoque, seventeenth- and eighteenth- and nineteenth-
century Japanese battle dress, and military clothing generally, as
well as uniforms worn by Japanese workers in at least two other,
more modern eras, 1980s punk and its appropriation of Scottish
clan costumes, the wrapped and tied peasant clothes of India and
Southeast Asia, African tribal headgear, medical prosthetic devices
and restraining hardware, commedia dell'arte, children's clothing

from the era of Little Bo-Peep, classical ballet, flamenco, and the Fellini of *Juliet of the Spirits*.

There are also numerous visual artists to whom her work invites comparison, from, most strikingly, Velázquez and Goya, to the drawings of Aubrey Beardsley, and on to Dalí, Arp, Miró, Bellmer, and Magritte, as well as Calder and his *Circus*; to Lee Bontecou, Eva Hesse, Louise Bourgeois, and Sheila Hicks (and fabric art in general), and then back to Rauschenberg's "combines," and forward again to more recent work like the fabric sculptures of Georg Baselitz, Kara Walker's spiky silhouettes, Rebecca Warren's figures in squeezed clay and bronze, and the arresting animatrons by the current enfant terrible Jordan Wolfson.

And that's just a partial list. Most of these names belong to the two movements in twentieth-century art history that seem to have most interested Kawakubo: surrealism and arte povera — or post-minimalism — the latter with its emphasis on materials and process, and on the often mysterious energy that, as the late curator Harald Szeemann put it, emerges when "attitude becomes form." Kawakubo's achievement could be encapsulated as the combination of these two seemingly irreconcilable approaches.

All this list-making perhaps gives the wrong impression. Kawakubo is no appropriationist magpie. For one thing, she has made so many different kinds of clothes out of such a searching and diverse body of ideas that any one aesthetic position might be contradicted by the next year's collection. The force of what she does with all these references and styles lies in her specific juxtapositions and recombinings. This is the stylist's art taken to a whole new, one wants to say philosophical, level. In our time, juxtaposition itself has become the engine of art, or rather, where art's inner energy becomes most visible. Kawakubo imbues the mixed metaphor with particular acidity and asperity. Never has pink-checked gingham, gathered and pulled tight over a non-anatomical protrusion, looked so uncompromising.

For this interplay of references to have real weight, there must be at least hints of a discernible visual syntax. How is it established, where does it reside? For Kawakubo, the answer lies in the relationship of image to form; it's the relationship of the *what* to the *how*. Regardless of the imagistic valences, the starting point for her clothes is often the fabric itself, the material fact of it. A tightly bundled bodice or derriere takes on a different meaning if the bundling is accomplished with black crepe de chine or with red-and-green wool plaid. In this orchestration of her effects, Kawakubo has the design equivalent of perfect pitch.

"It requires more imagination to be a sculptor than it does to be a painter," wrote the painter and critic Fairfield Porter. A painter can find the form, and subsequently the image, at the end of a brush. She may noodle around until eventually she finds something on the canvas that has vitality, but a sculptor must have more of an idea of where the work is headed, and she must master an often recalcitrant material to give shape to it. Whether the work is made by subtraction (cutting, chiseling, carving, etc.) or by addition (welding, sewing, stacking, binding, or just affixing a stuffed animal to a low brick pilaster), the sculptor at every turn must deal with an obdurate material reality. In Kawakubo's work, the final image derives in large part from research into what materials can be made to do.

In the mid- and late 1960s, turning further away from representation, postminimalism intensified art's focus on process, on the act of making, that was begun by the abstract expressionists, but without the melodrama. Draping, wrapping, clustering, layering, stacking, scattering, and scaffolding — all the verbs of postminimalist sculpture have their counterparts in the techniques of the needle trades. And if the traditional methods couldn't give Kawakubo the effects she was after, new ones were invented. The clothes are not just radical-looking, they are radically constructed, and some of the detailing and finishing that you can see up close in the more extravagantly shaped garments give an appreciation for just how complex and layered are the processes by which a form-in-cloth is made.

As a shape maker, Kawakubo starts with the body as an armature, an upright support on which to slash, mold, gather, and bind, the same as any designer, but she has in general steered clear of the tight-to-the-body mania that has dominated fashion over the last twenty-five years. One of her radical reimaginings is a "one size fits all" attitude toward body size that challenges the conventional idea of sexiness as a matter of display — showing more skin. Kawakubo is philosophically un-"size-ist," and many of her clothes provide the wearer with a kind of open volume of fabric that takes different shapes depending on who's inside.

Yet even when her dresses involve voluminous convexities that take up a lot of space, in the manner of traditional bell-shaped gowns, they are often conjoined with acts of restriction and compression: tying, binding, lacing, wrapping, or winding. She is interested in the redistribution or realignment of mass, and will sometimes use shapes to hold other shapes in place, or let one shape expand provocatively while corseting others, like squeezing your fist around the middle of a plastic bag full of Jell-O.

Or shapes are resolved by well-placed and artfully tied knots: straps, laces, strings, all pulled tight and tucked in. Much is made of the techniques of knot tying, and the methods of wrapping up little parcels. Packaging, and the presentation of gifts generally, has long been elevated in Japan into a not-so-minor art form called tsutsumi, of which there are different schools and myriad forms. In Kawakubo's version: take a crisp white bedsheet, throw in a big pile of bulky but soft-edged objects, gather the four corners of the sheet together, and tie them into a beautiful bow. Repeat six or eight or ten times, and place your parcels about the body: one on a shoulder, one at the hip, one on the collarbone, etc. Top off with a little black lace draped over the head. Voilà!

Especially in her earlier years, two foundational images have carried over from collection to collection, sometimes clearly delineated, at other times as more of a pentimento. The first image is of a bundle of cloth, such as a peasant farmer might carry hanging from a pole, now balanced on top of two sticks, or legs, like attenuated columns. A pile of hair, a twisting of cloth bags and sacks hung about the body: a modern vagabond. This is the folkloric, more overtly Japanese side of Kawakubo's designs, and it recurs throughout her oeuvre in various guises. The other image, also folkloric, is the marionette. In this part of her vocabulary, the focus is on the hinge and the strap. Arms held akimbo, knees flexed, head tilted — the posture of the puppet, strings pulled taut or draped about the floor.

Unlike most of the major fashion brands, Kawakubo is not part of the cult of the model. There is no "face" of Comme des Garçons — and she is not dressing "the modern woman," whoever that person might be. She exposes and directly challenges our ideas about beauty, and even coherence, as nothing more than culturally received attitudes. Many of her creations seem to stem from questions a child might ask: *What would happen if . . . ?*, or *Why not try . . . ?* A dress with four sleeves and multiple armholes? Jackets worn as pants, pants worn back to front — why not? This is art that says, "What, you only have two armholes? What a pity! Why should pants only fit your waistline? How boring!" Why should a dress be worn by only one person at a time? Why not wear two dresses at once? Why not cover your face in cellophane, or sew a giant stuffed toy onto your dress front, or attach big lumps to your shoulders and fanny, and pull your hair up into the shape of a candle flame? *Why not??*

Kawakubo says, "Nothing new can come out of a situation without suffering" and "There is very little creation without despair." Some of her clothes from the last few years, the ones that feature arm-hiding, hobbling, and other movement restrictions, including more or less complete body-obscuring, call to mind the last scene from *Story of O,* in which the heroine is totally submerged in her bird costume and paraded around on a leash. How can a sensibility and a work ethic that is so generous and unstinting also have a whiff of cruelty?

That's one side. The other side of Kawakubo's artistic nature is humorous and self-affirming, almost jaunty, expressed in collections with highly evocative, witty, and thought-provoking names like "Not Making Clothing," "Body Meets Dress — Dress Meets Body," and "Two Dimensions." This side is expressed in clothes that come closest to traditional sportswear. Plaid jumpers, bright colors, tulle skirts, and knee-length cropped pants like hiking shorts — these are also signature looks. Kawakubo asks us to imagine a world in which Pauline Réage, author of *Story of O,* companionably coexists with Claire McCardell, creator of American sportswear. Wait, you might say, that *is* our world.

Though there are many possible comparisons between Kawakubo and the art world, there are obvious differences in the ways that fashion and art are carried out. The biggest one is the coordinated talents of a large number of skilled artisans, the highest-level practitioners of the so-called needle arts. The process of turning ideas into clothes is intuitive, complex, and experimental, involving a seemingly magical translation on the part of the patterners, and Kawakubo has at her disposal an atelier full of cutters and shapers, finishers, sewers, and weavers, many of whom have worked with her for the duration of her career. Her chief patterner, Yoneko Kikuchi, who has become managing director of production, is quoted in the exhibition catalog: "It takes time exploring ideas in Kawakubo's mind and giving them form . . . It becomes crucial to have creativity from every one of us . . ."

The process at times resembles a game of "Guess what I'm thinking," a kind of inspired charades-meets-zen-koan. Another patterner relates how Kawakubo once brought into the studio a crumpled piece of paper and directed the team to make something that had the same quality. It is truly a collaborative art, and such a group of cocreators would be the envy of many artists, myself included, but of course one must know what to do with such skilled people.

Kawakubo's decades-long collaboration with her lead cutters and pattern makers also says something about time and longevity in relation to an artist's imagination. One of the revelations of the exhibition is just how many of the most original designs were made within the last five years — the ones least tethered to notions of taste or even functionality, in which the whole history of fashion seems to have been digested and reinvented as one mind-blowing dress after another, each completely different from the one before. It is among the most sustained sprints of creativity seen in any of the arts over the last fifty years.

There is a kind of art experience that seems to anticipate our reactions, and beyond that, our yearning for a certain kind of feeling, essentially one of being taken to a more rarified place. The art got there first, so to speak. Yes, we think, we didn't realize it before, but this is what it feels like to be alive at this moment. It might be triggered by a surprising juxtaposition, a new use for an old material, combined with a harking back, a vestigial memory of a mostly lost classical past. The feeling is complicated; it can be gut-churning, because of what it demands of us, or piercing, as when attached to, say, a Rauschenberg combine painting.

The sensation is even more unsettling when it's produced by an article of clothing. A dress, a pair of pants, a smock — how much could they mean? Kawakubo's clothes, especially for someone who has not closely followed her shows from season to season, instill a sense of coming late to the story, of being able to grasp only a piece or an outline. So much has already been decided before you got there. Once made, the decisions are somewhat familiar: they make use of elements one recognizes, and the logic of the materials themselves, but the sum of their effect when combined in one garment leaves you playing emotional and aesthetic catch-up.

Kawakubo named her most recent collection "Invisible Clothes," an ironic or koan-like title. *Get your mind around this,* they say. Circling back to her original black and white, or just black, with white used as an accent or punctuation, these clothes have the severity of some of her earliest collections, but with the sublime and mysterious quality of the best art. One dress from that collection takes the shape of a giant, ragged-edged ravioli, rendered in matte-black quilted satin. Running vertically up the middle of this dark, glimmering pasta is a vertical dimple, two deep folds in the cloth that reveal the silhouette of a woman, flaring at the hips and narrowing at the waist, before ending in the inspired, perverse gesture of a vastly oversized, round-edged, brilliant white Peter Pan collar. The dress is shown in the catalog with the model's face covered in what looks like Saran wrap, with white ribbon tangled about the hairline — one of the many photographs by Paolo Roversi that made me gasp as I turned the pages. Its effect can't really be explained, but it left me with a feeling of elation. Another piece from the collection resembles a cylindrical upholstered pumpkin. And yet another is a cross between Little Red Riding Hood and a beach chair with its own awning. No other designer has made clothes that come so close to a feeling of madness.

Kawakubo's work embodies a potent wish-drama, the same one that has gripped virtually every avant-garde artist from Manet to the present: the wish to be radical, undermining, wholly original, and also to claim, somewhat miraculously, the unself-consciously egotistical personality of the artist. The modern artist says, *Love me for hating what you love, and love me for not needing you.*

How could such an intense fashion theoretician with seemingly no particular desire to please have enjoyed such a success as a brand? She tells Bolton in the catalog interview: "It's for others to interpret what I create." "I've never liked my clothes being interpreted." "Basically, I've never wanted my work to be understandable." If there were ever any doubt that fashion designers are the true inheritors of the surrealist legacy, that last statement is the kind of thing that could have been said, with perhaps a more sociable tone, by Luis Buñuel.

The exhibition's nonlinear layout underscores the melancholy feeling that attaches to the clothes themselves. There's a loneliness to them that stems from the isolating effect of high principles. As great domestic architecture can make most homes look careless and dull, these are clothes that make everything else we're wearing seem mundane at best, unthought-out. Looking at her work, I've seldom felt such a strong sense of missed opportunity. Being confronted with such a novel idea of beauty pushes us past the point of detached amazement — it's destabilizing.

There has been a certain amount of talk in the fashion press as well as by Kawakubo fans about how her clothes only really come alive when worn. Without disputing that obvious truism, it felt to me that many of Kawakubo's shapes and forms seem to derive from an inner intensity that does not shirk even from the malevolent. I didn't miss the human presence; there were plenty of ghosts in the room. The clothes are for people unlike us, but looking at them reminds us of memories and emotions that are so intense as to sometimes be painful, at which point the ghost-wearers become like us, but a little too late. Rather than celebrating the *now* and congratulating us on our modernity, this is work that wears the heaviness of time. Like Noh theater, like the best art, it implicates us emotionally while also leaving us behind. These are clothes that you may need, but they definitely do not need you.

LUC SANTE

Maybe the People Would
Be the Times

FROM *VICE Magazine*

ALMOST EVERYTHING OF interest in New York City lies in some
degree of proximity to music. If you are in your teens or twenties — and who isn't — pretty much everything you do apart from
your day job has something to do with music. And it isn't even just
the permanent soundtrack on your stereo and in your head. The
music is your spur. You were led to the city by music. You were
fourteen or fifteen and wanted to crawl inside the music. The music was immense, an entire world immeasurably different from the
sad one you were born into. If you could figure out how to get in,
the music would suffuse you. You wouldn't even need an instrument: you would become one with the music and it would pour
from you like light through gauze.

The search led through record stores: the cavernous Times
Square markets with their tens of thousands of titles, the little
downtown storefronts with inventories calibrated to the changing
tastes of one local clique, the flyblown neighborhood shops where
they might have back stock neglected since 1962, the doo-wop
museums manned by savants in obscure subway arcades, the head
shops purveying bootlegs from a curtained alcove in the rear, the
oldies row on Bleecker Street where all the clerks are critics and
the discourse alternates unpredictably between impassioned and
sardonic. It wound past clubs that are just bars with a stage in the
back, or lightly redecorated union halls, or resurrected chantoosie
joints from another era, or ex-vaudeville palaces with paintings
on the ceiling, or hotel ballrooms with a thousand conspicuous
fire-code violations, or sawdust-floored folkie taverns with an aura

of everybody having missed the bus a decade earlier, or jazz lofts in semi-industrial parts of downtown so remote there's no place within a mile to buy cigarettes after dark. It flittered across underground newspapers and teen-gossip rags and lifestyle glossies and quickie paperback bios and radio interviews and industry-promo artifacts stacked near the cash registers and hazy orally transmitted lore of dubious provenance.

But 1975 is a new world, somehow. Everybody gets a haircut that year, and no one can say exactly why. Psychic emanations are big; you can feel change peeling off the walls but can't really name the form of that change. The year is a laboratory. Anything is possible. At stake is a future that might at least superficially look more like a past. Which is to say that the hippie order of knowledge has been overturned. The haircut is an affirmation of this. The time has come for us to assume our own place in the music, and that will involve an overthrow of what has come before. Life is suddenly black and white with a thin stripe of red running through.

The year begins when Marvin Gaye calls in sick and the Apollo gives us our money back. The alternative option is a rumor, really, although it's been going on for half a year. After a very long subway ride we arrive at a tunnel of a bar under a bum hotel on the Bowery with a pool table and a stage in the back: CBGB. Onstage four guys in shirt-jacs, conspicuous lack of overt theatrics, shaker bars on the guitars: Television.[1] The poster has a blurb from Nick Ray,[2] of all people — four cats with a passion — and another from someone named Scott Cohen: killers. sharp as tacks. they made me cry. This is something else, we think, as they blast into a cover of "Psychotic Reaction," by the Count Five. At first glance they're channeling 1966: the clothes, the covers, and when they talk they sound like Mitch Ryder or somebody, that not-quite-black hepped-up hoodlum corner talk affected by all the guys who wore winklepickers in 1966. The words to the songs likewise convey mod menace: "I look at you / I get a double exposure" or "Prove it / Just the facts / Confidentially." The bass player, who seems to enjoy jumping up and landing on his knees, has a ditty with a chorus that goes: "I belong to the [*pause*] blank generation." But it's also about how the twin leads snake around each other as if they are each holding knives, how lyrical passages turn without warning into dissonant slashing fury, how the drummer carves the beat out

of flurries of paradiddles, like he's been absorbing Elvin Jones[3] —
how the unstable field of noise constantly threatens to crash and
burn.

And that makes the music right for the world outside: the per-
sistent breakdown of all structures, the vacated certainties and
the welcoming randomness, the retreating future and imminent
prehistory. Tom Verlaine[4] sings about how "Broadway / Looks so
medieval," and so it is, our moment the great shipwreck of time.
All the contents of previous decades and centuries are heaped up
on the sidewalks for us to pick through and select and repurpose
or discard. Nobody else seems to want this lurching hulk of a city,
headed to the honor farm like a former star given to paregoric
and shoplifting, so it has de facto been ceded to us self-appointed
guttersnipes, and maybe someday we will rule it, although for now
we're content to pick at its scabs. The Bowery is our ancestral
home, that broad empty boulevard running from nowhere to nowhere lined with pedigreed hovels inhabited by ghosts, where in
one tiny establishment every night is New Year's Eve and we're all
contestants for Miss Hitchhiker of 1976.

But information flies in erratically from other parts of the
globe. For a few years now the strongest signals have been emanat-
ing from the unlikely island nation of Jamaica. Unlikely because
we didn't know anything about it until a great mass of its seething
cultural products appeared on our doorstep circa 1973, notably
the desperado epic *The Harder They Come* — as tough and cheap as
a spaghetti western, as taut as an epigram — and then its glisten-
ing soundtrack (nobody can make out the words to the Maytals'
"Sweet and Dandy," and we only figure out it's about a country wedding long after we've given ourselves over to its perpetual-motion
groove, like a Slinky if it could go up the stairs as well as down),
and then a whole profusion of records. Much of it is mysterious
at first, especially the style that involves poets possessed by spirits
talking and chanting over a backing track mined with sound effects and giant echo and instruments dropping out and detached
fragments of a sung melody drifting through like lost birds. Big
Youth is splendid and so is U-Roy, but it is thanks to Patti Smith
(who has her finger firmly on the pulse of the moment) that we
know about reigning Rasta surrealist Tappa Zukie, whose every recording sounds like the primal struggle of man versus radio. Zukie
shouts from inside a room he has hewn himself from a bass line

as tall and dense as trees, runs a zigzag course over a shifting terrain of percussion, summons phantom armies of brass instruments to come riding over the crest. In "Jah Is I Guiding Star," Horace Andy's plaintive "My Guiding Star"[5] is stripped down to glittering shreds as Zukie, transfixed, reaches the peak of his sermon: "Have mercy upon those who have mercy upon themselves / Don't get me mad y'all." Then his torrential rant, like one immense release of breath over three and a half minutes, trickles down into ellipsis: "The automatic clicker with remote control / the dennis / the menace / the mattress all / the dread dem sleep and the baldhead a-peep / and the dread dem wake and the baldhead creak how you mean . . ."

This is music that gives us seven-league boots to walk the streets in, loping twenty-block miles faster than taxis, or else we dance in somebody's bare loft decorated with foil-sided insulation panels, with clamp lights scattered on the floor pointing up the walls, a single pole-mounted fan moving the air around the 1500-square-foot oven, the turntable hooked up to a guitar amp and the music's echo redoubled by the cavernous echo of bricks and mortar. We dance to reggae and we dance to soul, or disco, or R&B. Marvin Gaye's "I Want You" and "Got to Give It Up," the Floaters' "Float On," Chic's "Le Freak," James Brown for days but especially right now "Papa Don't Take No Mess," and it's also the inaugural year of Funkadelic's anthem, "One Nation Under a Groove." Someday they will swap out Francis Scott Key's Bavarian drinking song for this stepping march that gathers all the strands — it's a chance to dance our way out of our constrictions, on a national scale. The song already seems to be under way when the needle hits the groove, and it might as well never end, since we keep taking the needle back to the start when it starts edging near the run-out. It's a whole circus parade of sounds and effects: brass band, clowns, aerialists, prancing horses, confetti showers, giant papier-mâché monster heads. It will teach you how to dance if you don't know how. You let your ass fall into the central bounce path carved out by the bass and the handclaps, and then the rest of your body can align with whatever you want for however long you want: the half-tempo crooner, the squeaking synth, the chuckling guitar monologue, the drum fills, the whistles, the calls and interjections by what sounds like two dozen different voices. It's maybe on the sixth reprise that those of us who aren't completely fucked up start to notice that the floorboards are visibly moving up and down on the one, and this is no joke when you're talking about century-old joists and beams. We start to edge toward the walls, where long tables are covered with empty bottles and cans. From there the crowd looks like one body with four hundred limbs. The air, redolent of sweat and spilled beer and tobacco and cannabis and unnamable musks, is maybe a third of the way toward transmuting into a solid. Somebody screams along with the falsetto wail that turns into "You can dance away." Just then the fuse blows.

Because we are nineteen or twenty-two or twenty-four and in the great city we are living in the great moment, the very forefront of now. Nothing can happen that we won't know about at least a week in advance. There are no media to cover our scene — TV and radio and newspapers and magazines all equally indifferent — but we know everything anyway because we are plugged into the great invisible telegraph of youth. A club will open in some distant and untrafficked neighborhood; a 45 will come out that is for sale in just three stores; a band will form and rehearse but not yet have played out; a bar in far-flung midtown will change its jukebox offerings to include the few available records made by our people — we know all these things instantly. For that matter there is no one on the scene with whom you don't have at least one mutual friend. We are in the heart of the great city, and yet our scene is a little village, where all the people we saw in the club last night, including those onstage, will be having breakfast in the same Ukrainian coffee shop this morning.

So we know that our now is the big Now, yet also that that conviction is shared by a scant few hundred people. Among those are some who think that it really is 1966 all over again, and that their band is just one lucky break away from permeating every jukebox and radio station and drive-in and high school dance across the land and across the sea. Some of us, though, see the ever-growing wreckage piled up at our feet, wreckage we cannot look away from, the detritus of so-called civilization, and we wonder if we are not being propelled instead toward the collapse of time. The end may be at hand, or it may just be going sideways. There are other cities within this city, and all of them are following different temporal routes. We see ours as a palimpsest of succeeding nows, like wheatpasted posters blithely and unendingly covering up yesterday's posters on boarded-up storefronts, while they measure theirs in workweeks or lunar months or fiscal years or a relentless thud of falling decades. The aged gingerly set forth from their residential hotels in search of bananas and condensed milk, braving all the dangers of the street, self-protectively oblivious of the dateline, still inhabiting a shimmery haze of 1937 within themselves, and as we pass them by we are fleetingly pulled into their orbit. Or else we walk by a radio and hear the Jesters and the Paragons and the Flamingos and the Moonglows because a calendar next door or down the street still reads 1957. Julius McMichael's spectral falsetto lead on the Paragons' "Florence" casts us off the shore of the speculative present and maroons us in a pillowy intertime, all velvet and sateen and crushed corsages on the scarred basketball dance floor, a ballad that keeps falling into dirge cadence, hovering between the aurora borealis and the void.

We all paid heed to that English tatterdemalion's cry[6] of "No future" in different ways, and if the word "future" didn't portend a lifetime's career opportunity in the mills gone south, or a cracked vision of needle-nosed high-rises connected by space taxis against a blood-red sky with three moons, what mostly remained in our heads was "no." Our fill-in-the-blank generation has had its blank filled by "no." There is a No Wave, and it is coming to your town but not really. Your town could not take it. You want your big guitars and hummable melodics and never-ending teenage idyll. Those things look delusional from where we stand. They were washed away by wars and assassinations and riots long ago, and if you don't understand this you are huffing stronger drugs than we possess. Our aesthetic is *destroy,* as the French say, who have converted the English verb into an adjective. Not for nothing are the faces of this instant those of Ulrike Meinhof and Andreas Baader,[7] lately deceased. Bands are forming of people who have never before picked up a musical instrument and aren't sure which end of it you stick in your mouth. They manage to produce sequences of noise that are two minutes long and have some sort of semi-consistent beat, but that's your only guarantee. It might be a lot better than that, but you can always count on a large quotient of rage and consequent distortion and lacerating atonal shrieks you can almost see graphically represented above the stage as cartoon notes with a shudder running through them. You climb the stairs to Max's[8] one night and find Bradly Field thumping on something with one stick and Gordon Stevenson emitting a two-note sine wave on his bass and in front is sixteen-year-old Lydia Lunch, producing circular-saw effects on some kind of junkyard guitar and squalling: Teenage Jesus and the Jerks. "Little orphans running through the bloody snow," she raves, evoking Victorian horror (although even after the record comes out you are convinced she has them rampaging through the Blarney Stone; you have done likewise in that chain of old-man bars). Lydia is small but she commands. She has everybody in the joint nailed to the wall. She could do anything onstage, and frequently does. Sure, she is just a teenage poet denouncing Mom and Dad and God and Society, but she has a force field of death-dealing noise to back her up and no one is about to get cute with her or deny a word.

Poetry is a thread that runs through this neighborhood, connecting the decades. Beat poets moved in back when it was an enclave of working families with zero flamboyance and few comforts — they liked that, and the fact that it was cheap. Through the hippie years and afterward more poets kept coming, filling the bookstores with side-stapled chapbooks mimeographed on typing paper, their authors lined up along the counter at Gem Spa, high on pills. Coffeehouses with reading series came and went, and then the Poetry Project, which cemented the connection between poetry and music: Patti Smith read there many times, Lou Reed read there, the Fugs performed, younger poets started their own bands — Television was one of them. Nowadays poetry still permeates the place, although the music has made it less conspicuous, which is crazy since poetry permeates the music. For that matter you walk around with a bass line in your head since that is your fuel, and then you naturally put words to that walking bass, words that come at you from stray talk or newspaper headlines or the memory of sentences that drift in unbidden. The mighty strophes of Linton Kwesi Johnson[9] (weirdly unnamed on his first record, simply attributed to Poet and the Roots) fly across the ocean from a place much more unsettled than our reasonably tranquil acres of ruins. He patiently enunciates the lyrics, the reggae band following his tempo — the inverse of the toasters who follow the riddims — and he is in no way engaging in hyperbole. "Five Nights of Bleeding" is a vast canvas of knifings and brawls and riots, where the music is a witness to both racist police violence and the propensity of victims to turn on their own. The words are hard, sculpted, scorched, three-dimensional, epic: "Inside James Brown

was screaming soul / Outside, the rebels were freezing cold." That
comma weighs as much as a wall. We can feel it from here, even
though our lives are nursery school.

The beatniks called our neighborhood "the set," which is apt
since that is where the strutting occurs. There are people who do
not seem to exist except on the St. Mark's sidewalk between Second and Third, and that number has increased as the population
has expanded. You see outfits that make you look twice — useless
to enumerate, since there are even more outrageous ones out
there right now — and then you never see them again. But by this
time there are scenesters in every hole. The epoch when you'd sort
of nod when passing a compatriot you didn't know is long gone.
People have moved in wholesale, in contingents from around the
world — the Texans, the Germans, the Australians, the Irish, the
enormous number of people from northeast Ohio, the bounce-
backs from San Francisco. There were two clubs for the longest
time and now there are as many as twenty, although the number
is constantly shifting. You've lost count of how many clubs you've
attended — sometimes with lights and pageantry and bouncers
behind a rope — that were shut the next day by the cops or the
firemen or the creditors. You pass clusters of photocopied posters everywhere — on every stretch of nonresidential unoccupied
wall, pretty much, and you rarely see an intact poster more than
two or three days old. Sometimes you can't tell the band posters
from the conceptual-art posters or the nutjob conspiracy posters.
The posters build up into clumps day after day after day, and when
they reach a critical weight they calve off like icebergs. You go out
wheatpasting sometimes, and it's a mess. The glue freezes in the
winter and gets all over your clothes and in your hair in the summer, and you're always keeping an eye out for the cops, and you're
trying not to cover other people's posters but often can't help it,
and you wonder whether yours won't be covered over by daybreak.

The bass these days is often physically present, issuing from
bars and passing cars and parked cars and pizzerias and record
stores and clothing shops, but it is always in your head because it
is indelible. On your rounds you are motored by Robbie Shakespeare on Junior Delgado's "Fort Augustus," and Bootsy Collins
on Parliament's "Flashlight," and Lloyd Parks on Dennis Brown's
"Equal Rights," and Jamaladeen Tacuma on Ornette Coleman's
"Voice Poetry," and Jah Wobble on "Swan Lake" by Public Image

Limited,[10] and so many others you can't name since you heard them in a club or on a twelve-inch single with the most minimal information rubber-stamped off-center and half-inked. It's all about the body nowadays, and you fling yours to hell four to five nights a week. You are stepping and hot-dogging like a wizard, executing moves you amaze yourself with, sure that everybody around must be eyeballing you, master of the polyrhythms, freestyling to the lip of the world without ever falling off. You favor the clubs with the least number of people on the floor so you can truly strut, open out, work your arms, jack your footwork. You look over at your partner and you briefly sync on the chorus, and then you both spin off into separate waves again, honoring the high-hat or that guitar that sounds like a rubber band, clairvoyantly anticipating the next chord change or even the next item that segues in with a counterintuitive slow shimmer. You knew that would happen. You are omnipotent because you are so deep inside the groove you might have been born there. You are the one most like the music, and your inner being shines forth like a beacon slicing across the floor, illuminating the corners. Also you are high as fuck.

You have arrived where you once wanted to be, in the dominion of music, the kingdom of the groove, the empire of rhythm. For better or worse you are living in youthville, where nine-tenths of the people you register in your field of vision are your age and more or less on your team, even though the scene long ago fragmented into affinity groups — this one eternally rocking, that one given to costume parties, others to champion-level drinking or filming themselves naked or experimenting with electronics or drafting militant screeds or following everything that is going on in London with painstaking fidelity to detail. One day everybody on the street is wearing horn-rimmed glasses and businessman raincoats buttoned up to the neck, the next they are all dyed blond and sporting cowboy neckerchiefs and big hats pushed back on their heads, and those go for all sexes. You go to clubs with polysyllabic names where all you can see is a strip of blue light at belt level. You find yourself in big-ass clubs with the ambiance of airports. You might be ushered into clubs with door policies so restrictive there are more people outside than in. You follow cryptic instructions to clubs on rooftops or in cellars or on the seventeenth floor of featureless office buildings, or to whoop-de-doos in public parks that might last an hour or five minutes depending on when the cops show up. You make your way to clubs that open at 4 a.m. and close their doors sometime around noon. There's the one in the alley far downtown where you get yourself into a fistfight for reasons you can't begin to fathom, the one in the ancient condemned theater on Fourteenth Street where jokers on line on the firetrap staircase start flicking lit matches at one another, the one in the decommissioned bar and grill where the personnel from all the other clubs go after closing, where you belly up to the counter and order not drinks but rails of uptown.

You get your poetry in snatches now, because it shows up as croaked lines deep inside the groove or buried in the mix or mumbled through a sleeve. You might register them only subliminally, maybe pick them up in daylight sometime later and wonder where you caught that sentence. Mostly you recall single barked chorus phrases that rattle around your head while the rest of the number might as well consist of doos and dahs, "She's lost control again" and "The cassette played pop tones" and "Tanz der Jesus-Christus." But lately poetry has been filtering down from the Bronx on stray 12s you can sometimes buy in that place on Union Square where they seem to rotate the stock every other day. "I was spanking and a-freaking in a disco place," says Spoonie Gee,[11] who is the smooth talker, the midnight stalker, the image of the man they call the J. D. Walker, bouncing to the Patty Duke riddim as it shuffles from side to side, his voice track intermittently so flanged it hurts your ears, and that phrase takes on a power and significance you can't account for except by reference to its reminiscent tense, somehow a harbinger of how all of this will one day fade into sepia, since golden lads and girls all must, as chimney sweepers come to dust. But that won't come anytime soon, since you are young and have been young all your life and live in the land of the young and have made no arrangements to ever be anything but young.

But as fate would have it, forces are even now making arrangements for you, since you and everybody else you know have been steadily increasing your consumption of substances, primarily powders. There was a time when these showed up rarely, then irregularly, in the pocket of some cosmopolitan friend, or in the pages of a book mailed from Thailand, or purchased from a dapper gent who also traded in vintage men's shoes, or paid as commission by an acquaintance who wanted to use your kitchen table as a place to tap a vein. But lately you have surprised yourself outside a slot in a door in some ruin a couple of blocks over in the empty quarter and handing over cash in exchange for bags. You tell yourself you will never be one of those people who stand for hours in the rain being toyed with by the lookouts, shuffled from one side of the street to the other, made to show track marks at the base of the steps, suffered having the slot slap shut definitively just as you are finally stepping up to it. You like boy the best because it unties every knot in your nerves and fills you with a glow you can carry to every occasion, making you the nonpareil you think you are on the dance floor. But your friends all seem to have unaccountable piles of girl lying around, and you cannot in good conscience refuse hospitality, so you inhale line after line, even if it makes you kind of jangly and causes every cigarette to burn up in three seconds. "I'm a dyn-o-mite," states Dillinger confidently. "I've got cocaine running around my brain."

He also cites the ancient rhyme: "A knife and a fork, / A bottle and a cork, / That's the way / To spell New York," and that sounds about right. All around us property is being carved up. The unlucky are being turned out of their homes on technicalities. Storefronts are being unboarded so people can sell trinkets to inquisitive tourists. Clubs are catering only to the slim and the rich, or have ballooned into funfair malls with three stages and eight dance floors and sixteen bars and VIP rooms inside VIP rooms. What was formerly given up to the street for common scavenging is now being put up for sale on flattened cardboard boxes on the sidewalk. People are flooding into the set just to gape. People are paying money to sleep in closets and backyard sheds and doctors' examining rooms. People are selling T-shirts advertising the neighborhood, or bands that have already broken up, or telling one and all to go fuck themselves. Suddenly cops appear on foot patrol in select areas. Suddenly beggars are fighting for turf. Suddenly beggars have gimmicks. The weird are turning pro. The pros are moving to more discreet zip codes. We realize we are absolutely unprepared for any of this, which as far as we know was brought about by the music. We thought the music would change the world, and we were correct except in the matter of specifics.

You check out the people on the street and note the year when they stopped: this one with the death's-head rictus 1973, that one in the Perfecto jacket 1977, her friend in the vinyl T-shirt 1979, those people looking like drunken ballroom dancers on an ocean liner 1980 — and that's when you realize you have a year written on your own forehead and it's not the one that tops the current calendar. You have aged out of the struggle just in time for the struggle to be done with you. You will never again inhabit the great Now, only a small and fragile instant that flips over every time you blink. Music will keep happening and you might like some of it or even a lot of it but it will no longer be yours. You will never be a star if you have failed to achieve that goal by now. All you can do is head to the dance floor in the burning disco where Chic is playing on an endless loop. These, the singers assure you again and again, are the good times.

Notes

1. The band founded in 1974 by Tom Verlaine and Richard Hell, who built the club's stage and effectively transformed Country Blue Grass & Blues into CBGB.
2. Director of films including *Rebel Without a Cause* and *Johnny Guitar.*
3. Post-bop drummer, most famous for his work with John Coltrane (1960–66).
4. Television's singer and lead guitarist.
5. A wistfully crooned reggae ballad.
6. Johnny Rotten in the Sex Pistols' "God Save the Queen."
7. Leaders of the ultra-left guerrilla organization Red Army Faction, who with two other members were found dead, ostensible suicides, in their cells at Stammheim Prison in West Germany in 1976 and '77.
8. Max's Kansas City, on Park Avenue South near Eighteenth Street, famous in the 1960s as the hangout of Andy Warhol, the Velvet Underground, and others of the Factory set, which enjoyed a second life during the punk '70s.
9. Jamaican British poet known for his published poems as well as his performances with musical backing, beginning around 1974. His first album, *Dread Beat an' Blood* (1978), was based on his second book, of the same name, and chronicled black British life in terms both poetically rich and journalistically detailed.
10. The genres represented are, in order: dub reggae, R&B, dub reggae, harmolodic jazz, and post-punk.
11. Né Gabriel Jackson, Harlem-based rapper whose "Spoonin' Rap" (1979) was one of the very earliest hip-hop recordings.

KATHRYN SCHULZ

Losing Streak

FROM *The New Yorker*

A COUPLE OF years ago, I spent the summer in Portland, Oregon, losing things. I normally live on the East Coast, but that year, unable to face another sweltering August, I decided to temporarily decamp to the West. This turned out to be strangely easy. I'd lived in Portland for a while after college, and some acquaintances there needed a house sitter. Another friend was away for the summer and happy to loan me her pickup truck. Someone on Craigslist sold me a bike for next to nothing. In very short order, and with very little effort, everything fell into place.

And then, mystifyingly, everything fell out of place. My first day in town, I left the keys to the truck on the counter of a coffee shop. The next day, I left the keys to the house in the front door. A few days after that, warming up in the midday sun at an outdoor café, I took off the long-sleeved shirt I'd been wearing, only to leave it hanging over the back of the chair when I headed home. When I returned to claim it, I discovered that I'd left my wallet behind as well. Prior to that summer, I should note, I had lost a wallet exactly once in my adult life: at gunpoint. Yet later that afternoon I stopped by a sporting-goods store to buy a lock for my new bike and left my wallet sitting next to the cash register.

I got the wallet back, but the next day I lost the bike lock. I'd just arrived home and removed it from its packaging when my phone rang; I stepped away to take the call, and when I returned, some time later, the lock had vanished. This was annoying, because I was planning to bike downtown that evening, to attend an event at Powell's, Portland's famous bookstore. Eventually, having spent an absurd amount of time looking for the lock and failing to find it, I gave up and drove the truck downtown instead. I parked, went to the event, hung around talking for a while afterward, browsed the bookshelves, walked outside into a lovely summer evening, and could not find the truck anywhere.

This was a serious feat, a real bar-raising of thing-losing, not only because in general it is difficult to lose a truck but also because the truck in question was enormous. The friend to whom it belonged once worked as an ambulance driver; oversized vehicles do not faze her. It had tires that came up to my midriff, an extended cab, and a bed big enough to haul cetaceans. Yet I'd somehow managed to misplace it in downtown Portland — a city, incidentally, that I know as well as any other on the planet. For the next forty-five minutes, as a cool blue night gradually lowered itself over downtown, I walked around looking for the truck, first on the street where I was sure I'd parked, then on the nearest cross streets, and then in a grid whose scale grew ever larger and more ludicrous.

Finally, I returned to the street where I'd started and noticed a small sign: NO PARKING ANYTIME. Oh, shit. Feeling like the world's biggest idiot, and wondering how much it was going to cost to extricate a truck the size of Nevada from a tow lot, I called the Portland Police Department. The man who answered was wonderfully affable. "No, ma'am," he veritably sang into the phone, "no pickup trucks from downtown this evening. Must be your lucky day!" Officer, you have no idea. Channeling the kind of advice one is often given as a child, I returned to the bookstore, calmed myself down with a cup of tea, collected my thoughts amid the latest literary debuts, and then, to the best of my ability, retraced the entire course of my evening, in the hope that doing so would knock loose some memory of how I got there. It did not. Back outside on the streets of Portland, I spun around as uselessly as a dowsing rod.

Seventy-five minutes later, I found the truck, in a perfectly legal parking space, on a block so unrelated to any reasonable route from my house to the bookstore that I seriously wondered if I'd driven there in some kind of fugue state. I climbed in, headed home, and, for reasons I'll explain in a moment, decided that I needed to call my sister as soon as I walked in the door. But I did not. I could not. My cell phone was back at Powell's, on a shelf with all the other New Arrivals.

*

My sister is a cognitive scientist at MIT, more conversant than most people in the mental processes involved in tracking and misplacing objects. That is not, however, why I wanted to talk to her about my newly acquired propensity for losing things. I wanted to talk to her because, true to the stereotype of the absent-minded professor, she is the most scatterbrained person I've ever met.

There is a runner-up: my father. My family members, otherwise a fairly similar bunch, are curiously divided down the middle in this respect. On the spectrum of obsessively orderly to sublimely unconcerned with the everyday physical world, my father and my sister are — actually, they are nowhere. They can't even *find* the spectrum. My mother and I, meanwhile, are busy organizing it by size and color. I will never forget watching my mother try to adjust an ever so slightly askew picture frame — at the Cleveland Museum of Art. My father, by contrast, once spent an entire vacation wearing mismatched shoes, because he'd packed no others and discovered the mistake only when airport security asked him to remove them. My sister's best TSA trick, meanwhile, involved borrowing her partner's laptop, then accidentally leaving it at an Alaska Airlines gate one week after 9/11, thereby almost shutting down the Oakland airport.

That's why I called her when I started uncharacteristically misplacing stuff myself. For one thing, I thought she might commiserate. For another, I thought she might help; given her extensive experience with losing things, I figured she must have developed a compensatory capacity for finding them. Once I recovered my phone and reached her, however, both hopes vanished as completely as the bike lock. My sister was gratifyingly astonished that I'd never lost my wallet before, but, as someone who typically has to reconstruct the entire contents of her own several times a year, she was not exactly sympathetic. "Call me," she said, "when they know your name at the DMV."

Nor did my sister have any good advice on how to find missing objects — although, in fairness, such advice is itself difficult to find. Plenty of parents, self-help gurus, and psychics will offer to assist you in finding lost stuff, but most of their suggestions are either obvious (calm down, clean up), suspect (the "eighteen-inch rule," whereby the majority of missing items are supposedly lurking less than two feet from where you first thought they would be), or New Agey. ("Picture a silvery cord reaching from your chest all the way out to your lost object.") Advice on how to find missing things also abounds online, but as a rule it is useful only in proportion to the strangeness of whatever you've lost. Thus, the internet is middling on your lost credit card or Kindle, but edifying on your lost Roomba (look inside upholstered furniture), your lost marijuana (your high self probably hid it in a fit of paranoia; try your sock drawer), your lost drone (you'll need a specially designed GPS), or your lost Bitcoins (good luck with that). The same basic dynamic applies to the countless websites devoted to recovering lost pets, which are largely useless when it comes to your missing Lab mix but surprisingly helpful when it comes to your missing ball python. Such websites can also be counted on for excellent anecdotes, like the one about the cat that vanished in Nottinghamshire, England, and was found, fourteen months later, in a pet-food warehouse, twice its original size.

Perhaps the best thing that can be said about lost entities and the internet is that it has made many of them considerably easier to find: out-of-print books, elementary school classmates, decades-old damning quotes by politicians. More generally, modern technology can sometimes help us find misplaced objects, as you know if you've ever had your girlfriend call your lost cell phone, or used that little button on your keys to make your Toyota Camry honk at you. Lately, we've seen a boom in technologies specifically designed to compensate for our tendency to lose stuff: Apple's Find My iPhone, for instance, and the proliferation of Bluetooth-enabled tracking devices that you can attach to everyday objects in order to summon them from the ether, like the Accio spell in the Harry Potter books.

These tricks, while helpful, have their limitations. Your phone needs to be on and nondead; your car needs to be within range; you need to have the foresight to stick a tracking device onto the particular thing you're going to lose before you've lost it. Moreover, as anyone who's ever owned a remote control can tell you, new technologies themselves are often infuriatingly unfindable, a problem made worse by the trend toward ever smaller gadgets. It is difficult to lose an Apple IIe, easier to lose a laptop, a snap to lose a cell phone, and nearly impossible *not* to lose a flash drive. Then there is the issue of passwords, which are to computers what socks are to washing machines. The only thing in the real or the digital world harder to keep track of than a password is the information required to retrieve it, which is why it is possible, as a grown adult, to find yourself caring about your first-grade teacher's pet iguana's maiden name.

Passwords, passports, umbrellas, scarves, earrings, earbuds, musical instruments, W-2s, that letter you meant to answer, the permission slip for your daughter's field trip, the can of paint you scrupulously set aside three years ago for the touch-up job you knew you'd someday need: the range of things we lose and the readiness with which we do so are staggering. Data from one insurance-company survey suggest that the average person misplaces up to nine objects a day, which means that by the time we turn sixty, we will have lost up to two hundred thousand things. (These figures seem preposterous until you reflect on all those times you holler up the stairs to ask your partner if she's seen your jacket, or on how often you search the couch cushions for the pen you were just using, or on that daily almost-out-the-door flurry when you can't find your kid's lunchbox or your car keys.) Granted, you'll get many of those items back, but you'll never get back the time you wasted looking for them. In the course of your life, you'll spend roughly six solid months looking for missing objects; here in the United States, that translates to, collectively, some fifty-four million hours spent searching a *day*. And there's the associated loss of money: in the US in 2011, $30 billion on misplaced cell phones alone.

Broadly speaking, there are two explanations for why we lose all this stuff — one scientific, the other psychoanalytic, both unsatisfying. According to the scientific account, losing things represents a failure of recollection or a failure of attention: either we can't retrieve a memory (of where we set down our wallet, say) or we didn't encode one in the first place. According to the psychoanalytic account, conversely, losing things represents a *success* — a deliberate sabotage of our rational mind by our subliminal desires. In *The Psychopathology of Everyday Life*, Freud describes "the unconscious dexterity with which an object is mislaid on account of hidden but powerful motives," including "the low estimation in which the lost object is held, or a secret antipathy towards it or towards the person that it came from." Freud's colleague and contemporary Abraham Arden Brill put the matter more succinctly: "We never lose what we highly value."

As explanations go, the scientific one is persuasive but uninteresting. It sheds no light on how it feels to lose something, and provides only the most abstract and impractical notion of how not to do so. (Focus! And, while you're at it, rejigger your genes or circumstances to improve your memory.) The psychological account, by contrast, is interesting, entertaining, and theoretically helpful (Freud pointed out "the remarkable sureness shown in finding the object again once the motive for its being mislaid had expired") but, alas, untrue. The most charitable thing to be said about it is that it wildly overestimates our species: absent subconscious motives, apparently, we would never lose anything at all.

That is patently false — but, like many psychological claims, impossible to actually falsify. Maybe the doting mother who lost her toddler at the mall was secretly fed up with the demands of motherhood. Maybe my sister loses her wallet so often owing to a deep-seated discomfort with capitalism. Maybe the guy who left his *Hamilton* tickets in the taxi was a Jeffersonian at heart. Freud would stand by such propositions, and no doubt some losses really are occasioned by subconscious emotion, or at least can be convincingly explained that way after the fact. But experience tells us that such cases are unusual, if they exist at all. The better explanation, most of the time, is simply that life is complicated and minds are limited. We lose things because we are flawed; because we are human; because we have things to lose.

Of all the lost objects in literature, one of my favorites appears — or, rather, disappears — in Patti Smith's 2015 memoir, *M Train.* Although that book is ultimately concerned with far more serious losses, Smith pauses midway through to describe the experience of losing a beloved black coat that a friend gave her, off his own back, on her fifty-seventh birthday. The coat wasn't much to look at — moth-eaten, coming apart at the seams, itself optimized for losing things by the gaping holes in each pocket — but, Smith writes, "Every time I put it on I felt like myself." Then came a particularly harsh winter, which required a warmer jacket, and by the time the air turned mild again the coat was nowhere to be seen.

When we lose something, our first reaction, naturally enough, is to want to know where it is. But behind that question about location lurks a question about causality: What happened to it? What agent or force made it disappear? Such questions matter because they can help direct our search. You will act differently if you think you left your coat in a taxi or believe you boxed it up and put it in the basement. Just as important, the answers can provide us with that much coveted condition known as closure. It is good to get your keys back, better still to understand how they wound up in your neighbor's recycling bin.

But questions about causality can also lead to trouble, because, in essence, they ask us to assign blame. Being human, we're often reluctant to assign it to ourselves — and when it comes to missing possessions it is always possible (and occasionally true) that someone else caused them to disappear. This is how a problem with an object turns into a problem with a person. You swear you left the bill sitting on the table for your wife to mail; your wife swears with equal vehemence that it was never there; soon enough, you have also both lost your tempers.

Another possibility, considerably less likely but equally self-sparing, is that your missing object engineered its own vanishing, alone or in conjunction with other occult forces. Beloved possessions like her black coat, Patti Smith suggests, are sometimes "drawn into that half-dimensional place where things just disappear." Such explanations are more common than you might think. Given enough time spent searching for something that was *just there,* even the most scientifically inclined person on the planet will start positing various highly improbable culprits: wormholes, aliens, goblins, ether.

That is an impressive act of outsourcing, given that nine times out of ten we are to blame for losing whatever it is that we can't find. In the microdrama of loss, in other words, we are nearly always both villain and victim. That goes some way toward explaining why people often say that losing things drives them crazy. At best, our failure to locate something that we ourselves last handled suggests that our memory is shot; at worst, it calls into question the very nature and continuity of selfhood. (If you've ever lost something that you deliberately stashed away for safekeeping, you know that the resulting frustration stems not just from a failure of memory but from a failure of inference. As one astute internet commentator asked, "Why is it so hard to think like myself?") Part of what makes loss such a surprisingly complicated phenomenon, then, is that it is inextricable from the extremely complicated phenomenon of human cognition.

This entanglement becomes more fraught as we grow older. Beyond a certain age, every act of losing gets subjected to an extra layer of scrutiny, in case what you have actually lost is your mind. Most such acts don't indicate pathology, of course, but real mental decline does manifest partly as an uptick in lost things. Dementia patients are prone to misplacing their belongings, and people with early-stage Alzheimer's often can't find objects because they have put them in unlikely locations; the eyeglasses end up in the oven, the dentures in the coffee can. Such losses sadden us because they presage larger ones — of autonomy, of intellectual capacity, ultimately of life itself.

No wonder losing things, even trivial things, can be so upsetting. Regardless of what goes missing, loss puts *us* in our place; it confronts us with lack of order and loss of control and the fleeting nature of existence. When Patti Smith gives up on finding her black coat, she imagines that, together with all of the world's other missing objects, it has gone to dwell in a place her husband liked to call the Valley of Lost Things. The shadow that is missing from that phrase darkens her memoir; in the course of it, Smith also describes losing her best friend, her brother, her mother, and that husband (at age forty-five, to heart failure).

On the face of it, such losses fit in poorly with lesser ones. It is one thing to lose a wedding ring, something else entirely to lose a spouse. This is the distinction Elizabeth Bishop illuminates, by pretending to elide it, in her villanelle "One Art," perhaps the most famous reckoning with loss in all of literature. Anyone can become skilled at losing, she claims; the trick is to begin with trivial losses, like door keys, and practice until you can handle those which are tragic. No one could take this suggestion seriously, and we aren't meant to do so. Through its content as well as its form, the poem ultimately concedes that all other losses pale beside the loss of a loved one.

Moreover, although Bishop doesn't make this point explicitly, death differs from other losses not only in degree but in kind. With objects, loss implies the possibility of recovery; in theory, at least, nearly every missing possession can be restored to its owner. That's why the defining emotion of losing things isn't frustration or panic or sadness but, paradoxically, hope. With people, by contrast, loss is not a transitional state but a terminal one. Outside of an afterlife, for those who believe in one, it leaves us with nothing to hope for and nothing to do. Death is loss without the possibility of being found.

My father, in addition to being scatterbrained and mismatched and menschy and brilliant, is dead. I lost him, as we say, in the third week of September, just before the autumn equinox. Since then, the days have darkened, and I, too, have been lost: adrift, disoriented, absent. Or perhaps it would be more apt to say that I have been *at a loss* — a strange turn of phrase, as if loss were a place in the physical world, a kind of reverse oasis or Bermuda Triangle where the spirit fails and the compass needle spins.

Like death more generally, my father's was somehow both predictable and shocking. For nearly a decade, his health had been poor, almost impressively so. In addition to suffering from many of the usual complaints of contemporary aging (high blood pressure, high cholesterol, kidney disease, congestive heart failure), he had endured illnesses unusual for any age and era: viral meningitis, West Nile encephalitis, an autoimmune disorder whose identity evaded the best doctors at the Cleveland Clinic. From there, the list spread outward in all directions of physiology and severity. He had fallen and torn a rotator cuff beyond recovery, and obliterated a patellar tendon by missing a step one Fourth of July. His breathing was often labored despite no evident respiratory problem; an errant nerve in his neck sometimes zapped him into temporary near-paralysis. He had terrible dental issues, like the impoverished child he had once been, and terrible gout, like the wealthy old potentate he cheerfully became.

He was, in short, a shambles. And yet, as the ER visits added up over the years, I gradually curbed my initial feelings of panic and dread — partly because no one can live in a state of crisis forever but also because, by and large, my father bore his infirmity with insouciance. ("Biopsy Thursday," he once wrote me about a problem with his carotid artery. "Have no idea when the autopsy will be and may not be informed of it.") More to the point, against considerable odds, he just kept on being alive. Intellectually, I knew that no one could manage such a serious disease burden forever. Yet the sheer number of times my father had courted death and then recovered had, perversely, made him seem indomitable.

As a result, I was not overly alarmed when my mother called one morning toward the end of the summer to say that my father had been hospitalized with a bout of atrial fibrillation. Nor was I surprised, when my partner and I got to town that night, to learn that his heart rhythm had stabilized. The doctors were keeping him in the hospital chiefly for observation, they told us, and also because his white-blood-cell count was mysteriously high. When my father related the chain of events to us — he had gone to a routine cardiology appointment, only to be shunted straight to the ICU — he was jovial and accurate and eminently himself. He remained in good spirits the following day, although he was extremely garrulous, not in his usual effusive way but slightly manic, slightly off — a consequence, the doctors explained, of toxins building up in his bloodstream from temporary loss of kidney function. If it didn't resolve on its own in a day or two, they planned to give him a round of dialysis to clear it.

That was on a Wednesday. Over the next two days, the garrulousness declined into incoherence; then, on Saturday, my father lapsed into unresponsiveness. Somewhere below his silence lurked six languages, the result of being born in Tel Aviv to parents who had fled pogroms in Poland, relocating at age seven to Germany (an unusual reverse exodus for a family of Jews in 1948, precipitated by limited travel options and violence in what was then still Palestine), and arriving in the United States, on a refugee visa, at the age of twelve. English, French, German, Polish, Yiddish, Hebrew: of these, my father acquired the first one last, and spoke it with Nabokovian fluency and panache. He loved to talk — I mean that he found just putting sentences together tremendously fun, although he also cherished conversation — and he talked his way into, out of, and through everything, including illness. During the years of medical crises, I had seen my father racked and raving with fever. I had seen him in a dozen kinds of pain. I had seen him hallucinating — sometimes while fully aware of it, discussing with us not only the mystery of his visions but also the mystery of cognition. I had seen him cast about in a mind temporarily compromised by illness and catch only strange, dark, pelagic creatures, unknown and fearsome to the rest of us. In all that time, under all those varied conditions, I had never known him to lack for words. But now, for five days, he held his silence. On the sixth, he lurched back into sound, but not into himself; there followed an awful night of struggle and agitation. After that, aside from a few scattered words, some mystifying, some seemingly lucid — "Hi!"; "Machu Picchu"; "I'm dying" — my father never spoke again.

Even so, for a while longer, he endured — I mean his himness, his Isaac-ness, that inexplicable, assertive bit of self in each of us. A few days before his death, having ignored every request made of him by a constant stream of medical professionals ("Mr. Schulz, can you wiggle your toes?" "Mr. Schulz, can you squeeze my hand?"), my father chose to respond to one final command: Mr. Schulz, we learned, could still stick out his tongue. His last voluntary movement, which he retained almost until the end, was the ability to kiss my mother. Whenever she leaned in close to brush his lips, he puckered up and returned the same brief, adoring gesture that I had seen all my days. In front of my sister and me, at least, it was my parents' hello and goodbye, their "Sweet dreams" and "I'm only teasing," their "I'm sorry" and "You're beautiful" and "I love you" — the basic punctuation mark of their common language, the sign and seal of fifty years of happiness.

One night, while that essence still persisted, we gathered around, my father's loved ones, and filled his silence with talk. I had always regarded my family as close, so it was startling to realize how much closer we could get, how near we drew around his dying flame. The room we were in was a cube of white, lit up like the aisle of a grocery store, yet in my memory that night is as dark and vibrant as a Rembrandt painting. We talked only of love; there was nothing else to say. My father, mute but alert, looked from one face to the next as we spoke, eyes shining with tears. I had always dreaded seeing him cry, and rarely did, but for once I was grateful. It told me what I needed to know: for what may have been the last time in his life, and perhaps the most important, he understood.

All this makes dying sound meaningful and sweet — and it is true that, if you are lucky, there is a seam of sweetness and meaning to be found within it, a vein of silver in a dark cave a thousand feet underground. Still, the cave is a cave. We had by then spent two vertiginous, elongated, atemporal weeks in the ICU. At no point during that time did we have a diagnosis, still less a prognosis. At every point, we were besieged with new possibilities, new tests, new doctors, new hopes, new fears. Every night, we arrived home exhausted, many hours past dark, and talked through what had happened, as if doing so might guide us through the following day. Then we'd wake up and resume the routine of the parking garage and the elevator and the twenty-four-hour Au Bon Pain, only to discover that, beyond those, there was no routine at all, nothing to help us prepare or plan. It was like trying to dress every morning for the weather in a nation we'd never heard of.

Eventually, we decided that my father would not recover, and so, instead of continuing to try to stave off death, we unbarred the door and began to wait. To my surprise, I found it comforting to be with him during that time, to sit by his side and hold his hand and watch his chest rise and fall with a familiar little riffle of snore. It was not, as they say, unbearably sad; on the contrary, it was bearably sad — a tranquil, contemplative, lapping kind of sorrow. I thought, as it turns out mistakenly, that what I was doing during those days was making my peace with his death. I have learned since then that even one's unresponsive and dying father is, in some extremely salient way, still alive. And then, very early one morning, he was not.

What I remember best from those next hours is watching my mother cradle the top of my father's head in her hand. A wife holding her dead husband, without trepidation, without denial, without any possibility of being cared for in return, just for the chance to be tender toward him one last time: it was the purest act of love I've ever seen. She looked bereft, beautiful, unimaginably calm. He did not yet look dead. He looked like my father. I could not stop picturing the way he used to push his glasses up onto his forehead to read. It struck me, right before everything else struck me much harder, that I should set them by his bed in case he needed them.

So began my second, darker season of losing things. Three weeks after my father died, so did another family member, of cancer. Three weeks after that, my hometown baseball team lost the World Series — an outcome that wouldn't have affected me much if my father hadn't been such an ardent fan. One week later, Hillary Clinton, together with sixty-six million voters, lost the presidential election.

Like a dysfunctional form of love, which to some extent it is, grief has no boundaries; seldom this fall could I distinguish my distress over these later losses from my sadness about my father. I had maintained my composure during his memorial service, even while delivering the eulogy. But when, at the second funeral, the son of the deceased stood up to speak, I wept. Afterward, I couldn't shake the sense that another shoe was about to drop — that at any moment I would learn that someone else close to me had died. The morning after the election, I cried again, missing my refugee father, missing the future I had thought would unfold. In its place, other kinds of losses suddenly seemed imminent: of civil rights, personal safety, financial security, the foundational American values of respect for dissent and difference, the institutions and protections of democracy.

For weeks, I slogged on like this, through waves of actual and anticipatory grief. I couldn't stop conjuring catastrophes, political and otherwise. I felt a rising fear whenever my mother didn't answer her phone, hated to see my sister board an airplane, could barely let my partner get in a car. "So many things seem filled with the intent to be lost," Elizabeth Bishop wrote, and, as much as my specific sadness, it was just that — the sheer quantity and inevitability of further suffering — that undid me.

Meanwhile, I had lost, along with everything else, all motivation; day after day, I did as close as humanly possible to nothing. In part, this was because I dreaded getting farther away from the time when my father was still alive. But it was also because, after all the obvious tasks of mourning were completed — the service over, the bureaucratic side of death dispatched, the clothing donated, the thank-you cards written — I had no idea what else to do. Although I had spent a decade worrying about losing my father, I had never once thought about what would come next. Like a heart, my imagination had always stopped at the moment of death.

Now, obliged to carry onward through time, I realized I didn't know how. I found some consolation in poetry, but otherwise, for the first time in my life, I did not care to read. Nor could I bring myself to write, not least because any piece I produced would be the first my father wouldn't see. I stretched out for as long as I could the small acts that felt easy and right (calling my mother and my sister, curling up with my partner, playing with the cats), but these alone could not occupy the days. Not since the age of eight, when I was still learning to master boredom, had life struck me so much as simply a problem of what to do.

It was during this time that I began to go out looking for my father. Some days, I merely said to myself that I wanted to get out of the house; other days, I set about searching for him as deliberately as one would go look for a missing glove. Because I find peace and clarity in nature, I did this searching outdoors, sometimes while walking, sometimes while out on a run. I did not expect, of course, that along the way I would encounter my father again in his physical form. To the extent that I thought about it at all, I thought that through sheer motion I might be able to create a tunnel of emptiness, in myself or in the world, that would fill up with a sense of his presence — his voice, his humor, his warmth, the perfect familiarity of our relationship.

I have subsequently learned, from the academic literature on grief, that this "searching behavior," as it is called, is common among the bereaved. The psychologist John Bowlby, a contemporary of Elisabeth Kübler-Ross, regarded the second stage of grief, after numbness, as "yearning and searching." But I had never knowingly engaged in it before, because, in my experience, my dead had always come looking for *me*. After other people I'd loved had died, I had often felt them near me, sometimes heard their voices, and even, on a few exceedingly strange occasions, been jolted into the uncanny conviction that I had encountered them again in some altered but unmistakable form. (This, too, turns out to be common among the grieving. In his wonderfully matter-of-fact poem "Alone," Jack Gilbert writes about the strange way that his late wife "has returned / as somebody's Dalmatian.")

These experiences, to be clear, do not comport with my understanding of death. I don't believe that our loved ones can commune with us from beyond the grave, any more than I believe that spouses occasionally reincarnate as Dalmatians. But grief makes reckless cosmologists of us all, and I had thought it possible, in an impossible kind of way, that if I went out looking I might find myself in my father's company again.

The first time, I turned around after five minutes; I have seldom tried anything that felt so futile. After he lost his wife, C. S. Lewis, who had likewise previously felt the dead to be near at hand, looked up at the night sky and, to his dismay, knew that he would never find her anywhere. "Is anything more certain," he wrote, in "A Grief Observed," "than that in all those vast times and spaces, if I were allowed to search them, I should nowhere find her face, her voice, her touch?" Between his late wife and himself, he felt only "the locked door, the iron curtain, the vacuum, absolute zero."

Thus do I feel about my father. "Lost" is precisely the right de-

scription for how I have experienced him since his death. I search
for him constantly but can't find him anywhere. I try to sense some
intimation of his presence and feel nothing. I listen for his voice
but haven't heard it since those final times he used it in the hospital. Grieving him is like holding one of those homemade tin-can
telephones with no tin can on the other end of the string. His
absence is total; where there was him, there is nothing.

This was perhaps the most striking thing about my father's death
and all that followed: how relevant the idea of loss felt, how it
seemed at once so capacious and so accurate. And in fact, to my
surprise, it *was* accurate. Until I looked it up, I'd assumed that,
unless we were talking about phone chargers or car keys or cake
recipes, we were using the word "lost" figuratively, even euphe-
mistically — that we say "I lost my father" to soften the blow of
death.

But that turns out not to be true. The verb "to lose" has its tap-
root sunk in sorrow; it is related to the "lorn" in forlorn. It comes
from an Old English word meaning to perish, which comes from
a still more ancient word meaning to separate or cut apart. The
modern sense of misplacing an object appeared later, in the thir-
teenth century; a hundred years after that, "to lose" acquired the
meaning of failing to win. In the sixteenth century, we began to
lose our minds; in the seventeenth century, our hearts. The circle
of what we can lose, in other words, began with our own lives and
one another and has been steadily expanding ever since. In consequence, loss today is a supremely awkward category, bulging with
everything from mittens to life savings to loved ones, forcing into
relationship all kinds of wildly dissimilar experiences.

And yet, if anything, our problem is not that we put too many
things into the category of loss but that we leave too many out.
One night, during those weeks when I could find solace only in
poetry, my partner read "Crossing Brooklyn Ferry" aloud to me.
In it, Walt Whitman leans against the railing of a ship, exalting
in all he sees. So expansive is his vision that it includes not just
the piers and sails and reeling gulls but everyone else who makes
the crossing: all those who stood at the railing watching before
his birth, all those watching around him now, and all those who
will be there watching after his death — which, in the poem, he

doesn't so much foresee as, through a wild, craning omniscience, look back on. "Just as you feel when you look on the river and sky, so I felt," he admonishes, kindly.

And, just like that, my sense of loss suddenly revealed itself as terribly narrow. What I miss about my father, as much as anything, is life as it looked filtered through him, held up and considered against his inner lights. Yet the most important thing that vanished when he died is wholly unavailable to me: life as it looked *to* him, life as we all live it, from the inside out. All my memories can't add up to a single moment of what it was like to be my father, and all my loss pales beside his own. Like Whitman, his love of life had been exuberant, exhaustive; he must have hated, truly hated, to leave it behind — not just his family, whom he adored, but all of it, sea to shining sea.

It is breathtaking, the extinguishing of consciousness. Yet that loss, too — our own ultimate unbeing — is dwarfed by the grander scheme. When we are experiencing it, loss often feels like an anomaly, a disruption in the usual order of things. In fact, though, it *is* the usual order of things. Entropy, mortality, extinction: the entire plan of the universe consists of losing, and life amounts to a reverse savings account in which we are eventually robbed of everything. Our dreams and plans and jobs and knees and backs and memories, the childhood friend, the husband of fifty years, the father of forever, the keys to the house, the keys to the car, the keys to the kingdom, the kingdom itself: sooner or later, all of it drifts into the Valley of Lost Things.

There's precious little solace for this, and zero redress; we will lose everything we love in the end. But why should that matter so much? By definition, we do not live in the end: we live all along the way. The smitten lovers who marvel every day at the miracle of having met each other are right; it is *finding* that is astonishing. You meet a stranger passing through your town and know within days you will marry her. You lose your job at fifty-five and shock yourself by finding a new calling ten years later. You have a thought and find the words. You face a crisis and find your courage.

All of this is made more precious, not less, by its impermanence. No matter what goes missing, the wallet or the father, the lessons are the same. Disappearance reminds us to notice, transience to cherish, fragility to defend. Loss is a kind of external conscience, urging us to make better use of our finite days. As Whitman knew, our brief crossing is best spent attending to all that we see: honoring what we find noble, denouncing what we cannot abide, recognizing that we are inseparably connected to all of it, including what is not yet upon us, including what is already gone. We are here to keep watch, not to keep.

JOHN SEABROOK

My Father's Cellar

FROM *The New Yorker*

MRS. HALL, MY third-grade teacher at St. John's Day School, had given the class a homework assignment: draw a floor plan of your parents' house or apartment. Our house was big, but I did my best to include all the rooms on the first floor — kitchen, dining room, breakfast room, library, drawing room (a funny name for the room where the adults sometimes played cards), living room, two powder rooms, and bar.

I had to restart a couple of times until I got a feel for the proportions. I liked the way the assignment made me think. I was momentarily outside the familiar rooms and the lives we lived there, looking in. Eventually, I managed to fit all the rooms into the square boundaries of my plan. I was proud of my work, and showed it to my mother.

"Oh dear," she said, and laughed.

"What's so funny?"

"It's just the size of the bar, darling." She laughed again — light but with a hint of tension. "It's so big. Mrs. Hall will think we're alcoholics!"

My bar, labeled *BAR* in big, blocky letters, was a large rectangle exactly in the middle of the plan, as big as the kitchen.

The bar was a narrow passageway off the dining room which connected the front of the house with the back. Although small, the room produced maximum merriment per square foot. The bar was like a magic hat from which a magician pulls impossibly long scarves of colored silk. It sounded big — the violent rattle of the martini shaker and the muted explosion of a champagne cork reverberated throughout the house. The liquor cabinet was a men's club of masculine archetypes: someone's ornery grandfather on the whiskey bottle; on the gin, a British Beefeater, dressed like the real ones we had seen at the Tower of London, in a bright-red jacket and round black hat, holding a long spear. There were chrome-plated grippers and squeezers and shakers that my father washed and laid out on a dish towel before the guests arrived. There were the names of cocktails: martinis, daiquiris, manhattans, old-fashioneds. My favorite, the bullshot (it sounded like "bullshit") — Worcestershire sauce, beef broth, and vodka — was for the morning after, if someone had a hangover.

I dutifully erased the rectangle marked *BAR* and made it smaller, but now it was smudged, and more of a focal point than ever.

So I redid the whole plan, trying to draw the bar to scale, but it still came out larger than it actually was. "That's better, thank you, darling," my mother said, but I could tell she was worried about Mrs. Hall.

Most of my father's alcohol was secured in a cellar somewhere in the basement. Its location was a mystery to me, at first. Clearly, the wine and the champagne he served at dinner and at parties came from somewhere. There was no wine in the bar except for a few bottles of lesser whites in the fridge, for those sorry guests who preferred a glass of wine to a cocktail before dinner.

My father, John M. Seabrook (called Jack), was the scion and president of Seabrook Farms, a large frozen-food company that operated on more than fifty thousand acres in southern New Jersey — a kind of feudal empire that resembled, in his mind, at least, the venerable inherited estates of Great Britain. He had seen the wine cellars in some of those places, and he had set about building one for his own demesne, in Deep South Jersey. But by the time I was born, in the late 1950s, the frozen-food empire was no longer his — C. F. Seabrook, the owner of the company, had sold the business to a wholesale grocery outfit from New York. Soon my father became the CEO of a public company in Philadelphia. *"Cee Eee Oh"* was among the first sounds I recall hearing at the dinner table. It was like whale talk.

There was a key marked wc that was kept in the drawer of a side table in the dining room. My father said that WC stood for "water closet," which was what they called the bathroom in England. But what bathroom door did the key fit? Most of the doors didn't even have locks on them. My father often said that there was no reason anyone should lock doors in the house.

After some time, I realized that the bland, trust-me look on his face when he explained about WC meant that he was joking, and, moreover, that he wanted me to see that he was joking. He was going to show me his wine cellar. And one day he did.

"You can help me pick the wine for tonight," he said one Saturday afternoon before a dinner party, when I was seven or eight. Thrilled, I followed him down the steep, curving steps that led to the basement. He was dressed in his casual weekend clothes: widewale corduroys the color of straw, a pale-yellow dress shirt, beautiful brown ankle boots with pink socks poking out of the tops. He moved carefully on the stairs, gripping the right-hand railing and lowering his foot slowly onto the next step, then stamping down with his heel to make sure it gripped before putting his weight on it. Years before, while riding alone one Sunday morning, he'd been thrown from his horse and landed on an irrigation pipe, cracking his pelvis. The horse had run back to the farm, and the men had gone out looking for my father, not finding him until several hours later, lying in a ditch. That was one of the few stories he told in which he was ever at a disadvantage. It wasn't heard often.

At the bottom of the stairs was a low-ceilinged passageway that led to the basement's outdoor entrance. Along one wall was some cabinetry for storing excess kitchenware and picnic stuff, and, next to that, a floor-to-ceiling plywood bookcase, painted white with green trim, holding books that had belonged to my older half sisters, Carol and Lizanne — *Eloise, Black Beauty, The Happy Hollisters.*

He stopped in front of the bookcase.

"See anything?"

I looked at the books. Among them was *The Boy Who Drew Cats*, a Japanese folktale about a rebellious artist-boy who defeats a goblin rat that lives in the temple and has killed many mighty warriors, simply by drawing pictures of cats on the walls and going to sleep. In the morning, when he finds the terrible rat dead in the temple and can't explain it, he notices that the cats' mouths in the drawings are dripping with blood.

My father grasped the shelves and pulled to the right, and the whole bookcase slid noiselessly into a recessed pocket behind the cabinetry. Before us was a wide, arch-shaped wooden door, painted glossy gray, with a brass key plate. He fitted the WC key into it and pulled the door toward us just enough to catch the edge with his fingers, being careful not to pinch them against the edge of the now hidden bookcase.

The heavy door swung open, drawing the cool air of the cellar behind it. The viny scent of wine, cut with the stringent reek of strong alcohol, enveloped us. It was pitch-black within, and, in the moment it took my father to find the light switch, I imagined a demon rat rushing past us and disappearing into some other part of the house.

Then the lights blazed up on a square room, about fifteen feet per side, filled from floor to ceiling with wine and liquor, resting in sturdy wooden bins stacked four high, stained dark-brown and built around three sides of the room, along with a two-sided row of bins in the middle, forming two bays. It was like stepping into King Tut's tomb.

The first bay held champagnes on the left and bottles of liquor and port on the right. There were exotic bottles such as framboise, calvados, and Poire Williams, and drinks I'd later come across in Hemingway — Campari, Armagnac, Pernod, marc — as well as liqueurs in garish colors, such as Chartreuse. I knew that "proof" meant percentage of alcohol by volume in the liquor: 100 proof was 50 percent. Most potent of all was the 151-proof rum, which my father used to set alight crêpes suzette on New Year's Eve. There was a cache of those bottles down here.

Although my father told stories of epic drinking events from his youth, it was clear that they belonged to mistakes he had made in his first iteration as a husband and father, when he was in his twenties and thirties. All that remained of those days, apart from the stories, were these exotic bottles, their labels brittle and foxed.

In the next bay were the red and white wines, all French — great châteaux such as Cheval Blanc, Latour, Margaux, and Palmer. American wines did not interest my father, because the British aristocrats he modeled his tastes on, and whom he wished to impress, were ignorant of Yank vineyards. His wine was the juice in the illusion that he was one of them.

The wines in the bins were sorted by château, with six or eight bottles of like vineyard and vintage occupying each bin. They lay on their sides to keep the corks moist, and you could not right them lest you disturb the sediment. Latour had a picture of an old tower with a lion on top of it. Cheval Blanc did not have a picture of a white horse, which seemed like an oversight. If a bottle was upright in front of the bin, it meant that that wine was ready to drink. The bottles of Burgundy, whether white or red, had gently sloping shoulders and expansive, deeply dimpled bottoms. The red Bordeaux wines, with their shrugged shoulders and skinnier butts, were called clarets, a word I knew from Dickens which made me picture a man with whiskers dining on mutton in a tavern.

Many of the red wines were older than I was. It pleased my father greatly that the year of my birth, 1959, and that of Bruce, my brother, 1961, were shaping up to be first-rate vintages, in both Burgundies and clarets. Later, after the wines had further matured and become famous vintages — wines that Gordon Gekko might have sent Bud Fox as thanks for an insider tip in *Wall Street* — they featured prominently in our early-adult milestones, homecomings, and victories. My father opened a lesser 1959 Bordeaux on my twelfth birthday and proposed a toast in which he compared me favorably to the wine. I would always be measured against my birth wine; the wines kept getting better. It's hard to compete with "excellent and utterly irresistible," as the 1959 Cheval Blanc was described in a recent review.

The bottom row of the reds contained the magnums — two bottles of wine in one. There were also a few double magnums, and one jeroboam: six bottles. My father said that there were much bigger bottles, including a Balthazar (sixteen bottles) and, the biggest of all, a Nebuchadnezzar — twenty bottles. No way! When we learned in Sunday school about how the Babylonian king Nebuchadnezzar cast the Hebrews Shadrach, Meshach, and Abednego into the fiery furnace, I pictured a giant bottle of wine, tipped forward aggressively, towering over those godly men.

Propped up against the small pyramids of bottles in each bin was a three-by-five-inch Rolodex card with the wines' vintage and terroir, the number of cases ordered, price per case (in francs as well as dollars), plus importer's commission, the wine merchant he had used (Sherry-Lehmann, on Madison Avenue), and the dates purchased and delivered, all transcribed in his oddly third-grade penmanship. This information was cataloged at a sort of standing desk that was built into the end of the central aisle, with cards, different-colored pencils and pens, and a pencil sharpener. A map of the wine-growing regions of France was tacked up above the desk.

Another map showed the Saint-Émilion area. Behind the standing desk, along the fourth wall, were shelves that held baskets of single-shot bottles of gin, whiskey, and vodka — Lilliputian miniatures of the big bottles in the bar. These were for horse-drawn picnics.

In the back corner of the room was a narrow bricked-up archway. A few years later, during the addition of a major new wing to the house, my father added a second secret cellar here, replacing the bricks with a faux-brick door; the keyhole was concealed behind a dustpan hanging from a peg. The door opened onto a long rectangular room with wooden crates stacked along the walls, leaving an aisle between them. These were the cases of wines for "laying down," still years away from drinking, the crates branded with the images of the labels inside.

Why the elaborate deception? We lived among farmers and hired hands who preferred a six-pack of Bud. A burglar was unlikely to be looking for a great wine to pair with fish. What was he so worried about?

My father was the dispenser of all alcohol in the house (and out of the house; he always carefully studied the wine list, even in a Greek coffee shop). He decided what wine his guests were drinking, and how many bottles of it. Although my mother eventually learned to drink a cocktail in the evening, so that her husband wouldn't have to drink alone, she was by nature abstemious. She had seen the damage caused by her older sister's "problem," as she referred to alcoholism in letters to their mother. Wine interested her not at all, except to make coq au vin, one of her signature dishes. Once, she went to the wine cellar by herself for a bottle of red wine and chose a Cheval Blanc '55. "And she cooked with it!" my father would cry — the punch line of the story — as his dinner guests shook their heads and moaned "Ohh noo!" and my mother smiled gamely and played along as the simpleton housewife, which she most certainly was not. My mother was a beautiful, brainy woman from Spearfish, South Dakota, who by her early thirties had established herself in New York as the nationally known Elizabeth Toomey. She wrote a column for the United Press. She met my father while covering Grace Kelly's wedding to Rainier III, Prince of Monaco, in April 1956. My father was a guest of the Kelly family. By October, my parents were married, and my mother's journalism career was over. Her new career was to be Mrs. John M. Seabrook, which she took very seriously.

After the coq au vin disaster, my father reserved two bins in the cellar for my mother, labeling two Rolodex cards, in red marker, *ETS Red* and *ETS White*, and placing a few bottles of his most ordinary wine in each. Later, when I started coming home from college with friends and we would help ourselves to a bottle or two, we knew to avoid the ETS selections. ETS Red and ETS White became our shorthand for inferior wines everywhere.

An hour before dinner each evening, my father would go into the bar to open and decant the red wine he had brought up from the cellar. Using the corkscrew's collapsible knife with a curved edge, he sliced away the foil around the rim, exposing the cork, and embedded the point of the screw in the still-firm pith. With a few deft motions the cork was out. With older corks, infinite care had to be taken, but rarely did I ever see him break a cork in the bottle. When he did, it felt like a crisis.

Decanting was always done by candlelight, because only when the decanter was lit from below could the sediment be seen properly. My father explained this to me while he was decanting a bottle, his voice hushed with concentration as he poured the crimson liquid through the little glowing circle of candlelight and onto the broad glass lip of the decanter, watching for the first dark bits of wine waste — the hated sediment — at which point he stopped. Sometimes, with an old bottle, a whole glass of wine was left, so thick was the crud.

White wine, of course, you didn't need to decant; the bottle sat in a clay sleeve that kept it cold. If the wine was a chilled Beaujolais, which was served on those fall days when the new vintage arrived, the bottle sat on the table, its shoulders streaming, in a pewter coaster inscribed with the words A DINNER WITHOUT WINE IS LIKE A DAY WITHOUT SUNSHINE. A smiling Provençal sun split the sentence in half. I spent mealtimes listening to the adults talking, staring at that bit of alcoholic wisdom. It became my watchword.

After the wine was decanted and people were seated, my father would pour. Pouring wine properly, a practice later passed along to my brother and me, requires considerable skill. The right hand cradles the decanter below its waist and underneath, while the left hand grasps its throat with a white linen napkin. Approaching over the diner's right shoulder, the pourer's left forearm near the seated person's right ear, the left hand holds the lip of the decanter over the near wall of the wineglass (never touching it) while the right arm comes up to initiate the flow of wine. When the proper level in the glass is reached, which varies depending on the size of the glass, the wine, the number of people at the table (not counting my mother, who wouldn't have any), and those likely not to want a second glass (a calculation the pourer must make afresh on every occasion), the right wrist rotates laterally, decanter neck spinning in the curved fingers of the left hand, so that the wine drips are held by centrifugal force, keeping any drops from falling onto the white tablecloth, while the napkin in the left hand slides up to blot the lip. The slightest breakdown in muscular coordination results in spreading crimson stains of your ineptitude on the spotless tablecloth for all to see.

I don't remember my first taste of wine. I know I feared it. The smell of beer was off-putting but tolerable; wine, while aromatic, smelled of real alcohol, and my body judiciously sensed poison, even as my brain scented fun. But I knew on some level that I would learn to drink wine, and I was eager to get started. It was like learning to speak French, at which I would also fail miserably.

I was allowed a full glass of champagne when I turned thirteen, in January 1972. I had a glass set at my place at the table, and, as a special honor, I got to try the 1959 Bollinger. Before this, I had been permitted to take small sips of champagne from my father's flute. The bubbles were nice, but the shocking dryness of the grape practically gagged me. The champagne bottle had the letters EXTRA BRUT printed on the label. *Brut,* my father explained, meant "dry" in French, and that was what I was tasting. But how could something wet be dry?

As he poured the wine into my glass, I heard the faint whistling of breath in his nostrils and caught a whiff of his aftershave. I kept perfectly still, not even daring to breathe, lest a micro-flutter cause him to pour me any less wine than he intended to.

And then a toast I can't remember, except that it concluded, "1959 was a very good year."

I took a sip, then another. I felt something. What? Did anyone else feel it? I looked around. The adults were talking about what they always talked about — how the wine tasted (notes of peach, white pepper, and chocolate), where the grapes were grown, and how it had rained at the right time on the 1959 crop. They talked about everything but the most basic fact about the wine: the feeling it gave you. It felt as though my good spirits had emerged from a cave in my lower jaw where they usually hid away, like Puff the Magic Dragon breathing flaming 151-proof rum. It was a revelation, but no one at the table spoke a word about it, and I quickly learned to conceal the feeling. That was my first lesson.

I felt proud that I had been judged "grown up" enough to drink wine. And although my mother more than once questioned whether thirteen was too young, my father claimed that he had been drinking whiskey by twelve (probably not true), and, anyway, if I was grown up enough to work in the fields weeding peppers and moving irrigation pipe in the hot South Jersey sun, as I did in the summer and on weekends and after school in the spring, I was grown up enough to drink wine.

Wine became a once-a-week thing, at Sunday "dinner," which we had in the middle of the day, at 1 p.m., like British aristocrats. People in America watched the NFL game on TV at that hour, which was what I wanted to do. But attendance at these family dinners was mandatory. We had our assigned places and we sat in them, year after year. Although the table was circular, my father's place was clearly at the head, not only because it was aligned with his portrait, on the wall behind — a close-to-life-size, full-length study of him in a tailcoat, his top hat nearby — but also because on the side table under the portrait sat the platter holding the Sunday roast for him to carve.

My father liked to drink red Burgundy with beef and Yorkshire pudding, and claret with lamb and roast new potatoes. In early May, when it was soft-shell-crab season, he would open a Meursault — ten years old and perfect for drinking with shellfish, he'd say. In November, it was new Beaujolais with roast chicken. (With steak, he drank beer.)

At first, he poured me no more than a quarter of a glass. Acting grown up was the way to get more — carrying on a conversation about one of the issues of the day, such as Vietnam, Nixon, whom my father supported (he scolded me for calling him "Tricky Dick"), or the election of '72. Buoyed on a pink cloud of fizz, I sounded off on these themes, as well as holding forth on, say, an amusing incident that occurred in Mrs. Fenessy's Latin class. The more I talked, the more my estimation increased in my father's eyes, and the more wine he poured into my glass the next Sunday, firing my powers of conversation to still new heights.

All went well through the spring of 1973, until one Friday evening in June. The Devon Horse Show was going on, an annual ritual of the horsy set in the preppy parts of southeastern Pennsylvania, and there was a large tailgate picnic, with horses and horse vans, in a big open field with an eighteenth-century house nearby. Alcohol was everywhere. I had never seen people drink like that — drinking just to get loaded, the way I would one day.

An older boy I knew, whose father was one of my father's friends, brought me a Budweiser and said we should chug one together. The first one was pretty hard to get down, but then I drank two more in quick succession, easily. Not long after that, my parents said it was time to go.

My father had recently bought my mother a maroon Jaguar XJ6. It smelled like a new car, almost like a ripe melon — leather and a cleaner of some kind. It wasn't long after we set off along the twisty, hilly roads alongside the Brandywine Creek that the smell began to curdle the beer in my stomach. I lay back, my eyes open, hoping to ride the wave of nausea. I got the spins. Suddenly, my stomach flipped and I knew I was going to throw up. I fumbled for the window control, but I couldn't find it, discreetly hidden next to the ashtray, and I puked all that beer and whatever I'd had for dinner into the leather map holder on the side of the door.

My parents were shouting as I finally found the power-window switch and, too late, hung my head out the window, the night air cooling my blazing shame. The blurred lights became fixed as my father pulled over.

After they had done what could be done, we got back in the car and went to a gas station for paper towels and water, then drove home with all the windows open, in roaring silence. I went immediately to bed. The next morning, I was on the floor of the upstairs bathroom, leaning my pounding head over the bowl, suffering the first of many hangovers, when I heard my parents' voices coming from the breakfast room, which was directly below. My mother was talking about the incident, but I couldn't hear her words. My father's devastating judgment, however, was loud and clear:

"I guess Johnny is not as grown up as we thought he was."

*

Just what was my father up to, in introducing me to alcohol? He was passing along something he loved, and, moreover, something we could do together for the rest of his life (and did). He was always generous with his extensive knowledge of clothes, horsemanship, and alcohol. But he was unwilling or unable to engage in my preoccupations and fears. He didn't care about sports — except for riding, shaking a martini was his only routine physical exercise. Nor did he like board games; he couldn't stand losing, my mother explained, so he didn't play. Many years later, when I was visiting my parents with my wife, Lisa, and our son, Harry, my father agreed to a round of Celebrity, the after-dinner parlor game. Each player thinks of ten celebrities and puts their names into a hat, for a team of other players to act out. My father wrote his own name, including his middle initial, ten times, requiring the opposing team to enact him again and again. The idea that anyone could be more celebrated than he was apparently did not compute.

Perhaps he was trying to educate a thirteen-year-old in the gentlemanly art of drinking? I would be going off to boarding school in the fall of 1972, exposed to new alcohol providers, and maybe he thought he needed to instruct me? Possibly, but I doubt it ever occurred to him that his namesake, John Jr., might have a weakness for alcohol. Alcohol was not about weakness in our family. It was about strength. I understood early on that what was important was not how much you drank but how well you held it.

It was as though the only way he could express his love as a father was to teach me to be just like him, starting by giving me his name. That's what it meant to be "grown up." My father didn't anticipate that when it came to alcohol I was not going to be like him. Our house sat atop a Fort Knox of alcohol, and, at least as far as I could tell, he never had one glass more than he should. But for me alcohol offered an escape from control, his and everyone else's. A glass of wine gave me a kind of confidence I didn't otherwise feel — the confidence to be me.

I got started on my drinking career with the mistaken notion that alcohol revealed the real, feeling me, when in fact it was the alcohol I was feeling. This flawed logic would take more than forty years to root out.

I did indeed meet a surplus of new alcohol providers in boarding school and college. Arriving in New York in the fall of 1983 as a twenty-four-year-old would-be writer, at first I drank vodka martinis, which horrified my father; eventually I came to prefer what John Cheever describes in his journals as the "galling" taste of gin. I'd switch from clear liquors to brown in the winter months, to ward off seasonal affective disorder. After cocktails, I always drank wine. I started out buying, by my father's standards, budget wine, planning to start a cellar of my own as soon as I had the space. Once, when I was twenty-seven, while reporting a piece for *GQ* about the young sommelier at '21,' I won a case of Château Palmer for guessing the relative amounts of Cabernet and Merlot in one of the vineyard's blended wines. "An excellent foundation for a cellar!" my proud father declared. The wine was soon gone.

For a quarter of a century, I averaged a twenty-dollar bottle of wine almost every night, buying most of them individually at a nearby liquor store. I also bought cases of wine for parties and for weekend houses, and plowed through those, too — oceans of wine washing over us and our friends as the children played under the table. Even though I had been drinking three hundred and sixty-five days a year since I was twenty-four, it never occurred to me that I might be an alcoholic. I didn't think of myself as a particularly heavy drinker.

At the very Jag-defiling beginnings of my drinking career, it was clear that I could hold only a certain amount. That mark increased over time, but only up to a point: two highball or water glasses full of ice and either gin or bourbon, followed by up to a bottle and a half of wine. Any more and I'd get sick. My gut always had my back.

In 2009, when my family moved to a town house in Brooklyn, I had a cellar of my own, at last. I loved the vaulted basement, which was dry and high-ceilinged enough for me to stand in. Just after we moved in, I ordered a top-of-the-line redwood wine case, with room for 128 bottles, installed it under one of the vaults, and filled it with an exotic collection of vintages I had acquired from my brother-in-law's online wine business, which was going out of it. Night after night, I went down to my cellar and drank a bottle by myself, because Lisa was cutting back on drinking, and supposedly I was, too.

By 2000, my parents had started to relocate, from New Jersey to Aiken, South Carolina, for the climate, medical care, and horses.

My father had much of his wine crated and packed into a horse van, and driven more than six hundred miles south on I-95, and then west on I-20 to Aiken. There were no sliding bookcases in the Aiken cellar, but the climate control was superior.

After my mother died, in 2005, when she was eighty-three and he was eighty-eight, he entertained much less. He lost interest in drinking wine — he said he couldn't taste it anymore. Still, during my long stays in the Palmetto State, which I would take in rotation with my siblings Bruce and Carol, we went through the nightly ritual of discussing the upcoming meal and what wine (which he wouldn't touch) would go best with it. Perhaps a creamy 1996 Meursault, if we were having fish, or a firm La Tâche '90, with beef. Or, hell, why not open the biggest bottle you've got, Dad? (I was already loaded at this point, on two generous Maker's Marks.) No, no, he would shake his head vigorously and close his eyes in horror at the prospect.

Nightly, I would make my unsteady trip down the basement stairs to fetch yet another bottle of his wine. Standing among all the glorious bottles my father would never drink, I felt some of the beauty and grace that I had imbibed as a child begin to leak out of me. He was dying, and the rituals that went with the cocktails and the wine would die, too. My legacy was the leftover booze. I finally came to understand why my father had gone to such lengths to conceal his cellar. It wasn't to keep people out. It was to keep the alcohol in.

After I uncorked the bottle — decanting was pointless; what did I care? — I'd go through the motions of pouring him a glass; he'd refuse. So I just kept the bottle next to me and slopped it into my glass, sediment and all. To get through the after-dinner portion of the evening, which involved either Fox News or reruns of *Law & Order*, I might require a large slug of Rémy Martin. After the home-health aide had got him into his wheelchair and taken him to bed, I would get angry and send e-smites to my siblings about treatment of the help. My brother wrote back, "Lay off the vitriol and the bourbon."

When my father died, at ninety-one, in early 2009, slipping away when none of us happened to be visiting, many hundreds of bottles remained in his cellar. Fortunately, my brother arranged to have them auctioned. Had it been left up to me, I'd still be drinking them.

*

Back in Brooklyn, every night I went down the steep steps to my man cave in the basement and tanked up, before joining the family upstairs for a pretend-to-be-sober dinner that did not fool Lisa. She scoffed at me when I acted innocent of any drinking issues, and threatened an intervention. I agreed to try "moderate" drinking. When that didn't work, and when faced with the ultimate ultimatum from Lisa, I tried lying, and kept my drinking secret. In those dark moments of mendacity, I thought about the giant rat from *The Boy Who Drew Cats* that I had imagined escaping from my father's cellar on that first visit long ago.

Obviously, I had to stop drinking. If I stopped, I would feel like a man again when Lisa looked at me, rather than a rat. But stopping seemed like the hardest thing I could possibly do. Each time the subject came up, I'd agree to work toward stopping, but would hardly even pause, and sometimes would correct in alcohol's favor, as a reward for negotiating another extension of my license to drink.

Lisa found a therapist, and I submitted — at first reluctantly, then wholeheartedly — to the three of us untangling alcohol from my life. "You came by it honestly," the therapist, also named Lisa, said when we started, of my drinking. Part of the work involved going back, in my mind, to the wine cellar behind the bookcase and figuring out how I came to drinking. I felt that if I could just stay there, at the beginning, with all the bottles nestled in their bins, it would be okay. Eventually, at the therapist's suggestion, I started writing about my father's cellar. Writing became a way of laying down wine as my heritage without actually having to drink it.

I took what I hope will be my last drink on what would have been my father's ninety-ninth birthday, April 16, 2016. Here's to you, Dad, I silently said, as I emptied my final bottle of twenty-dollar Oregon pinot noir from the corner liquor store into a water glass and glugged it down. It was no Cheval Blanc '59.

ADAM SHATZ

No Direction Home: The Journey of Frantz Fanon

FROM *Raritan*

In memory of Jean Stein

I WAS A teenager when I first saw a picture of Frantz Fanon, on the back of my father's hardcover copy of *Black Skin, White Masks*, a 1967 Grove edition. He appeared in a tweed jacket, a freshly pressed white shirt, and a striped tie, with a five-o'clock shadow and an intense, somewhat hooded expression; his right eye slightly turned up to face the camera, his left fixed in a somber gaze. He seemed to be issuing a challenge, or perhaps a warning, that if his words weren't heeded, there would be hell to pay.

Who is this man? I remember thinking. The jacket explained that he had been born in Martinique in 1925, had studied psychiatry in France, had worked at a hospital in Algeria during the French-Algerian War, and had eventually joined the Algerian independence struggle, becoming its most eloquent spokesman, before dying of leukemia at age thirty-six. I was intrigued by the way that Fanon connected different worlds — France, the West Indies, North and sub-Saharan Africa — and by the link that he forged between psychiatry, a discipline devoted to care and healing, and revolution, an attempt to transform the world by means of creative destruction.

I was no less intrigued by *where* I found *Black Skin, White Masks* and *The Wretched of the Earth,* often described as the bible of decolonization. In the small library of radical literature that my father kept in our basement, Fanon's books were sandwiched between *The Autobiography of Malcolm X* and Isaac Deutscher's *The Non-Jewish Jew:* the former a classic memoir of black nationalism, the latter an essay on socialist internationalism. This location may have been an alphabetical accident, but the more that I read Fanon, the more I became convinced that he belonged in between the political traditions broadly represented by Malcolm X and Deutscher; that he spoke to their questions, their tensions, and, not least, their internal contradictions.

"I do not come with timeless truths," Fanon writes in his introduction to *Black Skin, White Masks*. But when I began reading him, in the late 1980s, during the death throes of the apartheid regime in South Africa and the eruption of the first intifada in occupied Palestine, his observations about the humiliation of colonial domination and the psychological dynamics of anticolonial revolt had lost none of their immediacy. Not surprisingly, his work was undergoing an extraordinary revival in the university, where he was being rediscovered — in a sense *discovered* for the first time — as a major thinker of postcolonial modernity, rather than as a propagandist of violent revolution, or as the "theoretician" of the Algerian Revolution.

Since then, Fanon's work has made significant inroads beyond the academy. There are allusions to, and echoes of, Fanon in the writing of Kamel Daoud, Claudia Rankine, Ta-Nehisi Coates, John Edgar Wideman, and Jamaica Kincaid; in the art of Glenn Ligon, Isaac Julien, and John Akomfrah; in the cinema of Ousmane Sembène, Raoul Peck, and Claire Denis; even in jazz and hip-hop. (The trumpeter Jacques Coursil, a Martinican trumpeter and linguist, draws on passages of *Black Skin, White Masks* in his haunting oratorio *Clameurs*.) His name has also been invoked by members of the Black Lives Matter movement, in part for its talismanic aura, in part because Fanon's writings on the vulnerability of the black body apply with eerie power to the extrajudicial killings of young black men. In the aftermath of Eric Garner's death by choke hold, the contemporary resonance of Fanon's remark that "we revolt . . . because . . . we can no longer breathe" hardly needs to be spelled out.

The power of Fanon's writing lies not only in its perceptiveness or topicality, but in its unusual rhetorical force. Fanon was somewhat ambivalent about appeals to emotion. In this he was very much a product of the French schooling system. His mentor at the Lycée Victor Schoelcher in Fort-de-France was the writer Aimé Césaire, who had taken part in the creation of the Négritude movement with his fellow poet Léopold Senghor, later Senegal's first president. But Fanon was skeptical of Négritude's lyrical claims about a shared black consciousness that unified Africa and the diaspora, and he especially recoiled from Senghor's claim that "emotion is Negro just as reason is Greek." He aimed, rather, to dismantle the edifices of racial prejudice and colonialism in a French of classical rationality. Yet for all his fierce disagreements with Césaire, Fanon remained his disciple, and both his first book, *Black Skin, White Masks,* and *The Wretched of the Earth* contain passages of feverish prose poetry. As he explained to the philosopher Francis Jeanson, who edited *Black Skin, White Masks* and would later become Fanon's ally in the Algerian liberation struggle, "I am trying to touch the reader emotionally, which is to say, irrationally, almost sensually . . . Words have a charge for me. I feel incapable of escaping the bite of a word, the vertigo of a question mark."

Reading Fanon, one sometimes has the impression that mere expository prose cannot do justice to the impulsive movement of his thought. I use the word "movement" advisedly: Fanon did not write his texts; he dictated them while pacing back and forth, either to his wife, Josie, or to his secretary, Marie-Jeanne Manuellan (who has just published a memoir about the experience). This method of composition lends his writings an electrifying musicality: restless, searching, and, as he fell prey to the leukemia that would kill him, otherworldly in its call for a new planetary order, cleansed of racism and oppression. The black British filmmaker John Akomfrah set his remarkable portrait of Stuart Hall to the music of Miles Davis. Were he to make a film about Fanon, he would surely set it to Coltrane, whose classic quartet was formed the year that Fanon died, and who died just six years later. Fanon's sentences remind me of Coltrane's famous "sheets of sound": cascades of arpeggios, rapid, dense, ever in pursuit.

Forged in perpetual movement, Fanon's writing holds up a mirror to his peripatetic life. He was not, by profession, a writer. He was a doctor, and later a revolutionary spokesman and diplomat. Yet nothing, arguably, mattered to him more than writing. For someone who left Martinique at twenty-one, never to return; who was expelled from Algeria, his adoptive country, at thirty-one; and who spent his last five years as a revolutionary exile roaming throughout North and sub-Saharan Africa, writing was his only home.

It was his way of wrestling with the problems he confronted in his difficult, dangerous life. Albert Memmi, a Tunisian Jewish psychologist and critic of colonialism who was in many ways Fanon's foil, described Fanon's life as "impossible." Perhaps it was. But there is no doubt that Fanon *chose* his life, as much as it is possible to do so. In that sense, Fanon's life bore little resemblance to those of his contemporaries and friends, anticolonial patriots like Patrice Lumumba of Congo, Felix Moumié of Cameroon, and Abane Ramdane of Algeria, all of whom sought to liberate their countries from foreign domination. Fanon, by contrast, never considered returning to Fort-de-France, and felt disappointed, even betrayed, that Césaire, his mentor, had campaigned for Martinique to become a department of France, rather than an independent country. Not long before he died, Fanon confessed to Simone de Beauvoir that he dreaded becoming a "professional revolutionary," and spoke movingly of his desire to set down roots. But where? That was the problem. He was a man without a country — except a country of the future, or of the imagination. As painful as this must have been to Fanon, his statelessness, the migratory nature of his life, has lent his writing a uniquely global relevance that the speeches of Lumumba and Moumié noticeably lack, and that not even the work of his great Martinican peers, Césaire, Edouard Glissant, and Patrick Chamoiseau, can match.

Fanon's career as a revolutionary psychiatrist has given his writing an irresistible allure, but this peculiar intimacy of life and work has also been the cause of considerable misunderstanding. Healer, soldier, martyr: much of the literature on Fanon amounts to little more than a praise song. As an icon of "Third World" resistance, Fanon has been adopted by groups as various as the Black Panthers, Palestinian secular guerrillas, Islamic revolutionaries in Iran, and the alienated *banlieusards* of France, who feel as if the Battle of Algiers never ended, but simply moved to the metropole. Lost in this process of sanctification have been the complexities of Fanon's life; the unfinished, ambiguous, sometimes agonized nature of his writing, particularly its relationship to the Western tradition; and, not least, the ironies and contradictions that history would impose on his words. Lost, too, has been the central thrust behind Fanon's life and work: not the struggle against French rule in Algeria, but the struggle for what he called "dis-alienation," the emancipation of people's repressed capacities and the achievement of a humanism worthy of the name.

Fanon bears some responsibility for the abuse of his writing. He contributed many of the jingles that would later provide Third World liberation struggle with its exhortatory soundtrack. The slogan for which he is best known, however, is one that he did not write, the claim that "killing a European is killing two birds with one stone, eliminating in one go oppressor and oppressed: leaving one man dead and the other man free." It was Jean-Paul Sartre, not Fanon, who wrote this, in his famous preface to *The Wretched of the Earth,* a powerful critique of Eurocentrism that, alas, did no service to Fanon's reputation by exulting in self-flagellation and celebrating terrorism as a kind of Dionysian carnival of the oppressed.

In fact, violence was never Fanon's remedy for the Third World; it was a rite of passage for colonized communities and individuals who had become mentally ill as a result of the settler-colonial project, itself saturated with violence and racism. His clinical work was the practice that underpinned his political thought. He considered colonialism a deeply abnormal relationship; the colonizer and the colonized were locked together — and constructed — by a fatal dialectic. There could be no reciprocity, only war between the two, until the latter achieved freedom. But this was no more a "celebration" of violence than Hegel's account of the master and the slave, which inspired it.

The other charge often leveled against Fanon is that he was a defender of what, today, we call "identity politics," a black nationalist who insisted upon the irreducible "fact of blackness," the supposed life force of black authenticity. In fact, Fanon saw blackness not as a fact but as the phantasmagoria of a racist white society: "the fact of blackness" was a misleading translation of *l'experience vécue du noir,* "the lived experience of the black man." Fanon regarded Négritude as a "black mirage," a flight into an imaginary, mystical past, a retreat from a future that remained to be invented. The solution to being forced to wear a white mask was not, for Fanon, proudly adopting a black mask. As a student he was so determined to overcome Césaire's shadow that his first writings, allegorical plays deeply indebted to Sartre, altogether avoided the topic of race. Even as he became an advocate of revolutionary struggles in the Third World, he remained highly critical of nostalgic attempts to revive traditional African culture.

That Fanon has been so widely misread makes a kind of poetic

230 ADAM SHATZ

sense. For *mis-recognition,* and the violent alienation it produces, is the plot on which most of his work turns. His first important psychiatric paper, published in 1952 in *Esprit,* described the psychosomatic distress experienced by North African workers in France. Perplexed by their accounts of pain without lesion, French doctors had concluded that these men suffered from cerebral and cultural deficiencies. Fanon saw their illness very differently: "They have had France squeezed into them wherever, in their bodies and in their souls," only to be told, "They are in 'our' country," a reproach that the French-born descendants of these men are still hearing today.

Nor was Fanon himself immune from racism, as he discovered not long after arriving in Lyon in 1947. Raised by middle-class parents in Fort-de-France, he had fought and nearly died serving in the Free French Forces, and received the Croix de Guerre with a bronze star. He had worn the same uniform as the metropolitan French, unlike the Senegalese members of his battalion, the so-called *tiralleurs sénégalais.* As far as he was concerned, he was a West Indian French man, from a respectable home. "Negroes" were Africans, and he wasn't one of them. He had even made a point of studying in Lyon, rather than in Paris, one of the capitals of the Black Atlantic, since he wanted to be somewhere "more milky."

In milky Lyon, however, a little white boy saw him pass by and cried out: "Look, Maman, a Negro! I'm afraid." The experience of seeing himself being seen — of being fixed by the white gaze — provided Fanon with the primal scene of *Black Skin, White Masks.* Although he found his life partner in a left-wing, white French woman — Marie-Josèphe Dublé, known as Josie — he described his life in Lyon as a series of what, today, we would call microaggressions, from patronizing compliments on his French to well-meaning praise of his mind.

What Fanon suffered in his encounter with the little boy on that "white winter day" was, as Louis Althusser puts it in his classic essay on ideology, the experience of being "hailed" or "interpellated." That this primal scene takes place outdoors is crucial to its power. As Althusser writes: "What . . . seems to take place outside ideology (to be precise, in the street), in reality takes place in ideology. What really takes place in ideology seems therefore to take place outside it."

Fanon was not a follower of Althusser, much less a philosophical antihumanist, but in *Black Skin, White Masks* he attempts to do something that Althusser might have appreciated, namely, demonstrate the way that ideology interpellated French West Indians as racialized subjects. *Black Skin, White Masks* is not a memoir, but it is obviously the product of Fanon's time in Lyon, his first experience as a member of a black "minority." Interestingly, two of the chapters explore how racial ideology disfigures interracial relationships, a subject that would have been of acute personal concern to Fanon.

The problem of "love" in a racist society lies at the heart of *Black Skin, White Masks,* nearly as much as it does in the work of James Baldwin, who in 1956 would hear Fanon address a conference of black writers organized by *Présence Africaine* in Paris. Baldwin, who sailed to Paris a year after Fanon arrived in Lyon, does not mention Fanon in his report on the conference, but he would later invoke Fanon in his 1972 book *No Name in the Street.* The title of *Black Skin, White Masks* could have been *Notes of a Native Son,* for Fanon, like Baldwin, was grappling with the obstacles to black citizenship in a white-dominated society. His principal quarrel in the book is not with colonial domination and exploitation, but with the racial limits of French republicanism: it is a Frenchman's hopeful protest for inclusion, not a bitter repudiation of the *métropole.* Fanon seems confident of his ability to achieve "nothing short of the liberation of the man of color" not only from white supremacy, but from the restrictive conceptions of Négritude: "The Negro is not. Anymore than the white man." Fanon's language here should be familiar to anyone who has read Sartre's 1946 essay "Anti-Semite and Jew," which argues that the idea of "the Jew" as the Other was an invention of the anti-Semite. For Fanon, a person of African descent became black, became a "nègre," through and only through the white gaze. The so-called black problem was no less a phantasm than the Jewish question.

Yet Fanon was not content simply to dispatch with race as an analytic concept, and to prove that it is a mere construction, unlike, say, class. This argument has had its liberal defenders, including the political philosopher Mark Lilla, who, in a widely cited *New York Times* op-ed article (later expanded into a book, *The Once and Future Liberal*), belittled what he called "diversity discourse" as an "identity drama" that "exhausts political discourse" and divides a polity that could otherwise be unified around supposedly real things like "class, war, the economy, and the common good."

In Fanon's view, however, race is always already a refraction of ideas, fears, and anxieties about "class, war, the economy, and the common good." It is a fiction, yet one so pervasive and so powerful as to produce profound real-world effects. It may seem to be "a very trivial thing, and easily understood," as Marx wrote of the commodity, but "it is, in reality, a very queer thing, abounding in metaphysical subtleties and theological niceties." Like the commodity, race is the ghost in the machine of an apparently disenchanted society, never fully exorcised, a tribute not only to enduring inequities but to the enduring power of the gaze, of unreason and ressentiment. And its worst injuries, for Fanon, are psychological: violations of dignity, especially the "shame and self-contempt" it implants in its victims. Even a relatively privileged, "assimilated" black man like himself was "damned": "When people like me, they tell me it is in spite of my color. When they dislike me, they point out that it is not because of my color. Either way, I am locked into the infernal circle." But how was he to liberate himself from this infernal circle and — as Ta-Nehisi Coates puts it in *Between the World and Me* — "live free in this black body"?

Looking to free himself from the white gaze, Fanon was briefly drawn to the racial romanticism of Senghor, tempted, he says, to "wade in the irrational," as the Négritude poets had urged him. When he read Sartre's introduction to *Black Orpheus*, a 1948 anthology of Négritude poets, he was taken aback by the condescension: Sartre defended black consciousness as an "antiracist racism" — what Gayatri Spivak would later call "strategic essentialism" — but downgraded it to a "weak moment in a dialectical movement" toward a society free of race and class oppression. Yet by the end of *Black Skin, White Masks,* Fanon has come to agree. The "only solution," he declares, is to "rise above this absurd drama that others have staged around me" and "reach out for the universal," rather than seeking refuge in some "materialized Tower of the Past." If anyone is making that leap, he adds, it is not the Négritude poets, but the Vietnamese rebels in Indochina, who are taking their destiny into their own hands.

Fanon's dissatisfaction with the political moderation of the Négritude movement, and with his mentor Césaire, who had become a senator in the overseas department of Martinique and an opponent of independence, may help to explain one of the great mysteries of his life: his decision not to return home to Fort-de-France after completing his residency at the psychiatric hospital of Saint-Alban-sur-Limagnole in the Massif Central. François Tosquelles, Fanon's mentor at Saint-Alban, was both a doctor and a resistance fighter, having headed the Spanish Republican Army's psychiatric services before crossing the Pyrenees in 1939. He had pioneered institutional or social therapy, which tried to turn the hospital into a recognizable microcosm of the world outside. The idea underlying social therapy was that patients were socially as well as clinically alienated, and that their care depended on the creation of a structure that relieved their isolation by involving them in group activities.

In 1953, after more than a year at Saint-Alban, Fanon took up his post at Blida-Joinville, a psychiatric hospital about forty kilometers south of Algiers. He was responsible for 187 patients: 165 European women and 22 Muslim men. He found some of them tied to their beds, others to trees in the park. They lived in segregated quarters, with the women in one pavilion and the men in another. The hospital's former director, Antoine Porot, the founder of the so-called Algiers School of colonial ethnopsychiatry, had justified this segregation on the grounds of "divergent moral or social conceptions." Several of Fanon's colleagues shared Porot's view that Algerians were essentially different from Europeans, suffering from primitive brain development that made them childlike and lazy, but also impulsive, violent, and untrustworthy. As a West Indian atheist who was neither a Muslim "native" nor a white European, Fanon stood at a remove from both the staff and the residents at Blida. Since he spoke no Arabic or Berber, he relied on interpreters with his Muslim patients. His closest friends in Algeria would be left-wing European militants, many of them Jews.

To instill a sense of community among the staff — and perhaps to break out of his solitude — Fanon created a weekly newsletter. In a striking article published in April 1954, he questions the spatial isolation of the modern asylum, anticipating Foucault's 1961 *Folie et déraison: Histoire de la folie à l'âge classique:*

> Future generations will wonder with interest what motive could have led us to build psychiatric hospitals far from the center. Several patients have already asked me: Doctor, will we hear the Easter bells? . . . What-

ever our religion, daily life is set to the rhythm of a number of sounds
and the church bells represent an important element in this sympho-
ny. . . . Easter arrives, and the bells will die without being reborn, for
they have never existed at the psychiatric hospital of Blida. The psychiatric hospital of Blida will continue to live in silence. A silence without
bells.

Restoring the symphonic order of everyday life was the goal of
social therapy, and Fanon pursued it with his usual vigilance, introducing basket weaving, a theater, ball games, and other activities. It was a great success with the European women, but a total
failure with the Muslim men. The older European doctors told
him, "When you've been in the hospital for fifteen years like us,
then you'll understand." But Fanon refused to understand. He
suspected that the failure lay in his use of "imported methods,"
and that he might achieve different results if he could provide his
Muslim patients with forms of sociality that resembled their lives
outside. Working with a team of Algerian nurses, he established a
café maure, a traditional teahouse where men drink coffee and play
cards, and later an "Oriental salon," as he put it, for the hospital's
small group of Muslim women. Arab musicians and storytellers
came to perform, and Muslim festivals were celebrated for the first
time in the hospital's history. Once their cultural practices were
recognized, Blida's Muslim community emerged from its slumber.

Fanon's curiosity about Algeria led him far outside the hospital gates. Deep in the *bled* of Kabylia, the Berber heartland, he
attended late-night ceremonies where hysterics were healed in
"cathartic crises," and learned of women using white magic to render unfaithful husbands impotent. He discovered a more merciful
attitude toward mental illness: Algerians blamed madness on ge-
nies, not on the sufferer. In his writings on these practices, Fanon
never uttered the word "superstition." Yet even as he insisted on
the specificity of North African culture, he was careful to avoid the
essentialism of the Algiers School. He wanted to pierce the frozen,
apparently natural surface of reality, and to uncover the ferment
beneath it.

On November 1, 1954, that ferment erupted, when the Front
de Libération Nationale (FLN) carried out its first attacks, launch-
ing a war of independence that would last for nearly eight years.
The FLN was a small organization that had grown out of a split in

the banned Movement for the Triumph of Democratic Liberties, a group led by the founding father of modern Algerian nationalism, Messali Hadj. Winning over the Muslim majority to its cause, and, not least, persuading them that they had a chance against one of the world's most powerful militaries, required no small effort and no little coercion. Their case would partly be made for them by massive French repression: the razing of entire villages, the forced relocation of more than two million to "regroupment" camps, widespread torture, and thousands of summary executions and disappearances; as many as three hundred thousand Algerians died during the war. Fanon, however, needed little convincing. When the rebels contacted him in early 1955, he had already chosen his side; according to his biographer David Macey, his first thought was to join them in the maquis.

Fanon took great risks to help the rebels, opening the hospital to FLN meetings, treating fighters at the day clinic, and forbidding the police from entering with their guns loaded. At the same time, he was treating French servicemen who were involved in torturing suspected rebels. He did not hand over their names to the FLN for they, too, were victims of a colonial system whose dirty work they were required to perform. Eventually, however, Fanon concluded that he was helpless to effect change at Blida: Algeria's Muslims had been subjected to what he called "absolute de-personalization," and to remain in his position was to perpetuate a spurious normalcy. He resigned from his post in a protest letter to Resident Minister Robert Lacoste in December 1956; a month later he was expelled from Algeria. But before he left, he had a brief meeting with Abane Ramdane, an FLN leader from Kabylia who powerfully shaped his vision of the Algerian struggle. Ramdane, sometimes described as the Robespierre of the Algerian Revolution, was a kindred spirit: a hardliner opposed to any negotiations prior to France's recognition of independence, and a genuine modernizer with progressive, republican values.

After a stop in Paris — his last visit to France — Fanon settled in Tunis, where the FLN's external leadership was based. He divided his time between the Manouba Clinic, where he resumed his psychiatric practice under the name "Dr. Fares," and the offices of *El Moudjahid,* the FLN's French-language newspaper, which he helped edit. As the FLN's media spokesman in Tunis, he cut a glamorously enigmatic figure. Living in an independent Arab country sympathetic to Algeria's struggle, Fanon no longer had to conceal his loyalties. Yet, paradoxically, he learned to tread even more carefully than in Blida. For all its claims to unity, the FLN was rife with factional tensions, and Fanon was a vulnerable outsider with no official position in the leadership. His most powerful ally in the movement was Ramdane, the leader of the "interior," but Fanon was now on the other side of the border, working for the FLN's "external" forces, who saw Ramdane as a threat to their interests.

Fanon's contributions to *El Moudjahid* were not always appreciated by his colleagues in the FLN, particularly his fiery denunciation of the "beautiful souls" of the French left who denounced torture but refused to support the FLN because of its attacks on civilians. The FLN's leaders in Tunis were pragmatic nationalists, and their goal was to intensify the divisions in France over Algeria, not condemn France as a nation. Unlike Fanon they didn't have to prove that they were Algerians. There is no doubting the sincerity of Fanon's writing for *El Moudjahid:* he tended to gravitate to the most militant positions, and he had an old account to settle with the French intelligentsia. But his fervor also expressed a longing to be accepted as a fellow Algerian. According to the historian Mohammed Harbi, a left-wing FLN official who crossed paths (and swords) with Fanon in Tunis, Fanon "had a very strong need to belong."

Fanon upheld the FLN line even when he had very strong reasons for doubting it, as in the case of the Melouza massacre. In a small hamlet outside Melouza, the FLN had killed hundreds of sympathizers of a rival nationalist group, and then tried to blame the massacre on the French. In his first public statement in Tunis, made at a press conference in May 1957, Fanon denounced the "foul machinations over Melouza," insisting that the French army was responsible.

He exercised a similar discretion, when, a year later, *El Moudjahid* announced that his friend Abane Ramdane had died "on the field of honor." In fact, Ramdane had been dead for five months, and he was not killed on the battlefield. His erstwhile comrades had lured him to a villa in Morocco, where he was strangled to death. The external leadership had long wanted to seize control of the revolution, and Ramdane, the figurehead of the internal struggle, stood in the way. Real power now lay with the external elements of the FLN and the so-called army of the frontiers. Fanon, who was close enough to the intelligence services to know the truth of his friend's murder, said nothing. Shaken by Ramdane's death, he made his peace with the army of the frontiers, both for the sake of the revolution — the military leadership, in Tunisia and Morocco, was increasingly the dominant force — and to protect himself: according to Harbi, his name was on a list of those to be executed in the event of an internal challenge to the FLN leadership.

He was scarcely more secure in his medical work at the Manouba Clinic, where he began to introduce the social therapy he had practiced in Blida. The clinic's director, Dr. Ben Soltan, called him "the Negro" and accused him of being a Zionist spy and of mistreating Arab patients on Israeli orders. The proof was his denunciation of anti-Semitism in *Black Skin, White Masks,* and his close friendships with two Tunisian Jewish doctors. Dr. Fares managed to hold on to his position, but shifted his energies to the Hôpital Charles-Nicolle, where he created Africa's first psychiatric day clinic.

He was most at ease, as ever, when he was writing — or rather, dictating. His first book on the Algerian struggle, *L'An V de la révolution algérienne* (translated as *A Dying Colonialism*), was composed over three weeks in the spring of 1959. It is a passionate account of a national awakening, as well as a document of the utopian hopes it aroused in the author, who had come to think of himself as an Algerian after three years in Blida. I don't think it is an exaggeration to say that Fanon had fallen in love with the Algerian people. As John Edgar Wideman writes in his novel *Fanon,* "Fanon is not about stepping back, standing apart, analyzing and instructing others but about identifying with others, plunging into the vexing, mysterious otherness of them, taking risks of heart and mind, falling head over heels in love whether or not there's a chance in the world love will be requited or redeemed."

L'An V is Fanon's love letter to the Algerian Revolution, and it often feels like an expression of Ramdane's views — or fantasies — about postindependence Algeria. In *L'An V,* the Algerian Revolution is not simply an anticolonial uprising, but a social revolution against class oppression, religious traditionalism, and patriarchy. For all the appeals to Islam, Fanon argued, Algerian nationalism was a nationalism of the will, rather than of ethnicity or religion, open to anyone willing to join the struggle, including European democrats who renounced their colonial status and the country's Jewish minority.

In fact, Ramdane's vision was rapidly losing out, partly because the French army had crushed the FLN's interior leadership during the Battle of Algiers. After independence, women in the maquis would experience a painful regression, and the *pieds-noirs* would flee en masse to France, along with Algeria's Jews. Those who envisaged a multiethnic Algeria were always a minority, and their numbers diminished with every *pied-noir* or army atrocity. The single consensual demand inside the FLN — aside from independence itself — was the reestablishment of Algeria's Islamic and Arab identity. Fanon was correct that France's attempt to "emancipate" Muslim women by pressuring them to remove their veils had only made the veil more popular; what he failed (or refused) to see was that influential sectors of the nationalist movement were keen to reinforce religious conservatism. We know from a letter that Fanon wrote to a young Iranian admirer in Paris — the revolutionary Islamist Ali Shariati — that Fanon viewed the turn to Islam as a green mirage, a "withdrawal into oneself" disguised as liberation from "alienation and de-personalization." But he shied from expressing these views in public, and leftists within the FLN were furious that Algeria's pious bourgeoisie had, in Mohammed Harbi's words, "found in Fanon a mouthpiece who presented its behavior as progressive." Fanon "the Algerian" saw what he wanted to see — or what Ramdane wanted him to see.

Nevertheless, he brilliantly captured the psychological impact of revolt on an oppressed people, their transformation into historical subjects. In effect, the revolution was achieving what he had hoped to do inside the walls of Blida: the "tense immobility of the dominated society," he wrote, had given way to "awareness, movement, creation," freeing the colonized from "that familiar tinge of resignation that specialists in underdeveloped countries describe under the heading of *fatalism*." Revolution, it turned out, was the cure for the "North African syndrome."

By the time *L'An V* appeared, Fanon had been pushed aside as the FLN's media spokesman in Tunis. His replacement was the information minister of the newly formed Provisional Government of the Algerian Republic (GPRA), M'hammed Yazid, a suave diplomat with strong ties to the French left, which Fanon had scornfully lectured. Fanon became a traveling ambassador and in March 1960 was appointed to Accra as the FLN's permanent representative. The United Kingdom of Libya supplied him with a *vrai faux passeport* that identified him as Omar Ibrahim Fanon. He took to his new assignment with characteristic zeal.

Algeria's liberation, he wrote in *El Moudjahid*, would be "an African victory," a "step in the realization of a free and happy humanity." Fanon saw Algeria's war of decolonization as a model for all of Africa and first made his case — against the more conciliatory positions of his host, Ghana's leader Kwame Nkrumah — at the 1958 All-African People's Conference in Accra, where he led the FLN delegation and gave an electrifying speech advocating armed struggle as a uniquely effective route to national liberation. Few of Africa's leaders were prepared to sign up. Most were cultural nationalists like Senegal's president Léopold Senghor, who advocated African unity while accepting French interference in defense and economic policy — and siding with France at the UN against Algerian independence. Fanon was infuriated at having to argue the merits of the Algerian cause to Africans, and in one speech he nearly broke into tears.

Africa, Fanon believed, needed unyielding militants like his friend Ramdane. He was impressed by Sékou Touré, the ruthless dictator of Guinea, and once confessed that he had a "horror of weaknesses"; Touré appeared to have none. Fanon's closest allies at the conference in Accra were Patrice Lumumba, soon to be the first prime minister of independent Congo, and Félix Moumié, a revolutionary from Cameroon. In September 1960, Lumumba was overthrown in a Belgian-sponsored coup, a prelude to his assassination. Two months later Moumié was poisoned in Geneva. "Aggressive, violent, full of anger, in love with his country, hating cowards," Fanon wrote of his murdered friend. "Austere, hard, incorruptible."

In November 1960, hard on the heels of Moumié's death, Fanon undertook a daring reconnaissance mission. The aim was to open a southern front on the border with Mali, so that arms and munitions could be transported from Bamako across the Sahara. He was accompanied by an eight-man commando unit led by a man named Chawki, a major in the Algerian Army of National Liberation (ALN). They flew from Accra to Monrovia, where they planned to pick up a connecting flight to Conakry. On arriving

they were told that the plane to Conakry was full and that they
would have to wait for an Air France flight the following day. Sus-
pecting a trap by French intelligence, they drove two thousand
kilometers into Mali; later they learned that the plane had been
diverted to Côte d'Ivoire and searched by French forces. The drive
to Mali took them through tropical forest, savannah, and desert.
Fanon was beguiled; in his notes on the journey, he sounds like a
man possessed. "With one ear glued to the red earth you can hear
very distinctly the sound of rusty chains, groans of distress," he
wrote. The gravest threat to Africa's future, he said, was not colonialism, which was dying its inevitable death, but the "great appe-
tites" of postcolonial elites, and their "absence of ideology." It was
his mission, Fanon believed, to "stir up the Saharan population, in-
filtrate to the Algerian high plateaus. . . . Subdue the desert, deny
it, assemble Africa, create the continent." Unlike Algeria, Africa
could not create itself; it needed the help of men with energy and
vision. He was calling for a revolutionary vanguard, but his rhetoric of conquest was not far from that of colonialism.

The reconnaissance mission came to nothing: the southern Sahara had never been an important combat zone for the FLN, and
there was little trust between the Algerians and the desert tribes.
Reading Fanon's account, one senses that his African hallucina-
tions were born of a growing desperation. This desperation was
not only political, but physical. He had lost weight in Mali, and
when he returned to Tunis in December, he was diagnosed with
leukemia. Claude Lanzmann, who met him shortly after his re-
patriation to Tunis, remembers him as "already so suffused with
death that it gave his every word the power both of prophecy and
of the last words of a dying man." Fanon pleaded with the FLN to
send him back to Algeria. He wanted to die on the field of honor,
and he missed the fighters of the interior, whom he described to
Lanzmann as "peasant-warrior-philosophers."

The request was denied. Still, he made himself useful to the
soldiers in Tunisia. At an army post he gave lectures on the *Critique
of Dialectical Reason,* in which he devoted special attention to Sartre's analysis of "fraternity-terror," the feelings of brotherhood that
grow out of a shared experience of external threat. He had experienced this sort of fraternity in Blida and with Major Chawki in the
desert, and he saw it again in the soldiers of the ALN. Many were
from rural backgrounds, uncompromising people of the kind he

trusted to maintain the integrity of the revolution throughout the Third World. It was to these soldiers that he addressed *The Wretched of the Earth,* dictated in haste as his condition deteriorated.

In *The Wretched of the Earth* Fanon characterized decolonization as an inherently violent process, a zero-sum struggle between settler and native. Albert Memmi had made a similar argument in his *Portrait du Colonisé,* published in 1957 with a preface by Sartre. But Fanon dramatized this struggle with unprecedented force, as an inexorable, epic battle whose outcome was not only the destruction of the Western-dominated colonial world, but the destruction of the culture and values that sustained it. The future of world history was being written in blood by the peoples without history, the "blacks, Arabs, Indians, and Asians" who had made Europe prosperous with their "sweat and corpses." The initial stages of decolonization would be cruel and fumbling, as the colonized adopt "the primitive Manichaeism of the colonizer — Black versus White, Arab versus Infidel." But eventually, he predicted, they would "realize . . . that some blacks can be whiter than the whites, and that the prospect of a national flag or independence does not automatically result in certain segments of the population giving up their privileges and their interests." The war of national liberation, he said, must transcend "racism, hatred, resentment" and "the legitimate desire for revenge," and evolve into a social revolution.

The arguments in *The Wretched of the Earth,* particularly its romantic claims about the "revolutionary spontaneity" of the peasantry, were deeply influenced by Fanon's relationship with the ALN. The ideal of a rural utopia was, as Harbi notes, a "credo of the army," which depicted itself as the defender of Algeria's peasantry, and Fanon had persuaded himself that, unlike the proletariat, the peasantry were incorruptible because they had nothing to lose. In fact there *was* something to Fanon's claims about Algeria's peasantry: while the people who joined the maquis were not farmers, many of them were country people who had maintained their political and cultural traditions, and who had always regarded the French as invaders who would eventually be forced to leave. But Fanon's depiction of the peasantry as a population uncontaminated by French culture would help to underwrite a project he had always dreaded, the nostalgic "return to the self." Houari Boumediene, the leader of the external forces in Tunisia and later Algeria's president, may have dismissed Fanon as "a modest man who . . . didn't know the first thing about Algeria's peasants," but he grasped the usefulness of Fanon's position. Like his arguments about the veil, Fanon's celebration of peasant wisdom provided the army with — in Harbi's words — a "rationalization of Algerian conservatism," and a populist card to play in its power struggles with the urbane, middle-class diplomats of the GPRA, and the Marxists within the FLN.

The same was true of Fanon's claim that violence alone would lead to victory. By the late 1950s, the FLN understood that it could never defeat the French army, and that there would eventually be a negotiated settlement. International opinion became a critical battlefield, and the principal fighters on it were representatives of the GPRA: as the historian Matthew Connelly has argued, the war was as much a "diplomatic revolution" as a military challenge. But the heroic myth of armed struggle, which Fanon did much to burnish, allowed the leaders of the ALN to present themselves, rather than the GPRA, as the real victors, and impose themselves as the country's rightful rulers.

For all that Fanon meant his book to be a manifesto for the coming revolution, *The Wretched of the Earth* is perhaps most prophetic as an analysis of the potential pitfalls of decolonization. While Fanon defended anticolonial violence as a necessary response to the "exhibitionist" violence of the colonial system, he also predicted that "for many years to come we shall be bandaging the countless and sometimes indelible wounds inflicted on our people by the colonialist onslaught." He also knew that Sartre's "fraternity-terror" could turn inward, with lethal consequences. The idea that solidarity under arms would give way to social revolution was questionable, however. As Hannah Arendt pointed out in a perceptive critique of his work, the sense of comradeship in war "can be actualized only under conditions of immediate danger to life and limb," and tends to wither in peacetime, as it did after independence. The taste of power that violent revolt provided was fleeting; the suffering and trauma of national liberation wars would cast a long shadow. Fanon himself had seen that anticolonial violence was driven not only by a noble desire for justice, but by darker impulses, including the dream of "becoming the persecutor." He also predicted that leaders of postcolonial African states were sure to entrench themselves by appealing to "ultranationalism, chauvinism, and racism": he was anticipating the Mobutus and Mugabes of the future, the "big men" who would drape themselves in African garb, promote a folkloric form of black culture, and cynically exploit the rhetoric of anticolonialism — even, in the bitterest of ironies, Fanon's own words.

One of the earliest readers of Fanon's manuscript was his hero, Sartre. Fanon first contacted him in the spring of 1961 through his publisher, François Maspero, to ask for a preface: "Tell him that every time I sit down at my desk, I think of him." The admiration was mutual: to Sartre, Fanon was more than an intellectual disciple; he was the man of action Sartre never forgave himself for not having been during the Nazi Occupation. In late July 1961, they met for the first time in Rome, where they were joined by Beauvoir and Lanzmann. Their first conversation lasted from lunch until 2 a.m., when Beauvoir announced that Sartre needed a nap, much to Fanon's irritation. Over the next few days, Fanon spoke endlessly in what Lanzmann calls a "prophetic trance." He urged Sartre to renounce writing until Algeria was liberated. "We have rights over you," he said. "How can you continue to live normally, to write?" He was scornful of the picturesque trattoria where they took him to eat. The pleasures of the Old World meant nothing to him.

Fanon had recently undergone treatment in the Soviet Union, where he was prescribed Myleran, and was experiencing a brief period of remission. But in Beauvoir's account of the meeting in Rome, he comes across as a haunted man, beset by self-doubt and remorse, full of apocalyptic foreboding. The days after independence would be "terrible," he predicted, estimating that tens of thousands would die in power struggles. The score-settling among Algerian rebels seemed to horrify him nearly as much as French repression. He blamed himself for failing to prevent the deaths of Ramdane and Lumumba, and struck Beauvoir as "upset that he wasn't active in his native land, and even more that he wasn't a native Algerian." When Beauvoir shook his feverish hand, she felt as if she were "touching the passion that consumed it."

A week after Sartre filed his preface to *The Wretched of the Earth*, Fanon was admitted to a hospital in Bethesda, Maryland — his only visit to the United States, a country he called "a nation of lynchers." He was shocked, he told a friend, not that he was dying, but that he was dying in Washington of leukemia, when he "could have died in battle with the enemy three months ago." He died on December 6, 1961, just as his book was appearing in Paris, where it was seized from bookshops by the police. In New York, Algerian diplomats gave it as a Christmas gift. Beauvoir saw his picture on the cover of *Jeune Afrique,* "younger, calmer than I had seen him, and very handsome. His death weighed heavily because he had charged his death with all the intensity of his life."

Algeria achieved its independence in July 1962. It would soon become a leader of the Non-Aligned Movement, and play host to the ANC, the PLO, the Black Panthers, and other national liberation movements, many of them deeply influenced by Fanon. But over the years independent Algeria — austere, pious, socially conservative — bore less and less resemblance to the country Fanon had hoped for. Even if he had lived, it's not clear he would have ever been at home there, any more than Che was in postrevolutionary Havana. For all that he said to Beauvoir about his desire to put down roots, Fanon was too nomadic a spirit to remain for long in any one place.

The only country that he could have called home, besides the page, was the emancipated future, a secular messianism he shared with Walter Benjamin. He worried that newly independent countries would fall into the same trap as the advanced countries of the West: the fetishism of production rates and the despoliation of the environment that Adorno and Horkheimer bemoaned in *Dialectic of Enlightenment.* Fanon was not Jewish, but he had an elective affinity with the "non-Jewish Jews," many of them Marxists, who so powerfully shaped European critical thought during the 1930s and 1940s.

In Fanon's writing, the crimes of Nazism and imperialism are indissolubly linked: he saw colonized Algerians and Africans, like Jews, as victims of a hypocritical Europe. This linkage, which Fanon shared with Césaire in his *Discourse on Colonialism,* would recede with Israel's emergence as, in Deutscher's words, the Prussia of the Middle East, as an adversary of liberation struggles in the Third World. As the historian Enzo Traverso has argued in *The End of Jewish Modernity,* the "exhaustion of the Jewish cycle of critical thought" set in with Israel's conquest of the West Bank in the 1967 Arab-Israeli War, and Jewish intellectuals went from being the West's greatest internal critics to some of its most impassioned defenders. Since then, the traditions of Jewish critical thought and postcolonialism have gone their separate ways, with notable exceptions such as Edward Said, a Palestinian literary critic steeped in the writings of Eric Auerbach and Adorno, and his friend Tony Judt, a London-born Jewish historian who became an eloquent champion of a binational state in Israel-Palestine. Fanon, in retrospect, can be seen as one of the last threads connecting these traditions, and it is striking that Arendt defended him against caricatured interpretations of his writings on violence, and never once took issue with his critique of Western imperialism. She could have done so only at the risk of contradicting her *Origins of Totalitarianism.*

It is no wonder, then, that one of the most striking critiques of Fanon, by turns tender and damning, should have been written by a Jewish anticolonial theorist who converted to Zionism. Albert Memmi shared much with Fanon. He was a man in-between, and never quite at home, as a Jew from Tunisia, educated in Paris, who stood between the colonizer and the colonized. He wrote novels and nonfiction, worshipped Sartre, and practiced child psychology in Tunis when Fanon was stationed there for the FLN, although the two never met. In a fascinating essay, "The Impossible Life of Frantz Fanon," published in 1971, Memmi characterized Fanon's life as a thwarted quest to belong. The "germ of Fanon's tragedy," Memmi argued, was his alienation from Martinique, his homeland. Once the dominated man recognizes that he will not be accepted by the dominant society, "he generally returns to himself, to his people, to his past, sometimes . . . with excessive vigor, transfiguring this people and this past to the point of creating countermyths." This was what Césaire had done, he suggested, by returning home from the *grandes écoles* of Paris, inventing Négritude, and becoming his people's representative in the Assemblée Nationale. Fanon, however, had failed to return; instead, after realizing he could never be fully French, he transferred his fierce identification with the country that had spurned him to Algeria, the country that was battling France for its independence. Once Muslim Algeria proved too "particularist," it was subsumed by something still larger: the African continent, the Third World, and ultimately the dream of "a totally unprecedented man, in a totally reconstructed world."

In fact, Fanon never disavowed his Martinican roots, or his love of Césaire's writing, from which he drew his images of slave revolt in *The Wretched of the Earth*. Even so, Memmi captures something that Fanon's admirers in today's antiracist movements tend to overlook: his ambivalence about his own roots, and his relentless questioning of the "return to the self." For Memmi, a North African Jew disillusioned with Arab nationalism, identity had become destiny. And in his essay on Fanon, he wrote as if primordial ethnic identification — and the contraction of empathy it often entails — were the natural order of things, and Fanon an outlier, if not a failure, for defying it.

Fanon's great hope was that such identification could be replaced by a new, postnational culture, a Third World humanism that the philosopher Achille Mbembe has described as "the festival of the imagination produced by struggle." It was not to be. In much of the Third World, the dream of liberation from Europe has been supplanted by the dream of emigration *to* Europe, where refugees and their children now struggle for sanctuary rather than independence. Universalism, meanwhile, has turned into a debased currency: for all the talk of transnationalism, the only two postnational projects on offer are the flat world of globalization, and the Islamist tabula rasa of the Caliphate: Davos and *Dabiq*.

While writing this essay, I received an email from a friend, an African intellectual based in Munich. "To live in Europe today," he wrote me, "is to wake up every day to the drum beat of naked racial hostility, with politicians and their supporters lumping us poor black souls together as the wretched and dregs of the earth, vermin for which there is no legal protection or even empathy. Everywhere one turns you are a negative, a constant subject of dehumanization and depersonalization. I am sick of the claim of a common humanity. There is no such thing as a common humanity."

Fanon, the founding father of Third Worldism, shared my friend's bleak view of Europe, yet he insisted that if the world was to have a future, it lay in the struggle for a common humanity. For most people, the life he chose would have been a severe test, perhaps an impossible one: in conditions of oppression and exclusion, the bonds of nation, faith, family, and clan provide sustenance, and can't be wished away by revolutionary acts of will, as Fanon knew from his own work as a psychiatrist in Algeria. In *No Name in the Street*, James Baldwin writes that in all his years in Paris, he "had never been homesick for anything American," and yet, he adds, "I missed Harlem Sunday mornings and fried chicken and biscuits, I missed the music, the style . . . I missed the way the dark face closes, the way dark eyes watch, and the way, when a dark face opens, a light seems to go on everywhere." When Baldwin returned to Harlem in 1957, just as Fanon settled in Tunis, he experienced the peculiar feeling of being a stranger at home.

Fanon, who never returned home, attempted to do the opposite: to become a native in exile, in a country of the future. The emancipated future for which Fanon sacrificed his life now lies in ruins. The racial divisions, the economic inequalities, and the wars of the colonial era were not so much liquidated as reconfigured. The postcolonial world is no less divided between North and South, and no less shaped by spectacular violence, from the imperial exhibitionism of the "mother of all bombs" recently dropped in Afghanistan, to the low-tech shock and awe of throat slittings and stonings by the Islamic State. The boundaries that separate the West from the rest, and from its internal others, have been redrawn since his death, but they have not disappeared: if anything, they have multiplied. The coercive unveiling of Muslim women has reappeared in France, where burkini-clad women have been chased off beaches by police and jeering spectators. In the United States, the killings of unarmed black people by the police have furnished a grim new genre of reality television. The president has surrounded himself with white supremacists, imposed a ban on citizens from six Muslim-majority countries, and declared his intention to build a wall between the United States and Mexico, all to keep out the "bad hombres." The era of alternative facts and hypernationalism has been a breeding ground for the racialized fears that Fanon so brilliantly diagnosed in *Black Skin, White Masks.* The gated enclaves, surveillance cameras, and prisons of the liberal West have created cities nearly as compartmentalized as Fanon's Algiers. When John Edgar Wideman's imprisoned brother asked him why he was writing a book on Fanon, Wideman replied, "Fanon because no way out of this goddam mess . . . and Fanon found it." I am not sure that he did, but it was not for lack of trying, and the power of his example lies less in his answers than in his questions — questions that he was driven to ask as if by some physical necessity. How can Western democracies overcome the legacy of racial domination, so that black and brown citizens can experi-

ence the freedom enjoyed by whites? How can postcolonial societies avoid reproducing the oppressive patterns of colonial rule?
What might be the shape, the identity, of a genuinely free society,
an emancipated culture? As he wrote in *Black Skin, White Masks,*
"Oh my body, make of me always a man who questions!" The mess
of our postcolonial world is different from the one Fanon faced,
but it is no less daunting, and finding our way out of it will require
new forms of struggle, and no less imagination.

SHERRY SIMPSON

Lucky You

FROM *Harvard Review*

THE HUNDRED-DOLLAR BILLS tucked inside your wallet are so new, so stiff, that you could fold the three of them into elegant origami cranes, one for each day you'll be alone at the Silver Legacy Resort Casino. Celebrating your anniversary in Reno was your husband's idea, mostly, and before he left you here to relax for a few more days, you asked him to take your debit card. That's how well you know yourself. Not that you're a real gambler, one of those used-up-by-life people hunched over a poker hand, squinting through cigarette smoke as the dealer wings cards across the table, *shick, shick.* You're not excitable and giddy like the drunken college kids whooping and hollering around the craps table. Certainly you're nothing like the bored women sluicing money into $50 slot machines surrounded by red velvet ropes. Still, you visit Reno or Las Vegas once or twice a year, often enough that the *boop clang riiiinnngg beep* of a casino has become a toccata in the key of cash, a sound that strips the synapses raw and pinballs through the brain. You don't feel that rush in your head, though. You feel it in your chest, where anxiety and hope cinch together every time you risk a few quarters, a few dollars, a few hundred dollars — the amount doesn't seem to matter much.

On the first morning you vow to buy meals only with whatever winnings accumulate beyond your original bet. Fifteen minutes of intent but careful playing at video poker, and you've made $8, possibly the highest hourly wage you've ever earned. How triumphant you feel spending $1.95 for a tub of raspberry yogurt from the little convenience store that caters to people who'd rather not waste money on restaurant food. You might as well have slain a deer with your bare hands and eaten its liver raw right there on the casino floor. Not even noon, and already you're ahead a few dollars. Your husband will be so surprised when you come home with the original $300 and then some.

Ten hours later, your favorite slot machine, Hot Shot!, spins a thrilling combination of cherries and bells and fire and announces that you have won $277, which you could really use because the day's budget of $100 evaporated hours ago and already you've broken the second bill. A fire alarm clangs away and video flames flicker and sizzle, all of which would seem more exciting if Hot Shot! didn't fuss over your tremendous good fortune in exactly the same manner when the payoff is $2. But the amount of winnings isn't nearly as important as the need to ease this clenched, familiar feeling of losing.

A lady sitting one machine over gazes at the numbers totting up your riches cent by cent. "Lucky you," she says, and you smile modestly, savoring her envy as you sip from a weak — but free! — gin and tonic. As always, you hit the SPIN button a few more times in case you're on a streak, and damned if the bells and flames and cherries don't deliver another $54. Hot Shot! is hot, you're hot, and your lucky streak is hot, screw probability. Once the machine cools, you punch the CASH-OUT button, and a $250 voucher emerges serenaded by the tinny clatter of fake coins, a sound not nearly as satisfying as the avalanche of greasy quarters that slots once regurgitated in that prehistoric era when people like your grandmother lugged around plastic buckets filled with nickels. The moment you abandon Hot Shot!, the neighbor lady scooches into your seat.

When you flop into bed at 2 a.m., barely a hundred dollars of your winnings remain. You blame the waitress who took forever to deliver a free Corona, a beer that actually cost $84 if you include all the money you lost idly pulling the lever of a slot machine while you waited. Eighty-five dollars, counting the buck you handed her in the belief that failing to tip even the tardiest of waitresses is profoundly unlucky. Whether this is true, you have no idea. It's just one more theorem worth testing in your ongoing inquiry into the nature of the universe, one more proposition you'll interrogate the hell out of before this weekend is over.

For example, is it luck or is it chance when an infinite number of possibilities funnel into that glorious millisecond when the slot reels tick perfectly into place? Statistically, the outcome of any one spin does not depend on the previous spin's results — you know this — and a random number generator ought not to care whether you're a Pisces or a Sagittarius, whether you yank a lever or push a button, whether you choose a gaudy new video slot decorated with dancing leprechauns or a clanking workhorse stranded in a lonely corner of a dingy casino, a machine that surely hasn't paid out in ages, a machine that clearly has so much more to give. Of course the house usually wins, duh, you're not *that* stupid, but it doesn't *always* win, which you know because you've studied those grainy, blown-up photographs of slightly stunned past winners posing with giant foam-board replicas of checks, and if Jimmy S. from Elko, Nevada, could win $11,297 despite that unconvincing combover, then there's no reason you can't either.

And why not believe in luck, when chance offers only randomness, which implies chaos, which smacks of meaninglessness? To ward off an existential crisis, you have tried to outmaneuver chance in Jacks or Better video poker by memorizing charts that calculate which cards to keep and which to discard if you hope to achieve the theoretical return of 99.54 percent with a perfectly played hand. You have practiced these strategies for hours on risk-free internet poker sites with a studiousness you never mustered for your GRE exams. Even so, statistics don't stop you from drawing on an inside straight now and then. And it's not statistics that make you catch your breath when you're holding an ace, a queen, a king, and a ten, all in the suit of hearts, and you draw the final card already imagining the riches that will cascade through your life should that miraculous jack of hearts appear, which it doesn't and probably never will because chance is a stone-cold bitch.

But luck — luck is supernatural, persuadable, seducible. Luck notices how you comport yourself through life. Luck is like Santa and Jesus rolled into one. Luck knows if you've been naughty or nice, when you tip waitresses, what you deserve out of life.

"Did you win?" friends ask after these trips.

"I always win," you say, which is true. "The trick is trying to lose less."

How someone could just hand money over to casinos and corporations and billionaires and probably gangsters is beyond them. Gambling is like riding Space Mountain at Disneyland, you explain. You're not buying a physical object; you're buying a recreational experience minus the vomiting. Usually.

Sometimes you insist that gambling is an anthropological exploration of the fascinating behavior of humans. And you do notice when people try to summon luck by kissing a cross or arranging an audience of troll dolls or ritually stroking the glass above a reel of spinning symbols. You've shaken your head at ads for more outlandish charms — Gambler's Gold Lucky Seven Hand Wash, for example, or the penis bone of a raccoon. You know that you can no more harness luck with such tactics than you can siphon electricity into a jar. Luck is a state, a flux, a kind of ectoplasm that, under the right spiritual or mental conditions, oozes from your pores and recalibrates your future.

So, no coon dongs for you. You're a fan of Jungian synchronicity, the "meaningful coincidence." That's why you believe that the more brides you spot on the way to the casino chapel the more likely that you'll win big, a notion permanently cemented by a four-bride sighting coupled with a jackpot of $362.47 soon after. Encountering Elvis impersonators is also auspicious, especially if Elvis is driving a pink Cadillac convertible with the top down, which you once saw in Las Vegas on a particularly profitable evening. But crossing paths with brides or Elvises doesn't create luck, exactly. Winning simply means that luck is paying attention to the attention that you're paying.

On the second day in Reno, you pause at an ATM in Harrah's Casino and wonder if you remember the PIN for the credit card stashed in a hidden compartment of your wallet, the card that you assured your husband you'd use only for emergencies. This feels kind of like an emergency. And look! Nobody needs a PIN anymore. The casino is happy to dispense up to $500 in cash with nothing more than a driver's license and a zip code, both of which you possess. Teensy, almost unreadable print on the ATM describes usurious interest rates and outrageous bank fees, not that you bothered deciphering the details. The line at the cashier's window is long but not nearly long enough to change your mind before it's your turn to push a credit card and ID through the slot in exchange for three freshly minted hundred-dollar bills exactly like those you've already donated to some faceless billionaire/corporation/mobster.

At a cheerfully seedy casino called the Golden Nugget, you inadvertently play a slot machine that dispenses winnings in coins. You feed nickels into the coin slot three at a time, thinking, *Well, at least losing takes longer this way.* Scooping nickels into the plastic bucket blackens your fingers with the slick residue of all the gamblers who fondled them before you. Real money insists on the grimy truth. Either luck exists, or it doesn't. Either you have it, or you don't.

One thing you know for sure is that luck does not depend on how much money you have or don't have. Otherwise, why would Guadalupe Rodríguez, the mother of fabulously wealthy Hollywood star Jennifer Lopez, win $2,421,291.76 at an Atlantic City casino? In no way is this fair, but it's difficult to untangle the moral threads because Mrs. Rodríguez claimed that she'd use the windfall to open a $100,000 college fund for her two grandchildren. On the one hand, good for her. On the other, only $100,000? And, really, haven't the Lopez offspring already rolled lucky 7s simply by being born to Jennifer Lopez?

This kind of thinking raises uncomfortable questions about the role of Providence in your own life. Was it chance or luck that you were born into a white, mildly educated, middle-class family in these United States of America during the late-ish twentieth century? Chance or luck that you weren't home the morning that the electrical wiring shorted out and burned through the kitchen floor until it flamed into a conflagration that killed your cats and charred the house into ruins? Maybe if you'd been there you would have smelled smoke in time to save everything. Or maybe you would have died like the cats, hiding beneath the bed. How about when the massive grille of a semitruck missed your face by inches when the driver failed to see your tin can of a car as he pulled onto the road? One moment less dawdling in the bathroom, one fewer car ahead of yours at the stoplight — well, you can play this game all day.

So far, deliberate efforts to tilt the balance between chance and luck in your favor have failed, most notably the time you attempted telekinesis on a slot machine. After a half hour of beaming concentrated brain waves at the machine's innards in an attempt to force three cherries to align, you gave up and moved to a nearby bank of slots. Moments later, the man who claimed your seat won so much money that the red light on top spun wildly and a Klaxon blared through the casino and into the universe. Was that chance, or luck, or simply delayed telekinesis? You couldn't bear to go over and see exactly how much money he'd won; the naked envy on the face of every person in the crowd surrounding him was enough to sear your heart into a lump of smoking meat. Even now you find it painful to abandon a machine that's hoovering up your money because any minute now, the universe might pick you to win. Somehow it never occurs to you that the universe might be picking you to lose.

The casino's mad lullaby rockets around your skull as you lie in bed the second night wondering how to transfer $800 from the savings account to the credit card without your husband noticing. Standing in line at the cashier's window the next morning you promise yourself that you'll promise your husband that you will never, ever stay alone at a casino hotel again. You hope you mean it, you really do.

As you drift through the casino clutching the cash that will finally fix everything, you try to sense which machine will restore all that you deserve, and then some. You've always been bemused by the talismans and totems decorating individual slot machines — symbols that represent luck and money (the number 7, the color green), animals noble or whimsical (lions, wolves, lemmings), cultural references flattened into cartoons (Egyptian pyramids, Chinese emperors, American game shows). But now you dither between meerkats or dolphins, flags or flames, Pompeii or Rome. Hope perks up with every scatter win or wild card, sags with every impotent spin. You need to win — that is, you need to stop losing — but you haven't the willpower or character to simply retreat to your room until it's time to leave for the airport. Watching reruns of *Law and Order* won't help you retrieve all that money.

Perhaps, you reason, as yet another faithless machine confiscates money and hope, gambling is a useful way of practicing Buddhist nonattachment. Money is an illusion, when you think about it, a fluid metaphor that can mean anything you want it to mean. You want money, of course you do, but more than that, you want to win. What were you going to do with all that cash anyway, send it to Darfur? Save it for retirement? Give it to the cleaning woman who stops wiping ashtrays long enough to ask if those red flashing numbers mean pennies or dollars?

And now you wonder what it would be like to gamble as if it didn't matter, as if the teeter-totter of wins and losses didn't represent some kind of cosmic referendum, as if there were no need to worry that this disturbing episode is not just a story from your life, but *the* story of your life. Perhaps all this time you've mistaken destiny for luck. Surely there's a way to turn this loss into, if not a win exactly, then less of a rout. Maybe you could write the whole trip off your taxes as research for an article about the seductive gameplay of the new generation of slot machines, or the exploitive cynicism of credit card companies, or the desperation of middle-aged women who destroy their marriages during an inexplicable but all-too-common gambling fugue.

When you check out of the hotel, a single $20 bill occupies your wallet. Wait a sec — you'll need to tip the shuttle driver, so you'd better break it. Five minutes later, you salvage the remaining $9.75 from a poker machine, one last humiliation to tuck away for the long flight home.

When your husband picks you up at the airport, he doesn't ask how much money you won or lost. You look out the window at the familiar landscape, trying to think of the right words, but what emerges is the worst thing a married person can say to a spouse.

"I need to tell you something," you begin, "but you have to promise you won't get mad."

His face tightens. "How much?" he asks.

A long silence follows your answer, a silence in which you can still hear the Hot Shot! machine trilling its fiendish, unresolved melody. You're almost home before you say that after all these years, you finally understand something about addiction. When you were standing in line at the cashier's window borrowing money (again), you suddenly recognized the terrible emotional transaction under way: you felt awful about what you were doing, but the only way to stop feeling so bad was to continue doing the one thing that could help you forget how bad you feel. Now, you say, you realize how hard it must have been to quit drinking.

He doesn't answer, not because you mentioned the drinking — all of that is long past — but because he knows this grand epiphany doesn't mean shit. You're not promising to give up gambling. You're not claiming you'll change. You think you were unlucky, not stupid.

"I shouldn't have stayed there alone," you admit, eager to show that you've learned your lesson. "Just please tell me that you're not mad."

Unfortunately, he's not a liar, but he does say, "I guess it's not the end of the world."

Your thank-you is fervent, contrite, genuine. You barely stop yourself from adding, "I'm so lucky to have you." And the electronic tootling that sounds like winning and the hollow clink that means you're losing recede from your skull, leaving behind the deep hush of a universe that never, ever stops counting.

CLIFFORD THOMPSON

The Moon, the World, the Dream

FROM *The Threepenny Review*

I GREW UP in a Washington, DC, neighborhood called Deanwood, where daily life did not involve a sense of living in the most
important city on earth. Everyone in Deanwood was black, working class to working poor, some living in housing projects, others — including my family — in private semidetached brick homes.
We went to school or work in the mornings, came home in the
evenings; no one traveled far, for their jobs or anything else, the
exceptions mostly being trips "down the country" to families' even
more insular places of origin in Virginia, say, or North Carolina.
In December, in school, we put on Christmas programs, because it
was assumed, rightly, that everyone was a Christian in our world —
for us, the only world there was.

In my memory this sleepiness was at its sweetest in the spring
and summer, when the front doors of houses up and down my
street were routinely left open to let the breeze in, where, when
darkness came, people rocked on metal gliders on their small
porches, where sounds were mostly of cicadas whirring and crick-
ets chirping and the occasional car passing with a lazy roar up the
street, where the only other movement was of moths floating near
the yellow glow of the street lamps.

On the one such night that I'm recalling, in the warm months
of 1968, when I was five, the insularity of my world suffered a
brief, bizarre jolt. My brother, then nineteen, was beside me on
the porch and remembers what I remember, which for nearly half
a century was all that kept me from thinking of it as a dream.

We were gazing at the full moon. Then, beside it, part of the
sky began to change color, as if an invisible dial was spinning and

painting as it went around, until at the end of a second there was a perfect white sphere. Where a moment before there had been one moon, we now saw two.

Small children are, for the most part, rational beings, operating in the world based on their feelings but also on what they've learned. When children see things they want, they simply grab them, until they are told, and remember, not to. When pleased that things they've said have made others laugh, they'll say them again, soon filing away the lesson that funny lines almost never work a second time. And when confronted with things that go radically against their learned notions of how the world ought to work, children, like adults, become upset, even frightened.

Seeing what seemed to me the formation of a second moon, I ran screaming into our little house — trying, no doubt incoherently, to talk about what I'd witnessed. I don't recall that I was upset for very long. If, just beyond the screen door, the world was turning upside down, here in the house everything was as it ought to have been. There was my teenaged older sister, sitting calmly in a chair beside the dining room table; there, behind her, was my mother, applying a black, smoking-hot iron comb to my sister's head; here was the familiar crackling sound and the old smell of singed hair. Probably the TV was on. I felt safe again, back in the world I knew.

Clearly, though, I've never forgotten that other feeling.

If fear — and the accompanying fight or flight — is our first natural response to the unfamiliar, our second has to involve jokes. The most common response when I shared the second-moon story with friends recently was that I'd had too much of my beloved bourbon (never mind that I was five years old at the time I'm recalling). In case you're having doubts of your own, please know that I have never taken a mind-expanding drug or been diagnosed with a mental illness, and unless you count setting out to become a writer, I've never been known for giving way to delusions. (And even as regards that, a good friend told me once long ago that the problem with my becoming a writer was that I'm "not crazy enough.")

Plus, my story is corroborated by probably the most sober person I know: my big brother. "I was almost twenty, and it unsettled me," he said recently, "so I can believe you were scared." His explanation for what we saw? When I've mentioned it, every few years or so, his response has been reassuringly consistent if a little light on detail: "They" — whoever "they" are — "were testing chemicals in the sky." That was all I had to go on until recently, when I finally decided to dig a little deeper on my own.

I am hardly a conspiracy theorist, but I've long been intrigued by things that shake up my view of the world around me — specifically, things that awaken my sense that what most of us see makes up very little of what there is, that there's much more going on around us than we know. Some of the movies I've found memorable — Sidney Lumet's *Q & A*, Martin Scorsese's *The Departed*, and, for its Nazi submarine sequence, Woody Allen's *Radio Days* — appeal to my sense of a scarcely believable reality beneath the usual veneer, especially when it comes to human activity.

What I witnessed from my porch as a five-year-old, while not related to human interaction, definitely shook my settled view of things, an understanding based in part on the utter predictability of the night sky. The irony is that the world I lived in, the ground I walked on, the moon I saw at night were all formed by events so fantastic, and taking place on so indescribably large a scale, that the average adult mind — let alone the mind of a five-year-old — could not wrap itself around them.

The leading theory of the moon's formation is that, longer ago than most of us can comprehend, another young planet collided with our own, its core merging with our planet's, parts of its crust knocked loose along with parts of Earth's, the loose sections fusing into one with the heat of the impact as they spun away from the two now-joined planets to become our moon. In the summer of 1969, roughly a year after the fantastic thing I saw in the sky, humans went for the first time to this moon. I have very dim memories of watching the coverage on TV, and I still have a drawing of the astronauts I did in whatever summer school I was attending then. What now strikes me as significant about the moon landing — beyond the obvious — is that in light of the theory of the moon's formation, you could say that the astronauts were not only going to a new world: in the most concrete sense, they were returning home.

The moon, of course, continues to orbit Earth, rotating, as it does so, in such a way that we always see more or less the same side of it; it has been estimated that only 59 percent of the moon is visible, and not all of that is visible at once. One great thing about writing nonfiction is that you are free to *explain* your metaphors, and these facts about the moon seem to me applicable to all kinds of things. Recently, my younger daughter — the result, you might say, of the collision/merger of her mother and me — spun so far away from us as to enroll at a small midwestern college. Since she left, she has taken to emailing us videos of herself talking. In one of them, with her black-framed glasses, head wrap, and light brown skin, she looked strikingly like Zadie Smith. But even more striking, for me, was that I was suddenly looking at a woman. This was not the little person holding my hand and toddling beside me en route to Park Slope's Third Street Playground, the person about whom I knew, or thought I knew, everything; here was a young adult with as great a store of private knowledge as I have, one who shows me certain sides of herself but not others, and if I knew 59 percent of what was going on with her, I would know far too much. ("Don't you ever ask them why / If they told you, you would cry . . .")

Fifty-nine percent, of course, is more than I'll ever know about what's going on with the rest of the world, which brings me back to hidden human activity and forward to something I witnessed, not as a five-year-old, but as a young single man living in Harlem. One weekday afternoon in the late 1980s, I was in midtown Manhattan, on the first floor of the Citicorp building, with its shops and scores of people walking this way and that. I was relaxing with a cup of coffee, thinking and staring at nothing, when two men entered my line of vision from opposite directions, one of them carrying a shopping bag; the men passed each other with no acknowledgment, without breaking stride or turning their heads even slightly — but one of them dropped an object I couldn't see into the shopping bag of the other man.

To one extent or another, we create for ourselves the lives we envision, which means that each of us lives in a world of his or her imagination. The intrusion of another world into our own — analogous to the process that likely formed the moon — can be unsettling, for good or ill, on a small or large scale: seeing something strange in the sky, witnessing a mysterious handoff, falling in love.

For glimpses into other worlds, we need not turn to the heavens, or even to other people. There is the land of sleep. Except for my brother's presence on the porch that night in 1968, as I have said, I would have thought I dreamt what I saw; a second moon would not have been out of place in dreams, where one's own mind becomes a stranger, speaking of incomprehensible things in a language we cannot translate back in the waking world.

Here is Marcel Proust, in *In Search of Lost Time,* on the subject of dreams:

> ... our perceptions are so overloaded, each of them blanketed by a superimposed counterpart which doubles its bulk and blinds it to no purpose, that we are unable even to distinguish what is happening in the bewilderment of awakening ... that murky obscurity in which reality is no more translucent than in the body of a porcupine, and our all but non-existent perception may perhaps give us an idea of the perception of certain animals ...

And:

> ... in the chariot of sleep, we descend into depths in which memory can no longer keep up with it, and on the brink of which the mind has been obliged to retrace its steps.

And:

> ... sleep bore him so far away from the world inhabited by memory and thought, through an ether in which he was alone, more than alone, without even the companionship of self-perception, he was outside the range of time and its measurements.

Proust was a man who bent language to his will, whom words served as they served no one else — and even he doesn't quite nail it. Where Proust falls short, I would be wise not to try, except to say that if describing what happens in certain areas of sleep is beyond the power of the planet's preeminent master of language, then it is because there simply *is* no human language adequate to the task. Sleep-thought is based on the logic of the alien within ourselves.

All we can do, then, is to try to figure out some of what's going on in the world of waking life.

Several months ago I talked with my brother about that night in 1968. He said something I didn't recall his having said before: that prior to our second-moon sighting, there was a mention in the newspaper or on TV or radio about atmospheric tests. Armed with that knowledge, I spent a recent summer afternoon at the main branch of the New York Public Library, searching through the *Washington Post* database to see where the terms "atmospheric," "testing," "chemicals," and "NASA" appeared in articles published in the spring and summer of 1968, hoping to find a connection to what I witnessed. I came up empty. Disappointed, I went home and, in a spirit of what-have-I-got-to-lose, posted on Facebook a description of my childhood experience and a call for advice on how to solve this mystery. Amid the jokey responses was a suggestion that I contact a man named Derrick Pitts at a science museum called the Franklin Institute, in Philadelphia. That turned out to be a very good idea.

I learned from Derrick Pitts, an African American and the Franklin Institute's chief astronomer, that during the period of my second-moon sighting, NASA routinely conducted atmospheric tests involving what are called sounding rockets — which carry scientific instruments into space — launched from the Wallops Island Flight Facility, not far from Washington. Next, I sent an email to Wallops, whose news chief, Keith Koehler, informed me that what I saw sounded like a "vapor tracer experiment using a sounding rocket." According to information on the NASA page to which he sent me a link, vapor tracers are injections into the atmosphere of materials that either luminesce or scatter sunlight in order to reveal . . . I'm still working on understanding what they reveal.

One vapor, lithium, turns bright red when used at night; another, barium, is used only near sunset or sunrise and shows up as purplish-red. But then there is trimethylaluminum (TMA), which turns white — and which sounds like it might have produced what my brother and I saw. According to the NASA web page, "TMA releases are most often used to study the neutral winds in the lower ionosphere at night at altitudes of 100 miles (160 kilometers) or less." Searching online for a definition of "neutral winds," I found a paragraph of impenetrable science-speak; emailing two people in the field, I got back responses that seemed to me like descriptions of two different phenomena. I thought of how my late mother used to respond to unhelpful explanations: *Don't know no more'n I did before.*

So I'm left with three problems. The first — that I don't have a grasp of what neutral winds are — is perhaps not a real problem, since I don't know that even a definitive, plain-English explanation would benefit me much in the end. The second is that what I read about white TMA vapors, which is probably as good an explanation as I will ever have of what I saw, doesn't sound exactly like what I saw — the amorphous vapor cloud lacking the crispness of that quickly formed sphere I recall so clearly. So, did I witness something else? Or could it be that forty-eight years have distorted my childhood memory just a little? Do I think that the TMA vapor experiment accounts for what I witnessed? Let's say I'm 59 percent sure. More, even.

The third problem is that having (maybe, probably, I think) at last solved this mystery, I am presented with the one behind it. Why did I want so much to know the answer? Why have I talked about the subject so much to my wife and daughters that now, when I mention it, they smile, pat my shoulder, and head off to see if that pot of water is boiling yet? Maybe it's that having crossed the line of fifty — having nearly reached an age my father never saw — has given me the feeling that some mysteries of my life have to be solved soon, if at all; and maybe the question of what I saw when I was five, not critically important on its face, is a stand-in for something else I don't know about myself — a pretty benign substitute, as these things go. No doubt, having trophy wives, fancy cars, and other cliché trappings of midlife crises are not themselves what aging sufferers seek so much as seeing themselves *with* the wives and the cars; discovering what they themselves are like under these new and different circumstances; finding out at last, in this big, endlessly mystifying world, who they are. By shaking things up and seeing what remains in place, we hope to discover what in us is permanent, and what we've merely never bothered to toss away. If that is the real question, maybe I found part of the answer as a small boy. In a moment when the world around me suddenly seemed as scary, crazy, and unpredictable as any movie, as ill-intentioned as any conspiracy, as unfathomable as any dream, I went running toward my family, and I wanted to describe what I'd seen. At the moment when a long-standing mystery was introduced, a small area of darkness turned to light.

BARON WORMSER

Hannah Arendt in New York

FROM *Solstice*

SHE HAS WITNESSED rant that silenced every reproof. She has waited for some larger affirmation to arise, the vision of decency, but none came. She has heard the triumph of jackbooted certainty strutting to the mob's approving roar. The precious freedom that a republic cherishes, the freedom to seek truth in the face of falsehood, can dissolve like a book left out in the rain. Heinrich, her edgy, shrewd, passionate husband who fought on the streets of Berlin, is that precious, more precious, but without this freedom he would not be alive nor would she: two more corpses in the ideological charnel house of Europe. She does not doubt the burden: people must be ready to die for freedom, but the reasons must be honest ones. All the standard human debilities — greed, prejudice, sloth, ignorance, hypocrisy — are woven into freedom's cloth. Working as she does in the service of reason, she spends her life disentangling those threads, which is, in the twentieth century, a colossal joke. Some days she broods; some days she forgets. She is only human herself. At odd moments, Heinrich gently reminds her of that datum. He points out a tic in her German or a run in her stocking. They laugh together. There is something remarkable about their laughter. It is resonant with the distress and joy of time, moments that include kisses and years shattered by the hyphenated demiurge the two of them call "World-History."

History is the unexpected that is then parsed out as the expected. "Ah, yes, the world wars, Hitler, Stalin, revolutions, the atomic bomb, ah, yes, we saw it all coming. Here are some explanations." The human capacity for arguing backwards is as bottomless and frightening as the human capacity for accepting whatever comes marching down the disastrous pike. She and Heinrich are not mass people. The entertainments that light up Times Square could disappear tomorrow and for them there would be no loss. It isn't that they don't have fun — a word Americans are fond of. They are lots of fun — drinking, talking, and giving parties where people occasionally make tipsy fools of themselves. Their New Year's Eve parties are famous. But someone like Plato is likely to show up in their talk, a candle from the dim vault of profound endeavor. Would it be fair to say that Hannah is more at home with the philosophers than with the people down the hall? Sometimes she worries about that. She is an instinctively warm person. So many philosophers were cold men intent only upon the vigorous elaborations of their unhappy brains. They constructed intricate systems to catch flies.

She is safe in America — and thankful for that safety — but she is always looking over her shoulder. She turns around on a street off Broadway and sees only another New Yorker in his or her coffin of an overcoat. The sight reassures her. She goes forward on her errand, but for her larger errands there are no reassurances — nor should there be. Everything is fraught.

The person in the overcoat walks on unperturbed by the fraughtness. What would the German noun for that be? English is a terse, physical language incapable of those long words that gobble up short words. The German language was made for philosophizing. German honored the invention of entities. English was made for ordering fish.

She turns around again to watch the person. She has dwelled inside of life's fraughtness — love affairs, emigration, fanciful yet demanding conversations into the early hours of the morning — but she is outside, too. How could she ever have imagined she would be living here in New York City? Her childhood in Königsberg seems immeasurably far away. There were still landaus and teams of great, shaggy horses to pull them. There were rose gardens. There was the silence of a world before the advent of so many machines. German history, though, can clear any nostalgic vapors.

Juden raus!

How could a nation go so wrong? The first answer might be that it never was right. It wouldn't be a bad answer. Heinrich has proposed it to her more than once. Germany was never benign. As a nation, it had from the beginning too many dire myths rumbling in its stomach. The Jews always lived on a window ledge there. Good citizens, they partook eagerly of whatever crumbs were offered them; they made themselves comfortable on that ledge. They dressed properly, spoke properly, and educated their children properly. They loved German culture with an almost indecent passion. Hannah could quote Goethe and Heine with the best of them. If Jewish life was historically built on wariness then the belief in assimilation was all the more understandable. The Jews wanted to be part of the world that was Germany. Hannah *was* part of that world.

In her apartment are books and tobacco. Cigarettes give each day a harsh yet agreeable edge. A flourish of sorts, they intensify both the longueurs and flashes that go with thinking and conversing. One draws in and then expels. One reads and writes. Periodically she airs out the apartment but the city is dirty with the exhaust of smoke stacks and autos. That is as it should be. People are here to make money. The United States, as she once informed her mentor Karl Jaspers, is "a society of job holders." That is a fragile cohesion; everyone busy at whatever task they deem worthy of their precious hours. But maybe it is no more fragile than any cohesion. It emanates from the people. No king or church decreed this endless American labor. It makes for a bustling solace. Everyone has something to do. There are not so many grievances here. Yet she sees Negroes every day. There are plenty of grievances.

She has never been one for teleology. Ends tend to be lies that placate the means. Ends dwarf any mere life. What remains appalling to her about Germany was the eagerness of people to give themselves up to the ends and their indifference to the means. What happened there had nothing to do with the patient work of thinking but with faith gone wrong. Faith should be humble. Faith that is vengeful is a nightmare. So the ghastly assertion: Germany is a great country that must avenge itself, and part of Germany's greatness is its willingness to stand up against the forces that compromise its greatness. Murdering children — what a sign of greatness! Sometimes Hannah finds herself shaking her head on the street then she realizes other people shake their heads, too. They, too, have their inner conversations. They, too, carry within them the splinters of the past.

There is in this world no shortage of matters to despise. She can be a despiser. People that turn away from making judgments are at best too comfortable, at worst cowards. She has seen people be tested by history and fail. Many were friends of hers, people who, it seemed, shared her values and beliefs. One was once her lover. How hard for her to get that straight, to understand how a person of such depth could be susceptible to nothing more complex than the afflatus of hatred. Heidegger thought he was going to stand on a world stage. Trumpets would sound all around him. Spirits would levitate. The impulses that over two thousand years ago fashioned the tense embrace between the mystical and the rational would reappear with him as their emissary: a dream to mock all dreams. Yet something remarkable stirred inside of him. Though she was not much more than a girl when she went to bed with him, she knew that. Taking him into her body was like taking something imperishable into herself, something beyond flesh. If there was plenty there to shake her head about, there was nothing to regret. She had welcomed him. She had been flattered. And she had yearned for him. He trafficked in the impossible. He wasn't a modern man. When history knocked on his door, he thought it was his own legend summoning him. Alas, it wasn't. But "alas" was far too weak a word.

Juden raus!

Aspiration makes for a dangerous compound. That seems one of the beauties of living in the United States. There are no essences to aspire to. Beyond what a ballplayer can do, no one cares about greatness. The shop windows hold what is within reach. Money, in its fairy-tale potency, beckons and inveigles. She, too, enjoys lingering to look at a pair of shoes or a dress. The call to something higher has little appeal when considering a hemline or fabric. The vanity, whether mild or deep, that underlies every look in the mirror abets the commercial republic. That, too, is as it should be. People cannot escape their bodies nor should they want to. What destroyed Germany was the frightening mix of medieval and modern, obedience and degradation, kings and factories, everything wanting to be over and above and beyond, a *Götterdämmerung* of unsanctified emotion. Here, beyond the endless slogans, there are no sirens. The storefront medley of prices, bargains, and sales that accompanies her route along upper Broadway to the butcher, the grocery, and the five-and-dime is tawdry but blessedly mundane. Though no advertising agency is going to seek her out to pose for a photograph, she can appreciate the goods America dispenses: she is at home with her refrigerator as much as the next hausfrau.

How wrong that opponent of the mundane Karl Marx was! To think of him in the context of her daily life is almost humorous. A vengeful man, he could not accept the tangible rewards of capitalism nor could he believe that work might be more than a victim's begrudged labor. He lacked the combination of yearning, desperation, and common imagination that drove so many to America's shores. Instead, he sat in England and drove his pen to prove his loathing of the bourgeoisie. What he possessed, like many a Victorian, was a taste for fairy tales, only his fantasies ran elsewhere: the state would wither; labor would be replaced by higher activities; the working class would triumph.

The depredations of her adopted country are what they are. They have been practiced on the Negroes as something like a folkway, at once vicious and matter-of-fact. But there are laws and they can be brought to bear. There is a constitution. Marx, despite the shelter Britain afforded him, did not have a respect-for-the-rule-of-law bone in his prophetic body. He saw the careful precedents of justice as one more fraud. Those precedents can and do fail, as they have failed the Negroes, but democracy allows people to persevere. Such perseverance annoyed Marx. People with their quirks and peccadilloes annoyed him. A believer in the genius of theory and systems, he was one more progenitor of the false sciences that captivated the nineteenth century and set fire to much of the twentieth. He provided the justification for absolving any semblance of conscience: the masses — to say nothing of those who led the masses — have the right to bury the individual. *Bury* was not an exaggeration.

How many European intellectuals still worshipped at his sooty altar? Her husband once did. How many replaced God with history and a handful of exhortations? How many of them secretly believed that Soviet man and woman were better creatures? And how many despised America because it was irredeemably mediocre — the home of chewing gum and hair tonic?

Understanding the new nation has taken time. She would have been glad to live in France or, of course, Germany, but World-History ordained otherwise. America is such an unsettling mix of social friendliness and political covertness, of the prosaic and the idealistic, of oppression and freedom, of modern times grafted onto the world of 1776. For someone who has spent her life beginning many a sentence with "Why," America is bound to shock. That is the last question anyone cares for here. What matters is what you do, not what you think. It is hard for her to imagine a nation not as the complex sum of centuries but instead as an enterprise where everyone strives to achieve happiness. Happiness! Despite the brisk handshakes Americans exchange and the psychological explanations they lap up, happiness is no business. To found a nation based on the pursuit of happiness was to invite the personal into the political in ways no one could imagine. Hannah, who relishes etymologies, is quick to point out that "hap" means chance, luck, fortuity.

From chance to tragedy is a half step, as when her friend Walter Benjamin committed suicide because on the particular day in 1940 he tried to enter Spain, he was turned back. It is the trail of steps that led her sister to commit suicide. Clara had sought love she never found and wept often about her unhappy fate. Was it her fault the men she pined for did not respond? To talk of happiness can be very cheap talk.

Perhaps the lack of consolation is what the consolation of philosophy can best teach. Abstraction is a dubious consolation, more gauzy absence than actual presence. Jaspers likes the word "concrete" to describe what philosophy must be. The real rigor of philosophy is to keep the world in front of you and not elevate or subjugate it. The real consolation is the integrity that may reside in thinking and the choice of not surrendering to the hypothetical. In that sense she feels at home in America. The clamor about what irrefutably exists is genuine. If it is shortsighted, a species of perpetual-motion machine, it is preferable to some murderous, sovereign goal. "Everyone here is busy. Everyone here muddles along." That would be another conundrum to chew on as she walks the short blocks of Broadway.

Some days there is literally music in the air, not the classical music that her sister Clara practiced on the piano and that Hannah was taught to adore, but popular American music. Stores on Broadway sell radios, record players, and records. She has found herself standing outside a store on a warm day and taking in the sound. "Noise," poor Clara, who played the piano beautifully, would have called it: no rapture, no grandeur, no impassioned sensitivity. To Hannah, who to her mother's chagrin had no special musical aptitude, the songs, however thin they first appear, are wonderful. They lack the cabaret edge of Weimar but are blessedly free of indulgent German sentimentality.

Someone named Dinah Washington is singing "September in the Rain." Hannah stands there — it is July — and listens. The woman's voice is full and sweet, precise and gracious and, in its crisp yet feeling way, exquisite. What more, Hannah thinks, could we ask of life? A Negro woman stops beside her and also listens. Here is a spontaneous plurality.

Too often, politics, with its necessary focus on the plural that is the people, is wrongheaded. "Society," Tom Paine wrote and she has quoted, "is produced by our wants, and government by our wickedness." Our wants are like the songs: love me and understand me. But our living with one another, our plurality, is something else. Conceit and distrust bleed into our mutuality. Degradations become accepted manners; cultivated loathing overturns whatever modest civility a society may have achieved.

Maybe until you have lived fearing a knock on the door that will mean your death, until you have experienced how the arbitrary and wanton can be a law unto itself, you cannot understand the importance of civility. The United States of America is the result of a revolution — an uncivil act — but one the world has yet to understand, an obscured and partial revolution tied to the rights of the individual. How are such individuals from all over the globe supposed to make a political society devoted to something other than glorifying selfishness? Does one right get in the way of another right? Do individuals start to see themselves as compendia of rights? Do they invent new rights? How are the rights shared if they are rooted in the individual's actions and sense of life? Must the exigent force of economics make a travesty of rights? And who were the people who created this nation and its constitution? Who, compared to Hegel, Marx, and Heidegger, was the slave-holding gentleman named Thomas Jefferson? In trying to answer those questions she is trying to assess the nature of that revolution. The revolution in America rarely impressed her leftist, European friends. A tolerant, wary, eighteenth-century view of humankind seemed beside the point in modern times. Yet here was this nation.

If human nature is unknowable, like the German saying about jumping over your shadow, then every political system is a less-than-educated guess. The challenge is to balance your guesses based on what you know about human beings — their wants and their wickedness. One of the errors of modern times was to disbelieve in wickedness. On the shelf of idiot bromides, progress stood out as one of the most stupid. Hegel — to choose one of her German forebears — was barking at eternity: history had no immanent direction. As a man entranced by teleology, he lacked a feel for his own conceit.

She has seen the wickedness firsthand. *Juden raus!* Those two words are the gist of many lifetimes; grief and calamity linking hands over centuries. Though she never goes to a synagogue, she is adamant about being a Jew. Like many a modern person, she knows that she has replaced God with the world. She can't help herself. The thread that connected her to the divine was snipped. The political news she retails to Jaspers in her letters about Joe McCarthy or Adlai Stevenson or the dubious character of Lyndon Baines Johnson is not the stuff of piety. Too often, it is the stuff of low-minded democracy, of rumor, calumny, and supposition.

Does this mere spinning world give a person sufficient light in which to view wickedness? There are examples and reasons — some better, some worse — but the light is something different. She and Heinrich talk about that light. She, after all, wrote her doctoral thesis about Augustine. To dissolve human wrongdoing in the great encompassing light of God is terribly easy. God diminishes mankind. Mankind exalts God. God exalts mankind. Mankind diminishes God. Such a topsy-turvy relationship is awful and comfortable at the same time, like a child who will not stop shaking a rattle.

She has her particular fears, not only the mortal ones such as that Heinrich will die before she does, but ones that have no dimensions. Those are the modern fears bred in the bones of "banality," a word Jaspers used in a letter to her after the war. The word is an answer of sorts to the obedient wickedness of functionaries but not an answer, more like a gambit. The problem of evil, as she has termed it, is, however, no chess game.

How can a condition be a problem? How can myriad acts contain one seed? How can reason apprehend the depredations of spirit or worse, the blankness of spirit, the vicious emptiness of the bureaucrat Nazi Eichmann doing his job and complaining about his rivalries with other functionaries? And doesn't "problem" insinuate an answer? Doesn't "problem" contain a mocking overtone: Hannah hefting her small, resolute shovel before a mountain of confusion? Banal or not, evil is bred in human bones. Other animals cannot do it. So all the categorical human issues — will, volition, choice, responsibility, morality — congregate outside a philosopher's door and beg to be heard. Philosophy, as Heinrich's beloved Socrates demonstrated, is an unlucky and largely unwanted practice. To do it is to suffer it.

Hannah suffers gladly. She has that outsider gene. She is the one who will always ask the uncomfortable question, the one who falls, as she says, between the stools. There is some pride in her about this. There is some contempt for those who refuse to follow the trail of questions through the tenebrous woods. There is ardor, too, though, and something like love. Because she loves to be in the world, she feels she owes the world her complicated honesty. Whether the world wants such honesty is, as she would be the first to testify, another story.

Perhaps what ailed Germany has ailed her, which is one reason she went to Eichmann's trial. Amid the famous German efficiencies — getting trains to concentration camps on time — there is the metaphysical impulse, the belief that thinking can be more than window dressing for prejudice. Questions and problems beg for solutions: Hitler, though not a metaphysician, had a final one. Of course, to impugn philosophy in that regard would be unfair. Philosophy is provisional, part of a Western tradition of thought-work that has striven to be impartial, though not objective. Judgments are crucial to living on earth. Without the judgments bred by conscience human beings are lost. To be objective in matters of heart-feeling is to surrender one's birthright. It grieves her that so many have been so eager to do so. "Inhumanity" is not an idle word. It means something very exact.

Juden raus!

Adolf Eichmann seemed in that glass booth a small, middling person, in his earnest way ridiculous. His certified Jew-hatred — how else had he managed to occupy such an important position? — took a backseat. Time and again over the months of his trial, he spoke not to his zealousness but to his honor and his deportment. He scraped before his betters and looked down on ruffians. He admired Hitler for making something of himself. While extermination was being organized on a scale hitherto unimaginable, he worried and chafed about his career. He confessed himself happy at some times during the war and frustrated at others. He took satisfaction in doing a good job, in being an expert of sorts about Zionism. He relished the tepid oblivion of cliché. This Nazi, he declared, was "brilliant," that one was "untrustworthy." As a bureaucrat, officialese gave him great pleasure.

The deaths — to descend into the world of words — were ghastly but the fact of this man insisting on his career was also ghastly. Hannah Arendt's tone in her reporting on the Eichmann trial was tinged with exasperation and sometimes with sarcasm. Who could fathom the disproportion between men sitting at their desks with their requisitions and the naked men, women, and children waiting to take their death showers? Who could take the measure of modern times that promoted the genius of machines and machinelike behavior? Who could hold those euphemisms — "resettlement," "evacuation" — in his or her mouth and not choke? Perhaps what the world needed was not philosophy but a new Bible.

Despite her doubts — or because of them — she persevered as a free person is supposed to persevere. She touched on the obedience that the Jews were locked into, their filling out the endless paperwork the Nazis required of them, their standing in the lines that took them to their deaths. Many Jews howled at Hannah's written touch. They felt she was unfair, unfeeling, and little better than a traitor. Despite her intelligence, she was naive. There could be no qualifiers to the hideous, larger truth. But for Hannah, who was trained to consider the whole topography of truth and was steeped in the modern literature of desperation, there were such qualifiers, just as Eichmann had a grotesque, comic side as he sat there and clarified points of order about how he did his job. He was eager to speak and explain. He wanted to set the record straight. He may have been acting, putting on a performance while inwardly baying at the most horrendous of moons. To assert his enthusiasm as a Nazi would have been very bad form. Yet there he was, quite composed, ready to argue some peccadillo about the murderous protocols. He would, as they say in New York, "do anything to save his own skin." His testimony may have been nothing but lies but it still was testimony. He had been there. No one argued that point.

She thinks about this Eichmann as a representative of the human race. To assume that any given person has a conscience is a big assumption. To assume that the conscience has some depth and is something more than petty self-righteousness is a bigger assumption. The endeavor of philosophy, her life's endeavor, is to examine assumptions. Her husband, who is a living representative of the Socratic tradition, does that each day — one of many reasons why she loves him. His conscience is not so much pure as stalwart and restless. Like Jaspers, he grasps how much philosophy's posing of questions can matter. People need philosophy, its rigor and scope, but they don't know they need it.

Sometimes as she sat in that courtroom in Jerusalem she felt that she would explode with irony — a terrible feeling. The man in the dock was, as Americans put it, "a loser." He could not *think;* he could only follow directions or register his displeasure with those who didn't follow directions. He was not the person who should have been sitting there. Despite all the deaths he had orchestrated she felt that he was not the main act but an afterward. The horrific inspiration the Germans had derived did not emanate from this man who seemed in his vacant, responsible way nothing so much as narrowly ambitious. The enormous effort of the trial was spent on a hateful nothing.

But no — the trial (and she can't help but think of Kafka) showed what the word "conscience" could be. In that sense those who excoriated her were wrongheaded. To live in a world without conscience was unbearable. To say that one conscience equaled another was foolish. As Eichmann showed too well, one conscience did not equal another. The scales were broken. Or they never worked to begin with. Kafka would have understood.

To say "This is wrong" is as crucial as anything a human being can do. She gave examples in *Eichmann in Jerusalem* of people who paid with their lives for having a conscience. It was not complicated: the Third Reich was a nightmare they had to oppose. And yet she understands how easy rationalizing can be. Life is an extenuating habit. One Jew tells another Jew that things will be okay. Not all the rumors are bad. One Nazi tells another Nazi that a job must be done. There is honor. There is duty. There is the Fatherland. There is the Special German Way. Each abstraction is palpable. One German tells another German that the *Führer* knows what he is doing. "He has a plan." She thinks of the story about the German woman at the end of the war saying, "The Russians will never get us. The *Führer* will never permit it. Much sooner he will gas us." To which Hannah added: "There should have been one more voice, preferably a female one, which, sighing heavily, replied: And now all that good, expensive gas has been wasted on the Jews!"

Like more than a few of her Jewish brethren, Hannah could have had a career as a comic or a writer of what has been called "black humor." It comes with the burdensome territory inhabited by Job and Abraham and Sarah and Rachel, but she refuses to stay in that territory, much less indulge it. She is clear about being a Jew first and last but the identity doesn't buoy her. What buoys her is the patient, and, more likely than not, irritating quest for the truth of any small or large matter. What buoys her are the crowded streets of New York where people jostle each other, exchange greetings, gossip, wrangle, and mutter to themselves in various languages. The republic has no great task. Or its great task is to respect each person walking along Broadway, which is up to each citizen who constitutes the republic.

Again, she stands outside a record store and listens. Some young men with British voices are shout-singing about love. "Help!" Sweet yet ardent, the word throbs with imploring warmth. She nods as if to acknowledge this most basic of human pleas. Something always is rising from the demiurge's ashes. You wouldn't want to live forever — but you would.

Contributors' Notes

*Notable Essays and Literary
Nonfiction of 2017*

Notable Special Issues of 2017

Contributors' Notes

MARILYN ABILDSKOV is the author of *The Men in My Country*. She received her MFA from the University of Iowa's Nonfiction Writing Program. Her fiction and essays have appeared in *AGNI, The Southern Review, Colorado Review, Prairie Schooner*, and other magazines. Her work has received honors and fellowships from the Rona Jaffe Foundation, the Corporation of Yaddo, the Djerassi Resident Artists Program, and the Utah Arts Council. She lives in the San Francisco Bay Area, where she teaches in the MFA program at Saint Mary's College of California.

NOAM CHOMSKY, considered the founder of modern linguistics, is one of the most cited scholars in modern history. He has written more than one hundred books, his most recent being *Requiem for the American Dream: The 10 Principles of Concentration of Wealth & Power*. He has received numerous awards, including the Kyoto Prize in Basic Sciences, the Helmholtz Medal, and the Ben Franklin Medal in Computer and Cognitive Science.

PAUL CRENSHAW's essay collection *This One Will Hurt You* is forthcoming. Other work has appeared in *The Best American Nonrequired Reading, The Pushcart Prize: Best of the Small Presses* and other anthologies, *Oxford American, Glimmer Train, Ecotone, North American Review*, and *Brevity*, among others.

EDWIDGE DANTICAT is the author of several books, including *Breath, Eyes, Memory*, an Oprah Book Club selection; *Krik? Krak!,* a National Book Award finalist; *The Farming of Bones*, an American Book Award winner; and the novel-in-stories *The Dew Breaker*. She is the editor of *The Butterfly's Way: Voices from the Haitian Diaspora in the United States; Haiti Noir* and *Haiti Noir 2;* and *The Best American Essays 2011*. She has written six books for young adults and children, *Anacaona, Behind the Mountains, Eight Days, The Last Mapou, Mama's Nightingale*, and *Untwine*, as well as a travel narrative, *After the Dance: A Walk Through Carnival in Jacmel, Haiti*. Her memoir *Brother, I'm Dying*, was a 2007 finalist for the National Book Award and a 2008 winner of the National Book Critics Circle Award for autobiography. She is a 2009 MacArthur Fellow. Her latest book, *The Art of Death: Writing the Final Story*, was published in July 2017.

STEVEN HARVEY is the author of a memoir, *The Book of Knowledge and Wonder*, and three books of personal essays: *A Geometry of Lilies, Lost in Translation*, and *Bound for Shady Grove*. He is a senior editor at *River Teeth* magazine and the creator of the Humble Essayist website.

LESLIE JAMISON is the author of *The Recovering: Intoxication and Its Aftermath* and *The Empathy Exams*, both *New York Times* best sellers, and a contributing writer to the *New York Times Magazine*. She lives in Brooklyn and directs the graduate nonfiction program at Columbia University.

BETH UZNIS JOHNSON is a graduate of the MFA program at Queens University of Charlotte. Her writing has appeared in *Story Quarterly, Delphi Quarterly, Rumpus Readers Report, Southwest Review*, and elsewhere. She is the editor and senior writer of *Thrive*, the award-winning cancer lifestyle magazine at the University of Michigan Rogel Cancer Center. She lives in suburban Detroit with her husband and two sons.

HEIDI JULAVITS is the author of four novels and a work of nonfiction, *The Folded Clock: A Diary*. She is the coeditor of the best-selling *Women in Clothes* and a founding editor of *The Believer* magazine. A recipient of a Guggenheim fellowship, she teaches at Columbia University.

JENNIFER KABAT has contributed essays to *The Believer, BOMB, Frieze, Harper's Magazine, Virginia Quarterly Review, Granta, The White*

Review, and the *Los Angeles Review of Books,* among others. Awarded a Creative Capital/Warhol Foundation Arts Writers Grant for her criticism, her work has also been included in exhibitions at Arnolfini in Bristol, England, and Index in Stockholm, Sweden. Her ongoing collaboration with artist Kate Newby was featured at the Poor Farm in Little Wolf, Wisconsin, and research for "Rain Like Cotton" was supported by a grant from the University at Albany Art Museum. She is currently working on a book exploring how progressive values haunt places and history. She teaches at NYU and the New School.

SUKI KIM is the author of the *New York Times* best seller *Without You, There Is No Us: Undercover Among the Sons of North Korean Elite* and the novel *The Interpreter,* which was a finalist for the PEN/Hemingway Award. She is a contributing editor at *The New Republic,* and her investigative reporting and nonfiction have appeared in *Harper's Magazine,* the *New York Times,* the *New York Review of Books,* and elsewhere. She has been awarded fellowships in both fiction and nonfiction from the Guggenheim, Fulbright, and George Soros foundations, and a Ferris fellowship at Princeton University. She was one of the last writers to be featured on Jon Stewart's *The Daily Show,* and her 2015 TED Talk has been seen by several million viewers. Born and raised in South Korea, she lives in New York and Seoul.

DAVID WONG LOUIE is the author of *Pangs of Love* and *The Barbarians Are Coming.* He is the recipient of a Lannan Literary Fellowship and awards for a first book of fiction from the *Los Angeles Times* and *Ploughshares.* For twenty-three years he taught at UCLA before illness forced him to retire. He is working on a memoir about life with disease and the consequences of its treatment, tentatively titled *The Bartered Life: When What Saves Us Takes Away What Makes Us Human. Pangs of Love and Other Writings* will be published in 2019. He lives in Venice, California, with his wife and daughter.

AMIT MAJMUDAR's latest book is *Godsong: A Verse Translation of the Bhagavad-Gita, with Commentary* (2018). The first poet laureate of Ohio and a diagnostic nuclear radiologist practicing full-time, he is also a widely published poet and fiction writer. His work has appeared in *The Best of the Best American Poetry 1988–2012, The O. Henry Prize Stories 2017,* and the *Norton Introduction to Literature,* among other magazines and anthologies.

RICK MOODY is the author, most recently, of the novel *Hotels of North America*.

TIMOTHY O'KEEFE is the author of *You Are the Phenomenology*, winner of the 2017 Juniper Prize for poetry, and *The Goodbye Town*, winner of the 2010 FIELD Poetry Prize. His poems and lyric essays have appeared in the *American Poetry Review, Boston Review, Colorado Review, Massachusetts Review, Seneca Review, VOLT*, and elsewhere. He teaches writing and literature at Piedmont College, where he directs the creative writing program. He lives in Athens, Georgia.

Who is PHILIPPE PETIT? — A self-taught high-wire artist, magician, and street juggler. Author of ten books, Philippe speaks six languages, has built a barn with eighteenth-century tools, is an accomplished pickpocket and lock picker, gives lectures on creativity, plays chess, and was once sighted bullfighting in Peru. He likes the title "Renaissance man," will go well out of his way to taste a perfect chocolate mousse, does not suffer French fools gladly, and is a master at interrupting . . . He has been artist-in-residence of the Cathedral of Saint John the Divine in New York City for nearly forty years.

THOMAS POWERS is the author of *The Man Who Kept the Secrets: Richard Helms and the CIA* (1979), *Heisenberg's War: The Secret History of the German Bomb* (1993), *Intelligence Wars: American Secret History from Hitler to al-Qaeda* (2002; revised and expanded edition, 2004), and *The Confirmation* (2000), a novel. He won a Pulitzer Prize for national reporting in 1971 and has contributed to the *New York Review of Books*, the *New York Times Book Review, Harper's Magazine, The Nation, The Atlantic*, and *Rolling Stone*. His latest book, *The Killing of Crazy Horse*, won the 2011 *Los Angeles Times* Book Prize for history. Powers was one of the four founding editors of Steerforth Press, now based in Hanover, New Hampshire, which has been publishing trade books since 1994. He is currently writing a memoir of his father, who once told him that the last time he met Clare Boothe Luce was in the office of Allen Dulles.

DAVID SALLE is a painter living in New York City. His work is represented by Skarstedt Gallery, New York and London. He is a frequent contributor to the *New York Review of Books*.

LUC SANTE's books include *Low Life, Evidence, The Factory of Facts, Kill All Your Darlings,* and *The Other Paris.* He has been a frequent contributor to the *New York Review of Books* since 1981 and has written for a wide variety of other publications. His honors include a Whiting Award, an award in literature from the American Academy of Arts and Letters, a Grammy (for album notes), an Infinity Award for writing from the International Center of Photography, and Guggenheim and Cullman fellowships. He teaches writing and the history of photography at Bard College.

KATHRYN SCHULZ is a staff writer for *The New Yorker* and winner of both the Pulitzer Prize in feature writing and a National Magazine Award. She is currently expanding "Losing Streak" into *Lost & Found,* an exploration of disappearance, discovery, grief, and love.

With "My Father's Cellar," JOHN SEABROOK ushered in his twenty-fifth year of writing for *The New Yorker.* He has also published four books: *Deeper: My Two-Year Odyssey in Cyberspace; Nobrow: The Culture of Marketing, The Marketing of Culture; Flash of Genius and Other True Stories of Invention;* and *The Song Machine: Inside the Hit Factory.* But this is his first published piece of writing in sobriety. "Alcohol and writing are intimately entwined in both journalism and literature, but writing sober turns out to be more interesting. I believed I drank because I wrote; it turns out I was managing to write in spite of the limits that daily drinking imposes on a writer's mind. With this piece I got free of that. We'll see where it goes."

ADAM SHATZ is a contributing editor at the *London Review of Books.*

SHERRY SIMPSON's most recent book, *Dominion of Bears,* won the John Burroughs Medal in 2015. She teaches literary nonfiction in the MFA programs at the University of Alaska at Anchorage and the Rainier Writing Workshop at Pacific Lutheran University. Her essays appear in numerous journals and anthologies, including *Orion, AQR,* and *Creative Nonfiction.* Her first essay collection, *The Way Winter Comes,* is scheduled to be republished in paperback.

CLIFFORD THOMPSON received a Whiting Writers' Award for nonfiction in 2013 for *Love for Sale and Other Essays,* and in 2015 published a memoir, *Twin of Blackness.* His personal essays and writings on books, film, jazz, and American identity have appeared in publications including the *Washington Post,* the *Wall Street Journal,* the *Village Voice,* the *Times Literary Supplement, The Threepenny Review, Commonweal, Cineaste,* and the *Los Angeles Review of Books.* He is the author of a novel, *Signifying Nothing.* For over a dozen years he served as the editor of *Current Biography,* and he has taught creative nonfiction writing at the Bennington Writing Seminars, New York University, Columbia University, Queens College, and Sarah Lawrence College. His book *What It Is: Race, Family, and One Thinking Black Man's Blues,* is forthcoming. He lives in Brooklyn.

BARON WORMSER is the author/coauthor of sixteen books and a poetry chapbook. His recent books include *Tom o' Vietnam,* a novel set in 1982 about a Vietnam War veteran who is obsessed with *King Lear,* and *Legends of the Slow Explosion: Eleven Modern Lives,* biographical pieces about eleven crucial figures from the second half of the twentieth century. Wormser has received fellowships from the National Endowment for the Arts and the John Simon Guggenheim Memorial Foundation. From 2000 to 2005 he served as poet laureate of the state of Maine. He teaches in the Fairfield University MFA program and lives in Montpelier, Vermont.

Notable Essays and Literary Nonfiction of 2017

SELECTED BY ROBERT ATWAN

ANDRÉ ACIMAN
Underground, *Harvard Review*, #50

NAA BAAKO AKO-ADJEI
Why It's Time Schools Stopped Teaching *To Kill a Mockingbird*, *Transition*, #122

MARCIA ALDRICH
Wallpaper: A Parable, *Hypertext Review*, Spring

JASON ARMENT
White Whale, *The Iowa Review*, Spring

WHIT ARNOLD
Snap, *Midwestern Gothic*, Summer

CHRIS ARTHUR
Sleepers, *New Hibernia Review*, Summer

KENDRA ATLEEWORK
Dawn of Tomorrow, *Territory*, March

KAREN BABINE
Orange, *Zone 3*, Spring

JENNIFER BAKER
What We Aren't (or the Ongoing Divide), *Kweli*, June 23

BRUCE BALLENGER
Return to the Typewriter, *Fourth Genre*, Spring

JOHN BARTH
Out of the Cradle, *Granta*, #140

MOLLY BASHAW
Lebenslauf, *Crazyhorse*, Fall

M. BAYLESS
So Long, and Thanks for All the Fish, *Event*, 45/3

DAN BEACHY-QUICK
Even, *Zone 3*, Spring

GORMAN BEAUCHAMP
Open Casket and Cultural Appropriation, *The Antioch Review*, Fall

ELIZABETH BENEDICT
Do You Come Here Often? *Kitchen Work*, Winter

STEPHEN BENZ
Unapproachable Evanston, *Cream City Review*, Fall

EMILY BERNARD
Interstates, *The American Scholar*, Spring

DAVID BERSELL
My Father Is a Collection, *Hobart*, June 1

SVEN BIRKERTS
"What Next?" *AGNI*, #85

KATHLEEN BLACKBURN
Daughter Tongue, *Colorado Review*, Summer

RANA DASGUPTA
   Notes on a Suicide, *Granta,* #140
CAROL ANN DAVIS
   On Loose Thread, *The Georgia
   Review,* Fall
WILLIAM DERESIEWICZ
   On Political Correctness, *The
   American Scholar,* Spring
JAQUIRA DIAZ
   You Do Not Belong Here,
   KROnline, May/June
MIMI DIXON
   Breath, *Ploughshares,* Winter
JENNIFER DOE
   Any Woman Can Write This,
   Witness, Winter
BILL DONAHUE
   Painting the Fence, *Yankee,*
   March/April
BRIAN DOYLE
   Everyone Thinks That Awful
   Comes by Itself, But It Doesn't,
   The Sun, February
JACQUELINE DOYLE
   Family Pictures, *The Gettysburg
   Review,* Summer
ANDRE DUBUS III
   The Descent, *River Teeth,* Spring
IRINA DUMITRESCU
   Swan, Late, *Longreads,* February 7
MARTHA GRACE DUNCAN
   What Not to Do When Your
   Roommate Is Murdered in Italy:
   Amanda Knox, Her "Strange"
   Behavior, and the Italian Legal
   System, *Harvard Journal of Law
   and Gender,* 41/1

SUE EISENFELD
   Taking It, *Potomac Review,* #61
LUCY ELLMANN
   The Lost Art of Staying Put, *The
   Baffler,* #37
OSAYI ENDOLYN
   Another Country, *Oxford
   American,* Fall

JOSEPH EPSTEIN
   Hitting Eighty, *The Weekly
   Standard,* January 2/9
JULIET ESCORIA
   A Myth about Self-Harm,
   Catapult, August 11
G. C. ESSELSTYN
   Parents and Guardians, *New Ohio
   Review,* Spring

ANNE FADIMAN
   Jew, *The Yale Review,* October
BRUCE FALCONER
   Stuck in Winesburg, Ohio,
   Humanities, Fall
ALTHEA FANN
   Paper Houses, *Cimarron Review,*
   Spring/Summer/Fall
N'KENGE FEAGIN
   Dead Daddies and White Castles,
   Lunch Ticket, June 16
ANDREW FERGUSON
   Writer's Seat, *The Weekly Standard,*
   September 11
MATTHEW FERRENCE
   The Foxes of Prince Edward
   Island, *The Gettysburg Review,*
   Spring
LUCY FERRISS
   Meditation on Pain, *Prairie
   Schooner,* Summer
GARY FINCKE
   Inexplicable, *Cimarron Review,*
   Spring/Summer/Fall
MARIBETH FISCHER
   Damage, *The Yale Review,*
   January
NICK FLYNN
   Canopic, *Salmagundi,* Spring
ROBERT LONG FOREMAN
   Nothing Comes Back from the
   Dump, *Electric Literature,* January
   13
KRISTA FOSS
   Choosing Your Poison, *Prism,*
   Winter

ALISON KINNEY
  How Deep Is Your Love?
  Lapham's Quarterly, Fall
HANNAH KITTLE
  Ashes, Ashes, We All Fall Down,
  Lalitamba, 2017
PERRI KLASS
  I'm Not Talking to Anybody,
  Bellevue Literary Review, Fall
GEETA KOTHARI
  Dreams of Home, *Cosmonauts
  Avenue*, November
BRANDON KREITLER
  Thought-Work in the Glowing
  Field, *AGNI*, #85
RICHARD KREITNER
  Paterson: Alexander Hamilton's
  Trickle-Down City, *The Nation*,
  March 13
NAIRA KUZMICH
  Garni-Geghard, *Ecotone*, Spring/
  Summer

KATHERINE LAIDLAW
  A Place of Absorption, *Hazlitt*,
  March 16
MARK LANE
  Keeping Faith, *The American
  Scholar*, Spring
JOHN LANGENFELD
  Washing Clothes, *The Threepenny
  Review*, Summer
RICHARD SCOTT LARSON
  What "Halloween" Taught
  Me About Queerness, *Electric
  Literature*, October 31
EVAN LAVENDER-SMITH
  Post-its, *New England Review*, 38/4
DAVID LAZAR
  When I'm Awfully Low: On
  Singing, *The Normal School*, Spring
AMY LEACH
  The Green Man, *A Public Space*,
  #25
LAWRENCE LENHART
  If the Ferret Crosses the Road,
  Creative Nonfiction, Summer

E. J. LEVY
  Natural World, *Passages North*,
  #38
YIYUN LI
  To Speak Is to Blunder, *The New
  Yorker*, January 2
BRANDON LINGLE
  Stop-Loss, *The Normal School*,
  Spring
JIE LIU
  The Hug, *Emrys Journal*, #34
MEL LIVATINO
  Golf Dreams, *Under the Sun*,
  Summer
SONJA LIVINGSTON
  Like This We Begin: An
  Essay in Two Photographs,
  Ruminate,
  Summer
AMY LONG
  A Glossary of Terms: Excerpts
  from An Encyclopedia of
  Iatrogenic Opioid Addiction,
  Hayden's Ferry Review, Spring/
  Summer
VALERIA LUISELLI
  I Is Another, *Freeman's*,
  October

CARMEN MACHADO
  The Trash Heap Has Spoken,
  Guernica, February 13
SAIKAT MAJUMDAR
  The Critic as Amateur, *New
  Literary History*, Winter
ELI PAYNE MANDEL
  Footing Slow: A Walk with Keats,
  Ploughshares Solos, Fall
SARAH LAPIDO MANYIKA
  On Meeting Toni Morrison,
  Transition, #124
JANE MARCELLUS
  My Father's Tooth, *Sycamore
  Review*, 28/2
GREG MARSHALL
  Lies My Mother Told Me, *Tahoma
  Literary Review*, Spring

Notable Special Issues of 2017

Bellevue Literary Review, Finding
Home: Family & Connections,
ed. Danielle Ofri, Fall
Bennington Review, Threat, ed.
Michael Dumanis, Summer
Boston Review, Global Dystopias, ed.
Junot Díaz, October
Chautauqua, Invention & Discovery,
ed. Jill Gerard and Philip Gerard,
#14
Chicago Quarterly Review, The South
Asian American Issue, guest ed.
Moazzam Sheikh, #24
Conjunctions, Inside Out:
Architectures of Experience, ed.
Bradford Morrow, #68
Creative Nonfiction, Adaptation, ed.
Lee Gutkind, Summer
Ecotone, The Craft Issue, ed. Anna
Lena Phillips Bell, Fall/Winter
Fifth Wednesday Journal, Voices from
the Middle East and North
Africa, ed. Vern Miller and Hedy
Habra, Fall
Freeman's, Home, ed. John Freeman,
April
Granta, Journeys, ed. Sigrid Rausing,
#138
Grist, Tenth Anniversary Issue, ed.
Richard Hermes, #10
Hayden's Ferry Review, The
Marginalized and the Avant-
Garde, ed. Dustin Pearson,
Spring/Summer
Image, Life in the Dark: The Film
Issue, eds. Gareth Higgins and
Scott Teems, #93
Isthmus, Politics, ed. Ann Przyzycki,
Kelly Daniels, Jody Keisner, #6
Lapham's Quarterly, Home, ed. Lewis
H. Lapham, Winter
The Literary Review, Current Events:
The 60th Anniversary Issue, ed.
Mina Zallman Proctor, Fall

Little Patuxent Review, Prisons, ed.
Steven Leyva, Winter
The Massachusetts Review, Truth, ed.
Jim Hicks, Winter
The Nation, The Obama Years, ed.
Katrina vanden Heuvel, January
2/9
New Literary History, Aesthetics Now,
ed. Rita Felski, Spring
North Dakota Quarterly, Transnational,
guest eds. Cigdem Pala Mull,
Sharon Carson, Gayatri Devi,
Winter/Spring
Orion, Nature & Culture at a Turning
Point, ed. H. Emerson Blake,
Winter
The Point, What Is Comedy For? eds.
Jon Baskin, Ollie Cussen, and
Rachel Wiseman, Summer
Prism, Liminal, eds. Kyla Jamieson
and Shazia Hafiz Ramji, Fall
Room, Migration, ed. Nav Nagra,
40/3
Salmagundi, Better Living Through
TV, eds. Robert Boyers and Peg
Boyers, Summer/Fall
Texas Monthly, Hurricane Harvey, ed.
Tim Taliaferro, October
The Threepenny Review, A Symposium
on Neighborhoods, ed. Wendy
Lesser, Fall
Tin House, Rehab, ed. Rob Spillman,
#71
Transition, Roots Reconsidered, guest
eds. Kellie Carter Jackson and
Erica L. Ball, #122
VICE Magazine, The Music Issue, ed.
Ellis Jones, October/November
Water-Stone Review, Field. Body.
Country., ed. Mary Francois
Rockcastle, #20
Yellow Medicine Review, 10th
Anniversary Retrospective, ed.
Judy Wilson, Spring

ZYZZYVA, Art & Resistance Amid
   Turmoil, ed. Laura Cogan,
   Winter

Note:
The following essays should have appeared in "Notable Essays and Literary
Nonfiction of 2016":
Krista Christensen, Etymologies, *New Ohio Review*, #19
Maria Eliades, Leaving Istanbul, *The Puritan*, Fall
Amye Day Ong, Chest Percussions, *Image*, #91
Jeny Spinner, Those Stairs, *Kentucky English Bulletin*, Spring
Marian Ryan, Things I Never Told Her, *Granta*, Online ed., November 21

THE BEST AMERICAN SERIES®

FIRST, BEST, AND BEST-SELLING

The Best American Comics

The Best American Essays

The Best American Food Writing

The Best American Mystery Stories

The Best American Nonrequired Reading

The Best American Science and Nature Writing

The Best American Science Fiction and Fantasy

The Best American Short Stories

The Best American Sports Writing

The Best American Travel Writing

Available in print and e-book wherever books are sold.

hmhco.com/bestamerican